Outstanding Praise for the Novels of Rob Byrnes!

WHEN THE STARS COME OUT

"Hysterical, catty and dishy, Byrnes's new novel is a delectable take on the secrets of old Hollywood . . . A sweetly raucous tale.
—*H/X Magazine*

"Abounds with humor and poignancy . . . a really touching tale of what some people will give up for love."—*We The People*

"Never less than entertaining."—*Between the Covers*

"The novel is enjoyable and the writing smart."—*Envy Man Magazine*

"A hilarious, wickedly witty novel."—*Out Front Colorado*

"Cleverly written . . . outrageous and sexy . . ."—*EurekaPride.com*

"A smart, tart tale about learning to trust your heart . . . Under the breezily entertaining gloss of snappy wit, Byrnes has something substantial to say about how fine it is to come out of those darned closets."—*Pittsburgh's Out*

TRUST FUND BOYS

"Charming . . . well-paced."—*Booklist*

"Has a charming, bubbly class-consciousnes that makes it quite endearing."—*Books to Watch Out For*

"Just as he did in his first novel, *The Night We Met*, Byrnes brews a sexy, slippery, highly entertaining romance."—*Lavender Magazine*

THE NIGHT WE MET

"Clever . . . compulsively readable . . . The supporting cast is strong and the breezy dialogue exchanges are as authentic as they are hilarious. Byrnes adroitly combines a twist-filled plot, solid characterization, humor and steamy sex to create a nicely crafted, delightful debut that readers of any orientation will enjoy."
—*Publishers Weekly*

"A crowd pleasing delight."—*Booklist*

Books by Rob Byrnes

THE NIGHT WE MET

TRUST FUND BOYS

WHEN THE STARS COME OUT

Published by Kensington Publishing Corporation

WHEN THE STARS COME OUT

ROB BYRNES

KENSINGTON BOOKS
www.kensingtonbooks.com

KENSINGTON BOOKS are published by

Kensington Publishing Corp.
850 Third Avenue
New York, NY 10022

All Kensington titles, imprints, and distributed lines are available at special quantity discounts for bulk purchases for sales promotion, premiums, fund-raising, educational, or institutional use.

Special book excerpts or customized printings can also be created to fit specific needs. For details, write or phone the office of the Kensington Special Sales Manager: Kensington Publishing Corp., 850 Third Avenue, New York, NY 10022. Attn: Special Sales Department. Phone: 1-800-221-2647.

Kensington and the K logo Reg. U.S. Pat. & TM Off.

ISBN-13: 978-0-7582-1325-9
ISBN-10: 0-7582-1325-5

First Hardcover Printing: September 2006
First Trade Paperback Printing: November 2007
10 9 8 7 6 5 4 3 2 1

Printed in the United States of America

Kensington Publishing Corporation
Presents

a Rob Byrnes novel

Noah Abraham

Bart Gustafson

Quinn Scott

Jimmy Beloit

and

Kitty
Randolph

in

WHEN THE STARS
COME OUT

Introduction

My life has had three acts.

Act One began when I was born in Pittsburgh, Pennsylvania in 1934.

Act Two began when I was reborn on a soundstage in Los Angeles, California in 1969, on the day my eyes met the eyes of a stranger.

In those first two acts of my life—almost evenly split, chronologically—I led two very different lives. With my youth came a modest degree of fame; with my middle age came a great degree of love. And through those two acts of my life, I became a complete individual.

Now, as I enter my golden years, comes Act Three. The third act is where the plotlines are all drawn together, and you learn if you have been watching comedy unfold, or tragedy.

This is my story . . .

Los Angeles, California, September 1969

*S*tep *left. Step left. Turn to the right. Remember to keep a bounce in your knees. Step right. Turn to the left . . .*

He moved across the floor of the soundstage, and hundreds of hours of rehearsals ran through his head. If he wasn't particularly elegant or light on his feet, his movements were fluid, showing no trace of self-consciousness.

Turn right. Look at her. Hold the gaze. Smile . . . and . . .
She stopped singing.
Sing.

> *We have the moon, we have romance,*
> *We have to take this one last chance,*
> *So take my hand,*
> *And take me out,*
> *To somewhere where we'll see the stars come out.*

He sang his five lines to her in an unexceptional yet on-key baritone, and when he was done she picked up the song again. Then, again, he was dancing the steps that had been drilled into his head and his legs over hundreds—or was that thousands?—of hours of rehearsals.

Step right. Step right. Turn away. Remember to bounce. Slide to the right. Turn back. Turn away. Step . . .

He pivoted at the hip to look at her one last time, and when he turned away from her yet again, well . . .

That was when their eyes met.

For decades after that moment, they would describe it as "The Glance." It was immortalized on film, made timeless by the cameras that captured it that day. But that was just the bonus . . . the moment they could replay over and over again, watching themselves in all their youthful glory.

More importantly—much more importantly—The Glance would be forever immortalized in their hearts.

For decades, they would agree that it had been a good day on the soundstage, which was fortunate, because it was also one of their last days on a soundstage. The Glance began a relationship, ended another relationship, destroyed some careers, and began others. It drove some people apart and taught others how to love.

But whenever Quinn Scott and Jimmy Beloit thought back to that day when their eyes locked on that soundstage, it was as if nothing bad had ever happened in their lives. It was as if theirs were not the careers destroyed, and they had not been the ones evicted from Eden.

Because they had found each other. And that, they knew, was all that was important.

At least, for the first thirty-six years. The thirty-seventh year, on the other hand, would prove to be a bit more problematic.

New York City, September 1970

It was Friday, which meant it was Date Night.

Every Friday since they had returned from their honeymoon had been Date Night, and this Friday would be no different. Even though the husband was growing slightly bored with the marriage . . . even though the wife was growing impressively pregnant with their first child . . . even though the night in New York was cold and wet . . . it was Friday, and it was Date Night. If it had been a federal law instead of a married couple's custom, the Friday pattern could not have been followed more rigorously.

For Max and Frieda Abraham, Date Night followed a pattern that had, over the five years of their marriage, slowly evolved from a way to keep the relationship fresh into a numbing routine. They would dress and be out the door of their Park Avenue apartment— too expensive for their struggling budget, and too far uptown to be fashionable—no later than 6:30. They would indulge themselves with a cab, when they could find one, and travel to a movie theater somewhere north of Forty-second Street, the demarcation line at which they felt a cab ride would become cost prohibitive. They would almost always catch a movie, followed by a late dinner. And, after dinner, they would cab back to the apartment, arriving home no later than midnight. Frieda would go straight to bed, and Max would join her an hour or so later, first stopping to pore over the work he inevitably brought home in his briefcase, preparing for another long Saturday in the law office.

After almost 280 Date Nights, they both knew it was growing stale. Now, on most Date Nights, they barely spoke, except to review the movie they had just seen, or to review the food they were eating. Frequently, they both thought that they should tell the other that the routine-breaker had become a routine, but then they thought better of it, under the mistaken impression that their spouse still needed the break and that Date Night somehow continued to keep their relationship fresh and romantic.

Date Night on the third Friday of September 1970 started with a cab ride through rain-slicked streets to a theater near the Plaza Hotel, where they watched the colorful Kitty Randolph musical, *When the Stars Come Out.* For a new film, Max thought, it was already dated; a lavish Technicolor musical in 1970 seemed passé by a dozen years or so. American society had been transformed by Vietnam, Woodstock, rock 'n' roll, and marijuana. Even the gays were becoming visible in the wake of the previous year's Stonewall riot. The American musical had transitioned from *Oklahoma* to *Hair.*

But on the screen, girl-next-door Kitty Randolph was still being romanced by blandly handsome leading man Quinn Scott in a colorful, imaginary world devoid of real-world concerns. She was the new-to-the-big-city ingénue, bravely fighting the corporate structure in a San Francisco advertising agency and struggling to be taken seriously as a woman *and* a professional; he was the chauvinistic ad man won over by her charms and talent. They met, fought, flirted, fell in love, and, of course, sang unmemorable songs to each other.

The minor nod to female empowerment aside—already done better and more effectively by real life—the movie was an anachronistic crowd pleaser. And Kitty Randolph was no longer the fresh-faced child-woman of her early career. Now somewhere in the gray area between thirty and forty, her youthful appearance came largely courtesy of soft focus. All in all, *When the Stars Come Out* had the feel of desperation to it, as if the producers felt they could hold on to a past that was quickly fading away . . . if it had not already disappeared.

Or at least that was how Max reviewed the movie over dinner.

"Not a bad movie, but it feels like it comes from another era."

Frieda focused on her salad, gently poking the tines of her fork into iceberg lettuce. It annoyed Max when she did that.

"They're getting divorced, you know," she said finally, as she humanely speared a leaf at its corner and dipped it in the salad dressing pooled at the side of her plate.

"Who?"

"Kitty Randolph and Quinn Scott."

Max had not even known they were married in real life. For that matter, he had not even cared. Still, Kitty Randolph was America's girl-next-door, the kind of woman who did *not* get divorced. Even in racy, tumultuous 1970.

"Where did you hear that?"

"I read it," said Frieda, again gently poking her lettuce leaves. "In one of my magazines."

Max sighed. Her damn celebrity magazines, cluttering up the apartment. He hated them almost as much as he hated watching her poke the lettuce, and almost as much as he was growing to hate Date Night . . . but, of course, he would not say a word.

Frieda continued. "It's all very mysterious. No scandal, like Elizabeth Taylor and Eddie Fisher and that poor Debbie Reynolds. They just . . . split up. One day they were together, and the next, he was gone."

"He walked out on her?"

"He walked out. Or so they say. I read that he's quitting the movies and moving to Long Island or something. I think he has a house out there."

Max immediately decided that Quinn Scott was his hero. Any man who could just walk away had to be heroic, because most men—even hard-driving fourth-year associates at major law firms, like Max—were trained to just sit back and endure it for the rest of their lives. Like Max, they would marry at twenty-six, decide it was a boring mistake at thirty, and live silently with that mistake for another forty or fifty years.

True, Quinn Scott was not just any man. He was, like his wife, an actor, although not nearly as accomplished. He was that guy who

you sort of thought you knew from supporting roles in John Wayne
movies or insipid comedies, which, while not superstardom, put
him leagues ahead of all the actors you *didn't* sort of think you
knew. And for three years in the '60s he had played the lead in television's moderately popular crime drama *Philly Cop*, which certainly
counted for something, if not quite immortality.

So quitting the acting business? Max would believe it when he
saw it. He was probably just diminishing expectations, to better
make a graceful transition back to television. And anyway, there
were worse ways for a man to spend those last forty or fifty years.

"Max?" asked Frieda. "You're so quiet. Is something wrong?"

"No," he said, catching a sidelong glimpse of the curvaceous
cocktail waitress out of the corner of his eye as she passed and wondering not about her sexual voltage, but whether she, too, poked at
her salad, one lettuce leaf at a time. "Just thinking about the movie.
Go finish poking your salad."

"What?"

"*Eating* your salad."

She looked at him, not quite comprehending his words but still
knowing that there was something about the way she was eating her
salad that annoyed him. Her first instinct was to push the salad plate
away; her second instinct—the one she obeyed—was to finish the
salad at her own pace. She picked up the fork and began poking.

Max was saying something, but his words weren't registering with
her. Instead, she was thinking about how fabulous it must be to
walk in Kitty Randolph's shoes. Rich, famous, and now free to live
her life exclusively by her own rules. And if the world, like her husband, thought *When the Stars Come Out* was anachronistic, well, the *heck*
with them. Kitty Randolph didn't need a man, and neither did . . .

She felt something.

"Max," she said, in an instant forgetting her dissatisfaction as she
looked at her husband and beamed. "The baby! It kicked!"

Washington, DC, September 2005

Noah Abraham kicked, and the wastepaper basket toppled over.
Balls of crumpled paper poured out and rolled across the slightly
warped hardwood floor of his living room.

Damn The Project . . . damn The Project that was slowly but steadily frustrating him, destroying every last trace of his creativity.

Noah had months earlier stopped thinking of it quaintly as "his project." Now it had a capital T and a capital P: The Project. It was the quintessence of a good idea gone heartbreakingly bad and, in the process, consuming him. It cost him sleep, it brought on unfamiliar frustration, it stopped his creativity dead in its tracks. In short, it was a major pain in his ass.

He didn't consider himself a quitter, but The Project had been making him reconsider. He didn't quit when he sank a ton of family money on a weekly community newspaper in western Massachusetts, exposed a hotbed of municipal and business corruption, then learned belatedly that weekly community newspapers depend for their survival on the goodwill and advertising dollars of municipal officials and business leaders. Yes, the paper had to close, but he hadn't quit.

He didn't quit when his stint at an environmental group ended after a series of unfortunate run-ins with the executive director. The woman was an egotistical, incompetent jerk, running the organization into the ground and compromising its principles. Just because the board of directors unanimously if erroneously decided that he, not the director, was the problem, thereby bringing about his abrupt severance pay–free exit from the staff, he hadn't quit. And the fact that the executive director later took a job as a petrochemical lobbyist proved his point, in a sense. Yes, she remained on friendly terms with the not-for-profit board and had quadrupled her salary but, to Noah, it was a moral victory, and he moved on. He didn't quit.

And then came his project, which quickly morphed into The Project, and that, well . . . *that* made him want to quit. It was dead end after dead end, a string of furtive meetings and mumbled conversations offering neither insight nor depth. It was a maddening process yielding questionable results, at best.

And, worst of all, there was no one else to blame. No corrupt politicians, no incompetent executive director . . . Noah Abraham had only Noah Abraham's brainchild to blame. And his brainchild had grown into a very troublesome, morose, uncooperative, and disobedient brain-adolescent.

In his idealistic moments, he told himself he would push on, despite feelings of hopelessness and frustration. He had always moved on. He had moved on from the newspaper to the environmental group to The Project, and he would just keep moving.

But in his realistic moments, he thought, *Well, what the fuck did you expect when you decided to write a book about closeted gay congressional staffers?* To which his only answer was, "Seemed like a good idea at the time."

Noah picked up the spilled wastepaper basket contents and tried to press on, repeating his "you are not a quitter" mantra to the point where it became numbing. But it was too late; his eyes were now open. He had a great book idea, confirmed by a decent advance from a decent publisher, but there were good ideas and there were good ideas that are ultimately unworkable, and Noah was coming to the conclusion that his months of research would have no payoff.

He sat back on the couch, briefly closing his eyes and wishing everything would become clearer and easier. He wished . . . he wished he could understand.

Noah Abraham understood a lot of things—the AP Stylebook, the rules of most professional sports, the novels of Fitzgerald, the electoral college system, and on and on—but he did not understand the closet. He spoke a little Spanish, a little French, and even a little Russian, but he couldn't speak the language of those people.

He tried to hide it and project empathy, but more than a few of Noah's closeted subjects thought he was arrogant. That wasn't just his supposition; they had told him that in no uncertain terms. To their faces, Noah conceded the point and apologized, but in his head he was never apologetic. First and foremost, his premise was, *What is wrong with this person that, thirty-six years after Stonewall, he or she cannot come out?* If closeted Washington could not deal with that premise, then it was *their* problem, not his.

Noah had done it, after all. He came out to his parents during his junior year of college, and had lived a full and openly gay life for the fourteen years since that day with no repercussions. Now, a few months short of his thirty-fifth birthday, he hoped to learn what led other people to bury their sexual identities for the real— or, more likely, imagined—sake of a job, family harmony, and social acceptance. He would write about his new insights and maybe

change the world just a little bit for the better. He would help people embrace their sexuality and finally come to peace with themselves.

If only, he thought. If only . . .

*If only these fucking people would say something! If only they'd let them-
selves be visible!*

Racial minorities couldn't hide their race. The handicapped
couldn't hide their handicaps. Religion, well . . . yes, you could hide
your religion, but who bothered in 2005? As Noah saw it, it was only
too many of his fellow homosexuals who were hiding. They were
hiding, and they were mute.

Which made it his job to end the charade. Or so he saw it.

And The Project was to have been his tool to end the charade,
but . . .

He walked to the kitchen, poured a glass of merlot, and again
tried to wrap his head around his frustrations. It seemed like only
moments had passed before he refilled the glass. And then he decided that maybe watching a movie on HBO would be less frustrating.

A few hours later, somewhere in the latter half of the movie, he
felt no better. But at least he was a little bit drunk, which helped
him fall asleep on the couch. Because those nights in bed, sober,
torturing himself, were the worst.

Two hundred miles away, at the exact moment Noah was drifting off to sleep on his couch, Bart Gustafson strode into The Penthouse, a bar tucked onto a leafy side street on the Upper East Side
of Manhattan. From the safety of the doorway, he carefully assessed
the crowd before advancing forward, squeezing between patrons
who lined the narrow space along the bar until he reached the spiral staircase leading to an upper level. There, as a pianist sang to an
indifferent audience, the crowd was notably thinner. He easily found
an opening at the bar and ordered a drink.

"You're new here," said the youthful bartender, as he set the
scotch and soda on the bar. Bart couldn't identify his slight accent.
"I'm Paolo."

"Bart," he said in response, adding a friendly nod. "I've been
here before, but it's been a while."

Paolo smiled. "You've been here before and still you came back?"

Bart scanned the room and laughed. "I guess I'm a glutton for punishment." It was a joke, whether the bartender knew it or not. The Penthouse was the epicenter of the older gay bar crowd in New York, which was a demographic Bart felt comfortable with. He knew there were eyes in the room sizing him up—young, good-looking . . . was he new in town, lost, or a hustler?—but he paid them no mind. He was out for a friendly drink in a city that often overwhelmed him, and so he went for the comfort of The Penthouse and its gentlemanly clientele.

Bart waited until the pianist finished his unique version of *Son of a Preacher Man* to an almost unnoticeable smattering of applause before turning back to Paolo, who still stood nearby. "It's sort of quiet up here tonight."

"Mondays," Paolo said, as he emptied a departed patron's glass into the sink behind the bar. "It's busier downstairs, but every place uptown is dead on Monday night. If you're looking for action, I could recommend maybe a club in Chelsea."

Bart shook his head. "No, I'm fine. It just seemed quiet."

Paolo turned slightly while he straightened a row of stemware behind the bar, but kept his new customer in his peripheral vision. This kid was half the age of most of the men in the bar, and he didn't want to go to Chelsea? Well, if he thought he was going to make cash transactions in the bar, he had better think again.

The glasses straightened, the bartender walked back to where Bart sat on the other side of the bar. On an ordinary night he might not have bothered, but with seven patrons lining the polished wood bar—all of whom had full drinks in front of them—he had the time and, more importantly, he had the curiosity.

"So, what brings you out tonight?" he asked, when he had Bart's attention.

"Oh, I just came in from Long Island for the week. Sort of a mini-vacation."

"I see. A vacation from your boyfriend?"

"No, I'm single," Bart said, and he wondered if the bartender was trying to pick him up, which in turn intruded on his comfort level. "I just needed to get away for a few days."

"You live alone on Long Island?"

What was it with this guy? "No. I live with a couple of older guys." He hoped that would warn the bartender away.

Paolo smiled conspiratorially. "So you're like a houseboy?"

Bart sighed. "Uh . . . yeah, sure."

Now things began to make sense to Paolo, as he ticked off Bart's comments in his head. The kid's a houseboy for two older gentlemen, and he knew what *that* usually meant. Now he's in town for a few days and he wants to hang around with the older crowd. Probably looking for a little business on the side. And he'd almost certainly get it: he was very good looking and obviously well built, and he had that All-American Boy look working with his Ralph Lauren shirt and khakis. He would be considered totally fuckable if he wandered into one of the hotter bars in Chelsea or Hell's Kitchen . . . in fact, he could have any man in The Penthouse. He probably could have even had Paolo, had they met more innocently on one of those rare nights he wasn't working.

True, Paolo—who had seen his share of hustlers pass through The Penthouse doors—wasn't getting those vibes off him, but Bart was definitely getting the message . . . all the more so with every little bit of extra attention the bartender was giving him. And those messages made him uncomfortable.

For his part, Bart was now convinced that the bartender was, in fact, trying to pick him up. Why else would he be virtually on top of him, when he had a number of other patrons to talk to? Why else would he care about his relationship status? Or who he lived with?

He was relieved when Paolo finally excused himself to tend to another customer. But, sure enough, as soon as that drink was served, he was back.

"Another one?" he asked, motioning to Bart's almost-empty glass.

"No, thanks." He rose from his stool, dropped a few singles on the bar, and left. He really hadn't wanted to return to the couch on which he'd be spending the week so early in the night, but the bartender's attention was proving to be too much.

When he was gone, a regular customer seated at the other end of the bar asked Paolo, "So who was the cutie who just left?"

"Some 'houseboy.'" Paolo's eyes danced at the description. "He *said* he was just visiting. But I'm betting he's a hustler."

The man frowned. "Too bad he left. I wouldn't have minded getting a piece of that."

Paolo playfully swatted at the regular with his bar rag and said, "Yes, why should you be any different from everybody else?"

Chapter 1

I never set out to become an actor. It was something I fell into. I suppose that's understandable, since I grew up pretending.

The pretense began when I was just a child. My parents were on the lower end of the lower-middle class, but they made it clear that we were supposed to project a "certain image" to the good families of Pittsburgh. They were to think my father was hard working (he did most of his work on the edge of a stool in the corner tavern); they were to think that my brother and I were well mannered (we were hellions); and they were to think that our family was "comfortable," even though my parents were constantly hounded by bill collectors.

But we all acted, and the good families of Pittsburgh believed that we really were who we wanted them to think.

We were good actors. So good that sometimes we forgot that we were just playing roles . . .

Two hours into his semi-drunken nap on the couch his phone rang. Noah glanced at the clock on the VCR; it was almost midnight. The movie he had been watching was long over, and now Freddy Krueger was menacing a teenage girl on the television screen.

He toyed with the idea of not answering, but then curiosity got the better of him. Maybe, he thought, it was an interviewee, suddenly infused with gay/lesbian/bisexual/transgendered/two-spirited/questioning/whatever-else-had-been-added-that-week pride, who wanted to speak on the record. The sudden thought of an openly gay homosexual in Washington filled Noah with hope.

But when he answered the phone, it was his stepmother's voice on the other end of the line.

"Noah?"

"Tricia!" He was surprised to hear her voice, especially at that late hour. He had no problems with her—they had always gotten along just fine—but she *was* married to his father, which made her phone calls a bit suspect. That and the fact that, at thirty-eight, she was just four years older than Noah. The thought that if he were straight she would be dating material had always creeped him out a little bit.

"Did I wake you?" she asked.

"No," he lied, picking up the remote and muting the teenager's screams.

Tricia got right down to business. "It's your father, Noah. I'm afraid something has happened."

"Is he all right?"

"Yes, yes!" she said, a forced cheeriness suddenly in her voice. "I don't want you to worry, but I wanted you to know."

"What's wrong, Tricia?"

"He had a heart attack."

"He had a . . ." The words wouldn't come to him. "Is he okay?"

"He'll be fine. The doctors say that it wasn't all that bad." She paused. "It could have been much worse." Another pause—with each one, she was growing more honest—and she added, "They may have to do a bypass. We're still waiting to hear about that. But he's alert and responsive."

Another pause.

"And he sends you his love."

Noah stiffened. If Tricia had never told him that his father sent his love, he probably would have stayed in Washington, trolling bars in the name of research. But in his thirty-four years, he could only remember his father aiming the L word in his direction on four instances: his college graduation, the day his mother finally had the clarity of vision to leave his father, the night Noah cried when his first lover walked out, and one night when they sat all night at the kitchen table as Max poured his heart out when his second divorce became final. There was a fifth time, too, Noah suddenly remembered, but Max had only said the L word because Noah asked him point-blank, so he discounted it because he had forced the issue.

Noah knew that his father loved him. He showed it in a variety of ways. But where the words were concerned, he failed the verbal, but aced the math. The Abrahams were like a family of starchy WASPs, except that they were starchy Jews instead. Not Tricia, of course. *Tricias* were by definition not Jewish. But the rest of them were starchy Jews . . . although about as devout as your average Upper East Side Episcopalians.

So, Noah thought, if his father—the Episcopalian Jew; the Jew from *Ordinary People*—told Tricia to tell him he loved him, there was a problem.

"Noah?"

"I'm here. Now. But I'm leaving for New York"— he glanced at his watch; it was too late to do anything that evening—"in the morning. First train."

"That's not necessary. He's fine."

"He's not 'fine,' " Noah said evenly. "I need to be home."

"But your book . . ."

"It can wait."

"Really, Noah, it's—"

"I'll call you from the train," he said. "And please call me if anything changes overnight."

She surrendered. "I'll keep you posted."

"One more thing," Noah said, feeling incredibly brave. "Next time you see him, tell him I love him."

"All right." She paused yet again. "All right. I will."

After he hung up, Noah wondered if she paused because she knew that he wasn't all that good about using the L word himself. And he wondered if she knew he was scared. And, Noah being Noah, he wondered if she'd even bother to give his father the message.

The night passed without the tragic phone call Noah half expected, although he slept fitfully through a string of unsettling, if unremembered, dreams.

By 6:10 AM, he was at Washington's Union Station. He purchased his Amtrak ticket, grabbed a cup of coffee, stopped at a newsstand to pick up a copy of *The Washington Post* and—since it arrived at the last minute—*The New York Times*, and boarded the 6:30 bound for New York City before he had a chance to sit down.

He gave up on the newspapers before the train reached Baltimore. His mind was somewhere else. After a while, he took out the notes for The Project and tried to make sense of them.

But they were making no sense. The only consistent theme was evasiveness, and it would be difficult, if not impossible, to glean insight from dozens of interviews when the subjects were going out of their way to say as close to nothing as possible.

I am not a quitter, he told himself once again, to which—after a moment of reconsideration—he appended, *But I'm getting pretty damn pessimistic.*

His most recent pessimistic moment, the one leading to the up-ended wastepaper basket the previous evening, had come as a result of his most recent interview. Earlier in the day, in response to an ad he had run in the *Washington Blade*, a press aide to a United States senator from Ohio had agreed to meet him at a tiny, not-very-popular bistro in Georgetown. The aide—Noah agreed to refer to him as "G. C.," which were not his real initials—was nervous bordering on paranoid through their brief meeting, and only agreed to be taped after Noah assured him the tape would, eventually, be destroyed.

Later, back at home in his third-floor walk-up apartment on P

Street that almost overlooked Dupont Circle, if you stretched out the window and leaned to the right, Noah listened to that tape. And he didn't like what he heard. He had hoped that his immediate memory of the interview had been wrong, and that—once he listened to the tape—he would discover that G. C. had provided some useful information. But his memory was, regrettably, perfect.

G. C.:   So when I realized I was attracted to other men, I mean, exclusively, I became very, uh . . . I had a lot of fear.

NOAH: "Realized"? Or "admitted"?

G. C.:   Oh, I never admitted it to anyone. Not at first.

NOAH: Did you admit it to yourself? I mean, were you in some sort of self-denial? Or were you aware?

G. C.:   Denial? Oh . . . I suppose that's one way to look at it. Yes, I suppose that's the right term. Because I did realize it before, back when, I dunno, when I was a teenager, maybe. But I thought I could overcome it.

NOAH: But you couldn't.

G. C.:   I couldn't.

NOAH: And you tried?

G. C.:   *[Nervous laughter]* Oh, yeah, I tried. But then I went to work for Congress, and I, well . . . I guess you could say that I didn't have to try anymore, because I became completelashuel.

Noah stopped the tape recorder. "Completelashuel?" What the hell was it he had said, or tried to say, under the relative quiet of that unpopular Georgetown bistro? He rewound the tape and listened again.

G. C.:   Well . . . I guess you could say that I didn't have to try anymore, because I became completelashuel.

Noah closed his eyes and concentrated. That's what he had said. "Completelashuel." Complete . . . something? Complete lashuel? No, that didn't make sense. *Lashuel . . . lashuel . . .* a word that sounds like "lashuel." And goes with the word "complete."

Complete . . . *asshole.* G. C. had become a complete asshole. That would have almost made sense to Noah, given his work for a complete asshole of a United States senator from Ohio, except this particular Mormon would never use a word like "asshole."

Noah rewound the tape once again, the recorder playing a brief *wee-wee-wee*, then hit the "PLAY" button. Again, G. C.'s midwestern drawl came to life, tinny through the small machine.

> G. C.:   I tried. But then I went to work for Congress, and I,
> well . . . I guess you could say that I didn't have to try
> anymore, because I became completelashuel.

Noah tossed the tape recorder down on a lushly padded chair and stared at it for a moment with contempt, as if the inanimate object was the problem, not G. C.

And then, his frustration boiling over, he kicked the wastepaper basket, sending those crumpled balls of paper scattering across the floor.

Even now, with twelve hours or so to put things in perspective, he was no less frustrated. It was hopeless. It was useless. G. C. would forever be a completelashuel—whatever that meant, it couldn't be good—and there was nothing Noah could do about it, unless he disobeyed the interviewee's request—was it a request, or an order? More an order, he thought—and followed up on their interview.

Completelashuel. Fuck. "Completelashuel" was starting to sound like a good word to describe this entire project. Nearly ninety hours of taped interviews, most conducted in a low mumble mimicking G. C., hundreds of pieces of paper—from notebook pages to cocktail napkins—with scrawls in his sober and not-so-sober handwriting, documenting the phenomenon of the gay aides to the most powerful men in the United States of America, all justifying their decision to stay in the closet. The only real revelation he had was that party and ideology didn't matter in his decidedly unscientific survey. Noah may have been able to locate more gay Democratic aides than gay Republican aides, but they were closeted in what seemed to be proportionate numbers. More than a third of a century after Stonewall, career success for gay men—and a few lesbians— in Washington, DC was still all about passing as straight. Or at least asexual.

Asexual.

Noah reached for his bag, stashed under his legs, and rifled through it until he found the tape recorder. He searched the cassette until he found the offending part of the interview and hit PLAY and, yes, G. C. had obviously swallowed his words during the interview, fearful of being overheard. Finally, Noah heard him say that damn word, and closed his eyes in relief. "Completelashuel" was, in fact, "completely" (and he started swallowing on the "y") "asexual."

Yeah, that made sense.

He wanted to celebrate his detective skills, but Noah was suddenly gripped by a feeling that warranted no celebration. The whole project was useless. *The Project* was useless.

So G. C. had forced himself into asexuality. And he *still* couldn't talk about it. Again, Noah stared down the tape recorder, blaming it for the state of his world.

G. C. would never come out and tell his boss, the distinguished gentleman from Ohio, that he was gay. G. C. would never even buy Noah's book, should it ever actually be written, for fear of possibly being seen buying it in a bookstore, or having an online order tracked down, or having a guest see it in his home. Neither would L. G., Dennis (the real name), Dennis (the pseudonym), West Virginia Gary, Missouri Gary, Melissa E., Kay, the one-lettered K., or any of the others who had responded to his *Blade* ads or Craigslist solicitations.

Noah could document their existence, in an anonymous way, but it wouldn't make a bit of difference. They would always hide in the shadows, either furtively homosexual or, well, *completelashuel.* And there wasn't a damned thing he could do about it. His contribution to the advancement of gay and lesbian rights would be as futile as the insight he was not getting from his subjects.

The book—the book he once thought of as a career maker, an award-winner—might as well be a work of fiction, for all it would matter. His idea had bumped into reality and shattered. People who swallowed words like "asexual" would never allow themselves to be sexual beings. They could be leaders on arms control, the environment, war, peace, education, Social Security, Medicaid, health care, the pork barrel, the Brady Bill, NAFTA, and the nuances of constitutional law—and, on occasion, they could even guide their elected employers through a whole-scale defense of "traditional marriage," trading a defense of their sexuality for votes—but they would never, *ever* . . .

With a groan, Noah sank back into the train seat, trying to force away his frustration, and thought, *Why is this so fucking hard?* It was a question directed equally at himself and his reluctant subjects.

When he was honest with himself, Noah Abraham recognized that a strong streak of self-righteousness ran through him. He blamed that equally on nature (especially those genes from his father) and nurture (especially the upbringing by his father). When he was honest with himself, Noah Abraham blamed a lot of things on his father.

When he was dishonest with himself, he blamed his father even more.

He had been condemned to a life of openness and affluence. From an objective standpoint, that easy life made The Project so much more difficult for Noah. After all, if Noah was self-righteous, it was because his father had made life so easy. Maybe, just *maybe*, if he had a bit more fear, he could somehow wrap his head around G. C. and the men and women who lived like G. C.

He put the tape recorder back in his bag and stared out the window, contemplating the adversities he faced because, ironically, his life held almost no adversity. Out of the corner of his eye he saw a young man unsteadily returning down the swaying aisle from the café car, flashing Noah a smile as he passed, which only served to remind him of yet another personal advantage. If it wasn't enough that he was confident, intelligent, politically conscious, healthy, blessed with family money, and openly and comfortably gay, he also suffered with another intolerable lack of adversity: the knowledge that most people considered him quite good looking.

Gay, rich, smart, and good looking. Curse upon curse upon curse upon curse.

Noah didn't think twice about his desirability. He knew better, after almost fifteen years as an openly gay man. He knew he wasn't considered traditionally "handsome": that designation went to the Adonises with the square jaws, broad shoulders, and height. But he was universally considered "cute," and that was enough to guarantee him attention every time he wanted it, and often when he didn't. At five foot seven, he was on the slightly shorter side of male physiology, but even that seemed to work to his advantage. The rest of the package—the olive complexion, deep brown eyes, full head of wavy dark hair, trim frame, and even those dimples that lit up his face when he smiled—sealed the deal.

Over the years, Noah had not been the only person to speculate that perhaps he had been adopted. After all, his parents were not only taller, they were also not quite as "cute." But that speculation was put to rest by old family photographs, with their evidence of his remarkable resemblance to his maternal grandfather. Noah, of course, was disappointed, because if he had been adopted it would have meant that there had been one tiny bit of adversity in his life. But no. His family had even ruined *that* fantasy with those photographs. He was half Abraham and half Feldman, and he would have to live with that burden.

He wanted to struggle, but couldn't find anything to struggle against . . . so he chose to struggle with himself. As well as those people who displeased him: the closeted completelashuels of Washington, DC.

Noah noticed with a start that the young man who had smiled at him moments earlier was now sitting in the row of seats across the aisle. He gave him a polite nod, turned up his iPod, and turned to look back out the window, watching the fields and swamps and small villages of Maryland pass by.

At the moment Noah's train was departing Philadelphia's Thirtieth Street Station, Bart Gustafson awoke, tangled in sheets. He looked around the room in confusion before remembering that he was not at home in Southampton, but rather on a sleeper-sofa somewhere near Lincoln Center. He stretched, feeling an unfamiliar stiffness in his back brought on by the thin mattress.

"Jon?!" he called out to his host as he staggered to the kitchen. Jon wasn't there, but the coffee maker was turned on and the urn was half full. He poured a mug and sat, taking in the view of the traffic backed up on West Sixty-Fifth Street.

He wasn't disappointed that his host was out of the apartment. He was a nice enough man, but he was also close friends with Bart's employer . . . which meant that most of their conversation revolved around his employer. Bart didn't take many days off from his job, though, and talking about his boss on a rare vacation day didn't serve his vacation purposes.

The previous night had been a case in point. After Bart arrived back at the apartment—far too early, thanks to the unwanted attention of the bartender at The Penthouse—Jon had kept him up until after midnight reminiscing about "the old days." While Bart certainly appreciated the free place to crash while he was in Manhattan, he was beginning to wonder if it was worth it, since the point of his getaway was to *get away*.

Okay, he thought, as he refilled his coffee mug, it was Wednesday, the second day of his brief vacation, and he was in Manhattan, which meant he could not—under any circumstance—spend the day in front of the television. And, to the extent he could avoid it, he would also try not to talk about work or work-related people.

He drained his coffee and walked to the shower, determined to make a vacation for himself.

"You shouldn't have come." Thus spoke Max Abraham.

"I *had* to come."

Max shrugged. "Eh. So how's life?"

"That's not the big news here, is it?" Noah sat in the cold plastic chair next to his father's bed. "How are you?"

Max raised one of his bushy eyebrows in his son's direction. "My life continues. All in all, I suppose that's big news. It's certainly *good* news. For me, at least."

Noah smiled as he watched that bushy eyebrow hiked up on his father's forehead. For a moment, he wasn't just Max Abraham, father, but Max Abraham, New York City icon. In his frequent eagerness to be his own man, Noah sometimes forgot that he also enjoyed his status as the son of one of New York's most recognizable celebrities.

Max Abraham was one of the more flamboyant members of the New York City legal community. For several decades, he had represented actors, captains of industry, mob figures, cardinals, and politicians, and while it was true that his reputation for self-promotion exceeded that of his reputation for legal skills, he had managed to make untold millions of dollars in the process. Through pluck and nerve—and knowing when to call in the experts to shore himself up—he had managed to become so well known that not only was he a regular feature of the New York social scene, he was a recurring character on *Saturday Night Live* known as "Famous Lawyer Abe Maxham." Pure coincidence, the show's producers claimed, when Max threatened to sue. Pure coincidence . . . right down to those uncontrollable eyebrows.

Of course there had been no lawsuit. Max had bluffed, but would have never followed through. The *Saturday Night Live* parody validated his status as an iconic New Yorker, a status Max valued dearly. The lawsuit had been nothing more than a strategy to parley the SNL caricature into a few additional mentions on Page Six. It had worked—those things usually did—and even that morning as he rested in his hospital bed, Max was strategizing on how best to publicize his heart attack without scaring off potential clients.

"You gave us quite a scare," Noah said.

"I gave *you* a scare?" Again, an eyebrow hoisted. "Let me tell you about scary, Noah. Scary is when you're afraid your life might be determined by whether or not those asshole Manhattan drivers will get out of the way to let your ambulance up Third Avenue. *That* is scary."

Noah laughed. His father had been guilty of many things over the years—bad parent, worse husband—but his sense of humor always bought him forgiveness.

"And anyway," Max continued, "with a little luck I'll be out of here in a few days."

"You *should* get out of here. This hospital cramps your style."

In truth, he thought his father didn't look so bad for a man who had just suffered a heart attack and might undergo surgery. A bit pale and drawn, but that was understandable. Looking at him, Noah felt reassured that he would be around, making him crazy, for another couple of decades.

Max leaned toward Noah. "So tell me how the book is going."

"It's not." Noah let out a long sigh. "No one wants to talk. Not on the record. And when they *do* talk, it's . . . it's sad. Self-loathing justifications for why they won't come out, why they'd rather enable the enemy than—"

"Stop right there." Max punctuated his command with a sweeping hand-gesture. "Who is the enemy?"

"Anti-gay politicians. The ones they usually work for."

Despite his recent heart attack, the argumentative lawyer in Max began to take over.

"Define 'anti-gay.'"

Max was good, but—on this topic—Noah knew he was better. He began ticking off legislation. "The Federal Marriage Amendment. 'Don't Ask, Don't Tell.' Um . . . opposition to AIDS funding and information. Equating homosexuality with bestiality and pedophilia . . . Do I have to go on?"

"You have some good examples, Noah. And I'm not arguing with you. But is everyone who supports 'Don't Ask, Don't Tell' anti-gay?"

"Yes."

"Bill Clinton was anti-gay?"

"That was different. He was forced—"

"Yes!" Max rose from his prone position, and Noah could almost see him in a suit and tie, gesturing to hold the attention of the jury, instead of lying in a pale blue hospital gown under an industrial-grade sheet. "Yes, Clinton was *forced*. But he *did it*. He *conceded*. And in the process he both lost a battle *and* a war."

"If he didn't, it would have been worse."

"I'm not arguing with you against Clinton. Come on; you know that I'm friends with Bill and Hillary. Love them! All I'm saying is that you might want to remember that in politics, as in life, the palette has very little black and white, but a lot of shades of gray."

"The world doesn't look like that to me."

He sighed. "You're young."

"Thirty-four. Almost thirty-five."

"Young." Max grabbed a glass of water from the bedside table, drank, and continued. "Gays are the new Jews. I think you should fight for equality, but I don't think you should assume that everyone is going to get it, or that it's going to be easy. Take it from a Jew born in the Holocaust era. To me, it's insane to think that a lot of people didn't 'get it' about Jews just a few generations ago. It's better now . . . not perfect, but better. It will be better for you, too, but you have to realize that a lot of people—even a lot of *gay* people—are going to have a learning curve."

Noah shook his head. "It had better be a steep curve. Most of us don't want to wait, Dad."

"Ah . . ." Max closed his eyes and slumped back against the pillow. "The impatience of youth."

"I'm thirty-four," Noah reminded him. Again.

"Youth. You will learn."

Despite the fact that he had rushed two hundred miles to his bedside, Noah began to remember why they kept their distance from each other. Max Abraham was the ultimate negotiator, always willing to open with a compromise rather than stand on principle. Noah Abraham was someone altogether different. The only consolation, Noah thought, was that the negotiator and the idealist were mostly on the same side.

"How about," Noah said, "we change the subject."

His father smiled. "So I'm right?"

"Dad, I'm going to tell you that you're right. You are one-hundred-percent correct. And do you know why I'm going to tell you that?"

"Because I just had a heart attack."

"You are a very smart man."

Max laughed. "Play to your advantages, then take the victory and don't look back."

This time Noah laughed along with the fleshy, temporarily grayish man with the bushy eyebrows and the salt-and-pepper hair who, by some accident of biology, was his father. And he realized that maybe they were more alike than he liked to think.

When the laughter faded, Max said, "I updated my will—"

Noah stopped him. "We're not talking about that. *You'll* probably outlive *me*. Let's talk about something else. How has Tricia been holding up?"

Max shook his head. "It's tough. She's too young to . . ." He trailed off, realizing that the subject of Tricia's age was a bit of a sore point for his son. "She's doing all right. But why don't you tell me what's going on in your life. Are you still dating that architect?"

The architect would have been Harry. Noah and Harry had been more than "dating," and Max knew it, but he couldn't quite find the right words to advance a same-sex relationship to the next, more serious level.

And, in any event, Harry walked out of Noah's life one year earlier and was never heard from again, which was hard to do in Washington, but he had managed it. After Harry was gone, Noah didn't mourn; and he also didn't feel compelled to cry about it to his family. He merely mentioned it during a phone call, almost as an after-thought. The breakup had been dismissed with the briefest of mentions and Noah—as he always did—moved on with his life. It was just one of those things that he had to put quickly and silently in the past.

Although now, with his father seemingly not even remembering the breakup, he wished he had made a slightly bigger deal over it.

"No. Harry and I split up." He paused and added, "Quite some time ago."

"Sorry. He seemed like a nice guy." When Noah didn't reply, he added, "Are you dating anyone now?"

"I'm taking a breather. There's no rush, right?"

"Right." There were a few moments of awkward silence until Max understood that his son was saying nothing more on the subject, then he scrambled for a new topic. "So . . . back to your book."

Noah sighed. "I can't see how I can possibly finish it. No one will talk on the record, and when they do talk, they don't say anything. I wonder sometimes why they even bother talking to me."

"Maybe they *are* talking to you. Maybe you're just not listening."

"I beg your pardon?"

"You are the product of privilege, and you forget that sometimes. You've had a good life, but I'm not quite sure you appreciate exactly how good you've had it." Blood was suddenly rushing to Noah's head, but he decided to give his father a free pass for his heart attack and held his tongue.

Max continued. "Seriously. You've always had money and a roof. Don't get me wrong; I was happy to provide them. And you were also privileged to be born into a family that accepted you, gay and all. How old were you? Seventeen?"

"Twenty."

"Twenty. Young. But you told me you were gay, and still you were accepted and supported." He waved a steady finger in Noah's direction. "Twenty years old, and you were out, gay, and proud, with the full support of your family and no financial worries. Do you think that's the way it happens for everyone?"

"No. I know that I had it easier than a lot of people. But if people don't come out—"

Max slumped back into the thin pillows, dismissing the argument before Noah had a chance to start it. "I know, I know. If peo-

ple don't come out, Bush and Cheney will think no one except for
you and Rosie O'Donnell are gay and they'll put you in camps.
Blah, blah, blah."

Blah, blah, blah? Had his father, the famous lawyer and occasional social activist Max Abraham, really just dismissed his fears,
diminishing them to three nonsense syllables? A Jew born at a time
when millions of Jews were being exterminated in Nazi camps? A
man who lived through, and protested against, McCarthyism and
segregation? *This* was the man who was telling him that he was unrealistic to expect gay men and lesbians to show their faces?

Noah suddenly wished they were still talking about Harry.

The silence following his comment lasted an uncomfortably long
time, before Max finally—and correctly—said, "I think I've pissed you
off."

"A little."

"Eh, maybe it's good to get pissed off sometimes. Right?" Noah
didn't answer. "I'm sorry, but I'm a bit tired. I didn't mean to cause
a problem here. I was just trying to point out that it's easier for
some people—you, for example—to come out than it is for others." Max looked at Noah and winked, and Noah thought, *Did he
wink? Yes, he winked!* Which just pissed him off even more.

"You're a good boy," Max said. "You've got passion, and—most
importantly—you *are* right. I hope you succeed. Just . . . try a little
patience."

Noah could understand why other lawyers ran when his father
walked into a room, because he was by turns frustrating, charming,
infuriating, friendly, maddening, self-deprecating, and, finally . . .
well, he was Max Abraham. He did whatever he could to get your
goat, then embraced you before you could hate him. And then,
when all was forgiven, he would whip out the needle yet again.

In this case, though, Max Abraham was apparently going to wait
for the needle, because he went for the dodge . . . although it was
an understandable dodge.

He yawned.

"I hate to end such an . . . *interesting* discussion on this note, but
I'm getting tired, and I want to save some energy for Tricia. You
don't mind?"

In fact, Noah was relieved. "No, I understand."

"We'll pick this up later, okay?"

"Okay." Not that picking it up again was really necessary, but Noah knew his father wouldn't let the conversation end until he had won the argument unequivocally. They had been down this road before.

Back safely in the waiting room, Noah sent Tricia in, knowing that Max needed to talk to a young person with a more pragmatic sensibility.

And Noah wasn't that young person. He was just his son.

Noah sat in the waiting room while Tricia visited, mostly because he had nothing else to do at 1:30 in the afternoon in a city where he no longer lived. He made another feeble attempt to leaf through his notes, but, despite his father's avid advocacy on their behalf, still couldn't get inside the heads of the completelashuels.

Even as he stewed over his words, he knew he had to concede to his father one point: Max Abraham, as well as Noah's mother, had made his coming-out process an easy one. Even in their liberal and generally secular precincts of Manhattan's Upper East Side, the family dynamics involved in announcing one was gay were usually fraught with fear and loathing, both internal and external. But that wasn't Noah's experience. Maybe it was the innate decency of his parents, he thought, or maybe it was their interactions with openly gay men and lesbians predating Stonewall. Or maybe it was the distance they placed in their relationship—even when Noah was a child—that allowed his parents to step back and look at him not as the end product of their commingled DNA, but as just another person, the way they would have barely raised an eyebrow upon learning the same news about a neighbor's child. Whatever, he thought; the important thing was that after he gathered his courage and told his parents he was gay at twenty years of age, they had given him their support. The revelation didn't necessarily make them any closer, but it wasn't awkward, and it didn't drive them apart.

It just . . . was.

In that sense, Noah knew—once again—that he was privileged. He wasn't treated as an embarrassment, or even as the wayward son who was dating someone his parents didn't like. He was treated the same way he had always been treated, and while that also left something to be desired, he had always believed that a person can't miss something that they never had.

Still, he was perplexed. A lot of people faced bigger adversities than the completelashuels. But the complicity of the complete-lashuels in the great silence surrounding the lives of gay men and lesbians angered him. When they hid in their closets, and even worked against their own interests, they made people like Noah do all the work. They could feel safe celebrating a Friday Happy Hour at JR's because he did their work for them, and helped free their lives in the hours they weren't glued to both their desks and their self-denial.

In a sense, Noah felt he was working overtime to make their lives easier. And while Max Abraham had a hardworking son, he didn't like working quite that hard.

He glanced at a clock on the generic white wall of the waiting room and was surprised to see that a half hour had passed. Tricia would be ending her visit soon, which meant that Noah would have to prepare himself for an afternoon of strained small talk with his father's trophy wife. In his head, he began preparing topics, a task complicated by the fact that he really didn't know his stepmother all that well. Max and Tricia had been married for five years, a period coinciding with his self-imposed exile in Washington. They really hadn't had time to bond in the interim. This, Noah supposed, would have to be that time.

He ticked through possible small-talk topics in his head. Politics would be taboo, as would homosexuality. Family issues would also be verboten; the last thing Tricia needed to hear was a litany of his problems with her husband. However, *her* family was an option; Noah knew little about them, except that they were all still living a remarkably unremarkable existence in Buffalo. Of course, he also knew almost nothing about Buffalo, beyond snow, the Bills, and chicken wings, so if they had to go in that direction, Tricia would have to carry the conversation.

Since Noah had little interest in interior design, gardening, and social gossip—the usual interests of the Park Avenue Trophy Wife crowd—those topics were out. Pop culture could kill an hour, he thought, as long as she appreciated old movies and good theater. And the conversation would come to an abrupt end if she mentioned *Mamma Mia* or any boy bands. That was for certain.

He sighed. It was going to be an afternoon spent in light conversation about growing up in Buffalo. There was no way around it.

The squeaking wheels of a gurney snapped him out of his thoughts. Noah looked up to see the empty cot pass him, pushed by a short, cute, and very blond nurse. And since the nurse was also male, he offered a smile and received one in return.

Too damn easy, he thought, watching the nurse as he guided the gurney through the waiting room. The man gave him one last glance and smile as he left, and Noah returned to the Tricia dilemma.

It was not that Noah didn't like Tricia. But his father was sixty-four, she was thirty-eight, and Noah was thirty-four. To Noah, it was . . . strange. Uncomfortable.

At least when his mother remarried she had the decency to marry someone who was only a decade younger. Sixty-four related to fifty-four much better than sixty-four related to thirty-eight. As the son who had to relate to all of those people, Noah considered that an undeniable truth. A stepmother who was basically his own age was just . . . *wrong*.

He looked again after the departed nurse, wondering if an afternoon assignation would be appropriate while his father was in a hospital bed, before deciding that, although it would be more fun than forced conversation with Tricia, it would also be tacky. Propriety was so unfair in this sort of circumstance.

Minutes later Tricia walked into the waiting room and, spotting Noah, motioned for him to join her. Wordlessly, he obeyed.

They walked the few blocks from the hospital to Max and Tricia Abraham's Park Avenue apartment. The day was warm, the sidewalks were busy, and neither of them—lost in their own thoughts and not quite sure how to relate to one another outside of pleasant smiles and banal observations about the weather or the traffic— felt the need for conversation. When they reached the lobby of the white-brick building at the corner of East Seventy-third Street, Tricia excused herself to get the mail, which was as close as they came to conversation. Then, envelopes in her hand, they ascended in the elevator to the eleventh floor in silence.

Once inside the apartment, Noah dropped his bag in the foyer and awkwardly followed Tricia as she walked room to room, distractedly straightening things that didn't need straightening. It had been a while since he had been home, Noah realized, and—as he had expected—Tricia had been busying herself redecorating. Almost certainly through his father's influence, there was now a lot of leather in the apartment: couch, armchairs . . . even the padding at the edges of a set of end tables. He felt it made the large living room seem more closed and intimate, although the light curtains on the large south-facing windows and the tasteful use of flowers were clearly Tricia's efforts to soften the testosterone-driven room.

Tricia walked into the kitchen, all modern and metallic, filled with appliances Noah couldn't begin to identify, which uniformly bore the logos of what appeared to be an array of German and Swedish firms. It was only when she reached the refrigerator that she finally asked him, "Are you going to follow me *everywhere* for the next few days?"

He blushed. "Uh . . . I just thought you might need help."

"What I need," she said, opening up the refrigerator, "is a glass of wine." She took an uncorked white wine bottle from the shelf inside the door. "Care to join me?"

"Sure," he said, impulsively trying to forge a bond with her even though he really didn't feel like having a drink, especially so early in the afternoon.

She poured two glasses, offered him one, and motioned to the living room, where they sat an appropriate distance apart. She took the leather couch; he took one of the leather chairs.

"A lot of leather," Noah said, stumbling in his effort to come up with an ice-breaker.

"It was your father's idea. Obviously. Although I've come to like it. We bought the furniture last year, and I guess he was in a partic- ularly masculine frame of mind. Take this leather, throw in a bunch of red meat, add a high-pressure legal practice, and I guess you've proven your manhood without having to embarrass yourself with a mistress or a shiny red sports car." She looked at Noah and smiled. "You see? It was easier to get used to the leather than worry about the mistress."

It had never before crossed his mind that Tricia had been his fa- ther's mistress before she was his wife. But now it had, and he couldn't shake the thought. He wished she hadn't brought up his father's apparent recent need to reaffirm his masculinity, because it made him realize that his father had had decades in which to go through several midlife crises.

"So how is your mother?" she asked, moving the topic of conversation from one area of discomfort to another.

"Fine. She's . . . fine."

"I've always liked her."

Noah twitched. Did his father's third wife really just say something nice about his father's first wife? How would they have even—?

"We were both on a benefit committee for the Whitney a few years ago," she said, anticipating his reaction and, in fact, seeming to enjoy it. "So how does she like living in Florida?"

"Fine." He paused. "Just fine."

Noah's relationship with his mother was, if possible, even more complex than his relationship with his father. Divorced from Max just a few years after Noah was born, Frieda Feldman Abraham took her substantial settlement and started life anew, reborn as an Upper West Side social activist. Even as he was unable to shed it, he knew that his resentment about having been given everything too easily came directly from the mouth of his mother. While he never disliked his mother for that, he always felt wary and guilty in her presence. And he also wasn't sorry she had moved to Florida.

Also, he didn't like the way she ate her salad. That poke-poke-poking at each individual lettuce leaf made him want to scream sometimes.

Noah shook his head. "It's just sort of strange. I mean, my mother knowing my stepmother . . ."

Tricia wagged a finger in front of his face. "We've had this conversation before, haven't we?"

It took Noah a few seconds to understand what she meant, but then he remembered.

"Sorry. I mean, 'my mother knowing my *father's wife*.' Better?"

"Much," she said, offering no further information. Several times in the past she had warned him away from the word "stepmother" without explanation, and Noah now knew better than to ask. It was her title, so she had the right to be called what she wanted to be called, even if Noah felt that calling her "his father's wife" added even more distance to an already distant relationship.

They sat—uncomfortable among the leather-laden comfort—

for a long stretch of the mid-afternoon, vaguely looking out the window at the sliver of blue between the buildings, sipping wine, and wishing for easy conversation. Finally, Noah remembered his prepared topic.

"So your family . . . They're in Buffalo?"

After a half hour or so listening to what he came to think of as the Chronicles of Buffalo, conversation again wound down. Noah excused himself and, finally collecting his bag from the foyer, walked down a picture-lined hallway to the guest bedroom.

He was pleased to see that his former bedroom had not been leatherized in the redecorating process. In fact, the room retained a number of distinctly feminine touches. It was light and airy, the walls a periwinkle blue and the furniture spare and unimposing.

He tossed his bag at the foot of the bed, then tossed himself on top of the off-white comforter, where he tried unsuccessfully to nap. He stayed there for a long time, wondering how he could escape and where he could escape to.

A natural loner, Noah was not one of those people who prided themselves on collecting large numbers of close friends. He had a few friends—acquaintances, really—in Washington he could call when he really needed to get out of the apartment, but otherwise he was quite content to be on his own. His life had been quite similar when he lived in New York, but in the intervening years he had lost contact with his old crowd. He was now alone in Manhattan, and unless he went out by himself, he would be a prisoner of Park Avenue until it was time to go back to Washington and again face the hopelessness of The Project.

There were always museums, movies, and theater, but he couldn't think of them as solitary activities. Like dining alone in a restaurant, Noah felt uncomfortable flying solo at venues where everyone else came in multiples. Wandering the city might kill some time, but Noah had no great desire to wander.

He tossed and turned on the bed for what felt like quite a while longer, mulling his undesirable options and weighing them against the alternative, which was uncomfortable boredom. When he finally looked at the clock on the nightstand, only fifteen minutes had passed.

"Fuck," he muttered to himself. It was going to be a long visit. Even if he left the following day, it was going to be a long visit.

And because of those thoughts, he was actually grateful when he heard Tricia knock lightly on the guest room door.

"Come in," he called out, turning slightly to face her as she eased the door open.

"Are you as bored as I am?" she asked.

He blushed. Was it that obvious?

"Well . . . you know, it's not my house, and I didn't bring a book, so I'm sort of . . ." He smiled. "Yeah, I guess I'm a bit bored. Uh . . . no offense."

It was her turn to smile. "None taken. But I was thinking we should do something."

"Something . . . ? Something like what?"

She frowned. "Anything to get out of this house. I've barely had a breath of fresh air since your father went into the hospital, and once he comes home . . . well, I might as well forget about having a life for a while."

"But the doctors said he'll be back to normal in no time."

She blew a wisp of stray blond hair out of her eyes. "They always say things like that, but it never quite works that way. Your father was lucky, but he's still going to need some time to recuperate. Especially with *his* personality. If he were a laid-back, calm man, it would be a lot easier. But he's going to have to make an effort to relax, and I'm afraid there's going to be a lot of stress around here."

"Hire him a nurse."

She laughed. "I can't even keep a cleaning lady. Five years of marriage and not *one* has ever done a good enough job . . . according to him, that is. So let's forget about getting a nurse, because I'll be spending more time interviewing than he'll be spending recuperating."

Noah knew she spoke the truth. "So what do you want to do?" he asked, vaguely fearing something worse than boredom.

"I was thinking a bar."

That caught him by surprise. He thought she had been setting him up for a long dinner at whichever Upper East Side bistro was currently in vogue among the Park Avenue Trophy Wife set. Perhaps the glass of wine early in the afternoon should have been a warning to him. "His father's wife" had, in the course of just a few hours, surprised him several times: she might have been a mistress, and she might be a lush. Noah decided that he should neither dismiss her nor underestimate her.

He glanced at the clock on his nightstand.

"It's only four o'clock," he announced. "Isn't it a bit early?"

"Why, Noah! I didn't know you were such a stick-in-the-mud!" Tricia leaned against the door frame. "Never heard of Happy Hour?"

He was wary. "I've heard of it."

"I want to go." She affected a pout. "Take me out to Happy Hour."

"You are a very strange stepmother."

An index finger wagged in his direction. "Ah-ah!"

"Sorry. You are a very strange wife-of-my-father."

To which, she said simply, "Thank you," and—with a toss of her hair—left to change into more appropriate attire.

Chapter 2

People surprise you.

The ones you expect to be stuffy turn out to be down to earth. The ones you think you'll never see again become your best friends. The ones you hate, you learn to love, and the ones you love, well . . . maybe, maybe not.

When I first arrived in Hollywood I was twenty-three years old and had never been west of Cincinnati. And yet for some reason I was convinced that I could be an actor. After being cast in that school play when my knee injury kept me out of sports, I guess I thought I was a natural.

Fortunately, I wasn't the only one. After three months of waiting tables to put bread on *my* table I met a casting agent who looked me over, said I had just the "naivety" he was looking for to play a college kid in a movie he was casting.

I was fired two days into shooting. I guess he was wrong.

But right or wrong, that casting agent didn't give up on me. In fact, he went in a completely different direction, and one week after I was fired he slipped me into a stylish crime drama called *The Fresh Kill.* And a star was born, all because he had faith, and because he could see beyond that naïve twenty-three-year-old carrying trays and busing tables . . .

If Noah had any lingering doubts that their time together could still turn into a trophy-wife bistro excursion, they evaporated when he met Tricia in the foyer fifteen minutes later. He had used the time to freshen up and change into something more respectable; she, however, had used the time to dress down, exchanging the business casual attire she wore to the hospital for a casual jeans-and-top ensemble. And, in her designer jeans, he had to admit, in a gay sort of way, that his father's wife was kind of hot.

"So where do you want to go?" he asked. "I assume by the way you're dressed you want to mix with the masses this afternoon."

"I *am* the masses. I love being married to your father, and the way we live, but I'll always be a girl from Buffalo."

"Okay, Girl from Buffalo. Since you're apparently keeping it real this afternoon, where do you want to go?"

"Take me . . ." She paused and thought for a moment. "Take me to one of your places."

"*My* places?"

"Where do you go out when you're in the city?"

That was a good question. It had been so long since he'd been home that he struggled to recall the name of a bar. There was The Penthouse on the Upper East Side, but that would be too snooty for the dressed-down Tricia. There were the bars in Chelsea and the West and East Villages, but it had been so long, he was drawing a blank on specific locations, and at the rate bars came and went, he doubted that many of them were still in business. And in any event, all the bars he could think of—his old haunts—were gay, which he didn't think would hold much appeal for either of them.

"There are a few places," he finally said. "But I can't think of anywhere you'd be interested to go. Me, either, for that matter."

"You're such a snob. Do you think these bars are too downscale for me?"

"No. But all the ones that come to mind are . . . well, they're definitely too, um, *gay*."

"Perfect." With that, she flung open the front door and they were on their way.

They took the elevator back down to the immaculate, marbled lobby, where the solicitous doorman—even in September remembering that holiday bonuses were just a few months away—made a point of inquiring about Mr. Abraham.

"He'll be fine, Gustav," said Tricia, flashing a smile that she made sure also conveyed concern, lest the building staff start gossiping that she had poisoned him, as they had about Mrs. Jurgen in 5D when Mr. Jurgen suffered a stroke back in May. "But you'll be seeing a lot more of him for a while."

"Homebound?"

"For a few months," she said. "And if you know of any good home health care aides, I'd appreciate it."

Gustav, knowing the Abrahams's track record with cleaning ladies, nodded noncommittally, then turned his attention to a tiny, elderly woman entering the lobby, pasted on his bonus-worthy smile, and said, "Good afternoon, Mrs. Levy."

The older woman nodded, then, seeing Tricia, stopped and said, "I'm so sorry to hear about Max, dear. How is he?"

"He'll be fine," said Tricia, again employing her "not-guilty" smile. "Maybe this is God's way of telling him to slow down."

"Do tell him that Arthur and I send our best wishes," said Mrs. Levy, speaking to Tricia but sizing up the good-looking young man standing next to her . . . the young man whose hand the scandalously young Mrs. Abraham was now taking in hers.

"I'll do that," said Tricia, watching with satisfaction as Mrs. Levy's attention focused almost exclusively on her handclasp with Noah.

"Uh . . . yes, thank you." Mrs. Levy finally broke her fascination with their hands and looked directly at Noah. "I don't believe we've met. I'm Muriel Levy. 10C."

Noah was about to answer, but Tricia beat him to the punch. "This is Noah. You'll be seeing him around the building for the next week or so."

"I see." Mrs. Levy knew that she was scowling, and, after silently reprimanding herself for her rudeness, forced a thin smile on her face, which was deteriorating into a relief map despite the efforts of the best plastic surgeons in New York. "Very nice to meet you, Noah."

"Ma'am," said Noah, nodding politely.

Mrs. Levy walked toward the elevators, hoping she wouldn't burst before she had the opportunity to discuss with her friends in the building the good-looking, mysterious stranger whose visit with the very young Mrs. Abraham coincided with Mr. Abraham's hospitalization. And she was holding *his hand*! In *the lobby*!

At the same time, Tricia and Noah declined Gustav's offer to get them a cab, and walked together out onto the Park Avenue sidewalk.

"I don't think she realizes that I'm Max's son," said Noah, when they were out in the sunshine.

"I hope not," said Tricia, straining her eyes north up Park Avenue to see if any empty cabs were approaching.

"You're not concerned about building gossip?"

Tricia smiled. "Not at all. I've been dealing with it since I married your father. I think it's funny." She spotted a cab and stepped off the curb, hailing it from between two parked cars. "The building staff knows who you are, and that's all that's important. They're the only ones who can cause real trouble. The rest of it . . . well, it's funny."

When the cab stopped, Noah opened the door, allowing Tricia to get in first. He followed her into the backseat.

"So where to?" she asked, when they were strapped into the still-idle cab. "Any brilliant thoughts yet?"

"Not yet." He pointed south, where they could see thirty blocks down the broad avenue to the MetLife Building. "Let's just head south."

"Just drive south while we figure this out," Tricia told the driver, and the cab lurched into "drive."

"Sorry," said Noah. "But I'm still drawing a blank here."

"Well, at least we're heading in the right direction. The pickings will be richer south of Park and Seventy-third."

"Correct."

"I am just that in tune with gay culture."

Noah laughed. "I guess you are." He finally remembered the name of a bar. "There's a quiet place in Hell's Kitchen . . . sort of a neighborhood bar, except gay . . ."

"These days in Hell's Kitchen, that *is* a neighborhood bar."

Noah shook his head. "You go away for a few years, and look at how things change. Anyway, it's called Bar 51. Want to try it?" She nodded, so Noah told the driver, "Fifty-first and Ninth."

When the cab stopped twelve minutes later, Noah quickly spotted the rainbow flag identifying Bar 51 a few storefronts off the intersection. Over his objection, Tricia paid the driver, and when they walked through the front door at 5:00, they were customers number five and six.

"I hope you weren't expecting a wild Happy Hour," said Noah, as they ordered from the bartender.

"Happy Hour," she said, "is what we make of it."

And this is what they made of it: after one glass of wine, Tricia revealed herself to be a closet smoker; after two, she revealed herself to be a closet chain-smoker. And as the drinks flowed and cigarettes were smoked, she spent more and more time outside on the small smoking porch in front of the bar, befriending the slowly growing Happy Hour crowd.

And Noah kept tabs on her from his perch on the bar stool, watching her through the front window and marveling at Tricia Abraham: possible mistress, potential lush, and now a definite smoker.

But while he kept tabs on her, it was still a solo activity. Noah sat alone, once again vaguely bored, but now at least surrounded by people. It was not turning into an exciting experience, but he thought it was still preferable to being trapped in that sterile apartment in that sterile Park Avenue co-op. Which to Noah made Happy Hour at Bar 51 a very good thing.

At one point, and after a fifteen-minute absence on the porch, Tricia reappeared and Noah ordered another round of drinks.

"You're being very social tonight," he said to her, while the bartender filled their order.

"I've met some nice guys," she replied. "See those four guys out there?" She pointed out the front window where four men—still dressed for work, and ranging, to Noah's eyes, from their late-twenties to mid-forties—dominated a table on the smoking porch. "They call themselves 'the Stooges.'"

"Uh . . . okay. As in 'The Three Stooges'?"

"Exactly."

"I guess that's cool, but . . . there were three Stooges, and there are four guys out there."

"Yeah. One of them has to be Shemp."

"Uh . . . okay."

"Shemp is single, you know."

Noah sighed. "And which one is Shemp?" he asked, surveying the men on the porch.

"The young cute one."

"He's young and cute," said Noah. "You don't need a boyfriend when you're young and cute."

"Is that *your* excuse?"

Suddenly, Noah saw the turn the conversation was taking, and he didn't like it.

"Now, Tricia . . ."

"How long have you been single, Noah? Has it been a year since you broke up with Harry?" Noah nodded. Tricia had obviously paid more attention than his father. "Isn't it time for you to get back into the game?"

"Is that why we're out? Relationship counseling?"

She shook her head. "No, we're out because I had to get out of that apartment. The relationship counseling is . . . well, it's one of those things I'm prone to do after four glasses of wine. But while we're on the subject, would it be so horrible if you actually talked to someone? You're throwing out very antisocial vibes."

"I'm not antisocial."

"Okay," she said, realizing that she now had a fresh glass of wine waiting on the bar. "Let's not go there. Let's not even talk about sex."

"I would prefer not to talk sex with my stepmother," he agreed.

"With your *father's wife*," she corrected him. "Let's talk about friends. Nonsexual friends . . . people you just hang out with. Where are they?"

"I don't even live in New York anymore, so . . ."

"What about DC? Do you have a circle of friends there?" When Noah didn't answer, she said, "That's what I thought. Ever since Harry—maybe even before—you've carved out this solitary life for yourself. Why is that? You're good looking, smart, funny . . . you've got those cute dimples . . ."

"Tricia," he said, involuntarily flashing his cute dimples. "Happy Hour is not the place for analysis."

She blew the hair from her brow, sipped her drink, and said, "You're right. It's just that I get concerned about you. You should have close friends. Like the Stooges. You shouldn't be spending all your time alone."

"Don't be concerned," said Noah. "I'm not throwing my life away. I have friends, I have known love, and I also happen to be one of those people who *likes* to be alone."

"If you say so."

"I say so. Isn't it time for another cigarette break? Can't you harass Shemp out there and leave me alone?"

"What's your type?" she asked. Looking around the bar, she added, "What man here is the sort of guy you're interested in?"

"First, *not* a Stooge . . ."

Tricia shook her head, muttered something that sounded to Noah like "your loss," and headed back to her new friends on the tiny square of concrete outside the front door that passed as the bar's smoking lounge.

"Is your fag hag getting overly exuberant?" asked a voice behind Noah. He spun in his stool to face a man in his forties, his head shaved, sitting next to him at the bar.

"She's not a fag hag. She's my stepmother. Umm . . . my father's wife."

"I know what a stepmother is."

"No, I meant . . . she prefers to be called 'my father's wife.' I think she might have been scarred by Cinderella in her childhood."

"Ah!"

"Understand?"

"Not really."

And that, Noah thought, made two of them.

The man with the shaved head returned his attention to his friends, leaving Noah's eyes free to wander as he contemplated rewriting Tricia's role in his life. If asked, that was; he wouldn't offer. "Just a friend" seemed like an easy enough explanation, although, in a pinch, he supposed "fag hag" would do. Especially since that's what people would assume anyway.

Or maybe those Stooges would adopt her, and she could be their collective fag hag without the burden of a familial relationship. Yes, he thought, that might work.

She was right, of course. *Somewhat* right. He knew that. And the thought that the completelashuels were becoming the closest connections he had to intimate human contact sent a sudden chill up his spine. He looked at the liquid remaining in his glass, considered it briefly, and downed it in one quick gulp.

"You'd better slow down," said a man standing behind him. "Or else you're looking at a very short Happy Hour."

Noah turned, expecting to see the man with the shaved head again. Instead, he was greeted by the sight of . . .

Oh, hell, it was one of those tall, broad-shouldered Adonises. The type they reserved the word "handsome" for. And a young one, at that.

"I have it under control," Noah said, trying to get a good look at the man without appearing to stare. He *wanted* to stare, but . . . no, that wouldn't do. Noah was used to being the object of attention— or at least, lust—and he was uncomfortable being on the other side. Plus, he was deathly afraid he'd get caught looking.

The Adonis waved over Noah's shoulder, attracting the immediate attention of the bartender. After placing his order, he spoke again.

"I'm sorry for crowding you." His voice was a soft, mellow baritone. "I'll just be a minute."

"No problem." Noah turned again to take another look. He was tall—over six feet, maybe six two—with broad shoulders, a thick neck, and a handsome face framed by close-cropped light brown hair. The stranger had been watching the bartender fill his order, but, sensing Noah's eyes on him, he looked down at Noah. Noah's fears were realized—he had been caught in the act of staring—but the man merely smiled.

Again, Noah's instinct was to look away. But he fought it and managed to smile back.

"Is it always this slow here at Happy Hour?" asked the stranger.

"Uh . . . I really don't know. I'm not a regular."

"Oh." His eyes—brown, clear—returned to the bartender, who was now bringing him his drink. The stranger excused himself again to Noah as he reached past him to pay for the drink, then once more when he retrieved it from the bar. Noah felt a drop of condensation from the glass land on his pant leg, but didn't complain.

And then, drink in hand, the stranger nodded at him, smiled one more time, and slowly walked to the far end of the room.

Noah tried to think if he had been offered a conversational opening he had bobbled, decided that there was none, further decided that there was nothing he would have done about it anyway, and signaled for the bartender.

Still . . . *shit.* From a physical standpoint, the guy was perfection. Oh, he might turn out to be a real asshole, but physically: perfection. And really, after months without much human contact, the physical was all that was important at that moment.

After giving him the initial sexual impulse, though, Noah's brain went directly to rationalization mode.

He was with Tricia; it would be a bad thing to pick someone up while he was out with his step—uh, his *father's wife.*

And what if they clicked? He couldn't abandon Tricia in the bar to pursue a sexual conquest, and he certainly couldn't take the stranger back to the Park Avenue apartment. Even if Tricia was in-clined to look the other way, Gustav and Mrs. Levy would certainly spin that into something tawdry. Tawdri*er.*

And anyway, he could, indeed, be an asshole, which would make the physical encounter even more meaningless.

And, finally, even if all those other factors had a green light, the stranger could be very bad at sex. Very, *very* bad at sex. In which case the encounter would be less than meaningless.

Not to mention, he didn't seem interested in Noah at all. Yes, he had smiled . . . but he had also walked away without a backward glance. That was certainly an important factor.

Within thirty seconds, he had all but rationalized doing ab-solutely nothing about the stranger. So a good-looking guy reached past him to order a drink; Noah decided it was not an encounter worth noting. Even if the guy had handed him a phone number, Noah wasn't in the market. He had a book to write, and he wasn't even a New Yorker anymore. It wasn't worth wasting any more thought.

Still, he stole a glance to the other end of the room, where the stranger stood quietly, back against the wall, in his tight jeans and loose-fitting shirt with light blue stripes. And he let out an involun-tary sigh.

"And what have I missed?" asked Tricia, when she returned for a refill.

"Absolutely nothing," said Noah, fairly certain that he meant it.

They had another glass of wine, then decided it was time to leave Bar 51. As they walked out into the unseasonably warm September evening, Tricia stopped at the porch and waved to her new smoker friends. "Bye, Stooges! It was nice meeting you."

The Stooges, Shemp included, wished her safe travels and promised to get together again soon, but gave only the most perfunctory good-byes to Noah.

"I see who the popular one is," he said, as they walked down Fifty-first Street.

"That's because I put in an effort. Maybe if you went back there and talked to them . . ."

"Sorry." Noah rubbed his temple. "I'm just tired."

Something made Noah stop when they reached the corner of Ninth Avenue. He glanced back at the entrance to Bar 51, where the rainbow flag flapped in the gentle breeze and the Four Stooges held court on the smoking porch.

And he saw the handsome stranger walk out of the bar . . . directly toward them.

"Who's that?" asked Tricia, seeing him, too.

"I don't know," said Noah. "He came into the bar a while ago . . ."

"Did you talk to him?"

Noah sighed. "Not much."

"He's cute. He's not too young for you, is he?"

"He's not interested in me. Come on." Noah took Tricia's arm and walked her to the curb, where he started searching for a cab. As he stood at the curb, he felt compelled to take another backward glance . . . and when he did, the stranger was passing right behind him.

"Have a good night," he said, and he smiled as he walked past.

"Uh . . . you, too," Noah said softly.

"Hi!" Tricia shouted. The stranger glanced back over his shoulder and smiled broadly, but kept walking north up Ninth Avenue.

"Cute," she said approvingly. "I think you're wrong. I think he likes you."

"You're drunk," said Noah—not with condescension—as he took her arm to steady her.

"I should hope so. Seven glasses of wine. And I'm such a little thing . . ."

And then, with a particular elegance befitting a Park Avenue Trophy Wife, she tripped on the curb and collapsed in a heap.

* * *

Cute guy, thought Bart, as he walked up Ninth Avenue toward Lincoln Center, vaguely hoping he would encounter something interesting that would delay his return to Jon's apartment on West Sixty-fifth Street. Day Two of his vacation, like Day One, seemed to be ending far too early.

As he walked, he thought again about the man in the bar. Although Bart tended to like men a bit older—those in their late thirties or early forties were his ideal, and the man at Bar 51 was probably no older than his early thirties—he had the dark good looks and slim physique he was instantly attracted to. And he was so . . . handsome? No, handsome wasn't really the right word. He was *cute.* Yes, that was it.

Too bad he didn't seem very interested in Bart. He had looked, and he had smiled, but the minute Bart tried to talk to him, the cute guy had shut down.

He didn't understand that. New Yorkers could be such a strange breed.

Fifteen minutes later, Bart reached the busy intersection where Ninth Avenue—now Columbus Avenue—intersected with Broadway and West Sixty-fifth Street. There had been no distractions, and, as he crossed with the light, he accepted the fact that he would be spending another night chatting with Jon. He would have to make the following day, the third of his vacation, count.

Maybe a museum, he thought, as he searched his pockets for the key to Jon's building. He would have to see how Thursday shaped up.

Early the next morning Tricia and Noah learned that Max Abraham's doctors would only be keeping him in Lenox Hill until the following day. Things were looking good—the heart attack had resulted in minimal damage, and could be treated fairly easily—but, still, it *was* a heart attack. As bad as they felt for him, they were both secretly grateful for their own selfish reasons. In Tricia's case, she had an unforgiving hangover; in Noah's, he wasn't in the mood to deal with his father.

While Tricia spent large parts of the day in bed, Noah alternated between sitting in the guest room listening to music or wandering the apartment, looking for something to occupy his time. By late afternoon, he was once again feeling stir crazy and in need of fresh air, so he slipped out and took a brief walk around the neighborhood.

It was another pleasant day, and the walk was doing him a world of good. As he wandered the quiet brownstone-lined blocks, Noah pondered Tricia's words. Was he *really* closing himself off from human contact? Had the dissolution of his relationship with Harry *really* led him to a self-imposed solitude? Or worse, had he always walled himself off like that? Was he destined to be a loner—and to be lonely—for the rest of his life?

Then again, what did Tricia really know about his life? Both she and his father had made an effort to *not* get involved. It was one thing to know Noah was gay; quite another to know his partners, let alone his feelings about them. That could open themselves to all kinds of unpleasant possibilities. They might even have to envision him naked, in the arms of another man.

It was, Noah assumed, easier for Tricia—not a blood relative, at that—to drunkenly try to coax him into contact. It was quite another to cross the invisible line the family had placed in their relationships—the one that could not be crossed, because, like the edges of the flat earth in an early map, here be dragons.

Although he was breathing fresh air and clearing his head, Noah was not taking in the scenery; not until he approached the Whitney Museum on Madison Avenue and someone caught his eye.

Was that . . . ?

It was. It was the stranger from Bar 51, getting into a cab in front of the museum. Noah quickened his pace, hoping to catch up with the cab as it waited at the curb for a break in traffic.

Don't be too obvious, he told himself. *Walk quickly, but don't run.*

The cab began to pull away, and Noah—despite his best intentions—broke into a slow trot, drawing even with the vehicle moments before the driver punched the accelerator and sent it off into the northbound traffic. He looked through the rear passenger window . . . and there sat the stranger, looking back. A smile—of recognition?—crossed his lips as the cab angled into the left-hand lanes. Noah slowed his pace and watched it turn left at Seventy-ninth Street, a full two blocks away by the time he saw it disappear.

As he walked home, Noah tried to convince himself it was fate.

When that didn't work, he tried to convince himself it was just co-incidence. That was slightly more plausible—even in a huge city like New York, people ran into each other by chance—but he still felt there was something more to it. Two sightings in less than 24 hours, in two different parts of the city . . .

For perhaps the first time ever, Noah wished he possessed a spir-itual streak, because as implausible as fate seemed to him, he had reached the point where he needed to believe. In something . . . anything . . .

On an impulse, he hailed a cab, telling the driver to take him to Fifty-first and Ninth.

Bar 51 was crowded that early evening, its overflowing crowd pushing out onto the small porch where the smokers congregated. As Noah entered, the Four Stooges—anchoring their perch on the porch—greeted him with brief hellos and inquiries after Tricia. Noah felt slight regret that, up to that point, his father's mother was a more popular figure in a gay bar than he was.

Inside, the stranger was nowhere to be seen. Noah felt himself growing anxious as he scanned the room, hoping that he'd spot him somewhere in the crowd, hidden behind other patrons. But, no . . . Bar 51 was not that big of a place, and after four passes be-tween the front door and the bathrooms at the rear of the bar, it was clear that he wasn't there.

But just in case he was en route—delayed in traffic, or what-ever—Noah decided to stay for a drink. He made a mental note to give the stranger twenty minutes. Any more than that, he told him-self, would just mean Noah was being obsessive.

An hour later he left the bar. His only human contact was a quick good-bye to the Four Stooges, and Noah's promise to give Tricia their best wishes.

Bart's cab had been about to enter the Seventy-ninth Street Transverse and cross Central Park when he had a sudden impulse and changed his destination, telling the driver to take him not to Bar 51 in Hell's Kitchen, but to The Penthouse, which was much closer. The driver turned south on Fifth Avenue.

The car deposited him on Second Avenue in the lower East Sixties fifteen minutes later, and he took an unhurried stroll to the bar. It was still so early—almost *too* early—he was afraid he would be the only patron.

But even at that early hour of the late afternoon, the downstairs bar was lined with men when Bart pushed open the door and entered. Without more than the briefest scan of the customers, he walked to the spiral staircase in the back of the room, only stopping when he saw it blocked by a velvet rope.

"Sorry," the bartender called out to him. "We don't open the upstairs until six o'clock, so . . . another hour."

Bart turned and saw that the bartender was the same one who had made him so uncomfortable a few nights earlier. Was it Pablo? Paolo? He sighed and walked over to order a drink.

"It's you again," said Paolo, finally recognizing him in the dim lighting. He tried to keep the judgment out of his voice.

"It's me again," Bart agreed.

Paolo eyed him suspiciously, still not quite certain what the kid was up to, although he certainly had his suspicions. He was still sporting the same preppy look he had sported two nights earlier. Clearly, he was dressing to fit in—or rather not stand out—with The Penthouse crowd.

"Still not going out in Chelsea?" he asked, keeping his voice low to avoid being overheard by the other customers. Paolo didn't want it getting around the bar that he was trying to shoo business away from The Penthouse.

"No," said Bart, once again growing uncomfortable with Paolo's attention. *This guy never stops,* he thought. "I'd like a—"

"Scotch and soda. I remember."

While Paolo made his drink, Bart took one of the last available bar stools. The older man sitting next to him leered as he slid the stool tightly up to the bar, making no effort to hide his appreciation of Bart's physical appearance.

When Paolo set the scotch and soda in front of Bart, the man, never taking the leer off his face, set a twenty on the polished bar and loudly said, "That's on me."

Which made things even more uncomfortable for both Bart and Paolo, albeit for two very different reasons.

"Okay, then," said Paolo, gingerly lifting the twenty from the bar before walking off to the cash register.

"Uh . . . thanks," said Bart. "But you really didn't have to."

"It's my pleasure." The man continued to unsubtly eye him as Paolo returned with his change. "So do you have a name?"

"Bart."

"Pleased to meet you, Bart. I'm Morris."

"Nice to meet you." Bart shifted slightly and saw that, once again, Paolo had an eagle eye on him, watching his every move. When was the bartender going to get the hint that Bart wasn't interested?

"So . . ." Morris dropped his voice to a level at which only people within ten feet could hear. "So what's your story, Bart?"

"Just out for a drink."

"Any dinner plans?"

Well, *that* was abrupt, presumptuous, and inappropriate. And, based on the number of heads that swiveled in their direction, Bart knew he wasn't the only one who felt that way.

"Uh . . . thanks, but I think I have plans."

Morris continued, undeterred. "Because I have reservations for two at 7:00 at David Burke & Donatella, but my dinner companion cancelled on me, so I thought you might like to go."

"Well . . . I don't know you."

"What better way to get to know each other?" Morris's hand reached and found Bart's knee.

"I'll . . . uh . . . I'll have to think about it."

Morris stood, touched Bart on the shoulder, and said, "Nature calls. That gives you a few minutes to think."

When he was gone, Paolo leaned across the bar and motioned for Bart to join him. Bart sighed and leaned forward, hoping that Paolo wasn't about to try anything. One awkward situation at a time was more than enough.

"Listen," said Bart, deciding to be preemptory with the bartender. "I appreciate your attention, but I'm not interested in you."

Paolo raised his eyebrow. "You're not interested in me? Really? How sad."

"I'm sure you're a great guy, but . . . well, you're just not what I'm looking for."

"And what are you looking for?"

"Right now?" Bart thought about the answer to that question much more seriously than it deserved. "Right now I'm on vacation and just looking for some fun. Uncomplicated fun."

Still leaning on the bar, Paolo motioned for Bart to come even closer. When their faces were just inches away Paolo whispered: "I think maybe this isn't the right bar for you."

"I don't understand . . ."

"Understand this, then." Paolo's face conveyed intense seriousness. "We have a few rules here. The main one is, no hustling."

Hustling? It took Bart a moment to digest the word, but when it occurred to him that Paolo was calling him a prostitute, he reeled back. His whisper was now almost as loud as Morris's speaking voice. "I'm not a hustler. The guy bought me a drink, that's all."

Paolo took the scotch and soda off the bar and, in the same motion, dumped it in the sink. Bart's jaw dropped as he watched the liquid disappear down the drain.

"Good-bye," Paolo said with a dismissive wave, and Bart didn't wait for a second send-off.

Morris would dine alone that evening at David Burke & Donatella. It was just as well. After being accused of being a hooker, Bart was in a very bad mood for the rest of the night.

"How is he?" Noah asked Tricia, when he was safely back in the apartment, after a cab ride spent convincing himself that he hadn't really gone to Bar 51 *only* to find the stranger, but that he needed human contact. Even if, as usual, he hadn't actually engaged in any.

"He's sleeping," she said. "Thank God. He is the worst patient ever. Cranky, cranky, cranky. I couldn't wait to get out of that hospital."

Noah dipped his hand into a candy dish brimming with M&Ms, which Tricia had been struggling to avoid for the hour since she had left Lenox Hill. She frowned at him.

"You know my dad. He's an active guy. Being bed ridden is going to make him crazy."

"And him being crazy is going to make *me* crazy." She stared at Noah. "And you know what that means."

"Yeah. It means I'm going back to DC very soon." He popped a few pieces of candy in his mouth. "The Stooges were asking about you."

"You went back to the bar?"

"I was bored."

"Uh-huh. Bored or horny?"

Noah blushed. "A question I never expected from my step—uh, father's wife. But to answer your question . . . yes."

She looked at her watch, a slim, elegant, diamond-encrusted number Max had brought home for their most recent anniversary.

"You weren't out very long. I guess you weren't trying very hard."

He shrugged and grabbed another handful of M&Ms.

In turn, she shrugged, too. "Whatever. Not my life."

"No," said Noah. "It's not."

"Anyway, I'm glad you didn't tell me, because I would have probably wanted to go with you. And the last thing I need is more of that bad wine. My head was *pounding*."

Tricia looked at her stepson—her *husband's son*, she reminded herself—then at the candy dish, then back at Noah. Then back at the candy dish. Then . . . .

"Well, in other news, David Carlyle stopped by to visit your father."

"Oh, shit," muttered Noah. David Carlyle was his editor, and The Project—the stillborn Project—was already well past its contractual deadline.

"He asked for you to call if you got a chance."

"I'm sure he did."

With that, Tricia finally grabbed a handful of M&Ms.

David R. Carlyle III was not a punctual man. He was also not, in his very own self-critical estimation, the most responsible man on the planet. Although he held a senior editorial position at the publishing house Palmer/Midkiff/Carlyle, he knew that the fact that his last name was Carlyle had everything to do with it.

And he was fine with that. In the world of David R. Carlyle III, he was the rule, not the exception. A random twirl of his Rolodex would give up the names of dozens of other roman-numeraled scions of Manhattan, none of whom felt any special guilt for the good fortune of their birth. They lived well, they gave back from time to time, and they generally believed that if fate was going to smile on any individual, it was just as well it was them.

In fact, David Carlyle thought of himself as, perhaps, just a bit *better* than his peers. Because he *did* hold down a job, and he *did* go to his office more days than not, and he *did* contribute not only to the economic bottom line, but also to the nurturing of young talent. And although he was usually a genuinely humble man—one of his best friends was actually a young woman in the lower wage scales, and he loved bringing her to society events both for her company and the deflating effect her presence had on upper-class pomposity—he did have his moments when he thought of himself as a modern-day Medici.

But mostly he thought of himself as plain old David Carlyle, one of the good guys who just happened to have enough family money to keep him in homes on Fifth Avenue and in Southampton without ever giving a thought to his finances. One of the good guys who could afford to redecorate every year. One of the good guys who could go to the ballet on Tuesday, the bars on Wednesday, and, on Thursday morning, buy a book idea from an aspiring writer, before driving to the Hamptons for another long weekend. All in all, he thought, it was not a bad life for one of the good guys.

But if he wasn't extraordinarily punctual or responsible, he expected those attributes from his writers. Which is why Noah Abraham was beginning to piss him off.

One year earlier, Noah—the son of his lawyer, Max—had sat across from him in his office and promised to deliver a manuscript on closeted gay congressional staffers. Contracts were signed, and Noah had been given ten months to deliver that manuscript. In return, David had commissioned a contract and, eventually, an $8,000 advance, half of which was payable upon signing of the contract.

Noah had signed the contract, cashed the check, and then essentially disappeared.

And now, two months late on his delivery date, he had finally scheduled an appointment, which David knew was solely—if coincidentally—because he had visited his father's sickbed the day before. That wasn't why David had gone to the hospital, but if it spurred things along, all the better.

It was about time, too, because things were getting a bit awkward whenever he ran into Max and Tricia Abraham on the social circuit. Almost as awkward as that time a few years earlier, when David used a favor with Max to get legal assistance for one of his authors, and was repaid when the author ignored almost all of Max's advice before he vanished. Now *that* was an awkward period in the relationship between David and Max, assuaged only slightly—and exclusively on David's end—when the vanished author's book became a best-seller. Sometimes, vanishing is a good career move.

Noah, though . . . Noah had not been punctual, nor had he been responsible. Nor had he even had the decency to dramatically disappear. He had simply taken a relatively small amount of PMC money and not delivered. And it wasn't the money, David kept telling himself; it was the principle. As a gay man himself, David felt a special need to give back to his fellow gay writers, and when one of them didn't deliver—as occasionally happened—David Carlyle felt personally wronged.

But Noah *had* now taken the initiative to contact him, and although David was certain it was only because of the hospital visit, no one was holding a gun to the young man's head, so he felt slightly better. Maybe Noah would walk into his office with 100,000 words or so tucked under his arm and . . .

"David?"

David looked up from whatever it was he had been trying unsuccessfully to read and saw Noah in his doorway. Nothing was tucked under his arm. He frowned.

"Take a seat, Noah." The younger man sat. "Before we get down to business, how is your father?"

"No change overnight. He'll be fine. But he's driving everyone crazy right now."

"I can only imagine. Tell your father and Tricia I asked about them again, will you?" Noah nodded. "Anyway, on the matter of that manuscript . ."

"I know." Noah, his frown matching David's, glanced at the floor. "I'm far behind schedule. But it's not coming."

"Not at all?"

Noah summarized his problems with the book for David, who reacted not without sympathy. But business was business.

"Let me ask you a question," said David, when Noah concluded his narrative. "Do you think you'll be able to finish this book?"

Noah thought seriously about that. He wanted to say no, but was afraid that not being able to finish would speak to his abilities more than his topic. So he said, "Can I have another three months?"

"Will the manuscript be done in three months?"

"I think so," he lied.

"Then three months it is. But I really do need something by early January, at the latest."

"I understand," said Noah, trying not to think of the commitment he had just made.

They talked briefly and Noah excused himself, wishing he had never taken the $4,000 initial payment. It was not as if he needed the money, but his life at that moment would have been a lot easier without having to turn in a manuscript that he didn't want to write.

David Carlyle wished he had not taken the $4,000, too. Not because of the money, but because it had created all different levels of social awkwardness for him, and David *hated* social awkwardness. And even as he watched Noah leave, he knew he would not be seeing a manuscript by January, or at any point after that. There would be permanent social awkwardness, and that made him very unhappy.

Noah left the imposing Sixth Avenue building housing Palmer/Midkiff/Carlyle and began wandering aimlessly up the avenue, into the West Forties. Even though it was still technically the final days of summer, the tourists had largely decamped after Labor Day, and he was determined to enjoy the relatively uncrowded sidewalks. The holidays, with their maddening hordes, would arrive soon enough. After a dozen blocks, as he approached Radio City Music Hall, he saw something out of the corner of his eye that stopped him in mid-crosswalk.

It was that stranger, the handsome young man from Bar 51, walking south on the opposite side of Sixth Avenue.

Noah squinted, unable to believe that he was having this third coincidental encounter. As he stood in mid-crosswalk, the lights changed; two milliseconds later, a line of cabs and delivery trucks laid on the horns. Noah jumped and dashed for the opposite corner, narrowly avoiding a bicycle messenger in the process.

He looked back at the stranger, who now—thanks to the ruckus—was staring back at him. And when he smiled, Noah smiled sheepishly in return.

His view temporarily blocked by a row of passing tour buses, Noah tried to make a quick decision. Should he be bold, and dart across the street while he still had the light? Or should he walk away, and recognize this for what it was: a chance series of encounters?

The decision was one that, in the end, he didn't have to make. Because when the buses were gone, so was the stranger.

Anxiously, he scanned the sidewalk, looking up and down Sixth Avenue, but he had completely vanished.

Noah thought, *How the hell does someone disappear like that? Where did he go?* And he cursed himself again for letting opportunity slip through his fingers.

Well, *that* was strange, Bart thought, as he turned the corner and walked west on Fifty-first Street. Three days, three different parts of Manhattan . . . what were the odds?

As he approached Seventh Avenue, he thought about those odds a little bit more. Running into someone at Bar 51: common. Seeing that person a second time near the Whitney: not common, but not freakishly uncommon. But coming across the same man the next day on Sixth Avenue? Unlikely. *Very* unlikely.

Which left two possibilities: either Bart was meant to meet this man, or this man was stalking him. He hoped that this wasn't another stalker. The last one—the guy he had merely kissed outside an East Village bar one night, unfortunately after handing out his cell phone number—had called so frequently and persistently for months afterward that Bart was finally forced to change his number.

So if this new guy was a stalker . . . *no.* Bart tried to put the thought out of his head. It was good to be cautious, but bad to close himself off. He felt he led too cloistered of a life as it was.

As he waited at the crosswalk for the light to change, so he could cross Seventh Avenue, he had the strongest impulse to dash back to Sixth, to see if the guy from the bar was still looking for him in the shadow of Radio City Music Hall. If he *wasn't* a stalker, he might be as intrigued by the coincidences as Bart was. But he fought the impulse back. He had responsibilities.

He met his first—and, really, only—responsibility when he reached Eighth Avenue, where he popped into the parking garage in which he had hidden the car three days earlier for its five-night stay, checking it for any overnight dents or dings. He probably would have made this inspection if it were his own car; the fact that it was borrowed from his employer made the inspection imperative. After finding the car and giving it a careful eyeballing, he left the garage, satisfied that it had made it through the night intact.

His next responsibility, the optional one, was at the video store next to the garage, where he asked the clerk if some old movies were available yet on DVD. The clerk—young even to Bart, who still considered himself quite young—had never heard of the titles.

"*Sweet Svetlana? Darling, I'm Darling?*"

"Yeah." Bart was already impatient, having been on the hunt without success for months.

"Let me check."

The clerk went to work on his computer terminal, carefully confirming the spelling of the movies with Bart as he slowly typed. Finally, he looked up from the screen.

"I found the *Svetlana* DVD," he announced triumphantly.

"Is it out?"

"Mid-October. Part of the Kitty Randolph box set."

Bart frowned. "Can I order it without the Kitty Randolph movies?"

He couldn't; it was all or nothing, so—when the clerk couldn't tell him the names of the other titles in the set—Bart took nothing and let himself out of the store.

Responsibilities over, he walked another block west until he reached Ninth Avenue. Bart hadn't really intended to stop at Bar 51 again—not consciously, at least—but he had no better idea on how to kill some time, and he liked the place. At least no one at Bar 51 had accused him of prostituting himself.

He knew he could always go back to Jon's apartment but, much as he liked his host, there was still the problem of "employer talk." And now that he was into the fourth day of what could charitably be described as his worst vacation ever, Bart felt strongly that he had to take full advantage of the final forty-eight hours, especially since it was already Friday.

And, well . . . maybe that guy—Mr. Fate; Mr. Stalker, whatever—would show up, and he could try to figure out this string of coincidences. True, he was leaving New York in two days and didn't know when he'd be back, but it could be a harmless diversion. If there was something worth pursuing, he would only be a few hours away.

Not perfect, but workable. It wasn't as if there was a lot of competition, living as he did in virtual isolation in the Hamptons.

And if the guy really *was* a stalker, well . . . Bart could always get the car out of the garage and leave New York that night. *And* he'd be certain not to give out his cell phone number prematurely, just in case.

When he walked through the front door of Bar 51, he saw that the bartender he knew as Jason—"Young Jason," the regulars had informed him, as opposed to "Old Jason," who was also young but not as painfully young as Young Jason—was on duty. Bart ordered a Corona and took a stool at the midpoint of the bar. He was one of only a handful of people in the entire room, including Young Jason.

Although it was only 4:30 PM, he knew that he would have no more than three beers . . . even though he wouldn't even be driving. Bart was proud of his responsible, methodical nature . . . proud that he was always in control.

As the only child of strict midwestern parents, he was raised to be responsible. It was like that where he grew up: you could go one of two ways. The strict upbringing resulted either in responsible, no-nonsense children, or it resulted in wild, rebellious children. Bart was the former. He was babysitting while still almost a baby himself; a lifeguard at twelve who saved a life at thirteen; an exemplary son by any standard.

Any standard, that was, except that of his parents. They did not react well when their only child came out to them as gay. True, they didn't throw him out of the house or disown him, as so many others of their mindset would have done. But they dealt with the topic of homosexuality by strictly avoiding the subject, erecting an invisible wall in their house, behind which they hid away his sexuality.

In one sense, Bart was fine with the avoidance and neglect. He had no interest in discussing his sex life with them, anyway, and if it met their comfort level, it made *everyone*—including Bart—comfortable. Still, there were times—new love, heartbreak—when it would have been nice to share his life with his family.

Fortunately, he had a surrogate family to fill the emotional void left by his biological one. Bart had never intended to leave Toledo, but a job led to a relocation, and suddenly he was in Suffolk County,

New York, on the eastern tip of Long Island, the heart of the Hamptons, meeting yet another friend of a friend of a friend, leading him to his dream job. Now he was tucked away in a comfortable, if slightly lonely, life in Southampton, tending to the personal needs of a couple who were far too uncomplicated to need a personal assistant. But their money could afford one, so they thought. *Why not?* And Bart, as the beneficiary of the unneeded position, couldn't disagree.

Bart also quickly decided that he should enjoy it. A good salary, a huge house, a low-maintenance job, at least most of the time . . . they even let him borrow one of their cars on his occasional forays to Manhattan, which they called "Bart's Sanity Tour" to further prove their good humor. What was not to love?

It was perfect, he thought.

Except . . . well, it would have been nice to share it with someone.

But Bart was only twenty-eight years old. There would be time for all that.

He hoped.

And in any event, it was time for another Corona.

Tricia grabbed Noah by the arm as soon as he walked through the front door and onto the marble floor of the foyer.

"We're going out," she said. It was not a question, and it was not a request. It was an order.

"What? Why?"

"He's home," she said, referring to Max. "And he's making me crazy."

"He's home already? But . . ."

She clenched her jaw. "I *said* that we're going out."

"But . . ."

She waved him away. "Dr. Golden from 11G is with him. He can take care of any needs *your father*" not her husband; his father—"has. I've already cleared this with him."

"I should at least poke my head in," said Noah.

Tricia glanced at her watch. "You've got five minutes."

Noah walked down the corridor to his father's bedroom and, after knocking gently, quietly entered. The eighty-six-year-old Dr.

Golden from 11G sat next to the ailing Max, making his father look comparably healthy. Noah wondered if it was wise to leave his father in such decrepit hands.

Max's eyes were closed. Noah looked to Dr. Golden for permission to interrupt.

"He's awake," the old man grumbled, and Max's eyes opened.

"Dad? How are you feeling?"

"Not bad for an old guy who just had all sorts of tubes and catheters and balloons snaking through him." He smiled. "Tired, but good."

Noah offered him a faint smile. "Welcome home."

Max shifted, trying to find a comfortable position, and said, "So . . . how long are you staying?"

"Until I know we can leave you alone."

"No. I meant this afternoon." Noah didn't answer, so Max continued. "I know that Tricia wants to get out of the house. Why don't you take her somewhere?"

"Uh . . ."

"Go back to that bar you took her to the other night."

"She told you that?"

"I could see it on her face," he said. "In her eyes. I know she doesn't drink alone—a husband can tell that sort of thing—so she had to have gotten that hangover somewhere else."

"Uh . . ." Noah felt himself blush, outed as a co-conspirator in his father's wife's drunken evening at Bar 51.

"Please just take her out." He paused, and tilted his head conspiratorially. "Maybe she could drink a bit less, but still . . ."

Although Noah had already been dragooned into taking Tricia out, he was reluctant to admit it. There was something about the way the younger residents of the Abraham house were interacting that felt almost as if they were excluding the patient from their plans. Noah decided that another bar crawl with Tricia could wait for a day or two.

"I think I should stay here," he said finally.

"Noah." His father's voice took on the tone he always adopted— with family as well as in court—when he wanted to be obeyed. He dropped the volume a notch and said, "Your stepmother is making me a little crazy here, okay? I *want* you to take her out. I want a few hours without her hovering over me. Understand?"

"I can watch him, Noah," added Dr. Golden.

"See? It's that easy. Go out for a while and unwind. There's money on the top of the dresser."

Noah shook his head. "I have money."

"So take some more." Max shifted again, discomfort on his face. When he saw that Noah wasn't making the effort to take his cash, he again ordered him to take it.

"You're all crazy," said Noah, slowly backing toward the door, and, in the process, reaching out to take the wad of cash from the top of the dresser.

"Thank you," said his father. "That's the nicest thing anyone's said to me in . . . well, at least one week. So where are you taking her?"

Noah thought about Bar 51, and about that handsome man who seemed to be everywhere, but who, of course, had not been in the bar the one time he went to look for him.

"I don't know." And he didn't.

"Meaning, back to that gay bar?"

"Uh . . ." Noah glanced at Dr. Golden, who suddenly seemed very interested in that month's issue of *Architectural Digest*. "I don't think so."

"Do it. Let her see her Stooges again . . . have a few cigarettes and unwind . . ."

Noah was shocked. It was one thing for Tricia to be obviously hung over; quite another for her to tell him about the Stooges and confess bad habits that only appeared when she was drinking.

"You know a lot of things," Noah said, with appreciation.

"I'm a very good lawyer, which means I ask some questions, and very few things get past me."

"Agreed. But I don't know where I'm going to take her."

"Just do me a favor," said Max, as Noah prepared to make his exit. "Don't let her get so comfortable there that she becomes a lesbian. I'm sixty-four years old . . . too old to find a fourth wife."

No magazine had ever been studied as intently as the *Architectural Digest* in Dr. Golden's liver-spotted hands.

"So where would you like to go?" he asked Tricia, as they descended in the elevator. "Downtown? Uptown?"

She was decisive. "Bar 51."

In the lobby, the tiny Mrs. Levy eyed the couple carefully as they exited the elevator and crossed the lobby.

"Going out, Mrs. Abraham?"

"Barhopping," was Tricia's reply, and Mrs. Levy's jaw sagged as far as her breasts had.

"You really shouldn't do that," Noah whispered, as they walked out to the sidewalk.

"But it's fun."

He hailed a cab, and soon they were heading west toward Central Park.

"Your *husband* tells me that I should take you back to Bar 51," said Noah.

"Maybe your *father* is right. In which case, why did you give the driver an address on the Upper West Side?"

"Because I think I'm getting burned out on Bar 51."

She didn't buy that, but—not knowing what was going on in Noah's head, and not quite knowing how to ask—she quietly accepted his explanation and sat back for their ride across the park. When they emerged on the other side, the cab sped down West Eighty-first Street before pulling to a stop at the corner of Columbus Avenue.

"What's this place?" she asked, stepping out of the cab and eyeing the bistro in front of them.

"It's not one of my sort of places, and it's not one of your sort of places. So it should be perfect for the two of us."

It wasn't. The drinks were overpriced and the service was slow. But it gave Tricia the opportunity to ask a few questions, questions Noah was not used to hearing from a family member, even if the family member in question was not quite a blood relative.

"So," she said, settling on a very blunt opening, "when are you going to get over Harry?"

He looked up from his drink. "Excuse me?"

"It's been a year. Shouldn't you be dating again?"

He sighed. "This again? That's *my* business."

"Yes, it is." She looked out the bistro's tiny windows, watching a series of strollers pass, pushed by a series of fashionable mommies and less-fashionable nannies. "Do you ever think you'll want a baby?"

He almost spat out his drink. His back was to the window, so he didn't know what had brought that on, but—even if he had witnessed the stroller derby—he doubted that question would have occurred to him. "Where did that come from?"

"I've never had any desire to be a mother," she confessed, ignoring his question in the process. "And your father, well . . . you have to admit that, as a father, he's a great lawyer."

Noah was still confused, but that at least made him smile.

She continued. "I think that some of us just don't need that human connection. The parent-child one, I mean. But we still have to connect to *someone*, right?"

"Uh . . . I suppose."

"Take me, for instance. I have no interest in being a mother, but I *need* to be a wife. I need to have a man in my life. Otherwise I'm just . . . alone. And alone is no way to spend your life."

"Well . . ."

"Same thing with your father. I mean, he was there for you, and he tried the best he could, and he certainly wasn't a bad father, was he?"

"No."

"But fatherhood just wasn't his thing. He did his best, but Max just isn't hard-wired to be a parent. He still needs to be with someone, though."

"Which would explain the three wives."

She smiled. "Yes; exactly." Leaning closer, she added, "And how are you hard-wired, Noah?"

"Excuse me?"

"Are you hard-wired to be a parent?"

"No. Not at all."

"Do you need someone else? Or are you really that happy being alone?"

"Uh . . . I don't know, Tricia. When I'm in a relationship, well . . . it's nice to have someone to share my life with. But . . ."

"But what?"

"But to be in a relationship, there has to be another person. And ever since the breakup with Harry, the right man hasn't come along. That's all."

"You see, this is what I don't understand. You're outgoing, good looking, confident . . . Why is it that you can't meet anyone?"

"Because," he said, "I'm not trying."

She looked over her shoulder for the waiter, who was nowhere to be found.

"I would really like another glass of wine," she said. "Is that too much to ask?" Noah assured her he would watch for the missing garçon. "And what about sex?"

"Can't I keep any secrets?"

She gestured with her empty wineglass. "Oh, please. We're family."

"Okay," he said, wondering why he had never seen this side of her before, then realizing that until two days earlier, he had never seen her drunk. "Sex is good. I am pro-sex. But sex isn't everything."

She looked him up and down. "And you call yourself a gay man?"

"We're not all looking for sex."

"So what are you looking for?"

"Love."

Noah swallowed. Had he really just said that? On the surface—on a glib, cynical level—he wasn't even sure he felt that way . . . so why had he just made that confession to his stepmother? His father's wife? *Whatever* she was?

It didn't matter. Once again distracted by the absence of liquid in her glass, she was craning her neck, looking for the waiter. Noah had dodged the Freudian bullet.

"Okay," she said, finally returning her attention to him. "Let's get out of here."

"To where?"

"Anywhere but here. The service is terrible."

Noah nodded his agreement, and it was only then, as if alerted by silent alarm, that the waiter made his return appearance. It was also too late; Tricia was already slinging her purse over her shoulder.

Noah paid with his father's money, and they walked back out onto Columbus Avenue, where he held his arm out to signal for a cab.

"Let's see if the old man is any crankier," he said, scanning the approaching traffic for a lit "ON DUTY" sign.

"Home?" she asked, positioning her hands on her hips. "But we haven't even been gone an hour."

"You have a better suggestion?"

"Yes," she said. "That bar we went to the other day."

"Bar 51?" He shook his head. "Not again."

She affected a pout. "Please?"

He dropped his arm and walked her away from the curb. "Here's the story. There's this guy that I'm trying *not* to run into . . ."

"Who? Why?"

"It's sort of complicated. Remember the guy we saw the other night? The one who smiled at us when we were trying to get a cab home?"

"Vaguely. Remember, I was sort of drunk. He was tall, right? And he had a nice smile?"

"That's the one. Anyway, yesterday I saw him again. In a cab outside the Whitney. And if that isn't strange enough, I ran into him this afternoon near Radio City."

"So what's his name?"

"I . . . I don't know. We haven't really spoken. I just keep seeing him everywhere. And I'm afraid if I go to Bar 51, he'll be there again, and, well . . ."

"That's a good thing, though. Right?"

"Not really. I mean, there's obviously something that keeps bringing us to the same place—fate, or something. And that part is good. But I don't live here, and I won't be here for long, so I can't see any good that would come from pursuing it. And I'm afraid that if I go to the bar tonight and he's there, and something happens, well . . . I'm afraid that—"

"Yes," she said, with determination. "You're afraid."

"No! I'm not afraid, I'm just . . ."

"You said it twice. 'I'm afraid'; 'I'm afraid.' So you're afraid of meeting this man?"

"No, I just meant that the consequences, well . . ."

"Damn the consequences," she said. "Maybe you're fated to meet, and maybe you're not. But if you're going to stand here and tell me that you can't meet someone because some day you'll have to return to your lonely existence, well, that's just bullshit, Noah."

Which is how they ended up at Bar 51.

If Noah felt it was now no longer a surprise to see the stranger in random places, it seemed to him completely predictable that he would be at Bar 51 . . . and, as he had feared—and he had, indeed, *feared*—only moments after he and Tricia said hello to the Four Stooges, Noah saw him standing at the far end of the bar, holding a Corona.

"Is he here?" Tricia asked, looking over the crowd but not recognizing him.

Noah pointed him out.

"Go talk to him."

"Can we get a drink first?"

Tricia asked him to get her a glass of wine, and Noah squeezed into an almost-open spot at the bar, where he tried to flag down the bartender. It took a few minutes, but finally he was able to order.

"Two glasses of chardonnay."

"And a Corona," Tricia yelled out over his shoulder. Noah didn't have to look—he had seen the bottle in the stranger's hand when they walked into the bar—but he did anyway and there, standing behind him, were Tricia and her new companion.

"And a Corona," he repeated under his breath, instantly mesmerized by the stranger's shy smile.

Seconds later, Noah was handing Tricia her glass of wine, and the stranger his beer, and then Tricia was off to bum cigarettes from the Stooges.

And Noah was alone with this object of his . . . affection? Lust? Intrigue? He wasn't sure. He was only certain that whatever fate had in store for him, he was alone with it.

"I keep seeing you," said Noah, by way of introduction.

"I know." The stranger smiled. "Madison Avenue . . . Sixth . . ."

"Where did you disappear to this afternoon?"

"I had to take care of some things." The stranger smiled again and said, "You know, I almost crossed over to your side of the street when I saw you."

"Me, too!" said Noah, enthusiastically.

"I saw you here the other night, right?" He pointed out to the smoking porch, where Tricia was already highly animated through the large front windows. "With her?"

Noah nodded. "Tricia. My father's wife."

"Well . . ." The stranger's smile suddenly faded. "It's kind of wild that we keep running into each other."

"Uh . . . yeah." Noah struggled for conversation. "It's wild."

He tried to read the stranger's faded smile. Was he shy, or uninterested? For his part, Noah knew he was interested; he just didn't know if he could push himself to express that interest. Yes, he'd get grief from Tricia, but—really—what good could come of it?

Still, there *was* that grief from Tricia to consider . . .

"I'm Noah," he said abruptly, making direct eye contact with the man.

"I'm, uh . . . I'm Bart." He glanced around uncomfortably. "And it's nice to finally meet you."

"So, Bart . . . what do you do?"

For a moment, Bart's face registered panic. Did *everyone* think he was a hooker? It was only when he realized that Noah was asking about how he earned his living that he allowed himself to relax.

"Personal assistant. To an older couple."

"Oh. Great."

They sipped their drinks awkwardly, until Bart recognized that politeness dictated he ask Noah the same question.

"And what do *you* do?"

"I'm a writer."

"Oh." Bart nodded. He had heard that line before; everyone in New York who owned a computer called himself a writer, whether or not they had actually written anything worth publishing. "Writer" sounded vaguely professional, and interesting enough to supplant the real wage-slave jobs they always held. In fact, hadn't his onetime stalker claimed to be a writer? He thought so.

Another stretch of awkward silence followed, filled by the not-too-loud music coming from speakers at the rear of the bar. They each knew that they should fill the void, but neither one could think of an appropriate topic. The coincidence of their repeated encounters could only be discussed for so long.

It was Bart, finally, who not only broke the ice, he shattered it.

"Listen, Noah, I'm not a superstitious man, but . . . well, we keep running into each other, and . . . well, I'm running out of vacation days, so I apologize if this comes off as too forward, but I was wondering if you'd like to have dinner. Maybe tomorrow? Because I have to leave on Sunday."

There. That did it. Noah felt his heart race with the knowledge that, through no direct fault of his own, he had put himself in a place where—if he followed through—he wouldn't be able to deliver. Nothing could possibly come of it if he went on a date with this guy, no matter how much he might want it to work. They would just get started, and then Noah would have to leave town and return to his real life.

Bart saw the concern in Noah's face and realized he had gone too far. His dinner invitation was premature, but it really didn't warrant the look on Noah's face. He tried to joke his way out of it. "Is that a no? Because if it is, I'll accept it before you scream for the cops."

Embarrassed, Noah tried to shake off his apprehension.

"Do you always come on so strong?"

"You want to know the truth?"

Noah put a hand on his arm to stop him. "Listen, I'm sure you're a nice guy. It's just that I'm not really in a place where I can date."

"Well . . . I mean, okay, I can understand that. But I was just talking about dinner. *One* dinner."

"No, it's just . . ."

"Coffee? Would a coffee date be better? Less, um, commitment, or whatever?"

Noah shook his head. "Bart, you seem like a really nice guy. If I could, I'd like to get to know you better. But I'm only in the city for a few days, and it doesn't make sense to go on a date when I don't even know how long I'll be here, or when I'll have to return home."

Bart laughed to himself. Given his own situation, Noah's attitude was certainly ironic.

"So, no offense, but . . ."

"None taken."

"So you understand."

"I didn't say *that* . . ." Bart smiled. "Okay, yes, I understand."

With that, he retreated to the back of the bar, alone again with his Corona, and Noah walked out to the hazy porch to retrieve Tricia.

"How did it go?" she asked.

"We're more similar than I would have believed."

"That's good!"

"Uh . . . no. One big similarity is that we're both just passing through town. He leaves the day after tomorrow, and so it *really* doesn't make sense to get together."

"Did you ask where his home is? Maybe he's from DC, too!"

Noah shook his head. "Let's drop it, all right?"

* * *

It had been twenty minutes since his encounter with Noah the writer, and Bart Gustafson had spent seventeen of them regretting that, as impractical as the dinner date he had proposed would have been, Noah wouldn't take a chance. It had to be more than coincidence that their paths kept crossing. And it wasn't as if Bart was proposing marriage . . . although, he acknowledged to himself that he probably wouldn't object if the dinner date spilled over into a sleepover. That, at least, would rescue his vacation.

But maybe Noah was right. Bart, too, had his responsibilities, and responsibility dictated that he return to Southampton no later than Sunday. Maybe a date between two men who very likely would never see each other again wasn't a great idea.

Then again, was it that bad of an idea? If nothing else, maybe he'd even discover that Noah was really a writer. Whatever . . . Noah had made the decision for both of them, so there wouldn't be a date and they'd never know why fate kept bringing them together.

He glanced at his watch. It was early—only a few minutes after six—but he had already broken his three-beer rule. Now he had to try to justify extending it, making it a five-beer rule. It *was* the second-to-last night of Bart's Sanity Tour, after all. And, more importantly, he had no place better to be.

And then that woman, Noah's stepmother, was at his side. He smiled at her, noticing as he did that she was weaving slightly.

"Pardon me if I'm interfering," she said, "but Noah is a really nice guy."

"I'm sure of that," he agreed.

"And he's a catch."

Bart laughed. "Are you trying to be a matchmaker?"

"No!" she insisted, ringing a false note. "I'm just saying that he's a catch." She lifted up on tiptoe, steadying herself against Bart's solid body, and whispered in the general direction of his ear. "He's just a little . . . *wary* of getting involved."

"Did he tell you I asked him to dinner?"

"You did?" She looked out to the porch, where Noah was struggling in his attempt to finally bond with the Four Stooges. "No, he didn't tell me that. So what did he say?"

"I don't think he's interested."

She sighed. "Do you want me to talk to him?"

He thought about that before answering. "Honestly, I'm not sure. I mean, maybe he's right. If we're both just passing through New York, maybe it's not worth it. And I have had one hell of a bad vacation . . . besides meeting you and Noah, that is."

She put a hand on his back. "Vacations aren't supposed to be miserable. That's what people have jobs for." She took another glance at the porch and added, "Wait right here for a minute."

Bart's eyes followed her as she walked outside and started an animated conversation with Noah. He sipped his Corona, watching them for the next several minutes, until she began talking to the other smokers and Noah, clearly on the losing end of the discussion, walked back into the bar.

"About dinner," he said softly as he approached Bart. "Are you still interested?"

"Listen, don't feel obligated. Your stepmother sort of took this on herself. I didn't ask her."

"But it can't hurt, can it? And you've had a bad vacation, right? It's the least I could do as a guest New Yorker."

Bart smiled. "No, it can't hurt. And you don't know the half of my vacation."

"So," asked Noah, "do you like Italian?"

And so it came to pass that telephone numbers and last names were exchanged and reservations were to be made for 7:30 the following evening.

Maybe, Bart thought, as he climbed onto the sleeper sofa a few hours later after having once again revisited his employer's earlier years through another lengthy conversation with his host, the vacation would not be a *total* waste. At least he'd get to talk to a cute guy. That might not fully compensate for the months of deprivation, but it would be better than striking out completely.

He felt his penis stiffening, and realized that he was again getting ahead of himself. If Noah was already promising to be a reluctant dinner companion, it was far too premature to think of him as a willing sexual partner.

Don't get your hopes up, he told himself, as he struggled to sleep. *Don't get your hopes up . . .*

At the same time, Noah tossed and turned in his father's guest room, thinking similar thoughts. He wondered what Bart looked like under those clothes . . . if he was hairy, or smooth; if his muscles bulged as impressively under naked flesh as they had seemed to in the dim lighting of the bar; if he was experienced, or awkward . . .

And then a dim recollection of Harry—so different, physically, from Bart—popped into his head, and he remembered why he needed to exercise caution. With the memory of Harry quickly diminishing his erection, he shifted again in the bed, searching for both physical and emotional comfort.

Chapter 3

I first met Jimmy on the set of my last movie. He was a dancer, and the moment our eyes met I knew that we were meant to be together. I even followed him to his car on that first night, hoping to get his attention. Believe it or not, I never dreamed that he would be interested in me.

But he was, which thrilled me, but also opened up new challenges. After all, I had a wife and child. I had responsibilities.

It's never as easy to fall in love as it looks in the movies . . .

At 7:30 on Saturday evening they met at Viggio's, an Italian eatery in the West Forties. The pre-theater crowd was just clearing out and they were promptly ushered to a banquette in a quiet back corner.

Noah and Bart engaged in the smallest of small talk until the waiter took their order. The moment he departed, Bart set his elbows on the table and asked, "So is this date still comfortable for you?"

"Yeah, it's fine. But are we calling it a date?"

"Well, it *is* a date," said Bart. "It's just a date with no expectations."

"Ah, I see. An open-ended date."

"Exactly. Maybe it's a one-time thing, maybe more than once. We'll just take it as it comes." He looked at Noah, trying to gauge his comfort level, but his expression was unreadable. "So . . . you're a writer."

"Yeah."

"And what's your day job?"

Noah stiffened. "That *is* my day job. I'm a writer. I write."

"Sorry," said Bart, working to paper over the offense. "It's just that I meet a lot of people who say they're writers, but . . ."

Noah completed his sentence. "But they turn out to be untalented illiterates who have no hope of ever being published." He smiled. "Right?"

"Right."

"I'm one of the real ones, Bart. I have a real contract with a real publisher and everything. And I used to publish a weekly newspaper in Massachusetts. I know the people you're talking about, but I'm not one of them."

"Glad to hear it. I get tired of the bullshit." He paused, then asked, "So your book . . . Tell me about it."

Noah knew he had left himself wide open for that, even as he hoped he wouldn't have to discuss it. But since Bart had asked . . .

"I'm writing about closeted congressional staff members."

"That sounds interesting," said Bart, taking liberties with his definition of the word "interesting." "How's it coming along?"

Noah looked down and stared at his silverware. "Slowly." He deftly shifted the conversation away from his book by bringing up his father's heart attack. It was a cheap ploy, but he was much more comfortable talking about human mortality than literary mortality. Bart expressed his concern, Noah accepted it and assured him that the heart attack was mild, and then their food was on the table. Cannelloni in front of Noah; veal parmigiana in front of Bart.

"Okay," said Noah, after the waiter had once again departed. "So now you know what I do, but what about you?"

"Me?" Bart shook his head. "There's really not much to tell. Like I told you, for the past three years I've worked as personal assistant to this older couple in the Hamptons, and, well . . . I don't get out much. In fact, this was one of my big vacation weeks." He paused, and added, "Unfortunately."

"Yeah, you said you were having a bad week."

Bart sighed, and debated letting the subject drop. They were on a date—however they qualified it—and he was afraid his complaints about his week in New York would come across as whining.

Unless, that was, he could turn the minor tragedy into a funny story.

To his credit, the intense and ambivalent Noah Abraham found a great deal of humor in his tale of being ejected from The Penthouse because the bartender thought he was a hustler. Maybe too much humor, since his gales of laughter focused the entire restaurant's attention on their table.

"You know what?" Noah asked, as he dabbed tears from his eyes. "I'm glad we're having this . . . date, or whatever. And I'm really sorry right now that we're not both New Yorkers."

Now it was Bart's turn to stiffen. Noah seemed determined that this date could not possibly lead to anything else. That was logical, Bart acknowledged, but it wasn't hopeful. And Bart liked "hopeful" much better than "logical."

"It *is* too bad," Bart agreed, determined to play his own best hand and remembering the fantasies that had kept him up far too late the previous night. "Because I'd bet the sex would be phenomenal."

Noah's eyes darted to Bart. He looked so wholesome . . . "Did you just say what I think you said?"

"You don't believe in sex?"

Noah laughed. "Yes, you said what I thought you said. For the record, I believe in sex. In fact, I have believed in sex many, many times. You just caught me by surprise. I'm sort of off it at the present moment."

"Not permanently, I hope." A sly grin crossed Bart's lips, and, feeling bold, he rubbed his leg against Noah's under the table.

"Uh . . . no. And in case you wondered, your leg is having the exact effect I'm sure you intended." He took a bite of cannelloni and added, "Are you sure they made a mistake at The Penthouse?"

Bart laughed. "Am I being forward? Sorry about that. I've been deprived recently."

"Too bad we don't live closer together," Noah said again. "If we did, I promise you there would be a follow-up date."

Bart frowned. Even the allure of sex wasn't bending Noah. The man was absolutely, 100 percent determined to avoid a connection.

Which only made Bart try harder.

Across the table, Noah felt the swelling in his groin as Bart's leg slowly rubbed against his calf. He tried to mentally force it away, but knew he had lost the battle when he heard himself giggle. Noah *had* to change the topic, and quickly.

"So . . . tell me about this couple."

"Huh?" Bart had been distracted by the dimples Noah was now trying to hide.

"The people you work for."

"They're . . . they're nice." He pulled his leg back to his side of the table.

"Nice? That's it?"

"I just don't feel it's my place to invade their privacy. That's why I'm keeping them . . ."

"To yourself?" Noah hoped his smile was sincere.

Bart smiled shyly and shook his head. They returned again to their dinner and no more was said about the couple. Until, that is, Bart brought it up again, because Noah's silence—especially in the wake of his horniness moments earlier—was deafening.

"You think I'm holding back."

"You *are* holding back. But you have that right. We barely know each other. We don't have to rush into the sordid details. Although if we *don't* rush, well . . ."

"There's nothing sordid . . ."

"Just kidding. All the un-sordid details, if you prefer."

Bart leaned back heavily in the banquette. "Ah, shit . . . Okay, you know what? I do want to get to know you better, Noah. I don't want to start things off with you thinking I'm keeping secrets, like your congressional aides."

"I'd hardly equate—"

"I know, I know. But I think we both feel that something could happen between us." He stopped, then looked at Noah with alarm at the speed at which his thoughts poured out of his mouth. "Am I . . . uh . . . am I moving too fast?"

Noah reached across the table and put his hand on Bart's forearm. "You know how I feel. The geography is tough. But I'm trying to keep an open mind. Especially . . ." He looked down at the fullness in his lap. "Yeah, I'm keeping a *very* open mind right now."

Bart smiled . . . Noah smiled . . . The background music—something very operatic, heavy with strings—swelled. It was all very over the top and romantic, the way the realization that two people have just felt a mutual attraction is over the top and romantic, even when the food is hot dogs and the background music is traffic.

But, as he thought about what he wanted to say, Bart's broad smile wavered until it began to resemble a nervous tic. "Okay, I need to tell you something. You've heard of Quinn Scott, right?"

"The name is familiar." Noah struggled, then somewhat placed it. "Isn't he an actor? Umm, some television show? *The Brothers*, or something like that?"

Bart nodded, then shook his head in contradiction. "That's Quinn Scott, Jr: Q. J. He plays Mikey on *The Brothers-in-Law*."

"I think I've seen that," Noah confessed, with great humility. "He's one of the brothers-in-law who move in together when their wives leave them, right? And the other one is . . . uh . . . Jason St. Clair."

"Right. Quinn, Jr.—Q. J.—is the son of Quinn Sr., and that's who I work for. You might remember him from television, too. Or one of his movies."

Noah drew a blank. "Refresh my memory."

"*Philly Cop*?"

A ping sounded deep in Noah's memory. Had he watched that show in reruns decades ago, sitting cross legged in front of the huge television console? Yes, he thought he had.

"He was the detective, right? Tall, good looking, far-too-serious guy? And almost every week he and his partner ended up chasing some murderer over rooftops?"

Bart smiled. "That was the show. That was Quinn."

"Wow," said Noah, strangely comforted by those childhood memories. "How long ago was that?"

"Late '60s. Something like that."

"And what has he done since?"

"Not much."

"So he's been retired for a while?"

"You could say that. But he and his—" Bart stopped abruptly, thought for a split second and edited his response. "But he invested wisely when he had money, so he doesn't have any financial concerns. He's lucky. You know, a lot of actors blow their money when they make it, thinking the bubble will never burst. At least he was wise enough to hold onto his paychecks. He's sort of a financial genius."

"Why isn't he acting anymore?"

Bart, again, became thoughtful before speaking. "Let's just say that after *Philly Cop* went off the air . . . well, he went through a nasty divorce."

"A divorce? A divorce killed his career? It's Hollywood. I thought it worked the opposite way."

"I guess it depends on who you divorce," said Bart dryly. "In his case, Quinn was married to a woman with a lot more star power, and when things ended badly, she made him pay."

"Who?"

Again, a pensive look crossed Bart's face; but, again, he continued. "I'm sure you've heard of Kitty Randolph."

"Oh my God!" Realizing he had squealed, Noah tried to modulate his voice. "She's great!"

"I suppose. She's also Quinn Scott's ex-wife. *And* Q. J. Scott's mother, which is one of the reasons Quinn doesn't have much contact with his son."

"And you work for him? What's he like? He must have a lot of stories."

"Quinn is a very private man," Bart continued. "He doesn't talk about his old career much. It was   " Bart paused, searching for words. "Let's just say he has some painful memories."

Noah nodded. As the child of divorce—the child of several divorces, if you added in his father's second—he thought it only proper to convey sadness over the bitter breakup. "I understand. So tell me what he's like."

Bart shook his head. "I hope you don't take this the wrong way, but Quinn is very private, and I am very loyal, and I really don't feel comfortable right now."

Noah stiffened. Secrets had not been his friends recently. "Oh. Okay."

His mind began drifting back to the mess that was The Project. There was something about the way Bart protected Quinn Scott's privacy that brought those closed mouths in Washington to the forefront of his brain. He wasn't happy about the way it was consuming him at even the most inappropriate times.

Bart took a sip from his wineglass. He wasn't exactly sure what he had said, but he could see Noah go to a dark place, and knew that if the date could be rescued, it would have to be rescued quickly.

"So what are you thinking about?"

Noah snorted; an abrupt, derisive sound that he tried to pass off as something upbeat, making it all the more unreadable.

"I'm thinking," he said, "that I have a book to write, but nothing to write about."

"The political book?" Noah nodded. "It sounds interesting to me."

"You're just being nice."

"No. I'd tell you . . ."

"It's a mess. The only reason to write a book like that is to reach a conclusion . . . to make a difference. But I'm not learning anything, and if I'm not getting it, how can I expect readers to get it?"

"You're getting that some people are still afraid to come out, aren't you?"

Noah shook his head. "That's *not* news."

"I guess not."

Noah looked at Bart, determined to change the subject and get away from The Project. Slightly.

"And how 'out' are you?" he asked, in a tone he hoped wasn't confrontational.

"Excuse me?"

"This isn't a deal-breaker," Noah continued. "I'm just curious."

Bart smiled. "This is starting to sound like a real date."

"Was I getting too personal? Sorry."

"I'm out." Pause. "Enough. As for my family, let's just say that everyone knows, but it's sort of 'Don't Ask, Don't Tell.'"

"I'm not sure I know what you mean."

"They know, and I know that they know, and we don't really talk about it. It's too uncomfortable, so for all concerned it's easier if it's not discussed."

"That must be difficult."

"Surprisingly not. In fact, it's quite easy. I suppose if I ever meet the right man, that will change. But that hasn't happened yet, so there's no reason to make it a topic of conversation." He leaned forward, touching Noah's hand across the table. "Let's say, if you were the right man . . ."

Noah smiled. "Aren't you getting ahead of yourself? I don't know that we benefit from adding pressure to the date. Remember: I'm from Washington, and you're from the Hamptons."

"Uh . . . you're right." And Bart knew that while Noah was, technically, right, he felt something. And he was certain that Noah did, too. The very fact that he had not yet walked away told him that.

But Noah had issued a warning to slow down, so Bart would have to do his best to reel himself in.

"Sorry for bringing the topic up," Noah said. "I didn't mean to make our date too serious. But it's a subject that's near and dear to my heart, after all these months of dealing with people who hide in the closet."

"I know . . . I know . . . But maybe you'd be able to relate to them better if you had a little empathy."

Noah was shocked. "I have empathy!"

Bart shrugged. "If you say so."

"No," said Noah, with more insistence. "I have a lot of empathy. I really feel for those people."

"Uh-huh."

"I'm trying to help them, Bart. Not hurt them."

"I didn't mean to make you mad. It's just that I don't think you know what it's like to struggle with your sexual identity. I know you're trying to help the people you're writing about, but I don't think you know how to relate to them. And that's why this is so frustrating to you."

Noah thought about that for a moment. "You sound like my father," he said.

"Just my two cents." Bart smiled, trying to lighten the mood. "Take it or leave it. If I was that smart, I'd be writing my own book."

Noah tried to shrug off the criticism. After all, Bart himself had noted that it wasn't his area of expertise, and it certainly wasn't his father's, so their words carried only so much weight. Maybe, Noah thought, he could glean a little insight from them . . . but only a little.

"So . . . Quinn Scott. Are you out to *him?*"

Bart smiled and nodded his head. "Yes, Noah. I am out to Quinn. I am out to my family. I am pretty much out to everyone who would care in any way about who or what I sleep with. Now have I answered all your questions about this?"

"I'm just surprised that the macho Philly Cop would have an openly gay personal assistant."

"Why?" asked Bart. "He was an actor, after all. Even John Wayne probably knew gay people. He just doesn't care about these things."

"Sorry," said Noah, backing off.

"Ah, shit." Bart tossed his napkin on the table and looked into Noah's dark eyes, realizing that he was going to have to explain himself if there was any hope of *anything* transpiring between them. He would have to trust Noah, and hope that trust was not misplaced.

"Is something wrong?"

"No." He paused, giving himself one last opportunity to back out. He passed on it, forcing himself to forge ahead and trust.

"Sorry if I sound a bit defensive, but . . . here's the deal. Quinn is gay."

"*What?!*"

"Shhhh." Bart looked around the immediate vicinity of the table, only continuing when he was certain no one was eavesdropping. "It's sort of a secret, okay? He's not very open about it. But that's the reason Kitty Randolph divorced him and Quinn left Hollywood."

"I can't believe something like that is still a secret."

"Well, it is." Bart leaned closer. "Listen, I shouldn't be telling you any of this. So *please* don't spread it around, okay?" Noah nodded a silent agreement. "So now at least you know why I was being secretive and defensive. Part of my job is to protect Quinn and Jimmy's privacy."

"Jimmy?"

"Quinn's partner. Quinn's partner since 1969."

"That's commitment," said Noah.

Bart smiled. "I think it's great. And they're good to me, so please don't do anything that will cause me to lose my job."

"I think I can make that promise," Noah said, as he dabbed at the corners of his mouth with a napkin.

After Bart's revelation, any dark clouds that had threatened their date seemed to disappear, and, as both of them left their earlier guardedness behind through confession and drink, the evening continued on a much lighter note. Those touchy subjects—Quinn Scott, the book, and even the logistical improbability of a second date—were soon swept away as they indulged in some Hell's Kitchen barhopping.

By the time they finished at the third and last bar of the evening, both men had grown giddy in each other's company, to the point at which it was no surprise that even Noah—wary, ambivalent Noah—reached up, took Bart's face in his hands, and kissed him.

"I'm having fun," he said, after his lips left Bart's.

"Me, too."

Noah stared deeply and drunkenly into Bart's brown eyes. *Was he sure he wanted to say it? Yes, he thought he was.*

"Come home with me tonight."

"You're sure?"

"I'm sure."

"Okay. Oh, God yes, okay!"

They walked through the lobby, their heels making the slightest click on the polished marble floor. Gustav looked up from his newspaper as they passed his station, smiled in recognition, and returned to the *Post*'s write-up of the previous day's Yankees game.

After passing the desk, Noah took Bart's hand and led him down the central corridor to the bank of two elevators at the rear of the building. He pushed a button and the polished doors on the right opened immediately, revealing a diminutive woman and her leashed toy poodle.

"Good evening, Mrs. Levy," Noah said with a smile, as she stepped out of the cage.

"Good . . . good evening," she answered, first merely eyeing the two men suspiciously, then drawing a sharp breath when she saw they were holding hands.

Noah held his smile and addressed the dog. "Have a nice walk."

Mrs. Levy walked away, not quite comprehending what she had just seen. All she could process was that Mrs. Abraham's boy-toy was now holding hands with *another young man*, at which point her brain refused to work anymore.

When she was gone, Noah broke into drunken giggles, which infected Bart as they took her place on the elevator.

"I suppose I should ask why we're laughing," he said, as the elevator began to climb. "The hand-holding?"

"Well, yes, there's that," said Noah. "Mrs. Levy also thinks I'm having an affair with Tricia."

Bart burst into laughter. "Your stepmother? Oh, man, I guess *Desperate Housewives* has nothing on a Park Avenue co-op."

"Truer than you know, Bart. Truer than you know."

The doors opened and Noah, once again taking Bart's hand, walked quietly down the hall to his father's apartment. He slid his key into the lock and opened the door, revealing the dark foyer. Without a word, the men felt their way through the foyer and down an equally dark corridor, until they reached the guest room.

"You're sure no one is awake?" asked Bart, his voice hushed, as Noah closed the door.

Noah wasn't, but said he was. He flipped the light switch, illuminating a lamp on the nightstand.

Bart unbuttoned one shirt button then stopped.

"It's just that this seems so . . . high school. Don't get me wrong; I want to be here. But it's been a long time since I was smuggled into a boy's bedroom."

Noah approached him, an impish smile on his face, and pressed himself gently against Bart. "But it's kind of fun, right?"

Bart returned his smile. "Yeah. Kind of."

Noah unbuttoned Bart's second button and slid his fingers inside the shirt, feeling neatly trimmed hair bristle against his fingers.

"It's just that . . ."

"Shhhh." Noah put a finger to his lips, then, his hand still on Bart's chest, leaned up and kissed him.

Bart tilted his head down to meet Noah's kiss, and his reluctance—his nervousness, really—began to melt away. Noah's lips were soft, not demanding, as Bart had feared. Not aggressive, but welcoming.

He felt Noah's tongue slowly begin to probe inside his mouth, sliding along his teeth until it plunged deep inside, where Bart met it with his own tongue, first tentatively and then, as their intensity increased, hungrily. His strong hands found Noah's trim waist, and he guided him gently toward the double bed.

As they kissed, Noah continued unbuttoning the shirt, finally pulling it back to reveal Bart's well-defined torso. His chest was solid, and Noah instinctively moved his mouth to one of his small, reddish-brown nipples, slowly rolling his tongue over it until it hardened.

The shirt fell to the floor as they tumbled onto the bed, and Noah again found Bart's lips. They laid like that—side by side, kissing deeply—for a few minutes, until Noah broke away. Rising to his knees as the mattress gave slightly beneath his concentrated weight, he arched his back and pulled his own shirt over his head.

"Nice," said Bart, quietly, as Noah revealed his lean, wiry upper body.

Noah looked again at Bart's chest and said, "Obviously one of us spends more time with the weights than the other."

Bart looked down, an involuntary reaction to the compliment, and caught a glimpse of his pectorals. Yes, he had to admit that a decade at the gym had paid off in bulk, but it was the sinewy build of a man like Noah that he found most attractive. He reached over to him, cupping Noah's bare shoulder with one hand and pulling him forward as he said, "This is what I like. Come here."

The men continued kissing . . . touching . . . caressing . . . their lips alternating between mouth and body, until Noah finally rolled off Bart and said, "Okay, we're gonna have to do this now or I'm going to explode all by myself."

He reached for the top button of Bart's khakis, already tented from what was obviously an impressive and rock-hard erection. The button was popped, the zipper slid down, and then he saw it, defined through Bart's tight white boxer-briefs. He bent down and locked his lips on it through the fabric, feeling its warmth.

"Noah, don't." Bart pushed his head away.

"What's wrong?"

"Just take it slow, okay?"

"I can do that," Noah said, although he wasn't sure that was the truth.

He pulled the khakis off Bart's legs—noting that they were every bit as muscular and defined as his torso—then, standing at the foot of his bed, took off his jeans, which fell to the floor next to Bart's shirt. Socks followed, thrown carelessly around the room, landing wherever they landed. Underwear followed socks . . . two pairs of white boxer-briefs—one small, one medium—were tossed to the floor.

And then—Noah still standing, Bart still reclined on the bed— they took in each other's naked bodies. There was nothing left to hide.

"I think we should get this over with," whispered Noah, with a smile.

"Oh, yes. Please . . ."

Noah began to slide open the nightstand drawer, then unhappily remembered that this was no longer his bedroom.

"Shit," he said, looking around the room and hoping an inspiration would occur to him. "No lube."

"You didn't bring any with you?"

"No. It never occurred to me that I'd be having sex. You?"

Bart shrugged. "Same with me." He thought for a moment, then added, "Never mind. Come here."

Noah climbed back onto the bed, entwining himself with Bart. They kissed, and Noah closed his eyes in deep satisfaction.

"You know," said Bart, "if this were a movie, it would be the perfect moment to fade to black."

Taking his cue, Noah reached over and turned off the lamp on the nightstand, and the room went dark.

"Good morning."

Noah opened his puffy eyes and saw that the sun was, indeed, up. Meaning it was, indeed, morning. Hiking the comforter to his neck, he turned to see Tricia in the doorway.

"Sorry," she said. "I knocked, but you were out like a light."

His throat was dry. "What time is it?"

"Eight thirty," she said. "And if you want breakfast, you'd better get moving."

"I'm surprised you don't want kids, because you are *such* a mother."

"Thank you." Tricia smiled. "And Bart, if you want breakfast, you'd better get moving, too."

Noah panicked, suddenly remembering that he was not just in the guest room of his father's apartment; he was in the guest room of his father's apartment *with a naked man next to him.*

He glanced over, and saw Bart try to disappear under the covers.

"By the way," Tricia added, looking slightly unhappy and nodding to the pile of clothes and towels on the floor. "If you want that stuff cleaned, throw it in the hamper. I don't do maid service."

Noah's face reddened. He was not only in the guest room of his father's apartment with a naked man next to him; *there was also a pile of towels they had used to clean themselves up lying in the middle of the floor.* He tried to join Bart in making himself disappear.

When she was gone, the men drew their tired, naked bodies out of bed and began sorting through the clothes. With the exception of one of Noah's socks, which had mysteriously vanished after being tossed blindly the night before, everything was accounted for.

"So how embarrassing is breakfast going to be?" asked Bart, pulling his khakis over those muscular legs. "Maybe I should just go."

Noah shook his head. "Too late. She knows you slept here, and I'm sure she knows we had sex, so we might as well face this head on and get past it." He picked up one of the clean-up towels they had used. "Want a souvenir of last night?"

"That," said Bart, trying to straighten out his now-rumpled shirt, "is gross."

Noah grabbed a fresh pair of jeans from the closet. "I just thought you'd want a memento."

"How about you?"

Noah smiled. "Maybe I'll smuggle a towel out of here later."

"No, I meant how about if *you're* my memento?"

All noise in the world stopped. Noah turned to face Bart, and saw that he was serious.

He shook his head. "I can't be your memento, Bart. You've got to get home, and one of these days, I'll have to get home."

Bart frowned. "I sort of thought this was more than a trick."

"It was," Noah confirmed, as a nervous lump rose in his throat. In the daylight, sober, his common sense was starting to take over. "It was a date. We even had dinner first." He laughed, underscoring his joke, but stopped when he realized that Bart didn't find it all that funny. "I mean . . . look, Bart, we had a great time. If we both lived in New York, things would be different. But if I'm in DC, and you're out in the Hamptons, I don't see how it can work. It isn't practical."

"I just thought . . ." Bart's voice trailed away until he found the right words. "You see, I'm not exactly sexually inexperienced."

Noah smiled, remembering. "No kidding."

He was ignored. "But sometimes—not often, but sometimes—the chemistry is just right. And I thought we had that chemistry."

"Yeah, but . . ."

"Good conversation . . . we clicked . . ." A devilish smile was on his lips and his eyes sparkled. "Not to mention the great sex. I like you, Noah. I really think this could work."

"*Could* work," Noah said. "If we lived in the same city . . . yeah. It could be perfect. But after knowing each other for less than twenty-four hours, I think it's premature to say it *will* work. Especially with the geographic obstacles. Washington to the Hamptons . . . that's quite a distance."

Bart stopped him, a scowl beginning to cross his face. "If I ask you a question, will you give me an honest answer?"

"Shoot."

"Are you seeing someone else?"

"No! Not at all. Not since . . . well, it's been a long time. Let's just leave it at that."

"Me neither. So why not take a chance?"

"Bart . . ."

"Noah . . ."

Noah shook his head. It was crazy to think that after one date—and, yes, there had been a date involved, because there *was* dinner, and therefore Bart was not just a trick—and some admittedly fantastic sex, the two men should try to defy all the odds and start a long-distance relationship. Travel five hours every time they wanted to see each other? It was . . . crazy.

Still, he knew what Bart was talking about. He hadn't felt so comfortable with a man in a long time. Maybe even ever. They had opened up to each other and told each other things Noah was sure they had barely been able to tell themselves. And would it be such a bad thing to take a chance on an unlikely relationship?

"Let me think about this," Noah said finally, even as he strongly suspected that his answer would follow logic, not unrealistic emotionalism.

"If that's the best answer I'm going to get," said Bart, buttoning his shirt, "then that's the answer I'll have to take."

When they were dressed, Noah led Bart out of the room. Now, by light of day, Bart could admire the décor of the Abraham apartment. Even the overly leathered living room drew his seal of approval as they crossed through it on their shortcut to the dining room, although he couldn't let the moment pass without a comment.

"See what happens?" Noah said in response. "I move away for a few years and they let their fetishes take over."

In the formal dining room, Tricia sat casually at the table, sipping from a coffee cup. She looked up as she heard them shuffle into the room.

"Good morning again," she chirped. "Good to see you again, Bart."

His face reddened and he mumbled a good morning.

"Sleep well?"

Noah shot her a look, which she ignored.

The rough makings of a continental breakfast—bagels, a fruit bowl, miscellaneous pastries—sat on a platter in the middle of the table. Noah helped himself to a bagel, and Bart to some fruit, and, after pouring coffee, they sat.

"How's the old man this morning?" asked Noah. "Did he get any sleep?"

"He's doing better. In fact, you're going to see for yourself in a few minutes."

Noah almost gagged on his bagel. "You mean he's coming out for breakfast?"

"Did you think he'd be bedridden for the rest of his life?"

Noah felt a twinge of panic at the thought that his father would catch him in the apartment with Bart, who, as his hair alone would indicate, had clearly spent the night. And Tricia picked up on that panic as if she could read his mind.

"I wouldn't worry about having Bart here," she said. "He knows."

Now Noah *did* gag. "He knows?"

"He knows."

"*How?*"

Tricia reached over and patted his hand. "Your father knows sex noises when he hears them."

"Oh Christ," muttered Bart, wondering if he could possibly get out of the apartment before Noah's father made his appearance.

Tricia smiled. "Don't worry about it, Bart. Noah's father is very open minded. In fact, I think he's happy to know that Noah is getting *something*. We've been worried that he's become too much of a hermit lately."

Her husband's son stopped her. "That's enough, Tricia."

"What's the problem, Noah?" She set her coffee cup down. "We're all adults. You're almost as old as me, and if *I'm* allowed to have sex . . ."

Noah put his hands over his ears.

"Who's having sex?"

They all turned to see Max, clad in a navy blue bathrobe and matching slippers, his pale blue pajamas peeking out from under the robe, standing in the entrance to the dining room.

Noah took his hands away from his ears. "Uh . . . Tricia?"

"Not lately," said his father. "And not for a few more weeks or so. You don't want to kill me, do you?"

"No," said Noah, who was feeling very small. "Right now, I only want to kill myself."

Max wagged a finger at him. "Not in the apartment. You still expect everyone to clean up after you?"

Remembering the clothes and towels on the floor of the guest room, Noah and Tricia glanced at each other.

"No," said Noah, the lump in his throat returning. "Of course not."

Still standing, Max nodded to Bart and introduced himself. "I'm Noah's father, Max."

"P-p-p-pleased to meet you," stammered Bart. "I'm Bart."

"Oh, Bart! As in 'Oh, Bart, that feels fantastic!' You're that Bart?"

Bart closed his eyes and wished himself back to Southampton. He was disappointed when he opened them and he was still in the Abrahams's apartment, looking into the face of the now-cackling family patriarch.

"Just joking with you, Bart. Hey, could you pass me that coffee?"

"No coffee," said Tricia.

"You want me to fall asleep and drown in the shower? What is it with everyone trying to kill me so soon after my little incident?" He sat. "All right, then . . . juice?"

She nodded. "You can have juice."

"Thank heaven for small favors." Max turned again to Noah and Bart. "So what are you kids up to today?"

"No plans," said Noah. "Well, not for me, that is. Bart has to drive back to the Hamptons."

"I see." Max was silent for a moment, waiting while Tricia poured and delivered his orange juice. He knew he could have done the task himself, but he liked indulging himself with his convalescence. "And what do you do, Bart?"

"Personal assistant."

"Bigger than that," added Noah. "He's personal assistant to Quinn Scott."

Simultaneously, Max and Tricia spoke up, Max mentioning *Philly Cop* and Tricia mentioning *The Brothers-in-Law.* Then they looked at each other, puzzled by the other's reference.

Bart smiled, finally feeling some small level of comfort. "I work for the *Philly Cop* Quinn Scott. The actor in *The Brothers-in-Law* is his son, Quinn Jr."

"Never heard of him," said both Max and Tricia, each of them referring to the other Quinn Scott.

"Funny story," said Max, finally settling into his chair. "My former wife was pregnant with Noah here when his last movie was released. What was it called . . . *When Stars Shine?* Something like that?"

"*When the Stars Come Out.*"

"That's it. After the movie, we went to dinner, and that's the first time Noah kicked."

"And he hasn't stopped since," added Noah.

Max shook his head. "No, he hasn't."

Bart excused himself to use the bathroom, and seconds after he walked out of the dining room Max turned to his son and said, "He seems like a nice young man."

"Thanks. Yes he is."

"Sorry if I embarrassed him."

"What about embarrassing *me?*"

"You, you can handle the embarrassment. In fact, you should have more embarrassment in your life." He took another sip of juice. "So is this a serious thing?"

Watch it, Noah told himself; there was a minefield in his father's question. To say yes was to give his father—and Tricia, for that matter—free rein to turn it into a full-blown relationship. But to say no was to admit that he had dragged someone he barely knew back to their apartment for sex. And, dinner or no dinner, what looked like a trick looked like a trick.

"We'll see," said Noah, agreeable but vague. "We're feeling things out."

Max's eyebrows wiggled. "So we heard last night."

Noah's only response was an exaggerated sigh.

When Bart returned, his hair had been dampened and pushed back down into something not looking quite so obviously like bed head. He didn't sit, but instead placed his hands on the back of his chair and said, "It was nice meeting everyone, but I'd better get on the road."

Noah stood. "I'll walk you to the door."

Bart and the rest of the Abraham family said their good-byes, and Noah escorted Bart out.

"So," Bart said, when they were alone in the hallway, "am I going to see you again?"

"Yes. Of course." Noah was still not fully convinced, but the words came easily. "I've got your number; you've got mine. So, uh . . . just call me. Or *I'll* call *you.*"

Noah tried to read Bart's smile. It seemed forced; moreover, his eyes betrayed a lack of faith.

"I mean it, Bart," he said emphatically. "We'll be in touch."

"Okay."

Bart leaned into Noah, embracing him.

And for the first time that morning, Noah realized that he *was* going to call Bart. Maybe a relationship was crazy, but, as Bart had asked, why not take a chance on *something?* And if a phone call wasn't exactly a full-blown relationship, at least it was connection. Who knew where it could lead?

And in any event, no one had ever claimed that any of this would be easy.

Chapter 4

I have always been drawn to confident people. And I hate bullshitters. That pretty much sums up my philosophy of life.

As an actor, I've experienced a lot of bullshit. It comes with the profession. But after getting cheated out of money with a song and a dance on my first couple of movies, I decided to take financial matters into my own hands, and I never looked back . . .

After Bart was gone, Noah walked back into the dining room and flopped down on a chair across the table from his father.

"Nice boy," again said Max, who was trying to eat a piece of dry toast and wishing with all his slightly damaged heart that it was slathered with melted butter. "Then again, since my wife apparently set you up, I shouldn't be surprised."

"I have no secrets around this place, do I?"

"Apparently not. So tell me . . ." Max stuffed one small piece of the dry bread in his mouth and tried to swallow. "Tell me the truth. Are you going to see him again?"

"I told you I was."

"Your eyes said something else. And that boy, that Bart, he saw it, too." He chewed for a moment. "I mean, it's fine with me if it was a one-night stand, although I hope you don't make a practice of bringing those men into this house."

"It wasn't like that," said Noah. "I just . . . well, I've been trying to figure out what I should do. I live in D.C., he's out in the Hamptons . . . it's a complex situation. He wants to try dating, but . . ." As Noah fell into silence, his father hiked an eyebrow. "I know, I know, it's too soon to act like boyfriends. Dinner and sex doesn't . . ." Noah stopped. "Did I just start to say that?"

"Mmm-hmmm."

He blushed slightly. "Sorry. But you'll be happy to hear that I'm at least going to call him. And then we'll see what happens."

Max nodded, still trying to swallow.

"I like Bart," said Tricia. "You make a cute couple."

"Yeah, but . . . the distance."

She ran a hand through her bangs. "Noah, sometimes I think you'll grab at any excuse to be alone."

Max, still swallowing, again nodded his agreement.

"If it wasn't the physical distance," she said, without giving Noah a chance to respond, "it would be something else. For someone who's so outgoing, I'm surprised how closed-off you can be when it comes to men."

"I *said* I was going to call," he said, and realized he was whining.

"Yes, well, we'll see about that, won't we?" She looked at her husband and asked, "Max, are you all right? Do you want some water?"

With a great effort, the muscles in Max's throat finally pulled the food through his esophagus. He shoved the plate with the rest the dry toast away and said, "I'm fine. *Now,* I'm fine." He turned his attention back to Noah. "Do you even remember *Philly Cop*?"

"From the reruns . . . uh, syndication, I guess. It would have gone off the air around the time I was born, right?"

"Around the time Quinn Scott made that *Stars Are Coming Out* movie."

"What did you think of it?"

"Eh."

"I don't remember it, either," said Tricia. "In fact, I don't think I've ever seen it."

Max smiled and picked up his knife, intending to plunge it into butter the minute he could get Tricia out of the room for twenty seconds. "Quinn Scott as the toughest cop in Philadelphia. Every week, racing across rooftops to catch the bad guys." The butter knife in his hand was like a baton in the hands of a conductor, following the unseen Philly Cop as he leapt from roof to roof in pursuit of the Bad Guy of the Week. "As a lawyer, I can tell you that it was totally unrealistic. But it wasn't bad television, so why quibble?"

Noah laughed. "And who would ever believe that the toughest cop in Philadelphia was gay."

Silence. Until the knife so expertly wielded by Max hit the table and clattered off his other silverware.

"Excuse me?"

"Yeah," Noah said. "Quinn Scott is gay."

"That's ridiculous."

Noah looked in the general direction of the front door. If Bart knew that he was already sharing the carefully protected secret, he'd be appalled. "His personal assistant would know, wouldn't he?"

Max thought about that. "Quinn Scott is gay?"

"But he has a son," offered Tricia.

Noah countered her comment with, "Because no gay man has ever reproduced."

"He was married to Kitty Randolph," said Max, feeling suddenly argumentative. For some reason, he could accept that his own son was gay, but he couldn't accept that Quinn Scott—*Quinn Scott*—was gay. "I mean . . . Kitty Randolph!"

"Yes, he was married to Kitty Randolph. And they had a son, Quinn Jr. And then Quinn Sr. fell in love with another man, and they lived happily ever after." He thought about that for a moment before appending, "Well, at least as far as I know."

Max shook his head, trying to process the gossipy tidbit. He hadn't thought about Quinn Scott in . . . decades? He may not have even been cognizant that the actor was still alive. But it didn't matter; this Quinn Scott revelation had thrown him for a loop.

Maybe, he thought, the difference between the actor and his son was this: Noah was artistic, and sensitive, and perhaps not the most masculine man in any given room. Quinn Scott, though, well there was a man that every man wanted to be. Hearing that Quinn Scott was gay was like hearing that *Randolph* Scott was gay! The very thought of it was simply ridiculous!

But Max couldn't say anything like that, of course, because he would never embarrass his son in that manner and he would never, ever admit that he indulged himself with stereotypes. Instead, he looked Noah in the eye from his vantage point across the table and said:

"The story of Quinn Scott. Now *that* is a book I'd want to read."

The story of Quinn Scott. Now that is a book I'd want to read.
For the rest of the day, Noah heard his father's words in his head. The thought of a Quinn Scott book hadn't occurred to him when he was with Bart. Now it was the only thing that occurred to him. He didn't know why that was. The only thing he knew about Quinn Scott was that he really didn't know enough about him to have an opinion.

Fortunately, there was always the Internet.

Later that morning, Noah went to the home office—actually, a paper-cluttered alcove in the second, unused guest bedroom—and booted up his father's computer.

He did it in relative secrecy. While he told Tricia that he wanted to go online to do some research, he didn't want her—and he especially didn't want his father—to know that he wanted to research that shadowy memory of his youth: Quinn Scott.

First, though, he started with a search through various Web sites on the name "Bart Gustafson," not an uncommon step in the world of dating in the computer age. He found a high-school swimmer in Minnesota, a slot-car enthusiast in Palo Alto, and . . . that was it. *His* Bart Gustafson didn't seem to exist on the Internet. Satisfied with Bart's relative anonymity, Noah began typing the name "Quinn Scott" into Google, Yahoo!, and every other search engine he could find.

And Quinn Scott *did* exist.

His solid—if abruptly discontinued—career included not only *Philly Cop*, but a number of nondescript movies pumped out between 1958 and 1970 . . . 1970 coinciding with the release of his last movie, *When The Stars Come Out*, and the official end of his marriage to Kitty Randolph.

And then . . . nothing. Nothing, that is, besides a handful of cameos on guest-star-heavy television shows. Bart hadn't shortened Quinn Scott's professional resume as Noah had suspected; if anything, he had performed the amazing feat of making it seem much fuller than it really was.

Noah carefully looked up each of Quinn Scott's dozen or so movies, finding the usual combination of roles an actor aged twenty-four through thirty-six would have played during the era. He split time between playing the good guy and bad guy in a half-dozen forgotten film noirs—*The Fresh Kill*, *Port Richmond*—during the 1950s and early '60s. He fought alongside John Wayne in *Attack on Tottenville*, and acted with Kitty Randolph in several musical romances toward the end of his career. Then came the three brief television credits and then . . . nothing.

The only thing Noah found especially notable was that, despite Quinn Scott's filmography and famed costars, each and every film he appeared in was a decidedly lesser work. It was as if Kitty Randolph, John Wayne, and Ray Milland—seeing the handwriting on the wall, and recognizing that they had signed on for a cinematic flop—had grudgingly conceded to the casting of young Quinn Scott, recognizing that since a better and more marketable talent wouldn't be able to save the project, they might as well save the pro-

duction some money. Even when he did television, his costars were
low-rent. In fact, at its high-point—his appearance on an episode
of *Murder, She Wrote* in 1990 –Angela Lansbury didn't even appear
on camera, offering only a voice-over.

Noah also found a few pictures of the actor in his relative youth.
Quinn Scott was, as he remembered from watching *Philly Cop* in
syndication on weekday afternoons, blandly handsome. Even in stills
from his "villain" roles, he was clean cut, without a stray tuft in his
jet-black head of hair, his jaw jutting impressively toward the camera. What's more, there was little cinematic evidence that he ever
cracked a smile. Even in a Technicolor photo of Quinn as he romanced Kitty in 1969's *Sweet Svetlana*, he was dour, while Kitty—
dressed in a fluffy pink *something*—brightened things up with an
ear-to-ear smile. The only still Noah found of Quinn Scott smiling
was from the John Wayne oater *Attack on Tottenville*, in which he
stood behind The Duke, grinning at a bloody, body-strewn battle-
field.

So Quinn Scott *was* capable of smiling, but apparently only if he
shared the scene with a few dozen dead Injuns.

Noah began to feel sorry for the actor, without quite knowing
why. A dozen-year career had dried up overnight, save the extremely rare TV spot, and now he was all but forgotten. All because
he was gay and chased from Hollywood by his ex-wife, a *true* star.
Noah found that sad.

Damn, he thought. *The poor guy didn't even have a fan club!* There
wasn't even a Web site out there maintained by some film buff
where someone, feeling a slight moment of nostalgia, had asked,
"Whatever happened to Quinn Scott?"

Nothing. He was forgotten.

Noah shook off his contemplation of the actor's banishment. It
was sad, and it wasn't fair, but it was also thirty-five years in the past,
and everyone had apparently moved on. But, still curious about
why anyone, let alone his father, would want to read Quinn Scott's
biography, he began searching for more information on the other
members of the family; people who had retained or created their
fame during the computer age, and were therefore far more Google-
able.

Sure enough, Kitty Randolph and Quinn Scott Jr. were *every-*

where on the Internet. There was so much information, in fact, that Noah limited the notes he started taking to only the most basic biographical details.

While Quinn's marriage to Kitty was his only trip down the aisle, he was her second of three husbands. The marriage lasted, depending on the source, either four or five years, and resulted in the birth of the only child either of them had ever had. Quinn Scott Jr.—familiarly, Q. J.—was now in his mid-thirties and starring in the hit television comedy *The Brothers-in-Law*, and his mother had been making infrequent guest appearances on the show for each of the five seasons it had been on the air.

Kitty Randolph was now married to talent agent Dean Henry who—to Noah—certainly *looked* gay, even if he wasn't. Since they had kept their May-December marriage together for seventeen years, he gave Dean Henry the benefit of the doubt. For his part, Quinn Jr. seemed to date an awful lot of flight attendants, according to several gossip sites, but he had yet to take the plunge into holy matrimony.

Web page after Web page flickered across the monitor, and, as he read late into the afternoon, the idea of a Quinn Scott book never left his head. There was a lot of information—maybe too much—out there about Kitty and Q. J., but Noah's mission had nothing, really, to do with them, and everything to do with the words of his father that still echoed in his brain.

The story of Quinn Scott. Now that is a book I'd want to read.

And even though no one out there was asking it, Noah wanted to answer the question of "whatever happened to Quinn Scott?" He wanted to somehow let the world know that the Philly Cop was still alive and kicking.

He was into his fifth hour on the computer and his second hour reading dull fan sites devoted to Quinn Scott Jr.—and what was it about teenage girls that the Web pages they designed were invariably glaringly pink?—when Tricia's head popped into the alcove.

"Are you going to do that all day?"

Noah's eyes were dry. "I'm finishing up shortly."

"I just thought you might want to go out for a drink . . ."

He looked away from the screen, mock horror on his face. "Oh my God, Tricia! You're addicted to Bar 51, aren't you?"

"No!"

"Yes, you are!" Noah looked back at the pink screen and the photo of Quinn Jr., who was apparently his father's son, but didn't look it. "Okay. Give me ten minutes."

Doctor Golden once again assumed caregiver duties, and Noah and Tricia set off for Bar 51. When they walked through the front door, they noted that the Sunday Happy Hour crowd was almost as large as it had been on Friday. Painfully Young Jason poured their glasses of wine and they retreated to a space against the back wall, mostly out of the way of the other patrons.

"So what was up with the Internet?" asked Tricia, once they were settled in.

Noah shrugged, almost embarrassed to admit that his father was the inspiration for a day spent researching Quinn Scott. But he had to say *something*, so he told her.

"That's perfect," she said. "That gives you a great reason to call Bart!"

"Oh, Tricia . . ."

"Why not?"

"Because for one thing, I have to get back to DC."

"Oh, right," she said dryly. "Back to your writing."

"Uh . . ." Was that really all he had waiting for him in Washington? He sighed, realizing that it was.

After another glass of wine, she finally wore down his last stubborn trace of resistance. And once he let it slip that he liked Bart a bit more than he expected—even though their physical distance almost certainly precluded a *real* relationship—she was relentless.

And Noah did intend to call him, didn't he? Maybe his intent hadn't been to call a mere seven hours after Bart had left his father's apartment, but still . . .

Bart picked up his ringing cell phone and smiled when he saw Noah's name appear on the caller ID.

"Miss me already?" he asked, without so much as a hello.

Noah laughed. He was standing outside on the sidewalk, away from the noise of the bar. "The hours have passed like . . . hours."

"So you're a poet, too."

"Is there anything I can't do?" Noah waited for an ambulance, its siren blaring, to pass before continuing. "So, listen, I was wondering if you want to get together soon?"

"Of course! That's a stupid question." Bart thought for a minute before adding, "But I don't know when I'll be able to get back into the city."

"I was thinking of going out there."

There was silence, and Noah wondered if he had lost the connection before Bart's voice was back on the line. "To Southampton?"

"Sure. Why not?"

He practically gushed. "Okay! Yes!"

"Is next weekend too soon?"

Damn, Bart thought. *Noah certainly started slow then came on strong, didn't he?* But if he wanted to come out to Southampton in five days, that was fine with Bart, and he told him that.

"What about your boss? Will he be okay with it?"

"Don't worry about Quinn," said Bart. "Let me take care of that."

And then it was late afternoon on Friday. Bart borrowed a car and drove up to the highway, where he patiently waited in a parking lot for the slightly delayed bus. When the Jitney finally arrived and he saw Noah step out, small overnight bag in hand, his heart raced.

"Hey, handsome," he said, as Noah let himself in the passenger side door, then kept moving across the seat until he was almost on top of Bart. Their lips met, and both men closed their eyes, oblivious to the other disembarking passengers who had walked off the bus and straight into the private world of Noah Abraham and Bart Gustafson.

After a long time, although not quite long enough for the men, Bart playfully shoved Noah back to his seat with instructions to belt himself in.

"No fooling around," he said. "I'm trying to drive here."

The engine turned over and Bart cautiously merged into the heavy traffic, then made the second right. After he was off the highway he turned to Noah and said, "You can't believe how happy I am that you're here."

Noah smiled. "I think I can."

As they drove south, the houses and properties continued to grow larger. Noah watched the landscape pass, wondering how early Quinn Scott had bought into the Hamptons real estate boom. Bart had termed him a financial genius, a description that must have been on target if this was the company he was keeping.

Thinking of Quinn Scott—not an infrequent occurrence for Noah over the past week—reminded him:

"So listen, I have an idea for a new project."

"You're giving up on the book about Congress?"

"For now." He leaned back in his bucket seat. "I was thinking that your boss might be a good subject."

Bart laughed out loud. "Quinn? Get out of here."

They had talked every day since Noah asked for the invitation to Southampton, but he never knew quite how to bring up the subject. For one thing, he genuinely liked Bart, and he didn't want him to think he was using him—even though he was. For another, he knew how protective Bart could be of Quinn. But if this idea—*this* project—was going to have legs, Bart would have to know what was on Noah's mind.

"No, I'm serious. Think about it: here's this major star who's married to another major star, except he's gay. So he gets himself thrown out of Hollywood. But it's not a tragedy, because he finds true love. It's . . . it's . . . ."

"It's not going to happen."

Noah turned to look at Bart. He was smiling, but Noah could tell that he meant what he said.

"Sorry to burst your bubble, baby, but I've been with Quinn and Jimmy for a few years and I can tell you that they are *very* private people. There is no way that Quinn will let himself be your project. I'm just warning you up front."

Noah looked distractedly out his window. "Well, do you mind if I mention it?"

"I don't mind. I just don't want you to get your hopes up."

Noah was determined to be optimistic, but promised to take those words to heart.

Bart put on the right-turn signal and slowed as the car approached a break in a hedgerow, then eased into a turn. They drove through the open gate and up a double-wide driveway toward a large, if unassuming, white house.

"Welcome to Casa Scott," said Bart, looking straight ahead.
"Nice."

"You should see the inside. The place doesn't look like much from here—well, except *big*—but it's pretty interesting inside. I'll take you on a tour once we get settled."

Bart pulled the car up to the front of the three-car garage affixed to the right side of the house. Noah grabbed his overnight bag, then followed Bart through a windowed door into the garage. Inside, a pair of gleaming Mercedes—one hunter green, one silver—were parked side by side. They walked past the cars to another door, this one leading into the house, and, after Bart unlocked it, entered a short, dark entryway. One wall was overstuffed with outerwear bulging off wooden pegs, leaving little room for them to maneuver.

Without bothering to flip the light switch, Bart opened another door and stepped back as the door swung in, forcing Noah to wedge himself against the door to the garage until they could progress into yet another hallway.

"The kitchen," said Bart, pointing right, at a door to the rear of the house, "is that way. Chances are good that's where Quinn and Jimmy are." He pointed to the left. "So we're going this way."

Again, Noah trailed Bart as they walked down the long corridor, their tread near-silent on the worn but elegantly detailed carpet. No artificial lighting was needed now; sunlight spilled down the hallway from a large window at the end of the passage, which Noah assumed was the front of the house—an assumption that was confirmed when they reached it and he looked out over the front lawn.

Bart turned right at the end of the hall and they entered the foyer. The large room opened two stories to the roof, wooden beams crisscrossing the vast emptiness above them.

"Nice, huh?" asked Bart.

Noah made a 360-degree inspection. The room was low on décor: three small tables, each holding a vase of showy flowers but otherwise impractical; an intricate Persian rug covering roughly half the floor space; and a half-dozen small, oval mirrors mounted on the walls that Noah instinctively knew were antique. Besides the minimalist decorating, the two men were the only things in the room. But Noah had to admit that the foyer made for a grand entrance into Casa Scott—for those people who, unlike him, didn't have to enter through the garage, that was.

He had seen his fair share of Hamptons mansions, and Quinn Scott's was impressive without being overwhelming. He liked the openness and light in the foyer. There was that thirty-foot ceiling, for example, and the exterior wall with eight windows enhancing the feeling of size in the room by flooding it in natural light. The foyer was framed by two wide staircases, curving slightly as they rose to a second-floor hallway overlooking the foyer, exposed behind a wooden railing. Beyond that railing was a hallway into the building's interior, mirroring a similar entrance off the ground floor.

"So . . . you like it?" Noah abruptly realized that Bart had been trying to get his attention while he studied the room.

"Nice," Noah agreed. "It feels . . . airy."

"It *is* airy. The entire house is airy." Bart began walking toward the hallway off the foyer, and Noah followed. "Did I tell you that Quinn designed the place?"

"He's an architect?"

Bart laughed. "No. But he sketched out a design and hired an architect, in case you're afraid it's going to fall down on you."

Noah shook his head. "I'm really not concerned."

"Quinn and Jimmy had the house built in the early '80s," Bart continued, as they walked. "They used to live about a half mile away, but this is their dream house. The only way they're leaving here is feet first."

Twenty feet off the foyer, the hallway split. To the right, it opened into a formal dining room, and Noah could see that there were other rooms—had they wandered back to the proximity of the kitchen?—beyond it. To the left was the living room, decorated in neutral hues right down to the sand-colored carpet. It was into that room that Bart next led him.

"Wait here for a second," he said. "I'll find Quinn and Jimmy."

Bart walked through the living room, then, sliding open a glass door, stepped out onto the patio, leaving Noah behind. He dropped his overnight bag and stood almost motionless, scanning the titles on a bookshelf until . . .

"Who the fuck are you?"

Startled, Noah spun in the direction of the gravelly voice until he saw a familiar face he had never seen before.

Quinn Scott.

"I asked you who the fuck you are."

It was definitely Quinn Scott. He was much older now, of course, but it was him, dressed in jeans and a brown plaid shirt that looked as if it came straight from the men's department at Sears.

"I asked . . ."

"I'm Noah," he gasped, belatedly realizing he had not answered the man. "I'm . . . I'm a friend of Bart."

The older man studied him suspiciously, and Noah felt strangely as if he had stepped into a Quinn Scott film noir from the 1950s, and they were now in black and white, the villain of *Port Richmond* facing down the innocent hero. Until, that is, the villain hollered:

"*Bart!*"

From outside, they heard the sounds of someone rushing across the lawn toward the house, bumping into objects in his path in the process. And then Bart, panting for breath, slid open the glass door and stumbled back into the living room.

"Quinn!" he said as he struggled for breath. "I was looking for you outside."

A finger was jabbed in Noah's direction and the old man asked, "He a friend of yours?"

"That's Noah. The guy I told you was visiting for the weekend."

Quinn Scott kept a wary eye on the intruder. Again he sized him up carefully, then—seemingly satisfied—said, "Okay." With that, he turned and left the room.

They waited until he was out of earshot before speaking.

"So . . . now you've met Quinn," said Bart.

"Friendly guy."

"He's really not that bad. It just takes him some time to get comfortable." Bart looked in the general direction of Quinn's departure. "Grab your bag and I'll give you the rest of the tour."

"Will we be running into him again?"

Bart smiled. "It's a big house. Come on."

At the far corner of the living room was another staircase leading to the upper floor. They ascended, the steps emitting hollow squeaks under their footfalls, until they reached the second level and yet another hallway. This one ran along the back of the house, meeting the center hallway—the one that lead to the overlook of the foyer—in a T at its midpoint.

"This place is like a maze," Noah observed, trying to reconcile the layout of the house in his head.

"Nah. You'll get used to it. There's a pattern." Bart held out his hand, palm out, and with a finger tried to diagram the flow of the house. "The East Wing is where we came in. The garage, dining room, kitchen . . . they're all in the East Wing. The West Wing has the living room and study downstairs, and master bedroom upstairs. Follow?" Noah shrugged. "The guest rooms—and my room—are above the kitchen and dining room. Oh . . . and there are staircases in each corner." He pointed four times, indicating the approximate locations, and Noah thought he looked like a flight attendant pointing out the emergency exits.

"So where do we sleep?" Noah asked finally, and for the first time it occurred to him that, under this strange roof, they might not sleep together. He hoped that wasn't the case.

"Down here."

Bart escorted Noah to his room, pointing out one last staircase—or, as Noah now chose to think of it, another emergency exit—that led from outside his bedroom door to an alcove between the dining room and kitchen below. He took Noah's bag and set it next to the bed.

"And now," said Bart, taking the willing Noah in his arms, "I think we need to get reacquainted."

Quinn Scott didn't like having visitors. In all his years in Southampton, he had welcomed only a handful of people into his home. It was his private space, and every visitor stole another piece of his privacy.

Still, the boy was lonely. He knew that it couldn't be easy to be twenty-eight and leading such a monastic existence, trapped in an isolated house with two old codgers as his only regular companions. He could see it in Bart's eyes when he returned from Manhattan the previous Sunday, as he prattled on about the wonderful man he had met. And while Bart had not explicitly said they had had sex, it wasn't hard to read between the lines. Why the hell else would he have mentioned his date's "hot body"?

And if he needed confirmation, it came later that night when

Bart beamed for hours after Mr. Hot Body called him. It was all so sickeningly sweet that Quinn was considering never letting him out of the house again.

He hobbled toward the kitchen, where he knew he'd find Jimmy. If Jimmy wasn't on the patio soaking up sun, he was always in the kitchen. He was just that predictable.

And, yes, Quinn was hobbling, dammit. He was on his second hip, and it was no more comfortable than the original. He was only seventy-two, too young to be an invalid. Despite the discomfort, though, he resisted using a cane. If Quinn Scott was going to deteriorate, he was going to go down kicking, screaming, and unassisted.

Jimmy was in the kitchen, as he knew he would be. Their dog, Camille—half yellow lab and half shar-pei—sat at his feet, her pink and black tongue waiting for scraps to fall from the cutting board.

"Cocktail?" Jimmy asked, taking a sip from a glass of merlot before returning it to the counter.

"I'm not here for my health."

"I love it when you sweet-talk me."

Jimmy turned to the freezer, the former dancer's fluid movement every bit as graceful as it had been in his youth. And, with his partner's back to him, Quinn also had an opportunity to marvel *at that ass.* Sixty-two years old and still as firm as it had been when they met thirty-six years earlier. Jimmy was the opposite of Quinn: eternally youthful and able bodied. Sometimes Quinn resented him for that.

Jimmy grabbed an ice cube tray from the freezer, turned back, and began making Quinn's drink.

"So is Bart's friend here yet?" he asked as he poured.

"Mr. Hot Body? He's here."

"And?"

"Cute enough, I suppose, if you like them on the short side."

"So," said Jimmy, putting the finishing touches on the drink. "I guess we'll have to start calling him 'Bart's Little Friend.'"

Quinn smiled and accepted his cocktail.

The two couples largely kept their distance on the first night. Bart and Noah wanted their time alone, and Quinn and Jimmy—

well, Quinn, at least—wanted them to be alone. In fact, it was a few minutes after noon on the following day when all four of the men were in the same room at the same time, when their paths crossed in the kitchen.

"Where are you going?" asked Jimmy.

"We're just going to relax on the patio," said Bart. "Want to join us?"

"Not really," said Quinn, looking up from the newspaper spread in front of him on the counter.

Noah looked to the floor, where Camille sat, wagging her tail lazily.

"What a sweet dog," he said, reaching to pet her.

"I wouldn't do that if I were you," said Quinn. "Not if you want to keep that hand."

. . . the hand which Noah quickly retracted.

Even though September was about to become October, the sun on the patio was unseasonably warm. Bart and Noah put on sunglasses and settled into two of the six chairs ringing the glass table that dominated the patio.

After a few minutes of silent satisfaction in each other's company, Noah said, "I know you think he's going to shoot me down, but I'd still like to talk to him."

Bart glanced at the house, then his eyes returned to Noah. "When the time is right. I'll let you know."

Noah nodded, and retreated into silence.

The sound of the sliding door to the kitchen finally interrupted the quiet.

"Bart." They heard Quinn's voice before they had a chance to turn around. "We're out of tequila."

Bart sighed. "I didn't drink it."

"I know that. You're the last person in this house I'd accuse." He cleared his throat, loudly, and projected his voice back into the kitchen. "You think I don't know who the boozehound is around here?"

From somewhere unseen, Jimmy's voice sang out. "Before you go accusing, look in the mirror!"

Quinn snorted. "Listen to Princess Cuervo." Turning his attention again to Bart he tried as hard as possible to sound pleasant. "Bart, would you make a liquor store run?"

Again, Bart sighed. Without answering, he turned to Noah and said, "Even though it's my day off, I probably should go. Servitude never ends around here. Do you mind?"

"Do you want company?"

"Sit," said Bart, rising from the chair. "I'll only be ten minutes."

"We need limes, too," said Quinn.

"*Twelve* minutes."

Only when Bart was gone did Quinn finally limp away from his perch in the doorway, making his way slowly to Bart's still-warm chair. Quinn looked at Noah; Noah looked at Quinn; and then they both looked off to some distant spot in the lawn, far away from each other.

Quinn spoke first.

"So you're a writer."

"I've tried."

"Any good?"

"*I* think so."

Quinn smiled. "Good answer. I like confident people."

Noah took off his sunglasses and turned to Quinn, shielding his eyes from the sun with one hand. Bart had said he'd tell him when the time was right, but Noah preferred to take his opportunities when and where he found them.

"I think you've got a great story in you."

Quinn frowned.

"Maybe even a book."

Quinn's frown deepened. "Bart warned me about you," he said.

So Bart had tipped him off. Noah opened his mouth to object, but Quinn silenced him by raising one calloused hand in his direction.

"He told me you think I can be your project." Looking the younger man squarely in the eye he added: "Tell me, Noah, do I look like a project?"

Noah thought about what the right answer was, before deciding: "No."

"You're right. I'm not a project. So all I can tell you is that you're not going to write my book."

"But your stories," said Noah, ignoring the still-outstretched hand. "You're a part of Hollywood history!"

"I'm nothing. Just one of ten thousand people who had a moment . . . nothing more."

"Okay." Noah sat back in his chair, placing the sunglasses back on his face. Almost to himself he added, "It just seems like a shame."

"I suppose it does. To you." Quinn thought about that for a moment. "What do you mean, 'a shame.'?"

Hidden behind the dark glasses, Noah said, "Ten, fifteen years in film and TV. There are still a lot of fans who would like to read about those days, those experiences. And thirty-plus years with Jimmy, well . . . that's inspirational."

Quinn silently agreed. It was, indeed, inspirational. And maybe this young Noah Abraham was on to something. *Maybe.* "Inspirational? You think the story of Jimmy and me is inspirational?"

Noah turned to Quinn, slipping off the sunglasses again to better convey his sincerity. "More than inspirational. It's a love story for the ages."

He regretted those words as soon as they passed his lips.

Quinn's tone was mocking. "'A love story for the ages'? Good fucking God, where did you steal that line of shit from? I haven't heard anything described like that since . . . since . . . well, never mind. Son, if you're going to try to woo me, I'd prefer you'd offer me more than boring clichés." He closed his eyes and, to himself, repeated the line. " 'A love story for the ages.' What a load of crap."

Chastened, Noah closed his own eyes and tried to brainstorm his way out of the rhetorical hole he had dug for himself. He was a writer, dammit, and he *could* do better than offer boring clichés. In fact, he was obviously going to have to, if he was going to gain Quinn Scott's trust.

"Listen," he finally said. "I apologize for the choice of words. But . . . but . . . your story is amazing, and I think the world would like to read about it."

"I don't think so."

"I disagree," said Noah, suddenly feeling that he had just this small window of opportunity to sell his idea. "The people you've known . . . the things you've seen . . . And let's not forget your public image. You were the Philly Cop! You were shooting Indians next to the Duke! And all that time, you were gay."

"Except I wasn't," said Quinn. "Not really."

Noah looked at him, confusion on his face. "You weren't?"

"I was, but I wasn't. Follow me?"

Noah shook his head.

"I was gay, but I wasn't gay. Now do you understand?"

Noah clearly had still not grasped what he was trying to say. Quinn sighed and slid down just a bit in his chair.

"It wasn't as if I was being invited to pool parties at George Cukor's house. I wasn't dating Rock. Maybe I knew I was attracted to men—at least *some* men—but I didn't do anything about it. When I married Katherine, I really thought she was the one. Now do you understand?"

Noah gave him a slight nod. "I think so."

"A lot of the things I know, a lot of the stories I could tell, are second or third hand. I really wasn't part of the gay scene back then. It was only when I met Jimmy that, well . . ." His voice trailed off into silence until he concluded with: "I've really got nothing for you. In fact, all I have is that fucking 'love story for the ages' you were talking about."

Noah felt his trial balloon start to deflate. If, in fact, Quinn's life was composed of a short and mediocre career, a brief marriage to Kitty Randolph, and a thirty-six year gay relationship, the older man was right: he really had nothing for him. Without a little gossip, there was no hook. Noah could write an interesting book, but not a book that anyone would go out of their way to read.

Which meant that, again, he had nothing. Nothing for his publisher and, more importantly, nothing to stoke his creativity.

Again he heard the sliding screen door, and he instinctively looked in its direction, expecting to see Bart. Instead, Jimmy stood in the doorway.

"Um . . . tequila?"

"The boy went to the liquor store," said Quinn.

"And?"

"Yes, he's getting limes, too."

"Good," said Jimmy. "Because that blender isn't going to fill itself." He stepped out onto the patio, taking in the bright sunlight and warm afternoon. Turning to Noah, he said, "And will our guest be joining us for margaritas?"

Noah shrugged. He really wasn't in the mood, now that he had to face the sheer mediocrity of Quinn Scott's life.

"Oh, come on," said Jimmy. "If we can't relax on a Saturday afternoon, when can we relax?"

Quinn snorted. "What do you need to relax *from*, dear?"

"You, love of my life." Jimmy took a long look at the unsmiling Noah. "Is something wrong?"

"Sorry," said Noah, forcing a smile. "I was just thinking."

"We don't *think* around here, Noah. That's how we keep our sanity."

Still forcing his smile, Noah added, "I was trying to convince Quinn that he had a story to tell. He doesn't seem to think so."

Quinn slumped down just a bit in his chair and said, "I have no story."

Noah didn't really mean it, but still he said, "I don't know about that. A long-term relationship, a high-profile marriage . . . Even if you weren't part of the Hollywood gay scene, you still have a story."

"Excuse me?" said Jimmy, planting one hand on his chest. "Did I miss something? Did my husband regain his virginity when I wasn't looking?"

Noah raised an eyebrow and stole a look at Quinn, who slid even further down in the chair.

"There's not much to tell," Quinn grumbled.

Jimmy laughed. "Not much to tell? Oh, Quinn." He leaned into Noah and, with a finger pointed at his partner, said, "That old man might have taken his time coming out of the closet, but—let me tell you, honey—once I coaxed him out he made up for a lot of lost time."

"Jimmy . . ." Quinn grumbled, but Jimmy ignored him.

"Do some math here, Noah. We met in September 1969, and that shrew he was married to caught us in the act a few months later. But we weren't banished from the industry for another year or so. And why was that?"

"Jimmy . . ."

"Because *someone* didn't know the meaning of the word 'discretion.' I had to practically attach myself to him to keep him out of trouble."

"Jimmy . . ."

"Oh hush now," said Jimmy, flapping a hand at Quinn. "You

know it's true. If I wasn't watching you like a hawk, you would have *so* slept with Rock!"

Noah's eyes were now wide open. "Rock Hudson?"

"He was sniffing after my Quinn for months. 'I'm having a party; would you like to come over?' 'How about dinner Friday night?' Let me tell you, Noah, after word got out that hunky Quinn Scott was gay, half of Hollywood was chasing after him."

"That's not exactly true."

"It is *so* true. And thank God *I* got you first, because if it wasn't for my charm, skill, and patience, you would have gone through them like a kid in a candy store." When Quinn didn't respond, Jimmy cocked a hand on his hip and added, "His silence speaks volumes."

Quinn Scott was not a classically trained actor, but he knew how to hide the intense embarrassment he was feeling: he abruptly stood and walked back into the house.

"Call me when the margaritas are ready," he said in parting.

When he was gone, Noah said to Jimmy, "Those stories are true?"

"Swear to God."

Noah shook his head. "He told me he wasn't part of the Hollywood gay scene."

"Well, in a sense, he wasn't. It's true that gay men wanted him, and he did his fair share of hitting the party circuit after we became a couple, but he wasn't . . . well, he wasn't promiscuous. I do believe that he's a one-man man." He looked to the house, to make sure Quinn was out of earshot. "But they wanted him, and he loved the attention . . . until word got back to Kitty."

"You said she walked in on you?"

Jimmy was visibly energized, and took Quinn's vacated deck chair. "Now *that* was a scene! You know the story of how we met, right?" Noah shook his head. "It was on the set of *When the Stars Come Out.* He was starring opposite her—and let me tell you, I love Quinn dearly, but he should not have been doing musicals—and I was a dancer in the big musical number at the end of the show. Anyway, I had just ended a horrible relationship with an evil, evil man—dead now, God rest his soul—and I didn't think I wanted to meet anyone, but we were on the set, and our eyes met, and something just clicked."

"And . . . happily ever after?"

Jimmy threw his head back and let out a loud, high-pitched laugh. "Not exactly. Remember, Quinn was married to the top box-office draw in the nation, maybe the world. And up to that point, he had never even admitted to *himself* that he was gay. It was very complicated. Let me give you a brief flashback . . ."

Chapter 5

There are a lot of people in Hollywood who are trapped in loveless marriages . . . relationships that are more like business partnerships than love affairs. I know, because I used to be one of those people. Quinn Scott was all about his career, social standing, and financial comfort.

And let me tell you, that is not the way to go through life. There is nothing quite so liberating as freeing yourself to love, no matter what the consequences . . .

Los Angeles, California, September 1969

The scene had finally been shot to the satisfaction of the director and star Kitty Randolph alike, and the day was over. The last tweaks could be addressed in the editing room, and there was no need to keep cast and crew on the soundstage, eating deeper into a budget that was already keeping the studio executives up at night.

Jimmy changed back into street clothes in the dressing room he shared with the entire male crew of dancers and, bag over his shoulder, walked to his car, parked at the far end of the studio lot in a barren, treeless expanse that had been drenched in hot Southern California sunshine all day. He unlocked the trunk and threw his bag in, then slammed it shut. Fingering his keys, he walked to the driver's door, already dreading the furnace inside.

"Hey," said a deep voice behind him. "Nice work today."

The voice was familiar. He turned and saw Quinn Scott strut toward him from between parked cars.

"Mr. Scott," Jimmy said, more than a bit surprised. He heard his voice rise and tried to keep it in check. "I didn't expect to see you way out here."

Jimmy wasn't just making small talk. He had truly never before known of an actor of any consequence who had to park in the outlying lots . . . especially one the stature of Quinn Scott. This parking Siberia was on par with the public transportation that would have probably dropped him off much closer to the studio gates.

Quinn's eyes glanced off of him for the briefest of moments before absently scanning the lot full of heat-seared automobiles. "I think the '*When the Stars Come Out*' number went well, didn't it?"

"Oh, yes!" said Jimmy, still vaguely nervous at the encounter.

"Was I . . . too stiff?"

Jimmy smiled, wishing he could dare share the double entendre that was on the tip of his tongue. "Not at all. I mean, you're not a dancer, but you move well enough. I think you did quite well."

Quinn wasn't sure if he was being truly complimented, or damned by the faintest of praise. Sensing his discomfort, Jimmy added, "And you did a very good job singing, too."

The actor smiled. "Well, I don't think you're telling me the entire truth. But thank you. Anyway, this is Katherine's movie, and the rest of us are all window dressing, right?"

"Right. Uh . . . Katherine?"

Quinn corrected himself, changing from the legal to the familiar form of his wife's name. "Kitty."

Jimmy looked at him. The man was thirty-five or thirty-six years old, but he could still lie, shave five or six years off his age and get away with it. His broad shoulders, so unlike Jimmy's own lithe dancer's frame, slumped just slightly in the heat. Jimmy remembered the glance they had exchanged hours earlier on the set—the glance that seemed to say that they were the only ones in on the inside joke—and wondered if this masculine, handsome man could possibly be . . .

No. Impossible! Even the other male dancers—all but two of them as gay as gay could be; and the other two gay by association, going along to get along—even in all those catty hours on the set and in the dressing room, no one had ever thought to suggest that Quinn Scott could *possibly* be gay.

And yet . . .

And yet there was that glance on the set. And now here he was, standing under the sweltering sun in a parking lot far from any place he should have been found, asking Jimmy for a review of his song-and-dance performance.

It was . . . confusing. Not necessarily in a bad way, just in an unexpected way. And Jimmy didn't quite know what was supposed to happen next.

"Can . . . uh, can I give you a lift to your car?" Jimmy asked, as he slid his key into the lock. "It's too hot to walk all the way back to the lot."

Quinn smiled. "Thanks. But I'll just call a cab." When Jimmy raised an eyebrow he added, "Kitty already left with the driver. She has a party tonight and wanted to get ready."

"You aren't going to the party?"

He shrugged. "The key to our successful m-m-marriage"— Jimmy took note of the stutter—"is that we give each other room to breathe."

Jimmy nodded, as if Quinn had spoken some great wisdom. He pulled the door open and said, "Well, then, let me give you a lift home . . ."

The car, as he expected, was an oven. He rolled down his window, then leaned over the front seat and pulled up the lock to the passenger side door before scrambling back out of the car. Quinn followed Jimmy's lead, opening the door and rolling down his window, then retreating from the hot interior.

They stood outside in the waning sun, waiting for the seats to cool to a tolerable level, and Quinn offered Jimmy a cigarette and his lighter. Wordlessly, Jimmy nodded his appreciation, took one, and lit up.

"Damn, it's hot," said Quinn, finally breaking the silence.

"Sure is."

There was another awkward pause, during which both men struggled to come up with a topic of conversation.

"So . . . how do you like being a dancer?"

Jimmy smiled, and did a quick grapevine, despite the early evening sun that still beat down on the parking lot. "It's what I do," he said. "Well, for now. Some day . . ."

"Some day *what*?"

Jimmy hesitated, but decided to plunge right in. "Some day I'd like to do some acting, too."

There was an overlay of sarcasm in Quinn's chuckle. "You want to be a fuckin' *actor*? Sure about that?"

"Absolutely."

"Let me tell you something, Jim."

"Jimmy. Someone else in SAG is already a 'Jim.' "

"Okay, then, let me tell you something, *Jimmy*. Acting is bullshit, and trust me on this: I know. I do it twenty-four hours a day. Stick with dancing." For the first time in their entire conversation Quinn looked directly at him. "You have the moves, you know."

Jimmy shivered, and *that* certainly wasn't from the temperature. He tossed his cigarette to the ground, grinding it into the asphalt with a heel, and said, "The car should be bearable now. Let's get going."

While Quinn took his time getting into the passenger seat, Jimmy checked himself in the mirror. There were still the slightest traces of makeup at the edges of his mouth, melting in the heat, which he patted away with a tissue. Other than that, he was the same attractive twenty-six-year-old he had seen in the bathroom mirror that morning. If Quinn Scott really *was* gay—as simultaneously plausible and implausible as that seemed—he would, if nothing else, have some nice scenery for the ride home.

Finally, Quinn slid in next to him in the front seat. Jimmy turned the key in the ignition and the engine roared a bit too loudly to life. The men didn't speak as the car backed out of its space, then was maneuvered forward through the lot.

"So where am I going?" Jimmy asked, after they passed through the gate and he idled at the exit to the street, not knowing if he was making a left or right.

"Uh . . ."

Jimmy looked at Quinn and was surprised to see that the actor seemed nervous.

"Do I make a left here? Right?"

It turned out that they were making a right. That *was* the direction back to Jimmy's apartment, after all.

"I want to know your story, Quinn Scott."

He smiled. "I don't have a story."

Jimmy rolled away, pulling the sheets off Quinn's surprisingly smooth chest. For some reason—probably Quinn's hypermasculinity—Jimmy had expected a lot of hair; instead, his broad, muscled chest was as bare as Jimmy's own.

"Where are you going?" asked Quinn, pulling back on the crisp white sheets.

"Getting a cigarette. Want one?"

"Sure."

When Jimmy turned back to him, he was holding an ashtray, two cigarettes, and a Zippo. He set the ashtray—a piece of ceramic designed to look like a pond, complete with a tiny frog perched on the edge—between them on the bed, handed Quinn a cigarette, and lit it before lighting his own. After exhaling a plume of smoke, he looked at Quinn and said, "So you're not going to tell me your story?"

"I told you. There is no story."

"Do you do this often?"

Quinn smiled shyly. "Uh . . . believe it or not, this was my first time."

"I don't believe that," said Jimmy, inhaling again. "Tell me another one, handsome."

"No, it's true," said Quinn, sitting up and letting the sheet slide until it bunched in his lap. Jimmy looked again at his smooth upper body, pectoral muscles dancing in the glare of a streetlight filtered through cheap aluminum blinds. He saw the orange tip of Quinn's cigarette flare and waited for him to continue after he exhaled. "I've never done this before."

"Okay, let me get this straight: you have *never*—never *ever*—had sex with a man before."

"Nope."

"Cross your heart and swear on your mother's grave."

"Never."

"I don't believe you." Jimmy stubbed out his cigarette in the ceramic pond. "If this was your first time, then how did you get so good?"

"I didn't say I've never had sex before," said Quinn, as he extinguished his own cigarette. "Just not with a man."

"But . . ."

"It's all pretty much the same," Quinn added.

"It is certainly *not* the same! In case you didn't notice, that was *not* a vagina you just fucked!" Jimmy grabbed the ashtray from between them and set it on the nightstand, then slid over until he was pressed against Quinn's warm body. "You can tell me. Was it when you were in the army? A military academy? Uh . . . a seminary?"

Quinn laughed. "I've never been in any of those."

Jimmy sighed theatrically. "Please don't tell me that you learned to do that with your wife . . ."

Again came the laugh. "Oh, hell no! She'd castrate me if I even suggested it." Quinn reached over and began stroking Jimmy's taut stomach, feeling the soft trail of hair rising up from his groin in his fingers. "Maybe I'm just a natural."

Maybe, thought Jimmy. He still wasn't fully convinced, but Quinn's apparent aversion to some things Jimmy took for granted made a bit of sense in that context. Most men, for instance, couldn't keep their mouths off his rather large member, but Quinn, well . . . he *could*.

But *damn*, could he take care of everything else.

"Okay," said Jimmy, finally willing to concede the point. "So if I'm your first, do I get some kind of reward?"

"Uh . . ." Quinn pulled away. It was just a few inches, but it felt like miles to Jimmy. "We probably should have talked about this earlier, but . . . uh . . . I trust you're discreet."

"You mean, you trust I'm not going to fuck up your marriage to Kitty, don't you?"

"Yes," he confessed. "And this will . . . stay between us, right?"

Jimmy shook his head. "I can't even begin to tell you how many times I've heard those words in this town." Closing that gap with Quinn's naked body he said, "Yes, Quinn, I will keep this as our little secret. Your wife won't find out . . . other people won't find out . . . I won't be the man who drives your son into therapy for two decades . . . I won't even sell it to the tabloids. Even if I'm starving, I'll be discreet."

"Good," said Quinn, although he was not quite convinced enough to wash away his post-coital concern.

Jimmy kept Quinn's little secret quite well. When, upon returning to the set for a few more days of shooting at the demand of the perfectionist director, one of the other dancers made a remark about Quinn's tight ass, Jimmy obligingly told him, "You'd better make sure that he doesn't hear you, Mary, or he'll break your legs." When someone else said that Quinn didn't seem quite convincing as Kitty's love interest, Jimmy told him that he had no doubt of the red-hot passion in the Kitty Randolph-Quinn Scott bedroom, reminding them that only ten months earlier they had produced a child. And when yet another dancer giggled at Quinn's dancing, Jimmy joined in the laughter, even though he had been coaching Quinn twice a week, sometimes before and sometimes after their lovemaking.

They fell into a fairly predictable routine, which continued even after shooting ended and *When the Stars Come Out* wrapped. Every Tuesday and Thursday, precisely at 3:00 PM, which coincided with Kitty's biweekly appointment for her skin-care regimen, Quinn would park two blocks away from Jimmy's apartment down in Venice. He would don sunglasses to avoid being recognized, although at that hour of the day in Jimmy's quiet neighborhood, it was rare to encounter another pedestrian, let alone unwanted recognition. Quinn would walk briskly—but not *too* briskly, which could attract attention—to Jimmy's apartment, where they would spend the next two hours having sex and practicing dance steps, since—even after completing *Stars*—Quinn anticipated another musical in his future. Then they would shower and Quinn would hurry back to his car in time to avoid the increased scrutiny that would come as the neighborhood's rush-hour commuters returned home.

Other than that, there was no communication. No phone calls, no impromptu visits, no contact whatsoever.

Jimmy was disappointed in that. Young as he was, he had been around long enough to know not to expect much when having a clandestine gay affair with a married man. But there was something about Quinn that he found captivating. And as often as he told himself that this thing with Quinn was nothing more than a casual fling, he spent an equal amount of time wishing that it could be something more. Something permanent, even.

He wished that Quinn would leave Kitty and be a trailblazer: Hollywood's first openly gay leading man. Hadn't the closet doors been bulging lately, and weren't they about to burst open? In New York, not even three months earlier, gays had stood up for themselves at Stonewall. So many actors were gay, many of them growing impatient with hiding in the shadows. It was only a matter of time. Jimmy felt he could confidently predict that in the next handful of years, one leading man or another would step forward and not only declare his homosexuality, but show that his career would not suffer, and that he could continue to play a romantic hero on the silver screen.

Why shouldn't Quinn Scott be that pioneer?

Jimmy, of course, knew better than to broach the subject with Quinn. For now, Quinn was content to portray the character of "Mr. Kitty Randolph," and, in any event, all they really had was a twice-a-week arrangement.

Still, he could dream. And in the meantime he could also tutor, noting with satisfaction that Quinn was making slow but steady progress in both dancing and giving blow jobs.

* * *

If Jimmy had asked him, Quinn would have agreed that their life together—as secretive as it was—had become a routine. It was a routine he looked forward to; it was a routine he welcomed . . . but, in the end, the schedule had become agonizingly predictable.

He welcomed this new world that Jimmy had opened up to him. It was more than the sex, which—great as it was—was only part of what he felt with Jimmy. He felt, for the first time . . .

Love.

Too damn bad it was the love of another man, which would never do. Those four hours each week with Jimmy Beloit were beautiful in their tenderness and intensity, and painful in their brevity, but they were all Quinn could offer . . . and maybe more than he could afford.

And so, Tuesdays and Thursdays, week after week, Quinn Scott drove across LA, leaving behind his affluent Bel-Air neighborhood for Jimmy's modest digs, and feeling richer, yet more troubled, for the experience.

But it was still a routine, and routines breed regularity, and regularity breeds confidence, at first, and then sloppiness. It was late November, the Tuesday after Thanksgiving and some eight weeks since they had exchanged what they'd come to refer to as The Glance on that soundstage, before Quinn slipped up the first time.

It wasn't *really* a slipup. He had been courting the inevitable by following the same routine for two months with no deviation, expecting everything to always progress the way it had in the past. This time, though, the inevitability of disruption caught up to him, although he didn't know it at the time.

It was only after he had returned home that he learned of the slipup.

"You were in Venice today," Kitty said, sizing him up suspiciously as he walked into the dining room, where he had expected dinner to be waiting. There was no dinner; just Kitty Randolph sitting at the unset table, looking . . . not *angry*, really, but definitely perturbed. "What were you doing there?"

His first impulse was to deny it, but if she knew his car had been there, that wouldn't have been a good strategy. Compounding the lie could only lead to more trouble for him.

"I stopped to visit a friend," he said, with an even sureness that he hoped would put an end to the conversation. Before she had a chance to follow up he asked her, "How did you know?"

"Maria saw the car." From somewhere behind him, Quinn could hear Maria, their housekeeper, being noisily busy in the kitchen. He hoped she was making dinner, because sex with Jimmy usually left him famished.

Quinn smiled. "She's very observant."

Kitty didn't smile. "Which friend?"

"I don't think you know him."

She held her gaze, her eyes burrowing into his head, trying to read whatever secrets he wasn't telling her.

"Are you having an affair?" she asked, finally.

He felt himself blush slightly. "Don't be ridiculous, Kitty."

"I just can't imagine you would have a friend in Venice."

"From my struggling actor days." Hoping to put an end to the interrogation, he added, "Maybe you know him. Jimmy Beloit?"

She thought about that. The name *did* sound vaguely familiar. Had her husband mentioned him in passing once before?

"We ran into each other recently and he invited me over for a drink. Poor guy. His career just hasn't taken off." Quinn envisioned Jimmy's tidy, small apartment, keeping his mind away from that bed with the crisp white sheets. "And he lives in a dump. I really feel bad for him."

Kitty warmed slightly. Quinn *could* be lying to her, but he seemed sincere, and he certainly wasn't setting off her natural Bullshit Detector.

"And," Quinn added, "I think he might be a fag."

She furrowed her brow. "Did he say something?"

"Not directly. But I just got a few uncomfortable feelings." He shook his head. "Whatever. It's his business, right? Let's eat."

Dinner appeared just moments after the conclusion of Kitty's staged confrontation, and Quinn mentally complimented her on the way she set the scene. Through dinner, he wondered why he had thrown out the gay angle, let alone used Jimmy's real name. If she had demanded to meet him, it's true that there would have been a real person to go with the real name, but his elaborate story would have fallen apart when she either recognized Jimmy from the *Stars* set, or when she realized that the only way they could have known each other in their starving actor days was if Quinn was hanging out with twelve-year-olds at the time.

But he didn't think about any of it too much. The story, for all its elaboration, had worked, and Kitty was now far away from the topic of illicit affairs and well into a monologue on her favorite subject, which just happened to be the life and career of Kitty Randolph.

A few weeks later, though, Quinn made his second—and much more damaging—slipup. And this time he could not just blame it on bad luck, the way he had when his housekeeper happened across his car.

On a Wednesday night in mid-December, he and Kitty had stayed far too late at a prominent studio head's Christmas party. Generally well behaved in social situations, that particular night Quinn had had a bit too much to drink; not enough so that he made an ass of himself, but enough to render him extremely tired on the following Thursday. Still, he had a routine, so minutes after Kitty left to get her skin massaged, exfoliated, buffed, and moisturized, he climbed into his car and set off for his date with Jimmy, where the men spent their usual two hours in intimate union.

And then they both fell asleep in each other's arms.

For three more hours.

"Shit!"

Jimmy's eyes flickered open, only to spy Quinn scrambling frantically for his clothes.

"What . . . ?" he groggily started to ask, but then saw the clock on the nightstand.

"It's 8:00!" Jimmy had never seen Quinn lose his cool, let alone be reduced to panic. "It's eight-fucking-o'clock! I am *fucked!*"

"Just tell her . . ." Jimmy drew a blank.

"Tell her what?!" Quinn began buttoning his shirt. "How could you let this happen?"

Jimmy sat up in the bed, suddenly angry at the blame. "I fell asleep, too."

"Goddamn it!"

She was, as he knew she would be, waiting for him when he finally arrived home.

"Who is she?"

"Who is who?"

"Who are you seeing, Quinn? What's her name? I want to know her name."

"I . . . I don't know what you're talking about."

"Goddamn it, Quinn, I can smell the sex from here! You didn't even have the decency to clean yourself up!"

"Kitty, I—"

"You *what*, Quinn? You want a divorce?"

"No," he said. "Of course not. But you're wrong."

"I don't think so."

He knew he couldn't win. He was too rattled to think straight and, in any event, she was more right than wrong. *Far* more. Without a word, he left the room and went to shower the hours of sex and sleep off his body.

In the hot spray of the shower, as he soaped his body, he wondered if he had not done it on purpose, at least on a subconscious level. Had his suppressed longing for Jimmy led to his overindulgence at the studio honcho's party the night before, which, in tandem with his comfort in the dancer's arms, led to his ill-timed nap? Had the routine gone on too long? Was it time to confess to Kitty, and move on to the next phase of his life?

He let the steamy water course over him, hoping that it would wash away his sins.

Quinn and Kitty co-existed for the next few days. She was still angry, but no longer talked of divorce. He was contrite without being suspiciously *too* contrite. The subject of his late homecoming— the homecoming that "smelled of sex"—came up a few times, and each time he had dismissed the event as innocent, while offering no real details to clear his name. The simple fact was that he had been caught—he had let himself be caught—and the only way he hoped to survive the indiscretion was to maintain stony silence.

After all, he was a man, and hardly the first of his sex to stray. At some primal level, even Kitty would understand that. As long as it wasn't repeated—the "getting caught" part, that was, not the "cheating" part—Quinn felt they could get past it. They would hardly be unique in sharing a black moment, never quite going away but never being spoken of again.

And Quinn might have been right. But he wasn't.

On the Tuesday of the following week came the natural outgrowth of the previous Thursday's indiscretion. Six minutes after Kitty left to reinvigorate her skin, Quinn left to reinvigorate his life. Twenty minutes later, he held Jimmy in his arms; five minutes after that, they were in the bedroom.

And seven minutes after that, the doorbell rang.

"You have a visitor," said Quinn, as he slowly stroked Jimmy's erection.

Jimmy wasn't expecting a visitor. In fact, beside food deliveries and Quinn's biweekly visits, he couldn't even *remember* the last time he had been visited.

"Whoever it is," he said, taking Quinn's head in his hands, "will have to come back."

A minute later, the bell rang again. Jimmy, focused on the sensation of Quinn as he began to penetrate him, barely heard it. He only started paying attention when a fist started banging on his front door.

"Ah, fuck," he said, sliding off of Quinn. "I'd better get this before someone calls the cops."

As Quinn sank into the bed, Jimmy threw a robe over his naked body, pulling his erection flat against his belly with the belt. Partial-dressing accomplished, he marched out into the living room and swung open the door.

Kitty Randolph stood on the stoop.

She looked at him and gasped. And he looked at her and gasped, then slammed the door in her face.

While Kitty screamed for him to open the door, Jimmy raced, screaming, back to the bedroom.

"It's her!" he yelled, pouncing on the bed. "It's her!"

"Her?" Quinn's eyes widened. "Kitty?"

He sat, stunned, on the bed, as Jimmy began tossing clothes at him. From the living room they could hear her as she continued to angrily pound on the front door, each barrage of thuds louder and more demanding than the ones before. "You've got to get dressed and get out of here!"

"How?"

"The window. Crawl out the window!"

"That won't work." Although panicked and stunned, Quinn still knew that Jimmy's only windows—beside the one in the bathroom, which was too small to crawl through—were in clear view from the front stoop, where his wife was now standing and flailing at Jimmy's door.

"Then we'll hide you in a closet. Or under the bed."

Quinn shook his head. "It won't work. She'll find me."

"Well . . . what should we do?"

Quinn stood, gave Jimmy a short hug, took a deep breath, and said, "I guess we'd better let her in."

Chapter 6

You would think that revisiting my past—watching old movies or whatever—would be the last thing an old curmudgeon like me would want to do. You would think that I'd consider it a painful reminder of the industry I loved and was forced to leave.

But you would be wrong.

There is pain in revisiting the past, of course, but watching those old movies reminds me of a time when life felt fresh and perfect. It wasn't perfect, of course—it only became perfect when Jimmy came along—but, at the time, it was as close to perfect as I thought I would ever know. And anyway, Jimmy came from those old movies, too, and I can watch our celluloid memories over and over and over . . .

"Holy crap," said Noah, when Jimmy finished his story.

"The rest was sort of anti-climactic. Well . . . once she looked through the closets and under the bed, and figured out we weren't hiding another woman in the apartment. In fact, she was almost calm when she figured out that her husband was boning another man . . . although, come to think of it, she was a bit pissed off when she finally recognized me from the *Stars* set. But still, it wasn't as bad as I would have expected. It was almost . . . I don't know, a *relief* to her, or something."

"Maybe it was," said Noah. "If she caught Quinn with a woman, the divorce could have been sticky and expensive. With a man, though, she could make him go away quietly."

Jimmy nodded. "Which he did, in his own way. The divorce was painless, she gave him a tidy bit of money to keep his mouth shut, he signed over sole custody of Q. J., and everything would have worked out perfectly. He might have even been able to keep working. *Except* once he had tasted the forbidden fruit, he couldn't get enough."

"What do you mean?"

"The attention, Noah. Quinn fell in love with the attention he was getting from Gay Hollywood. There's a little—well, not so little, actually—shadow community out there, and after his divorce from Kitty was finalized and word started to seep out, he was the most in-demand man in that town." He looked away, lost in memories that were still fresh after thirty-six years. "You know, if Quinn really cared about women, deep down, he probably would have realized that every female in the industry had worshipped him for years. But he never noticed. So much for his heterosexuality, right? With the men, though, it was a different story. All of a sudden, we were invited to every gay dinner party in town . . . although when I say 'we,' I really mean 'Quinn.' I was only invited because I was the guy who was with Quinn." He paused, trying to decide how much he should confide before fixing on full disclosure. "And let me tell you, Rock Hudson was one persistent bitch."

Noah shook his head. "So much for Quinn not having a story to tell."

"He's got a story," Jimmy assured him. "I doubt it will ever be put on paper, but he's got a story."

It was then and there, in the seconds between the end of Jimmy's story and Bart's return from the market, armed with tequila and limes, that Noah Abraham decided firmly that he was not only going to write the Quinn Scott story, but he was going to make the actor like the idea.

He would no longer rely on fate or the goodwill of others; he would make his own luck.

The margaritas tasted especially good that afternoon.

At eleven o'clock the following Monday morning, Noah walked into the Midtown Manhattan offices of Palmer/Midkiff/Carlyle Publishing for his appointment with David Carlyle, beating him to the office by a full twenty minutes. When David did appear— flushed and breathing a bit too heavily from the combination of excess weight and a hot, humid day in New York—he asked Noah to wait another ten minutes before finally ushering him into his office.

"So what do you have for me?" David asked, getting straight to business.

Noah opened a manila folder, exposing three crisp copies of his proposal and a half-dozen printouts of Web pages. "Have you ever heard of Quinn Scott?"

He smiled warily. "Of course."

"There's a story there."

David sighed. "You've decided to substitute a serious study about the impact of homosexuality on personal politics with a pop-culture biography? Interesting choice. But I have to admit I'm not feeling it."

Noah took one copy of his proposal out of the folder and handed it to David. "Maybe this will convince you."

David took it and, without another word, began to read. Although he remained mute, Noah watched his eyes and saw them start to flicker with interest. When a smile crossed David's lips, he knew his editor had reached the money paragraph.

David finished reading and set the proposal faceup on his desk. "Interesting."

"And?"

"And . . . well, first, I owe you a bit of an apology. I thought you were talking about the television actor. The son, that is. I'm glad to see that some people still remember Quinn Scott Sr."

"A much better story, right?"

"If it can be published."

His abrupt statement puzzled Noah.

"Uh . . . but *you're* a publisher."

David sighed. "Noah, let me be quite blunt. A biography of Quinn Scott, in and of itself, would interest me only slightly more than one of his insipid son. But here you propose to out the father. You propose to publicly state that Quinn Scott is gay. That gets touchy, legally."

Noah cleared his throat. "My goal," he said, "is to have Quinn out himself."

David cocked an eyebrow. "You're talking about an auto-biography?"

"As told to me."

The editor again scanned the proposal.

"And he's willing to do this?"

"He's expressed interest." Noah hoped that David couldn't see through the transparent lie.

"I'm . . . uh, I'm not sure what that means. He's either willing to come out, or he's not."

Noah leaned forward, tenting his fingers on top of the desk. "I broached the subject with him, and he didn't reject it."

"Which doesn't mean he agreed."

"Not exactly. But he will."

David chuckled and sat back. "You are quite confident in your powers of persuasion, aren't you? Why would he do it now, when he hasn't worked in thirty years?"

"Because he hasn't worked in thirty years."

David conceded the point, even if he didn't quite agree.

Noah continued. "Decades ago, Quinn Scott dropped off the

radar, right? I'm sure some people still wonder what happened to him. Now we have the opportunity—"

"Not quite," David cautioned.

"*Almost* have the opportunity to tell his story. In the process, we not only show what a different world it is today to be gay in Hollywood—"

"A bit of an overstatement."

"But," Noah continued, ignoring him, "we get to tell his unique story and, in the process, put him back in the public eye. I mean, married to Kitty Randolph! Films with John Wayne and Robert Mitchum! *Philly Cop*! Think of the stories he has, the people he's known. And then we add his gay angle to the story, and I think we have an autobiography that's not only a big seller, but puts Quinn Scott back in the news and up on the screen."

His sales pitch over, Noah relaxed, easing back in his chair.

David was silent for quite a while, thinking things over. When he finally spoke, it wasn't to offer the deal Noah had anticipated. It was to offer another note of caution.

"*If* you can get Quinn Scott to publicly acknowledge his homosexuality, I'm interested. But there is another matter that will need to be addressed before I can make a formal offer."

"Which is?"

"Kitty Randolph." David paused to let Noah think about that for a moment, then filled the conversational vacuum. "Madame Randolph does not have the visibility she had forty years ago, Noah. But if anything, she's even stronger now than she was back in her glory days. In the fifties and sixties, when she was one of the top box-office draws, she made a lot of money, which is how she managed to all but blacklist your friend Quinn Scott. But she was nobody's fool, and she reinvested all that money right back into Hollywood. She may stay mostly behind the scenes these days, but she's a studio power-broker. And from what I understand, she's still nobody's fool."

"How do you know this?"

David shrugged and said, "I read *Premiere*, of course."

"She seems like such a sweet lady."

"I'm sure she's very sweet . . . as long as she's getting what she wants." David fixed a frosty smile in Noah's direction. "How she reacts when she's not getting what she wants is anybody's guess."

"So . . . okay, she can stop Quinn's comeback. But the book—"

David waved him away, and the smile disappeared. "If she disapproves, the book will vanish."

"It can still be published."

"It can," David acknowledged. "But without publicity, a book about a dinosaur like Quinn Scott—and I mean that with the greatest affection, of course—will vanish. The only way this book will be relevant is if we can book him on the talk shows, get him on *Oprah*, generate the publicity that will lead to the reviews that will lead to the sales. If Kitty Randolph wants this project to be buried, though, it will be buried. Quinn Scott will not get within one thousand feet of Leno or Letterman. Or even Dr. Phil. Trust me on this."

"You seem to have a healthy respect for her," Noah observed, stating the obvious.

David smiled, and this time it was genuine.

"To most of the world, she's just the sweetest thing. The adorable girl next door . . . the spunky career woman . . . the darling grandmother . . . But from what I hear, she's a tigress." He paused, then gushed: "I think she's *wonderful!* A true diva!"

"I'm glad you're a fan," said Noah. "But are you going to accept my proposal?"

David frowned and puttered around his desk for a moment before answering. "I'll make you a deal," he finally said. "If you can get Quinn Scott to formally agree to this project, and if you can get him to give me something I can sell, then I'll publish the book."

That seemed fair enough to both of them. They shook hands, sealing the not-quite but sort-of-almost deal.

So it was really all coming together quite well, Noah thought, sitting on the jitney on his way back to Southampton. All he had to do was convince Quinn Scott to cooperate; convince him to come out as gay in his eighth decade; convince Kitty Randolph not to squelch the biography; and convince America's booksellers and readers that the experience would be worth the $25 suggested retail price.

Oh, and he'd also have to write 300 to 350 pages in just a few months. But, compared to the other obstacles he faced, Noah felt that would be a comparatively easy task.

He knew it was a fascinating story; he just wasn't sure if Quinn would ultimately cooperate. It was one thing to get some juicy gossip from Jimmy; quite another for Quinn to go on the record with tawdry tales of his life in Hollywood.

And then there was the other important question: could Noah even write the damn book?

He had been every bit as enthused about the book on closeted congressional staffers, after all. Maybe more. He was confident, committed, and just knew that it would be significant. And yet, more than a year later, he had nothing . . . nothing except a sneaking suspicion that the closed mouths of his completelashuels were more an excuse than the cause of his writer's block.

What if he tried and failed to collaborate with the actor? In his imperfectly perfect life, Noah was confounded by the obstacle that was his writer's block. He knew he had to get beyond it; he just didn't know how.

The congressional book was dead. That was for sure. He would never finish that book, and couldn't even conceive of opening his notebooks again. His hopes all now rode on the Quinn Scott autobiography. It wouldn't be as prestigious as the original book, true, but it could still do good, and it could keep Noah motivated and propelled in a forward trajectory.

And if it didn't pan out—if Quinn refused, or Noah's writing demons again challenged him and again won—well, would it truly be *failure* to move out here to Long Island and become a wage slave?

Noah stared out the window, watching suburbia inch by as the bus crawled down the Long Island Expressway. All those people living normal lives; all those soccer moms and commuter dads and towheaded brats heading to the mall in their SUVs to shop at Sears and Macy's. In a sense, he envied their lives, devoid as they were of closeted congressional aides and faded homosexual actors and Hollywood divas. If he could keep Bart Gustafson and lose the rest, he thought, he might be quite content moving on to a cul-de-sac and taking a dependable office job. After all, if there was satisfaction in a book well written, there must also be satisfaction in a lawn well mown.

As for books, well, he'd pay for the sweat of the labor of other chumps when he took the SUV to the mall and made his monthly drop-in at Barnes & Noble or Borders or Waldenbooks. In fact, he would even read Danielle Steel without shame.

That is precisely how suburban-conformist he would become.

He and Bart would trade in circuit parties for the Friday fish fry circuit at the VFW post or the Elks Club. Maybe they'd adopt children. Maybe they'd even install lawn ornaments. Maybe even *garden gnomes!*

Noah smiled. There was something about taking this concept too far—to the garden gnome level—that was ever so slowly lifting him out of his malaise.

A convertible slowly passed on the left and he stared down into the interior. A young couple—he was tan, she was pale—sat in clear unhappiness as the wind tossed their hair. Watching them, Noah felt regret . . . and reality. He could have his fantasies—his snobbish, belittling fantasies, at that—but the fact was that all lives were complex. Hadn't decades worth of pop culture been devoted to exposing the tensions and secrets behind the façade of magazine-perfect suburban living? The couple in the convertible obviously had more going on in their lives than arranging a rock garden and buying garden gnomes, and would almost certainly trade lives with him if they could.

So what, exactly, was his problem? Why was he discontented? And now why was he feeling . . . shame? Was that what he was feeling as he watched the convertible pull away?

Noah felt his cheeks flush and realized that, yes, he *was* feeling shame. His father's words echoed in his head: he had had a good life and he was unappreciative of it, even as he took advantage of his many advantages.

He hated it when his father was right.

He slipped in his earbud, turned up his iPod, and let the voices in his head be drowned out by the music.

Forty miles or so down the road, his eyes opened, and he gasped in surprise at the realization that he had fallen asleep. He rubbed his eyelids gently, then looked back out the window. Now, the landscape was much more open; it was still suburbia, but it was the suburbia now dotted with farms, which eventually gave way to glimpses of larger houses partially hidden behind the tree line.

Which meant that the bus was slowly easing into the Hamptons.

And that meant he was almost back to Quinn Scott's house, which in turn meant that it was almost time to face his demons again.

He told himself that he *would* convince Quinn that the book should be written, and he *would* work with him to write it. And, together, they *would* record a bit of history and, in the process, improve a few lives.

And he also told himself that, try as she may, Kitty Randolph would *not* stop it.

Kitty Randolph. For all her fame, wealth, and power, was she bedeviled by the same demons that haunted Noah's subjects? Like his congressional staffers, cloaked in shadows and petrified to emerge from the darkness, was she also afraid of tales that should not be told? After all, according to Jimmy she had reacted fairly maturely, when all was said and done, to the revelation that her husband was gay. She had only gone ballistic when he was indiscreet, and stories started being passed around that she wanted buried forever. In trying to write this book, would Noah once again find himself cut off, shunned and stonewalled by those who wouldn't talk, for fear of angering the legendary Kitty Randolph?

Noah sighed and shook his head. He was still having a hard time reconciling the Kitty Randolph of Quinn Scott-Jimmy Beloit-David Carlyle anecdote with the Kitty Randolph of the screen. Those stories stood in such stark contrast to the wholesome image the world, including Noah himself, had of the actress. On screen, and in the celebrity-worshipping press, she was the girl next door, warbling her way through a series of sometimes memorable, more often not, Technicolor films; or being romanced by a succession of handsome leading men. And then there was her later reincarnation as the mother of the girl next door on the television screen, followed by her latest reincarnation as the wry older woman who now once again stole Hollywood's heart, this time by often playing against type. She was, in a less-sexual, less-threatening way, the embodiment of Stephen Sondheim's song "I'm Still Here"; "First you're another sloe-eyed vamp; then someone's mother; then you're camp." Except Kitty Randolph had never quite allowed herself to become camp. If there was a joke, she was not only in on it, she had orchestrated its setup.

When beloved Kitty Randolph swore like a sailor in the role of George Clooney's mother-in-law in the 2004 movie *Marriage Penalty*, it ran so counter to her image that *People* magazine rushed a new cover into production proclaiming, "Kitty and Clooney Cut Loose!" It was her equivalent to Julie Andrews's breast-baring moment in the movie *S.O.B.*—the legendary good girl gets earthy—and the world ate up every minute of screen time and every column inch of magazine puffery.

But Noah was learning the New Reality: Kitty Randolph was more than a force to be reckoned with. It was no wonder Quinn Scott gave up the fight so easily when their marriage dissolved and she chased him from Hollywood as word of his homosexuality spread. He had to have known that she held all the cards.

His gaze returned to the world outside the window of the slow-moving bus. The farm markets were now decidedly upscale, and the traffic increasingly heavy, which meant he was minutes from Quinn's house. And as he prepared to lay out his proposal for the crusty old actor, Noah felt a renewed sense of resolve.

He knew what would be in the book he had to write.

Quinn Scott had a story that needed to be told; that much was true. But the story was not, as he had initially believed, one as a role model for older gay men. No, the biography would be Quinn's one last chance to reclaim the public life Kitty Randolph had stolen from him. She had chased him into obscurity decades earlier, and this would be his long-delayed response.

As much as Quinn's story was one of survival, and as much as the story of Quinn and Jimmy was inspirational, the key to the story was their adversary: the wholesome, wily Kitty Randolph.

Lost in thought, Noah almost missed his stop. He grabbed his folder and darted from the bus, armed with a new project and an even newer sense of purpose.

"So here's what I'm thinking," said Noah forty-five minutes later, sitting on the couch across from Quinn in the living room, where the older man was watching a soap opera on television. After leaving Bart to his afternoon chore—cleaning the cluttered garage—he had wasted no time in tracking down his employer. "You know how we talked about writing a book?"

"I know how *you* talked about writing a book."

"Well, I was just talking to my editor, and . . ."

Quinn turned and glared at Noah; then, holding the remote control obviously in front of him, turned up the volume.

Noah decided to wait until the next commercial.

When the pitch for fabric softener finally began, he started again. Quinn wasted no time cutting him short.

"Not interested."

"But, Quinn . . ."

"*Not Fucking interested!* Those days are my past."

"I thought you were going to think about it."

"I did. I thought about it, and this is what I decided: no fucking book."

Now the television was trying to sell them term life insurance. Noah waited a moment for Quinn's storm to pass, then said:

"But the work is done. I mean, David Carlyle at Palmer/Midkiff/Carlyle is ready to publish. All we have to do is give him a manuscript."

Quinn sighed. This Noah kid was becoming more than a pest. All he wanted to know was whether or not Doctor Montgomery was going to come out of his coma, and he couldn't concentrate because—across from him on the couch—he was yammering on and on about an idea Quinn thought he had forcefully squelched.

Then again, at this particular moment he had no interest in term life, and people seldom kept talking after Quinn had shut them off, so maybe there was something worth listening to. He turned to Noah, nodded, and said, "You've got thirty seconds."

"Great." Noah began reeling off his spiel. "Here's the story: you're married to the world's best-known actress, but you only find true love with another man. She catches you in the act, and destroys you. But she can't destroy your love. Now, thirty-something years later and still in love, you reemerge to tell the world how you conquered her intolerance . . . how she isn't America's sweetheart, but rather embodies the worst impulses of the—"

Quinn had heard enough. "No."

"No?"

"No. No fucking way. Especially if it's going to be all about *her.*"

"Well, I mean, if we're going to look at your breakup and banishment from Hollywood as allegorical—"

"No."

"But this could be perfect! We can frame this like . . . like . . . like you stood up to the dark underbelly of American society!"

The soap opera was back on the screen, but it no longer held Quinn's attention. Instead, he was staring at Noah, who shrunk back a bit at his unforgiving stare.

"Are you some kind of Communist?" he asked.

"Uh . . . no."

"Then what's all this 'dark underbelly' bullshit?"

Noah watched as Quinn clenched his jaw, knowing he had already said too much and fighting an urge to say more. He had to look away from him, so he turned his eyes to the television. When he looked back, Quinn's own eyes were closed.

"Then she wins," said Noah, his voice a tentative whisper even as he braved one last comment.

Quinn's eyes opened again. "She always wins, son. That's what Katherine lives for: winning."

"And you're going to let her do this?"

Noah had expected Quinn to be angry, but the long-retired actor sounded, to him, far more regretful than angry. "What's done is done. For thirty-six years I've looked the other way, and there's no reason to go back and reopen the wounds." He swiveled in his recliner to get a better view of Noah, and to lock him in with those cool gray eyes. The tone of his voice was wistful. "Katherine can't be broken, Noah. And, you know . . . I was never really broken. She took away my career, but not my money. And not my love. She didn't get those things, which means she never really won, not by her terms, at least. And now, well . . . now it's been a long time, and Jimmy and I have a nice life, and I just don't see why we'd want to go through it all again."

"But . . ."

"Which is why I keep telling you *no fucking way!*"

And with that, the discussion was finally over.

Fortunately, Noah Abraham always tried to have a Plan B.

"So," Noah said, as he walked into the kitchen a half hour later, "How do you think I can convince him to write his autobiography?"

Jimmy Beloit looked up from the onion he was chopping. "Did he say no?"

"Yes."

"Then you can't."

As if to punctuate Jimmy's sentence, Camille let out a low growl. Noah took a step away from the dog.

"You see what a great opportunity this is, don't you?"

Jimmy chopped and didn't answer.

Noah raised an arm, sweeping his hand through the air as if spelling out a headline. "'After all these decades, Quinn Scott tells his story. All about why he disappeared from Hollywood . . . his secret love of thirty years . . .' "

"Almost thirty-six," said Jimmy, still chopping. "If I have to put up with him, I want credit for each and every year."

"It's a way for your love to be acknowledged. Thirty-six years. The two of you would be role models."

Jimmy stopped chopping and, using the edge of the knife, collected the diced pieces of onion and tossed them into a bowl. Task accomplished, he turned to Noah and said, "Role models to whom? Nobody remembers *him* anymore, and they never *knew* who I was."

Noah smiled. "That could all change so quickly. One book, and you both would become gay icons."

Jimmy removed a tomato from the refrigerator and began chopping again. "And suppose we don't want to be gay icons?"

"Why not?"

"Because maybe we just want to be an old couple living out of the spotlight. You know, neither of us has ever been to a gay pride parade. I'm sure it's fun, but that's not our lifestyle. Our lifestyle is this: cooking and gardening and going to assorted doctors for assorted ailments. Which seem to be coming on more frequently, by the way." He scooped up the tomato pieces with the knife blade and tossed them with the onions. "I don't think we'd ever be considered role models, except for maybe by the AARP."

That made Noah laugh, despite himself. Which was Jimmy's intent, and it had the side benefit of distracting Noah from his sales pitch for just long enough until they heard Bart entering the house from the garage.

"Hey," he said as he entered the kitchen. His face was streaked with dirt and oil.

"Well aren't you a sight," said Jimmy, as he began chopping the radishes. "You look so butch."

Bart smiled. "You can clean the garage yourself, if you want."

"No thanks. There are spiders out there." He looked up from the cutting board. "You boys should get cleaned up. Dinner will be ready shortly."

Bart left, and Noah heard his footsteps clomp up the stairs to his bedroom. He considered returning to his conversation with Jimmy, but reluctantly followed Bart upstairs. He was unsure of what to say to Jimmy and, well, the oil-smeared Bart really *did* look butch.

Alone again in the kitchen, Jimmy laughed to himself at the thought that he and Quinn could be gay icons. It was a ridiculous suggestion. And no matter how hard Noah had tried to sell the idea, he could no longer imagine Quinn in any kind of iconic way.

It hadn't always been that way, of course. When they first shared The Glance, and later that day when Quinn had appeared in the perimeter parking lot, Jimmy certainly thought of him as iconic. But at some point between that day and the day Kitty caught them in bed, he had lost his starry luster and become a mere mortal in Jimmy Beloit's eyes.

No; not a "mere mortal." That phrase was insufficient to describe the man he had loved for all those years. Quinn was something else altogether: a blustery, hard-edged pain in the ass on the outside, and the warmest, most loving man on the inside. They had given up a lot for each other, but over the years their sacrifices had proven more than worth it.

A simple book could never begin to convey the complex man who was Quinn Scott. And it could never make him an icon of anything near the stature he deserved.

But at least Jimmy could give Noah a glimpse; a slight taste of what Quinn Scott really meant to him. And he knew exactly how to do that.

After dinner, Jimmy stood and made an announcement.

"Since we have a special guest . . ."

"Again," Quinn grumbled.

". . . again, I thought it might be fun to have a movie night. Noah, have you ever seen a Quinn Scott movie?"

"I, uh . . ." Noah's first instinct was to say that he *thought* he had; his second was to lie. "Sure."

"Was it *When the Stars Come Out?*"

Since it was now clear where the conversation was going, he admitted he had not seen that particular movie.

"In that case, will you gentlemen be kind enough to accompany me to the screening room?"

As they rose from the dining room table, Noah whispered to Bart. "The screening room?"

"Downstairs. Don't get too excited. It's not exactly the Ziegfeld Theater down there."

The four men, accompanied by Camille, descended the dimly lit staircase off the kitchen until they reached the screening room, a small hideaway across the hall from the foot of the stairs. While Quinn strode into the darkness, Jimmy fumbled until he found the light switch. Moments later the room came to life.

"So is this going to be painful?" asked Noah, whispering to Bart.

"How painful can it be? You get to see Quinn Scott sing and dance."

"Oh dear . . ."

Noah turned and saw Jimmy in a tiny closed-off space at the back of the screening room, rifling through a box of videotapes.

"Can I give you a hand?"

"No," said Jimmy, as he carefully pulled a tape from the box. "I found what I was looking for."

Noah stared at the box. "Video? That's sort of . . . low tech, isn't it?"

Jimmy stole a glance at Quinn. Seeing that he wasn't paying attention, he laughed and said, "We're just civilians these days, hon. Any hope we had of furnishing this place with high-tech gadgets and professional film equipment disappeared back around 1970." He motioned around him at the small space in which he stood. "For instance, we call this the projection room, but that's tongue in cheek. It's really just a closet rigged with a VHS and DVD feed to the screen."

"Well, shouldn't you at least have these on DVD? I mean, tape is outdated. It disintegrates."

Jimmy held up the box. Kitty Randolph and, in the background, Quinn Scott—both eternally young as the stars of *When the Stars Come Out*—smiled back from the cover.

"I know this will come as a shock, but they decided to put *All About Eve* out on DVD before *Stars*. Go figure." He paused, then thought to add, "That's why Bart is kind enough to check the new release schedule every time he's back in civilization. And Bart and I check the Internet, and every other resource we can think of, whenever we have a chance."

"Oh, well . . . I guess that makes sense."

Jimmy leaned close to Noah's ear. "There *is* some good news," he said. "A 'Kitty Randolph Collection' is being released on DVD in a few weeks, and I'm not sure about this, because they haven't announced all the titles, but there's a chance *Stars* will be one of the movies in the set. Which would be perfect, because it will be just in time for Quinn's birthday."

"I'll keep my fingers crossed," said Noah.

"Appreciate it."

From the front row of the eight-seat theater that passed as his screening room, they heard Quinn holler. "Are you going to run the fucking movie? Or should I just go to bed?"

"Go to bed, old man," Jimmy muttered, but, responding for the benefit of Quinn, he yelled back, "Two seconds!"

"Go grab a seat," said Jimmy, shooing Noah out of the small room. Less than a minute later, the FBI antipiracy warning came on the screen as Jimmy hustled into the room, dimming the lights before he took a seat next to Quinn.

Music swelled and the bright opening credits began. Each screen title—beginning with the studio credit, then moving on to the lead actors and, finally, the name of the movie—appeared in a comic-style font before dissolving into twinkling stars. The theme continued through the end of the credits, when the deep blue background slowly turned lighter, and the camera pulled back to show that the blue had segued into a cloudless sky over San Francisco.

The camera angle dipped, and the bay came into view in the distance. It continued its descent until the camera was pointed down one of the city's hills at a lone figure walking up the center of the street.

Kitty Randolph.

And she was singing, because that's what sunny, happy, chipper, innocent Kitty Randolph did on the screen in 1970.

> *It's a day,*
> *That's meant for living,*
> *And so I say,*
> *That's what I'll do;*
> *My new home,*
> *My San Francisco!*
> *I'll make a pledge*
> *To do my living with you!*

Noah rolled his eyes, and Bart nudged him. They looked away from the screen and saw that Quinn and Jimmy were rapt, despite the insipid song and, oh, the little fact that the woman on the videotape had tried to destroy them.

Over the next two hours, fresh-to-the-big-city Kitty got a job at an ad agency, began flirting with the executive in the office next to hers—played by Quinn, of course—and battled sex discrimination. When Quinn accidentally got credit for one of her ideas, as well as the subsequent promotion, she scrunched up her nose and got huffily angry, but never hinted that she'd file suit or quit. This character had obviously not been off the farm long enough to have heard of Gloria Steinem.

Quinn's character, a laid-back ladies' man named 'Nick Butler'—eventually fell in love with Kitty's "Ann Fredericks," and, in time, made everything right when he discovered that she deserved his promotion . . . much to the blustery, sexist dismay of Gale Gordon as the advertising firm's president. And finally—their lives back the way they were supposed to be, with all resentment and jealousy banished and the lights of the Golden Gate Bridge shimmering against a dark, starry night—Quinn took Kitty in his arms while a diorama of passersby froze in their tracks.

"Ann," he said from the screen. "I think I love you."

"Is that the best you can do?" she asked. "Because I *know* I love you!"

He smiled. "I do love you, Ann. Will you be Mrs. Nick Butler?"

With that, he pulled a ring box from his jacket. She took it and opened it, then melted into his arms. And she sang.

When the evening falls, my dear,
And when my dream time calls, my dear,
You'll be with me,
Of that, no doubt,
I'll see your face when the stars come out.

Behind Quinn, the passersby in the street tableaux began danc-ing. Noah squinted and . . . yes, that was definitely Jimmy Beloit. It was a long, long time ago, and he was still in his youthful, boyish twenties, but that was definitely Jimmy who was taking the young woman in the blue dress in his arms and dancing just behind and to the right of the rather stiff, but not embarrassingly so, Quinn Scott.

Noah suddenly laughed, but it was lost in the screening room under the swelling music. He found it funny to be watching Quinn and Jimmy on the screen, roughly the same ages as he and Bart were, not knowing the storm that would envelop their lives in mere months. *When the Stars Come Out* might not have been great cinema, but it was a great time capsule.

His eyes wandered from the screen for a few short seconds, dart-ing back just in time to see it.

The Glance.

It really existed. If you never knew of its existence, you would miss it. But if you knew, you could plainly see the decades ahead of the two men being played out in that split-second when their eyes met, before they pulled away.

And despite his cynicism, despite the mediocrity of the movie they were just finishing watching, Noah felt his eyes well up at the sight.

He was still tearing when the end credits began rolling. Jimmy's name—buried in the middle of the other dancers, just before the crew credits began—flashed past, and then the formerly boyish dancer was turning the lights back on.

Bart looked at Noah. "Are you okay?"

Noah tried to laugh off the tears. The contrast in emotions made his head ache. "Yeah. Just . . . it was strange seeing them, so long ago."

"Christ," said Quinn, as he pushed past the younger men. "Turn off the waterworks. It was only a movie." He headed up the stairs.

Returning from the projection room after turning off the VCR, Jimmy had a tissue in his hand.

"Here," he said, and Noah took it. Jimmy leaned against the aisle chair across from Noah. "You saw The Glance?"

"I saw a lot of things," Noah said, grateful to feel Bart's arm reach around his shoulder. "But, yes, I saw The Glance."

"Well, first of all, don't listen to that asshole husband of mine. I can guarantee you that in just a few minutes he'll be locked in the bathroom, crying like a baby. He can be a bastard, but at least he's a *sentimental* bastard." Noah laughed. "And secondly, let it flow. It was a beautiful moment that led to the rest of our lives, and it's preserved forever on celluloid. That's sort of special, and if it's beautiful enough to make you cry a little bit, I think that's great."

Noah smiled, even though that made his head hurt even more. "Thanks, Jimmy."

Jimmy patted Noah, then Bart, on the shoulder. "I'm going to bed. Thanks for joining us for movie night."

They said their good nights. Then, when Jimmy was gone, Noah turned to Bart.

"You know what else?"

Bart smiled knowingly. "I think I know. They were young once. And now they're not." His hand squeezed Noah's shoulder. "I know, baby. I know."

Chapter 7

The hardest part about being in a relationship with another man was letting myself relax. Even though I was a relatively young man, I was old school. I still am, in many ways. I grew up believing that intimacies were for one man and one woman. A man and another man? Unthinkable!

It took work, and a lot of patience on Jimmy's part, to get me past that emotional block. Thank God he was—and remains—a persistent son of a bitch . . .

On Wednesday night, Noah boarded the jitney for his return trip home. The bus ride was uneventful until the final approach to Manhattan, when the panorama of skyscrapers took his breath away, as it always did. Even though he had grown up there and lived there for most of his thirty-four years, he still was in awe that all those people and all that glass and steel could sit on one tiny little island.

His father had retired for the evening, but Tricia was still up, watching television in the living room that, after a short stay at Quinn Scott's Hamptons house, seemed impossibly small. Noah dropped his backpack in the foyer and popped his head in to say hello.

"So how did it go?" she asked. "Are you making progress with him?"

Noah shrugged. "He doesn't seem to hate me quite as much, but he's getting pretty adamant that he doesn't want to do the book."

"I'm sorry." She gently pounded the couch pillow to her right. "Have a seat and keep me company."

He obeyed, sharing the couch with her.

"You never saw *When the Stars Come Out*, did you?" he asked, once he had made himself comfortable.

"No," she said. "Or at least I don't think so. I have to admit that a lot of those movies are sort of jumbled up in my head."

"Me, too," Noah confessed. "But we watched it last night. It was the movie where Quinn met his boyfriend."

"Boyfriend?"

"Yeah. Why?"

"It just sounds strange for two old men to call themselves 'boyfriends.' 'Boyfriends' sounds like such a *young* term."

Noah thought about that. She was right, in a sense, but . . .

"So what did you call my father before you dated?"

"Oh, Lord." She pursed her lips in a playful pout and pulled her hair back. "Do you really want to know?"

"Uh . . ." Noah remembered his fear that Tricia could have once been his father's mistress. "Do I? Because I really don't have to . . ."

"Mr. Big," she said, and she wouldn't meet Noah for eye contact.

Which was fine, because Noah didn't want to look her in the eyes either, after that revelation.

"I didn't have to know," he said.

She continued despite his demurral. "Like in *Sex and the City*. When I started dating your father, he seemed like this big, impressive dream . . . a man I could have never hoped to attract. So I took a cue from Carrie Bradshaw and started calling him Mr. Big."

"Uh . . . okay."

She paused, thought for a second, then blushed a bright red. "Oh, God, you didn't think I called him that because of his *penis*, did you?"

Now it was Noah's turn to blush. And cringe. And try to disappear into the cushions of the couch.

"Tricia, please don't make me think about things like that."

"Because that wasn't why I called him Mr. Big. I mean, he *is*, but that wasn't . . ."

"Please stop. Now."

In the morning, the thought of his father's penis mostly out of his head, Noah ran out to the closest Hallmark store and bought a card. When he was home, he retreated to the guest room and neatly hand-wrote his message.

Dear Quinn & Jimmy:

I wanted to drop a line to thank you for your hospitality this past weekend. My trips to Southampton are always a lot of fun, and getting to spend time with the two of you is a highlight.

Thank you, too, for sharing the magic of When the Stars Come Out *with me. The two of you are an inspiration, and I congratulate you for keeping the love alive over all the years. While I'm naturally disappointed that you won't let me share your story with the world, I'm thrilled that I, at least, have had the opportunity to witness long-term happiness and mutual support. If not the world's role models, you are mine.*

I look forward to our next meeting. And be nice to Bart!

With love,
Noah Abraham

Two days later, Quinn opened the card after carrying the day's mail into the kitchen.

"Look at this," he said to Jimmy, handing over the card. "The kid's pushy, but at least he has manners."

Jimmy read the card. "Role models. He really thinks of us as role models." Unconvinced as Jimmy had been by Noah's pitch, once the idea had been implanted into his head and he mulled it over for a few days, he had to admit—to himself, at least—that the thought held a certain appeal.

His partner, on the other hand, remained unconvinced.

"Must not get out much," said Quinn, as he began hobbling away toward the dining room.

"You know," said Jimmy, slowly following him, "maybe it's worth hearing him out. Maybe we *do* have a story that the world would want to hear."

"And maybe the kid is fucked in the head." Quinn stopped and turned slightly, the soreness in his hip preventing a full pivot. "We're nothing anymore. Remember that. We have a nice, quiet life, and we should appreciate that, because we've got it better than a lot of people."

Jimmy looked at the card again. "So you're afraid that a book would . . . roil the waters?"

Quinn shrugged. "It would probably change things, and I can't see how it would change them for the better."

"Let me ask you a question." Jimmy closed the card and used it to gently fan his face. "Is this at all about your ex-wife?"

Quinn's gray eyes bore a hole in Jimmy's skull, belying his words. "Of course not. That marriage was a lifetime ago. We haven't had any contact since Nixon was president. In his first term, at that. She doesn't carry any weight here."

Quinn semiturned back to his original position and began walking toward the living room. Jimmy followed at a respectable distance.

"Because here's the thing. We do have a nice, low-key life, but you know as well as I do that you're bored. This book would give you something to do. Something *different*."

"Bah."

"And so what if the world learns that the Philly Cop is gay?

Everyone out here—everyone we deal with on a regular basis—they all know. So what if a few anonymous fans out there get a surprise? Maybe that will be good for them. Maybe they'll start realizing that gay people can be anywhere, and can do anything . . . including playing tough cops on TV."

"You're wasting your time."

When they were both in the living room and Quinn was taking his place in the recliner, Jimmy, still standing, added, "Are you sure this doesn't have to do with Kitty?"

"Katherine is part of another life I once had."

"Or Q. J.?"

"Same thing. He belongs to his mother, not me. We've only exchanged Christmas and birthday cards for the past fifteen years."

"Uh-huh." With that Jimmy left the room, leaving Quinn to scramble out of the recliner unassisted if he wanted to follow him. Which he did.

"What do you mean by 'uh-huh'?!" he demanded. When Jimmy wouldn't stop he added, "Don't you walk away from me with an 'uh-huh'! I told you this has nothing to do with them, and it doesn't!"

Jimmy paused midway through the dining room and grasped the back of a chair.

"Okay," he said. "It has nothing to do with them."

"Not a thing."

"You just don't want to write a book . . ."

"Oh, Christ." Quinn leaned back against the dining room wall. *Damn, his hip hurt.* Trying to maintain his calm he said, "I just don't see why I should rock the boat. That's all. It has nothing to do with Katherine, and nothing to do with my son. It has everything—*every-thing*—to do with the fact that we have a nice life and I can't think of one good reason to do it. That's all."

"Uh-huh." Jimmy let go of the chair and started back to the kitchen.

"*That's all!*"

"Uh-huh."

Still leaning against the wall, Quinn called after him. "I want a drink. Is it noon yet?"

"Maybe," came the distant reply.

"Bitch," he muttered under his breath.

Jimmy's head, just vanished into the kitchen, popped out again from around the doorway molding. "I heard that. You're too deaf to talk to yourself."

Quinn hated the slow fade his body had started undergoing a decade earlier. Or was it two decades? The memory was another thing that tended to fade a bit. But he hated it even more when Jimmy reminded him of it. Almost a decade younger and always in better physical shape, Jimmy's body had thus far been spared many of the quotidian indignities of aging.

He just hated . . . the idea of mortality. Yes, that was it. His hip hurt—his *second* hip, at that—and his hearing was slowly failing. He was a mere human, and he would die someday.

Which is the thought process that brought on his epiphany.

He had become an actor in part because he wanted to leave something of himself behind. Ever since he had stepped onto that high-school stage and got his first taste of applause, he saw acting as a way to leave a permanent imprint that he had existed. Now there were his movies, of course, but they were only the first act of Quinn Scott's life. Shouldn't he leave the rest of himself behind, too?

Maybe that damn Noah had an idea worth pursuing. Maybe that was the way he could leave the rest of his life behind . . . and Jimmy's, too. Maybe the foolish idea wasn't so foolish after all.

"When you see Bart," he said, "tell him that I'll *consider* discussing this thing with Noah, and he should invite him back for a weekend."

Jimmy smiled. He didn't know it, but he was thinking exactly what Quinn was thinking.

"In that case," said Jimmy, "it's noon. I'll make you a cocktail."

Noah arrived by bus late the following Friday. Bart picked him up at the Southampton stop and, as they drove to Quinn's house, said, "I don't know what the turn-around is all about, but now he seems interested."

Noah put his hand on Bart's thigh. "So did you miss me?"

"Of course. Not that you've been away too awfully long." He smiled out the front windshield and added, "And you're the one who didn't want to date because you thought we'd never see each other again."

"I stand corrected," said Noah. "Happily corrected."

"You know . . ." Bart stopped himself.

"What?"

"Nothing."

"No, what?"

Bart's eyes didn't leave the road, and there was a nervous hesitation in his voice. "It's just that we've been seeing each other for a few weeks now. And if this works out with Quinn, you'll probably be out here a lot more often, or I'll be going with him to the city. And I was thinking it might be a good time to . . ."

Silence. Bart swallowed and kept his eyes on the road.

Noah waited for him to start talking again. It took twenty seconds—twenty long seconds in which he might as well have not been in the car—before Bart finally finished his thought. Sort of.

He swallowed again and said, "I know it's only been a few weeks, but I was thinking that . . . well, maybe it makes sense to . . ."

"Do you want to try to be boyfriends?" Noah asked, electing to put Bart out of his misery.

Bart smiled, happy that he hadn't had to do all the work. "Is that a bad thing?"

"No. I was thinking the same thing."

He hadn't really been thinking the same thing—not exactly—but given a bit more time, he thought he would have. However, since Bart had broached the subject, or at least *tried* to broach the subject, he made a snap decision. After all, Bart had been right once before, when he asked him to dinner. Now they were unexpectedly spending a lot of time together, and—if the Quinn Scott project broke his way—they would be almost full-time companions, so Noah thought that he might as well make an honest man out of Bart Gustafson. He was nice, and he was handsome, and he was kind, and he looked hot when his cheeks were smeared with motor oil, so why not?

As he drove, Bart felt incredible relief. Just a few weeks earlier he had left Manhattan convinced that Noah was never going to call him, and now they were going to be an official couple. He had fully expected him—*his boyfriend*, Bart reminded himself—to recoil at the suggestion, and call it premature. But he most definitely hadn't.

A laugh suddenly burst from Bart's throat. "God, I just realized that I haven't had a boyfriend since I was twenty-two. Isn't that sad?"

"I'm glad I could come along before you turned into an old maid."

And they both kept smiling the entire drive back to the house.

Once his immediate glee over his new relationship status had waned a bit, allowing him to focus on the immediate and important matters at hand, Bart warned Noah that Quinn was still skeptical about the book idea. Which is why, over dinner that night, Noah spent considerable time outlining his thoughts for Quinn and Jimmy.

"I know this won't be easy for you," he said, when he concluded his vision. "But, like I said before, you could become huge role models."

"That phrase keeps coming up," said Jimmy. He was silently supportive of the project, but wanted to make Noah work for it. "Aren't there enough role models out there?" He looked at Quinn for support.

"Jimmy's right," he said gruffly. "I think we're too damn old to be role models."

"There's always room for more role models," Noah told them. "And you're not that old. You're, like, my father's age."

"Thank you," Jimmy said dryly. "That's something every vain gay man wants to hear."

Quinn took up the argument. "If you want to write about an older role model, then why don't you write about your father? I'm sure you can find something inspirational."

"My father?" Noah smiled. "He's already inspired a *Saturday Night Live* character, so anything I try to do is bound to come up short."

"What?" said Bart. "You never told me that. Which character?"

"Famous Lawyer Abe Maxham."

Jimmy gasped. "Your father is Max Abraham?"

"I'm afraid so." Noah struggled to get the conversation back on track. "As far as the role model thing goes, don't worry about it. The goal here isn't to put you on the public speaking circuit. It's to put your story out there, and then let each individual do with it what he—or she—wants."

While they considered his words, Noah directed his next comments directly at Quinn. "Take Richard Chamberlain. When his bio came out a few years ago, I'm sure it inspired a lot of people— not just older folks, but young ones too—to embrace their sexuality. To not be ashamed. And it taught a lot of others that gay people are everywhere. Even on their television screens."

Quinn's skepticism bubbled to the surface. "Are you comparing me to Chamberlain?"

"Think about it. You were both television icons of the 1960s. What better comparison is there? You could be thought of tomorrow just like he is today: not only as a great actor, but also as someone who bravely told the world, 'I am gay.' Then we throw in a little gossip to spice it up and . . ."

"Ugh." Quinn's face wrinkled. "I *knew* you were going to gussy it up with dirt."

"*Clean* dirt," said Noah. "Not scandalous stuff. Just some snapshots of gay life in Hollywood, circa the late '60s and early '70s."

"I don't know. I'll have to think about it." Quinn rose from the dinner table. "I'm inclined to let my story be told, but there are a lot of considerations here."

"Please," said Noah, and he also rose from his chair. "Please *do* think about it. You've got to be comfortable with the project."

"I'll do my thinking in front of the television." Quinn nodded to Jimmy. "Care to join me?"

"In a minute. I want to clear the table."

When Quinn was out of the room, Noah turned to Jimmy and asked, "So what do you think?"

"About the project? Or about whether or not Quinn will cooperate."

"All of the above."

"I think he's almost there." He stood and began collecting the dirty dishes. "But 'almost' is not a yes. So good luck with it. On all counts."

The next morning, Noah looked out the window onto an obviously warm and sunny day. Even though it was now October, the temperatures were still not cooperating with the calendar. Not that anyone was complaining.

He was pulling on a pair of jeans when Bart walked into the bedroom, fresh from the shower and clad only in a towel wrapped around his waist.

"Oh, shit," said Noah, as he collapsed backward on the mattress with his pants pulled up only to mid-thigh. "Take me now."

Bart rolled his eyes. "Again? Sorry, dude, but after three times last night, it needs a rest." The towel dropped to the floor.

"But we're boyfriends now!" Noah playfully whined, still lying on his back. "I think that means we're supposed to have sex all the time."

Bart smiled and turned away, and Noah admired the wide shoulders which tapered down to a narrow waist. He thought he had been kidding when he asked Bart to "take me now," but suddenly he wasn't quite so sure.

"I'm going to have to leave you alone with them," Bart said, as he pulled a pair of briefs over his muscular thighs. "They have about six pages of errands for me to run. Will you be all right?"

"Not a problem. That gives me an opportunity to fine-tune this idea with Quinn and get us both on the same page."

Bart smiled. Noah still had no idea what he was getting himself into.

"Good luck with that." He glanced at his watch. "And you'd better get moving, Rip Van Winkle. It's closing in on noon."

"Noon? How did that happen?"

Bart winked. "Three times, baby . . ."

When Bart was dressed and gone, Noah finally finished pulling up his jeans, threw on a shirt and shoes, and descended the staircase to the kitchen, where he poured a cup of coffee. Then, pressing his face to the glass door, he found Quinn stationed at his usual post: the round glass table on the patio. Camille lay next to him, soaking up the sun through her blond fur.

Coffee cup in hand, Noah slid the door open and stepped outside.

"Good afternoon, Quinn. Nice day out here."

Quinn didn't answer. He took a deep breath—whether that was a sign of exasperation or he was taking in the fresh air, Noah didn't know—and stared into the distance, somewhere in the direction of his rosebushes at the far edge of the property line.

The silence continued, and Noah wondered if he had, again, lost Quinn and his cooperation.

Until Quinn finally spoke.

"Okay."

That was it: "Okay."

So Noah had to ask. "Okay?"

"Yup." Again, there was a long silence. Finally Quinn bothered to look in Noah's direction. "I'll probably do it."

"You'll do it?!" Adrenaline coursed through Noah. "This is great, Quinn."

Quinn's nostrils flared. "I said, I'd *probably* do it. Didn't say I'd do it. There's a difference."

As quickly as it surged, Noah's adrenaline rush subsided. "Of course there is. You'll *probably* do it."

Quinn again turned away from Noah, his eyes wandering back to the vicinity of the rosebushes, but he continued talking, in a slow, deliberate voice.

"We'll need some ground rules. You'll need a tape recorder."

"I'll get one," said Noah, remembering that his machine, the one still bearing the voice of G. C. swallowing his words, was at his father's apartment.

"Good. Everything I tell you will be taped. And *I'll* keep the tapes."

"Uh . . ." That wouldn't do. Noah understood Quinn's desire to cover his ass, but he also knew he would need those tapes. "I'm going to have to keep them, Quinn. The publisher will—"

"Then you'll make two tapes. Which means you'll need two tape recorders." Decision unilaterally decided, he moved on to his next demand. "Second, I don't want you to use Jimmy's name."

"But—"

"I also don't want you to use the names of any actors—any *person*, period—unless I explicitly tell you it's all right."

"I don't understand. The story of your life is more than just, well, *you*. It's the story of the people you've met and worked with through the years."

"I'm willing to out myself, or whatever you call it. 'Come out,' right?"

"Right."

"I'll do that 'coming out' thing for myself, but I won't be responsible for outing others."

"But—"

"If you can't make me those promises, this isn't going to happen."

Noah swallowed hard and did his best to be diplomatic. "I understand. But if this autobiography doesn't have anything to say, I don't think we'll find a publisher."

"PMC will publish it," he said firmly. "That's what you told me."

"I don't think so," Noah said, with equal firmness rooted in his experience in the industry. "At the end of the day, this is a business decision. And from a business perspective, no one wants to buy a biography that has nothing to say. David Carlyle is interested, but we'll have to give him *something*."

Quinn smiled, but it was not a smile born of good nature. It was a smile that said, Who the hell are *you* to tell *me* how to write my autobiography?

But what he actually said was, "I've got plenty to say, but there's no need to say it about other people. This is about me, son. *That* is the story."

Behind them, the sliding glass door from the kitchen *whooshed* open, and Jimmy Beloit—dressed for the sun in a straw hat, green-and-white striped shorts, and a loose white cotton shirt—walked out onto the patio, delicately balancing a martini and nodding to them as he passed.

"Don't let me interrupt."

"Can't stop you," muttered Quinn, and Jimmy smiled as he took up residence in a chaise lounge in the far corner of the patio, facing away from Quinn and Noah. When he finally sat, after an extended period of adjusting the cushion, only his straw hat was visible to the two men.

Returning his attention to Noah and the subject at hand, Quinn said, "Those are the rules. Live with them, or don't write the book."

Noah felt something heavy in the pit of his stomach. "And if the book is never written?"

He shrugged. "I guess it doesn't matter, does it? My life stays exactly the same as it's been for the last thirty-six years. I can live with that. As I recall, *you* are the one who thinks I need to do this to reclaim my life, and *I* am the one who doesn't think it's a great idea in the first place."

Noah had to concede his point. Quinn Scott could bitch about being bored, and he could bitch about being blacklisted, but he had a pretty damn good life out here in Southampton and he knew it. When it came to penning his autobiography, he held all the cards.

"Okay," Noah finally said, feeling a vague sense of frustration. "I think I can work with those rules. But . . . can we try to be a bit creative with them?"

Quinn frowned. "What do you mean?"

"What if we use the names of actors who are already publicly gay. Or dead. That wouldn't do any harm, right? I mean, it would be silly to protect Rock Hudson's sexuality at this point, right? The guy has been dead for twenty years."

Quinn thought about that. "I suppose . . ."

"And if you don't want me to use Jimmy's name, we can use a pseudonym. 'Johnny,' or something like that."

"Excuse me?" said the voice from the chaise, and the straw hat bobbed. "I am *not* a Johnny."

"Quinn asked me to protect your privacy."

"I *told* him to protect your privacy," Quinn asserted.

Jimmy's profile appeared at the edge of the chaise. "Oh, in that case . . . why not, Quinn? Why not? I gave up an acting career for you—"

"A *dancing* career."

"Which was going to grow into an acting career." Jimmy paused. "I would have had an acting career *in time*. I had a plan." He paused again. "Anyway, I gave up a *career* for you, so why shouldn't I *totally* disappear from history? In fact, when I die—which hopefully will be sooner rather than later, thank you very much—I hope you'll give me an unmarked grave. No, wait . . . take my body out to sea and dump it. Or, better yet, use it for chum. Get one last use out of me, then make sure that all evidence of my existence completely vanishes."

"Drama queen," muttered Quinn. "Sixty-two years of drama. Probably sixty-two years and nine months, because you were probably a fucking drama queen in your mother's womb." To Noah, he said, "Let me think about it. Maybe."

"I want to be in the book," said the chaise.

"Okay. Noah, you can use that asshole's name. Just make sure you describe him as old, fat, and out of shape."

"I obviously heard that."

"*And* bald."

"I obviously heard that, too."

Quinn pivoted slightly in his chair, straining to get a better view of his all-but-hidden lover. "As long as we all know you can hear me, I hope you can hear me when I tell you to put that martini down."

"You can come take it away from me. If your hip can make it across the patio, that is."

"Dr. Marcus says it will kill you."

"Screw Dr. Marcus. If you truly loved me, you'd let me enjoy myself while I still can, instead of forcing me to live a joyless existence for the next decade until I'm as old as you got to be, and I'm drooling and incontinent and convinced you're Napoleon."

A smile crossed Quinn's lips. Not the malevolent smile he had shown Noah a few minutes earlier, but a smile that showed he enjoyed the banter. Still, he made it disappear almost as soon as it had appeared.

"All right, then," Quinn said to the chaise. "Napoleon says you can have one martini. One."

"Oui, monsieur."

Returning again to Noah, Quinn said, "Be smart. Stay single." He stopped, turning to shake his head one more time in Jimmy's direction before continuing. "Okay, let's get back to the ground rules, because I have two more."

Noah sighed. "More rules?"

"My family. Rule number one: my ex-wife. Rule number two: my son. I don't want them involved. Obviously you'll have to mention Katherine, but I want her only mentioned in passing. I suppose we'll have to acknowledge my lack of judgment in marrying her, but, besides that and a mention of the movies we made together, I want nothing about her in the book."

"That's going to be tough," said Noah. "I mean, she's the reason that people will buy this book."

The moment those words flew out of his mouth, he regretted them. After all that playing to Quinn's ego, telling him that he would become a role model, and after having been warned off Kitty Randolph once before, Noah had set a bad hand down on the table and revealed that it was still all about . . .

Quinn's ex-wife.

Quinn's *hated* ex-wife.

Quinn glared at him, and there followed a long period of silence broken only when he muttered, "Excuse me?"

Noah cleared his throat and stared at the slate on the patio. "Uh . . . what I was trying to say is . . ."

"Oh, for chrissakes, Quinn," said Jimmy, interjecting himself again into the conversation but still not moving from his seat in the sun. "We've talked about this before. Who the hell is going to buy a book about you? Who even *remembers* you? Everyone who ever saw *Philly Cop* has been dead for twenty years."

Noah caught a glimpse of Quinn out of the corner of his eye. He was holding his position, poised to attack.

"Nobody asked for your input," he snarled at the chaise. "This is *my* book."

"There won't be a book if you don't listen to what Noah is trying to tell you. We are nothing more than two old gay men. We are not celebrities. You're not Rock Hudson, all right? The only reason anyone is going to buy your book is because you were married to Kitty Randolph. End of story."

Noah stole another glance and, this time, Quinn looked like he was softening. So, to share the burden with Jimmy, he added, "Like it or not, Jimmy is right. Kitty Randolph and Q. J. Scott—your ex-wife and son—are . . ." He trailed off and thought hard about the words he was about to use, knowing that they could doom the project. Still, they had to be said, so Noah pushed on. "Like it or not, your ex-wife and son are the reason most people will buy this book."

Quinn continued to glower at the man who hoped to cowrite his autobiography for an uncomfortably long amount of time, silence following silence.

"I'm sorry," Noah said, filling the void. "But that's the truth. No offense, Quinn, but you've been out of the business for more than a generation. The young people have never heard of you, and the older crowd has forgotten."

"But Richard Chamberlain . . . Yesterday, you were comparing me to him. What's different today? What happened to—?"

"Richard Chamberlain was Dr. Kildare," said Jimmy. "You were Philly Cop. Get the difference yet?"

Quinn ignored his husband and again asked Noah, "So what has changed since yesterday?"

Noah stopped him. "You had a decent career, but Jimmy is right. I was just making a comparison. I'm sorry, but you were no Richard Chamberlain. You were . . . you were . . ."

Be careful, he told himself. *Very thin ice here.*

But Jimmy again came to the rescue. Of sorts.

"You were more like the gay Darrin on *Bewitched,*" he said. "Whichever Dick that was . . . I can never keep them straight." He paused, adding, "Pardon all the totally intentional puns. So very Paul Lynde of me."

Noah waited for Quinn to explode—to go all Philly Cop on them—but he shocked him by laughing. *Laughing!* Noah said another silent prayer to St. Jimmy.

"Let me tell you something, son," Quinn said when that laughter subsided, which didn't take long. He looked Noah in the eye and tapped the tabletop for emphasis, making the coffee cup and iced tea glass shake. "I've spent more than thirty years on the outs with Hollywood, and I have a very realistic sense of my place in the world. This world and that world. I know that Katherine was—*is*—the meal ticket here, and that idiot I fathered is the gravy. I know that, from your perspective, they are the story."

"Well . . ."

"Let me finish. I know I'm not Chamberlain or Hunter or Hudson or Perkins or . . ." He turned to Jimmy's chair before continuing, his raised voice aimed at the figure who was now once again hidden behind the back of the chaise. "Or even the *goddamn gay Darrin.* But there's still a story to tell, without bringing all the rest of them too deeply into the mix."

"Go on," said Noah. He was unconvinced, but curious.

"Love."

"Huh? Love?"

"Exactly. Here's the story we're going to tell: a love story spanning almost forty years. A story about how a young actor and a very attractive young dancer found each other in their youth, when it was a much harder time to be gay. And a story about how they stayed together into old age."

"Old age?" said the chaise. "Speak for yourself."

"I always do." Quinn turned back to Noah and, as he began rising from his chair, said: "That's the story. Katherine and Q. J. are the icing, not the story. And they will be treated as icing. Their presence will be sweet . . . and spread thinly. Very, very thinly.

"Well, of course it will be *your* story. But . . ."

"I've told you the rules," he said. "Take them or leave them." Without another word, Quinn walked into the house, leaving his half-empty iced tea glass behind for someone else to bus.

Noah sat in relative solitude—relative in that Jimmy was there, but largely unseen—and thought about Quinn's rules. Maybe just a hint of the ex-wife and son would be enough for the readers . . . maybe the story of an enduring gay romance would have popular appeal . . . maybe it was workable . . .

But he knew the story would be so much better—and *sell* so much better—with more than a hint of Kitty and Q. J. The coming-out story of Quinn Scott could—*would*—be workable, and the romance between him and Jimmy would be sweet and life affirming. But its appeal outside the gay ghettoes would be another story altogether. A few literary body slams on Kitty Randolph could make all the difference between that all-important book review and entertainment industry buzz and a quick trip to the remainder bins.

His only hope was that Quinn Scott would eventually see the light. And even on such short acquaintance, he didn't peg him for the type of man who changed his mind.

Noah returned to Manhattan for clothes and supplies, and was back in Southampton for the following week, logging difficult hours of conversation with Quinn, then carefully transcribing the tapes. After thirteen hours of transcripts, he had mentioned Kitty Randolph only four times—all in passing—and he had yet to mention his son. And as far as Hollywood went, his most revealing true confession was his anger over being abruptly dropped from casting consideration as the doomed captain in *The Poseidon Adventure*, an event he refused to attribute for the record to Kitty, even though it occurred in the wake of their divorce.

Noah tried to draw him out . . . *oh, how he had tried.* But with every probing question, Quinn became more difficult. Their personal chemistry was nonexistent, and Noah was beginning to think that even the completelashuels had been more forthcoming with him.

It was Saturday night, as they talked in the living room after Bart and Jimmy had excused themselves for bed, when the explosion finally came. For days Noah had been listening to Quinn reminisce about gripping details such as how he and Jimmy had come to live in the Hamptons, and how they had quit smoking, and how he designed his house, and what it was like to have hip-replacement surgery, and now it was time for some meat.

"Tell me about your marriage," said Noah, sliding the microphones attached to the mandatory two tape recorders a bit closer to Quinn.

"It was brief."

"Talk about the day she caught you with Jimmy."

"This is bullshit," said Quinn, and he knocked the tape recorders off their perch on the ottoman. Noah jumped back. "That is *not* going in the book!"

"But, Quinn . . ."

His eyes burned a hole through Noah. "I thought we had an understanding."

"But there's got to be color."

"Fuck this book."

With that, he lurched from his recliner, pausing only to remove both cassettes, and stormed out of the living room.

Noah climbed into bed fifteen minutes later, silently drawing himself up against Bart's warm, muscular body. He felt Bart's hand reach for him . . . a welcoming touch. Still, he pulled away.

"What's the matter?" Bart whispered.

"I'm sorry. I'm . . . I'm feeling a bit deflated."

Bart pulled up the covers, flashing an impish smile. "Deflated? Let me see."

"Stop," said Noah, a laugh unexpectedly escaping from his lips despite his sour mood. "I'm . . . I just can't do it tonight, okay?"

"No problem. There will be plenty of other times." Bart rolled over on his back and stared at the ceiling. "Why don't you tell me what's wrong? Maybe I can help."

"I don't know . . ." Noah hoped that Bart would respect his desire for solitude, but he didn't, and when asked again he gave him an honest answer.

"It's Quinn. I don't know if I can work with him."

"Why?"

"He hates me."

"No." Bart's voice was soft. As he spoke, his soft hands slowly, re-assuringly worked their way across Noah's chest, brushing against the black curls. "Quinn doesn't hate you."

"The way he snaps at me . . . he won't cooperate. Maybe another writer . . ."

Bart shifted, propping himself up on an elbow. "What other writer would take on this book?"

Noah sighed. "I think this was a mistake. Maybe I should try to hang in there with my other project."

"It's not you, Noah. It's Quinn. That's just the way he is. There's more to him, though, and if you give this a chance . . ."

Noah felt a dull pounding in his head. "More to him? What, does he *kick*, too? Come on, Bart, I know the guy is your boss, but face it: he hates me."

"Hang in there. This will pass. He's . . . well, yes, he's a bit ornery, but he's a sweet guy. Really."

"I like Jimmy," Noah continued, not really answering his bed-mate. "He's a nice guy. But how he's put up with Quinn for thirty-some-odd years is beyond me. And the way he treats *you* . . ."

Bart's hands slid off Noah's chest. "Me? What do you mean?"

"Bossing you around . . . Complaining about everything . . ."

"Your problem," he said, and Noah could tell by the tone of his voice that he had crossed a line, "is that you take everything too personally. With a man like Quinn, you've got to let it roll off of you, because that's his public face. If you had ever seen the private face—and you will, Noah; someday, you will—you'd have a completely different opinion of him. And as for the way he treats me, you're wrong. But even if there were a problem, that's for me to determine, not you."

"Sorry."

The apology softened him a bit. Bart's voice was once again re-assuring. "Just hang in there, okay? You'll see."

Noah sighed. He really had no choice. "Like it or not, I'm going to have to hang in there. I don't see how I can cancel this. Not now."

"Oh, right," he said. "You'd have to return the advance money . . ."

"No, that's not it. Fortunately, money isn't one of my worries. But if I don't turn in a manuscript, well . . . it won't look good for me as a writer if I pull the plug on two straight projects with PMC. I've got a reputation on the line here."

Bart smiled. "All the more reason to give Quinn a few more chances."

"I suppose." Noah sighed and settled back into the bed, knowing that he not only had to give Quinn a few more chances, he also owed himself a few.

And, through Bart's best efforts, his deflation problem was soon corrected, too.

"Noah?" Bart's voice, barely a whisper, was close to his ear.

Noah stirred slightly before answering, catching a bleary glimpse of the alarm clock. It was 1:08 AM.

He finally managed to utter a "Huh?"

"Listen."

Noah closed his eyes again and listened. At first, he heard nothing but the vague sounds of nocturnal life outside the windows; the rustling of leaves in the breeze, a barking dog. When he concentrated, though, he could hear faint strains of music from somewhere in the distance.

"Do you hear it?"

"The music?"

"Yeah."

"I hear it. Why?"

Bart silenced him with a finger placed on his lips. "Come with me."

They put on robes and slippers and, leaving the lights off, navigated by moonlight filtered through the windows, creeping out of the bedroom and across the hall. They stopped when they reached the top of the staircase leading to the kitchen, Bart tugging on Noah's sleeve as if it were reins.

"I have a little something to confess," Bart said, his voice hushed in the darkness. "You know, I'm very loyal to Quinn and Jimmy . . . but I also violate their privacy from time to time."

"I'm not sure I understand," Noah said, h[...]
about to confess to, say, wearing their underwe[...]
that sort. Or, worse, peeping while they had sex.

He wasn't.

"A few months ago I heard that music and went to ch[...] [...],
and . . . well, ever since, I've come back whenever I hear it. It's always late at night, and it's always the same, and every time I see it—
no matter how bad my day has been—well . . ."

"What is it?"

Without another word, Bart took Noah's hand and led him
through the dark down the stairs. On the ground floor, Bart continued to guide Noah, leading him past the kitchen and into the
inky blackness of the dining room. They only stopped when they
reached a window overlooking the back lawn.

"This is the best vantage point. Stand back from the glass, so they
don't see you." After delivering those instructions, Bart pointed out
the window.

Out in the gazebo, lit only by the moonlight, Quinn and Jimmy
danced slowly in each other's arms, smiling and oblivious to anything and anyone else.

"That's the side of Quinn you haven't seen," said Bart, his voice
lost in a dream. "Until now."

Noah watched the men as they danced in the cool night air. "It's
very romantic."

"It is." They watched in silence for several more minutes until
Bart added, "That's happiness. True happiness. To be with someone you love . . . You know, I stand here and watch them and wonder if I'll ever be that lucky . . . to love someone, and love them for
so long that even in the older years, it's all still fresh and . . . and
joyful."

"I wonder if Quinn and Jimmy know how lucky they are."

"I'm sure they do. Look at them." Bart paused for a moment before again saying, "I'm sure they do."

They watched them for a while longer, until Bart gently pulled
on the sleeve of Noah's robe and said, "Let's go back upstairs. I
don't want them to catch me being a voyeur."

"Do you think they'd mind?" Noah asked, as he followed Bart
back through the dark dining room.

"Probably not. But they have their private moment, and they do it so well. And it's all theirs. Why let them know I intrude on it?"

And somehow, in a very subtle way, Quinn Scott seemed a lot less fearsome to Noah Abraham after that night . . . after watching him sweep his lover along in his arms as they danced to a rhythm of their own in the moonlit gazebo.

Chapter 8

The simple fact of the matter is this: the woman I married was petty, vindictive, and nasty. Yes, she had a tough climb to the top of her profession, and she had her share of disappointments. But she didn't handle any of that the way one of her charming screen characters would have: with a smile on her face and a song in her voice. No, she handled her challenges by attempting to destroy anything that got in her way.

And often, she succeeded. She nearly succeeded with me, too. Kitty Randolph wanted my head, and was probably disappointed that she had to settle for merely ruining my career . . .

Noah awoke early the next morning, invigorated by a cool, fresh breeze through the slightly open window. He watched Bart, his eyes still closed in sleep, for a few minutes, and thought that this was exactly the way he wanted to wake up every morning.

After an evening of slow, slow dancing in the gazebo.

Without disturbing him, Noah slipped out of bed and rushed through his shower and shave, suddenly eager to start the day. He threw on a pair of khakis and a loose shirt and, twenty minutes after rising, walked onto the patio. Although the temperature had finally started to drop, it was still pleasant in the backyard.

He greeted Quinn, who sat and sipped a cup of coffee at that round glass table.

"Good morning," Noah said.

Quinn considered that, then said, "If you say so."

Still, Noah pressed on. "Ready to do some reminiscing this morning?"

"Not really."

Noah swallowed and did what he knew he had to do. "About last night . . . I'm sorry about that. I was out of line."

"You were."

And that was that. Noah struggled to remember that magical image of Quinn and Jimmy dancing in the gazebo, because the magic was fading quicker than the dew in the morning sunlight.

The men sat in silence for an uncomfortably long time until Noah finally conceded and walked back to the kitchen, making a beeline to the coffee pot. He reached it just as Jimmy entered the room, the billows of his robe and Camille trailing behind him.

"Morning, sunshine," he said, as chipper as Quinn was gruff.

"Good morning." Noah held up the pot. "Coffee?"

"Please." He strained to look out to the patio. "And how is Mr. Happy-Pants this morning? Cooperative?"

"Not really," said Noah, as he poured. "I think he's still looking for his comfort level with me."

Jimmy rolled his eyes. "Get used to it, Noah. It's been a lifetime and I still don't think he's found one with me."

"Oh, I think he's . . ." Noah stopped, realizing almost too late that there was no need to confess to voyeurism, let alone implicate Bart, if he didn't have to. "I think he's just a bit cranky in the morning."

"Hmmph," grunted Jimmy, noncommittally. Then, brightening, he said, "I'm running a few errands as soon as I get some caffeine in me and get dressed. Need anything from the outside world?"

"You're leaving me alone with him?"

"Forty-five minutes," Jimmy said, laughing at what looked like terror on Noah's face. He would have to remember to tell Quinn to be a bit easier on the kid. "Plus, you won't be alone. Bart is somewhere around here, isn't he?"

"Yes, he is," said Bart, picking that moment to stroll into the kitchen, like Jimmy clad only in a robe. "I'll help keep the beast at bay, Noah."

"Thanks. Coffee?"

"Sure."

When Jimmy left the kitchen, Bart asked, "So how is he this morning?"

"Unforgiving."

Bart winked. "Just remember the dance."

And so, remembering the dance, Noah steeled himself and walked back to the patio.

"Do you feel like talking?" he asked Quinn.

"Maybe later. Right now, I'm not in the mood." With that, he stood and walked back into the house.

Moments later, Noah decided to follow him, but got only as far as the kitchen before Jimmy and Bart stopped him.

"I sent him upstairs for a nap," said Jimmy. "Let him sleep off that attitude." He looked off in the direction of Quinn's departure before continuing, making sure that he had actually left the room. "I can help you, you know."

"I wouldn't be so sure about that."

Jimmy continuing in a whispered, conspiratorial voice as he leaned in to Noah. "I don't want him to hear. He's not always as deaf as he lets on. But here's the deal: I have to take Quinn to physical therapy at 3:30. He'll be there ninety minutes. After I drop him off, I'm going to come right back home. You'll be here?"

Noah lifted an eyebrow. "Uh . . . why?"

"I have something to show you. I think you'll like it. It will put Quinn in a very good mood, and make him much easier to work with. But not a word of it to you-know-who, right?"

"Agreed." Noah cast his eyes downward. "Except . . . I don't know if it's such a good idea for me to keep living out here."

"Don't be silly," said Jimmy. "Take it from someone who's lived through it forever. It blows over. Plus, most of your clothes are here, and Bart won't let you leave with them, so we sort of have you trapped, don't we?"

"I guess you do."

Jimmy and Bart exchanged a smile. "I *knew* you'd see things our way."

That afternoon, after Jimmy forced the loudly complaining Quinn into the hunter-green Mercedes and drove off to his physical therapy appointment, Noah and Bart realized they had the house to themselves. For twenty minutes, at least.

Not a word needed to be spoken. They darted up the stairs the minute the car left the driveway, and, leaving a trail of clothing beginning at the midpoint of the staircase, had stripped to their underwear by the time they threw themselves on the bed.

Noah rolled onto his back and Bart straddled him, his powerful thighs pinning Noah's hips and, beneath the thin fabric of their briefs, their erections grinding together.

"No deflation problem this afternoon, I see," said Bart, as he lowered his upper body until his lips met those of his partner.

A short time later they lay in bed, their hands gently caressing each other after the hurried intimacy. Neither said a word, afraid of breaking the spell.

It was Bart who finally spoke. "What do you think of Quinn and Jimmy? I mean, together?"

"I think they fit. I guess you do that after thirty-six years."

"Do you ever see . . . ?" Bart stopped himself, and Noah knew that the words to follow would be edited for content. He was right. "Do you ever see *yourself* in a long-term relationship like that?"

Noah sighed and rolled onto his back. "I don't know. Decades of monogamy . . . it could get boring. Personally, I don't know if I can make a commitment like that."

"Oh." Noah felt Bart pull away from him. "Yeah, maybe . . ." He paused. "But I sort of like seeing it. In theory, I mean. Mutual support . . . growing old together . . . always having someone to watch your back."

"It's like you said: 'in theory.'" Noah propped himself up on an elbow and looked at Bart, whose eyes were now lost in wistful thought. "My father has been married three times, so I'm not sure that theory always becomes practice. I mean, it's a nice thing to aim for—that whole 'together forever' thing—but the reality is that people change over time. And it's rare when they change at the same time, and in the same direction."

"Maybe you're right," said Bart, distantly and without commitment. "But . . ."

"But what?"

Bart rolled slightly toward Noah. "Well, my parents got married four weeks after their first date, and they've stayed together for almost forty years, so it *can* be done."

"I know it can be done. I just don't know . . ." A sound from outside the windows—a slamming car door—stopped him. "Shit. He's home."

"That was quick," said Bart, with what Noah thought was too much distraction, as he rose from the bed. "Clothes!"

"I'm on it." Noah leapt from the bed, slid into his briefs, and darted out to the hall to collect their clothes as the sound of Jimmy's voice, calling for Camille, rose from the front yard. Ten seconds later, he deposited their jumbled clothing on the bed, and they separated the items and hurriedly dressed to the accompaniment of a slam from the front door. Jimmy Beloit *did* love to slam his doors.

He was clutching a brown-papered box and fluffing the flowers on one of the small decorative tables in the entry hall, whistling tunes from a string of unrelated musicals—something from *Rent* morphed into something from *Fiddler* morphed into something vaguely Sondheimian—when Bart and Noah finally walked down the stairs. The younger men waved as they descended with feigned casualness.

"That man," said Jimmy, chipper as ever as he fluffed the arrangement. "Twice a week for two years he's been going to PT, and twice a week for two years it's been an ordeal. I keep telling him 'Fine, don't go. Sit on your ass on your patio until your bones fuse into an

L-shape and your muscles atrophy. That way it will be easier for me to shove you down the basement steps and be done with you.' But does he listen to me? No. He keeps whining and bitching, but ultimately he keeps going to PT." He looked up from the flowers and said, "I smell sex."

On cue, Noah and Bart blushed and stammered.

"Oh, stop," said Jimmy. "Boys, I'm sixty-two years old, but I'm not dead." He finished his business with the flowers and, waving the box in their direction, told them, "Follow me. I have something to show you."

Noah and Bart trailed Camille, who trailed Jimmy, as they descended the stairs to the screening room. Once he flipped on the lights and they stood in dim fluorescence, he explained.

"I just picked up a package from the post office. Quinn's birthday present." He set it down on the floor.

Jimmy stepped into the projection room and opened the black-lacquer cabinet where he kept the videotapes. When he turned, he was holding the box containing *When the Stars Come Out*. Noah noticed for the first time that it was battered, showing the wear and tear of years of handling.

"This," Jimmy announced, handing the tape to Bart, "can go in the trash."

"The trash?"

Jimmy smiled and picked up the box from the floor. He began peeling the brown paper from the box. Freed from its taped edges, the paper fell to the floor, and Jimmy opened the package, revealing its contents: a selection of DVDs. On the top of the stack was the repackaged, re-engineered, and decidedly more high-tech version of *When the Stars Come Out*.

"And so the Scott-Beloit household joins the twenty-first century," said Jimmy.

"That's great," said Bart. "Quinn's going to love it."

Jimmy continued to hold the *Stars* case, setting the others aside. "Shall we give it a whirl?"

Bart looked at his watch. "Uh . . . we don't have time. Someone is going to have to pick up Quinn."

"Not the entire movie! I just want to make sure everything is working. I think we all know what we would be in for if I gave Quinn this present and the DVD didn't work, or I couldn't run the player. I'd rather do a test run and make sure everything is all right."

"I see your point," said Bart. "Why don't you just play the last scene. You know the one I'm talking about."

Jimmy smiled. "My thoughts exactly."

He disappeared into the projection room as Bart, Noah, and Camille took seats, and he stayed there as the screen lit up. After a few fumbles working the DVD player—skipping to a scene he hadn't wanted to; switching to the Spanish language option—Jimmy found the introduction to the *Stars* number and dimmed the lights.

Kitty Randolph, circa 1970, blond and wholesome in a white gown, was again on the screen singing:

> *When the evening falls, my dear,*
> *And when dream-time calls, my dear,*
> *You'll be with me;*
> *Of that, no doubt,*
> *I'll see your face when the stars come out . . .*

Noah turned to Bart and whispered. "Very crisp. And the color is much better than the video."

Young, handsome Quinn Scott was now on the screen, singing a serviceable response to Kitty. Then she sang back. And then they danced.

Noah stole a glance at Bart, whose attention was fully on the screen. He wondered if Bart saw himself up there, dancing with Kitty, waiting for Noah to appear—black tie around his neck and walking stick in hand—to steal him away.

"Oh, fuck!" Bart snapped, breaking the mood. "Un-*fucking-*believable."

Noah turned his attention back to the screen. "What? What did I miss?"

"That is so wrong." Bart's voice was angrier than Noah had ever heard. "Can she do that?"

Jimmy stood in the back of the room. Even in the dim lighting of the screening room, Noah could see he was ashen.

"What happened?" Noah asked. "What did I miss?"

"That *bitch*," snarled Jimmy.

"I missed it," Noah said once again, to which Bart merely sighed with . . . was that disgust?

"Here," said Jimmy, and Noah saw he was carrying the remote control in his hand. "Watch carefully."

"I don't think you have to watch all that carefully," muttered Bart, as Kitty once again began singing *When the Stars Come Out.*

And then, perhaps one minute into the number, Noah saw it. Or, rather, he didn't see it. That magical moment when the camera caught Quinn and Jimmy as their eyes met was now nowhere to be seen.

In fact, Jimmy was missing altogether. Not only had their brief moment been excised, but all evidence of Jimmy Beloit had now disappeared. The woman in the blue dress still danced, but now she danced with a sailor. The other dancers remained—the smiling blond guy, the swarthy one with the widow's peak, the others—but Jimmy had been disappeared from the film.

"She cut you out?" asked Noah, stating the obvious.

Jimmy paused the scene and sighed. "So it seems. I mean, I was there when we watched the tape the other night, and now I'm not."

"This is bad," said Bart. "Quinn will go ballistic."

"I don't understand how they did that," said Noah, studying the stilled figures on the screen, one of which was still *not* Jimmy, no matter how hard he stared.

"Me, either. But I'm a dancer, not a technician."

Noah turned in his seat and looked up at Jimmy, who still stood in the aisle, remote in hand.

"Are you all right?"

Jimmy's lower lip trembled slightly, but he held his composure. He set the remote on the back of a chair and said, "Yeah, I'm okay. But . . . why would she do this? It's been thirty-six years! Why can't she just leave us alone?"

Without another word, Jimmy turned and left the screening room, leaving Kitty, Quinn, and every dancer who wasn't Jimmy frozen on the screen.

"That sucks," said Bart, after he was gone.

"It's so petty and vindictive," Noah said, picking up the remote and zapping the images from the screen. He flicked the lights back on. "And why Jimmy? If she was going to gun for someone, why not Quinn?"

"Two reasons, I'd imagine. One, because she probably sees Jimmy as the gay male equivalent of the Other Woman. And two, because . . . well, let's face it; Quinn was a star. He was a somebody. Jimmy was just a dancer, and no one will ever notice that he's been erased from the scene."

"Nobody except Quinn and Jimmy," said Noah, and Bart grunted his agreement.

That night, three of the four men ate dinner under a cloud of sadness that Quinn couldn't understand.

"Is something wrong?" he finally asked, feeling as if he had been left out of something that had happened under his roof.

Jimmy tried to smile. "No, Quinn. Why?"

"You're all being too damn quiet."

Bart tried to rally. "You know, I've been feeling a bit under the weather all day. Maybe there's a bug going around." Noah and Jimmy quickly offered their concurrences.

"Ah, bullshit," grumbled Quinn, having none of it. He stood, tossing his napkin on the table, and said, "If no one is going to tell me what's going on, I'm going to watch some TV."

After he was gone, the silence in the room deepened, until Jimmy finally spoke.

"Okay, I've been thinking about this. I hate to admit this, but I'm still very angry about what happened to that movie. I can't seem to let it go . . . and I let *everything* go."

"Too bad we're powerless," said Bart.

"I know. But I think I can get a little satisfaction out of this. A little . . . *payback*. And the DVD is going to help me." He looked at Noah and Bart, and added, "It could help *all* of us."

"How?" asked Noah.

Jimmy looked up at the ceiling and pondered the question for a moment before answering.

"Noah, I mean no offense by this, but I've been a bit ambivalent about your project. Less so than Quinn, granted, but I sort of agree with him that it's probably best to let sleeping dogs lie. To the extent I've been in your corner, it's been because I want Quinn to be remembered for the star he once was . . . and because I know that you mean a lot to Bart."

Bart shifted uncomfortably.

"Ever since I was—what, banished?—from the business, I've been content to be with Quinn and lead a pretty anonymous life. It's a good life, don't get me wrong, but it's not the life I envisioned when I was singing and dancing on a soundstage. Because of Quinn—well, really, because of Kitty, but still—I gave it all up, and I would do it again if I had to." Jimmy realized that his voice was rising and, despite his best efforts, he was starting to tremble slightly with anger. He took a few deep breaths to keep himself under control and continued. "But this pisses me off for a few reasons. First, because *my* accomplishments—while modest—were still *my* accomplishments. Kitty Randolph chased me out of the business, but she had no right to make it seem as if I never existed."

"True," said Noah.

Jimmy ignored him. "More importantly, the look we gave each other is gone. She has erased The Glance. Forever. Well, except for VHS, but how much life does that tape have in it? She took a moment that was very special to Quinn and me and erased it forever. And I don't have to add that no one—*no one*—except for me, Quinn, and that *bitch* has ever or will ever notice that look. It was imperceptible to the public eye, but it meant everything to us. And she . . ." He stopped, unable to go on.

The room fell silent again for long minutes, each man afraid to look at the others. When Jimmy finally spoke, he was back in control.

"Anyway, enough about that. We can't undo what she's done. We can only use it."

"Use it?" asked Noah.

Jimmy laughed, but it was a cold laugh . . . the laugh of a man who really didn't think anything was all that funny. "I'm the cool, controlled half of Quinn and Jimmy, right? So if I feel this strongly about what she's done, just imagine Quinn's reaction."

"Oh, God," Bart muttered, hiding his face in his hands. "He'll be a wild man."

"Yes, he will," Jimmy confirmed. "And Noah will have his book."

Noah looked at Bart, then Jimmy. "Uh . . . I'm not sure I follow."

Jimmy tented his fingers and stared across the table at him. "Quinn doesn't want to do the book the way *you* want to do it, correct?" Noah nodded. "He wants to glide over his marriage to Kitty . . . he wants to keep her out of it. He wants to show her some respect. Correct?" Again, he was answered with a nod. "But if Quinn sees I was cut out of *Stars*, you know he's going to be angry and want to get back at her. Correct?"

This time, Noah didn't nod instinctively. This time, he actually understood where Jimmy was going.

Noah thought about Jimmy's suggestion. "I'm not sure that revenge is the way we want to go here."

"Suddenly noble?" Jimmy's voice dripped with sarcasm, and—for the first time—Noah realized that the agreeable former dancer and patient life-partner was not a pushover. Jimmy Beloit knew how to push back.

"No," Noah mumbled. "But it feels wrong. Like we're tricking Quinn or something."

"What we're doing," said Jimmy, "is getting him to do what he should have wanted to do in the first place. Don't consider anything we're discussing as an act of vengeance, Noah. Think of it more as . . . an incentive."

Bart suddenly spoke up. "You can't give *Stars* to Quinn for his birthday. It will ruin it."

"Don't worry," came the reply. "As far as everyone is concerned, the rest of the DVDs arrived as scheduled, but *When the Stars Come Out* is on back order."

They agreed. As Jimmy was about to leave the table, Bart said, "It's a good thing we took a look at *Stars* before you gave it to Quinn. This could have been a disaster."

A wry smile crossed the older man's face. "Quinn isn't the only one who values our one moment together on the screen." He stood and walked to the door, intending to join his husband for a restful night in front of the television set. But before he left the room, he turned to face Noah and Bart. "With luck and work, you'll understand one day."

A few nights later, as they prepared for bed, Bart looked at Noah and said, "I think you're wrong."

"About what?"

Bart climbed into bed and pulled the sheets over him. "About long-term monogamy. I've been thinking about that a lot since we talked the other day, and I've decided you're wrong."

Noah smiled. "*You've* decided? Well . . . thanks for that." He, too, climbed into bed, and pulled some of the sheets away from Bart for his own use. "But I'm not wrong."

Bart pulled back on the sheets. "I think I want what Quinn and Jimmy have."

"Ugh." This time, Noah didn't fight for the sheets. Instead, he turned to face away from Bart. "Listen, I'm sure what they have is very nice, but I'm not convinced it's for me. It's not for *most* gay men. Hell . . . it's not even for most *straight* men."

"So lifelong monogamy is only for women?"

Noah pushed his face into the pillow. "I don't know. I don't try to speak for women." When Bart didn't reply, he turned to look at him. "Why do we have to talk about this?"

Bart's voice was soft. "Because sometimes I wonder what the rest of my life will be like."

"I'm not sure I follow."

"I look at Quinn and Jimmy, and I see two people who love each other, and have been there to support each other. They've done it for decades, and—who knows?—maybe they'll be there for each other for another couple of decades. And I look at them, and I wonder who will be there with me when I'm seventy or eighty, and I need a new hip, or a ride to physical therapy, or even just a hug."

"You can hire someone. Like they hired you."

"For that hug, Noah? For love? It's not the same."

Noah sighed and began to roll back away from Bart, but stopped himself. Staring at the ceiling, he said, "You know what I think when I look at them?"

"What?"

"I think, 'God bless you.' Which is the same thing I think when I see my father with Tricia. *God Bless You.* Good job. Maybe the first one didn't work out . . . or the second . . . but good job on landing the third one, and good luck with her."

"You're very cynical tonight."

"No, baby," Noah said, turning to look at him. "Not cynical. Realistic. Happiness is . . . well, it doesn't come with guarantees."

"Nothing does."

"Can't we just take this nice and slowly? Can't we take things as they come along, without wondering what life will be like in forty years? I mean, we've only known each other for a month and a half or so. Then suddenly we're boyfriends . . . and now you're already planning the wedding. I know it worked for your parents, but it doesn't work for me. It's all going by too quickly."

"Yeah," Bart said tersely, and this time it was he who turned away.

Bart did know that their relationship was fresh . . . maybe too fresh to sustain such a deep discussion. But he also knew that he had found the man he wanted to pick him up at the hospital when it was time to go home after his hip was replaced.

And he wondered when Noah would know that, and *if* he would ever know that, well into the night.

At his intimate birthday party a few days later, held in a quaint Sag Harbor restaurant, Quinn was delighted to receive the package of DVDs from Jimmy.

"Oh, great," he exclaimed, looking over the titles. "*The Fresh Kills*! That was my first film!" He leafed through the cases. "*Attack on Tottenville* . . . that was the one I made with Wayne. *Port Richard* . . . *Mariner's Harbor* . . ." He came across the movies from the Kitty Randolph boxed set, unboxed by Jimmy to hide the fact that one title was missing. "*Sweet Svetlana* . . . *Darling, I'm Darling* . . ."

He stopped abruptly, a look of confusion on his face. Jimmy, Bart, and Noah leaned forward expectantly.

"Where's *When the Stars Come Out*? Hasn't that been rereleased? I mean, all these other movies are out . . ."

"Back-ordered," the three men answered in unison, and, so overwhelmed was Quinn by the gift, it never occurred to him to ask how all three of them would know that.

That night they sipped champagne and watched Young Quinn Scott take a bullet for the Duke in *Attack on Tottenville*, knowing he would rise from the dust to fight again.

In fact, they knew that would be happening quite soon.

After the movie, Bart and Noah—slightly buzzed from the champagne—excused themselves from the screening room and made

their way upstairs to Bart's bedroom, where, for the fourth straight
night, Bart proceeded to strip off his clothes, climb into bed, and
roll his body away from Noah. Unlike the other nights, this time
Noah stopped him, placing a hand gently on his shoulder and
rolling him partially back toward him.

"Is something the matter?" he asked.

Bart stared away, not immediately answering.

"Bart, if there's a problem, we should talk about it."

"There's no problem," he said finally. "Everything is fine."

Noah didn't accept his words. "There *is* a problem. You've been
pulling away from me for a few days, and I think we should talk
about it."

With a sigh and a shrug, Bart turned and looked at Noah, then
began speaking softly. "Sorry. I've just been . . . well, I've been having a hard time wrapping my head around the things you were saying the other day."

"What things?"

"About long-term, monogamous relationships."

Oh, Noah thought, regretting his comments, even though he
meant them.

"Here's the thing," said Bart, idly rubbing his hand back and forth
across his taut, naked stomach. "At the risk of repeating myself again
and again and again, that's what I want."

"Long-term monogamy?"

"Exactly. I want what Quinn and Jimmy have. I want to be them
in thirty, forty, fifty years. Not . . . not alone."

"Is the thought of being alone what scares you?"

"I think I'd be fine, and if that's how things end up, that's how
things end up. But if they don't have to be that way—if I can share
decades of my life with someone else—that's the ideal. That's what
I really want."

"I don't know," said Noah, sitting up in the bed, still covered waist-
down with the blanket. "I don't know if gay men are wired that way."

"Uh, Noah? We're staying in a house with two gay men who seem
to be wired *exactly* that way."

"Are you sure?"

Now Bart sat up. "What do you mean?"

"Thirty-some-odd years together, and you're telling me they've
never made accommodations?" Bart shook his head. "No three-

ways? No boyfriends on the side? No sex in the parks? Bathhouses? What about this flirtation Quinn had with Rock Hudson? Are you sure they never did the nasty when Jimmy wasn't looking?"

Bart's face looked pained. "Why do you have to tear everyone down to your level?"

Noah retreated slightly, realizing that he was going too far, and reached to place a hand reassuringly on Bart's back. "Listen, I'm not saying that they haven't been monogamous. I'm just saying—"

Bart stopped him and pulled away from Noah's hand, leaving it in midair behind him. "I don't think this is going to work."

"What?!" Noah was genuinely mystified.

"Us. It's not going to work. We want different things." He sprang from the bed, leaving Noah behind, mind reeling.

"Bart, I'm not sure what I said, but . . . but . . ."

Bart strode across the bedroom, and, sliding open a dresser drawer, took out a pair of olive cargo short shorts, which he proceeded to put on.

"Bart, what are you doing?"

"I think it would be for the best if I slept in the guest room," he said, as he pulled a T-shirt over his head. "We can talk tomorrow."

The conversation was over. Noah knew that he would not be able to talk himself out of this one . . . not tonight. He watched in frustrated silence as Bart let himself out of the bedroom.

And neither of them slept more than a few hours that night.

Bart's headstrong attitude, not to mention his defensiveness about Quinn and Jimmy, had stunned Noah. The next morning, as he lay bleary-eyed and alone in Bart's bed, lazily waiting for the sunlight streaming through the bedroom window to revive him, he tried to comprehend what, exactly, he had done or said to anger him so. He had merely done what he always did: he spoke his mind.

Okay, Bart wanted to be in a monogamous relationship for the rest of his life. While statistically unlikely, for homosexuals and heterosexuals alike, it was possible. It had not happened in Noah's family, true, but it had happened before in history. And it was nice—sweet, really—that Bart wanted that. But it wasn't Noah's fault that he had pointed out the truth.

And the adamant defense of Quinn's and Jimmy's fidelity could only be because they represented the personification of Bart's ideal. While it was true that he was closer to the men than Noah, Bart had no real way to know what had happened over the lifetime they had spent together. Especially since Bart had not even been born when they met.

The facts were these: Quinn Scott and Jimmy Beloit, like Bart Gustafson and Noah Abraham, were human. And humans make mistakes. And gay male humans, especially, make mistakes. Culturally and biologically, in fact, it was almost impossible that Quinn and Jimmy had never made a mistake. For God's sake, they came of age during the pre-AIDS era, when anonymous sex and bathhouses were the rule, not the exception.

No, Noah thought, *I was just being honest.* Just telling the truth. Bart could want what he wanted, but he shouldn't be surprised if he didn't get it. And he especially shouldn't hold up two older, apparently monogamous, gay men as his model, without knowing how they acted and what they felt before banishment and bad hips intruded on their lives.

Wisely, once Noah settled everything in his head and agreed with himself that he had been right all along, he decided to keep his mouth shut. Clearly, Bart was not predisposed to accept his logic. This would be one of those situations where an apology was in order.

Which is how Noah found himself in the guest room several minutes later. Bart, as he had expected, was already wide awake and, once again, staring at the ceiling.

"Good morning," said Noah, as he let himself into the room after a quick, light knock on the door.

Bart looked at him neutrally. "Morning."

"Sleep all right?"

Bart shrugged. His chest, bare above the sheet, rippled slightly.

"Uh . . . so how about that talk?"

Bart shrugged again.

Noah glanced at the floor, forced a smile, and looked back at Bart. "I've been sort of an asshole," he said, trying for as conciliatory a tone as possible. "And I apologize. I mean, I know how you feel about this, and, well . . . I agree. Uh . . . I agree that it's a great ideal, I mean."

Bart frowned. "But you don't think it's possible to have a long-term, monogamous relationship, do you? Which is a problem for us, I think."

"Does it have to be? Can't we just work toward it?"

"Not if you've already made your mind up that it can't work."

Noah heaved a heavy sigh and sat on the edge of the bed. "Can we try?"

"I . . . I don't know," said Bart, shaking his head. "I've . . . I've . . ." He stopped trying to come up with an answer and looked directly at Noah, knowing he had to say something he really didn't want to confess. "Listen, over the past few weeks, I've started to fall hard. And I never intended to, I just did. Ever since . . . remember that day we saw each other on Sixth Avenue? Near Radio City? And then later at the bar?"

"Of course."

"That was the day when I started thinking seriously about you. Even before I asked you to dinner, I was thinking about you. And do you remember the day when I was going to suggest that we become boyfriends, but you finished my thoughts for me?"

"Sure."

"That was the day I decided that you were the one. You're everything I've been looking for, Noah. Everything. And I let myself feel more than I should have."

Noah reached out to touch him, and this time his hand was not rejected.

"So this is mostly my fault," Bart continued, placing his own hand over Noah's, which now rested on his thigh. "I let myself get too far ahead, and . . . well, I know what I want, and I decided that you were the one who would give it to me. So it's not your fault that we're in this situation. It just . . . it is what it is."

"So now what?" asked Noah.

"I don't know. I've said what I've had to say, and . . ." He laughed. "Maybe more than what I had to say. But I guess it's best to get it all out there. At least we both know where we stand right now."

"Can we try to work this out?" Noah leaned close to Bart's face.

"Let's try," said Bart, kissing Noah gently and wishing it were so much easier. And hoping that one of them would come to see the light.

* * *

The timing was up to Jimmy. Returning from the gym two days later—where Bart had signed up Noah for a guest membership, reasoning that now that they were all but living together there was no reason to leave him home on training days—the younger men knew that the plan was about to unfold shortly after they walked into the house. They dropped their bags in the hall off the garage, walked into the kitchen, and immediately spotted the open box slapped with UPS labels on the counter.

"Looks like the back-ordered DVD has arrived," Bart said dryly, grabbing two bottles of water from the refrigerator and handing one to Noah.

"Looks like it." Noah held the bottled water in one hand and grabbed an energy bar with the other. "I wonder if we have time to shower."

"Maybe shower. Certainly not sex."

"Damn. And I was going to flex my new muscle for you."

They picked up their bags and were walking to the stairs when . . .

"GODDAMMIT!!"

"Think he's in the screening room?" Noah asked, hearing Quinn roar.

"No doubt."

"Should we go down there?"

"GOD DAMN HER! THAT BITCH!!"

"I don't know," said Bart. "Your call."

"Maybe we should wait."

"Then again, Jimmy is alone with him."

"I'LL KILL HER! I WILL BURY HER!!"

"I wouldn't think that Jimmy is the one in danger," said Noah.

"True. Then again, there could always be collateral damage."

Noah sighed and dropped his gym bag on the kitchen floor. "Okay, then. Let's see what's happening."

Bart followed Noah's lead and also dropped his bag, and then the men—armed only with water and an energy bar—descended to the screening room. As they approached it, Quinn bellowed again.

"MY LAWYER! GET MY LAWWYER! WHERE'S THAT FUCKING BART?! BART!!!"

"You called?" said Bart, stepping into the screening room, where the red-faced Quinn stood, and Noah thought that "enraged" would be the mildest adjective one could use to describe him.

"Where have you been?" Quinn demanded.

"The gym," Bart answered, calm in the face of Quinn's anger. "What's wrong?"

Jimmy appeared, wiping a tear from his eye and holding the DVD. "She . . . she cut me out," he said, choking on his words.

"Who?" asked Bart.

"*THAT FUCKING BITCH!*" screamed Quinn, his voice again at full volume. "*THAT . . . THAT . . .*"

"Don't say the C word," cautioned Jimmy.

"*THAT BITCH!*"

"That's better."

"Which bitch?" asked Bart, aware that he was only going to be able to carry the cluelessness so far. Already he worried that Noah might see that he could, when pressed, be quite a convincing actor in his own right.

"Kitty," said Jimmy, wiping an imaginary tear from his eye as Quinn struggled for words that weren't the C word. "She cut out our scene."

"In *When the Stars Come Out?* The scene where you guys locked eyes?"

"That's the one," Jimmy said. "The Glance! It's gone. I've been erased from the DVD version. It's like . . ." Jimmy worked up a choked and only semiconvincing sob. "It's like I never existed."

"Oh, God," said Bart, taking a step backward. "That's horrible."

Noah jumped in. "That's the scene you showed us a few weeks ago, right? The dance scene?"

"That's it. And now, I'm gone."

Bart creased his forehead. "I'll get your lawyer on the phone right away, Quinn."

"It won't do any good," said Jimmy, and the others looked at him expectantly, waiting for an explanation, which was quickly provided. "You're not used to this, Quinn. You were a star. But back when I was dancing, I was used to being cut out of the frame. Happened all the time."

"But you were there," Quinn said. "You made it on the screen. We have the videotape as proof."

Jimmy waved him away. "Look at all the films they're rereleasing these days. A lot of them have been recut. Director's cuts or restorations or whatever. Every single one of those versions—every single one—has meant some poor extra was edited out, and another one had his scene restored. It's the nature of the beast."

"But you weren't edited out," said Quinn. "Those scenes weren't recut. You were erased."

Jimmy shrugged. "If you could even find a lawyer to take this case, all Kitty has to do is say it was done for aesthetic reasons. There was something distracting about my performance, or whatever. We have no rights here."

Quinn thought about that. He knew that Jimmy was probably stating the truth, but he hated it that Kitty was still winning, still erasing him and Jimmy from the screen, after all these decades.

"Hey," said Jimmy, his arm now around Quinn's waist. "We still have the videotape, right? That's worth something. And you know what else? She can manipulate what's on the screen, but she can never erase the past thirty-six years of reality."

Quinn began to relax, seeing the wisdom in Jimmy's words. That was true; Kitty Randolph could forever delete that precious onscreen glance between the two men, perceptible only to them and Kitty herself. But she couldn't separate them from each other. And so he began to return Jimmy's embrace.

"It's just too bad," said Jimmy softly, as they held each other, aware that Quinn was calming down and not happy about that. "It's too bad that she always gets away with these things."

Quinn looked at his partner, realizing that, in Jimmy's arms, he had almost forgotten his anger.

"Not always," he said gruffly, and looked over Jimmy's shoulder. "Noah, let's talk."

Apparently, the Kitty Randolph who Noah Abraham and 99.99 percent of the world's population thought they knew was quite different from the Kitty Randolph who actually existed. And over the next few months, as her gay ex-husband dragged skeleton after skeleton out of closets that had been sealed for decades, Noah felt more and more secure that Quinn Scott's autobiography would be a winner.

The closest they came to an awkward moment was one afternoon when Quinn dictated: "The movies are nice—no, the movies are wonderful—but they aren't a substitution for life. The only thing they have in common is that you can have popcorn in both of them."

Noah rolled his eyes. "Okay, that line is going to have to go."

"Why?"

"Because it's stupid."

"It stays."

"But—"

"Remember whose story this is. It stays."

Noah decided to edit it out at a later point, when Quinn wasn't looking.

Noah's sentiment of the book's prospects was shared by his editor. No less than three times each week—more often, when Quinn was being particularly loquacious—Noah e-mailed David Carlyle summaries of the stories he was integrating into Quinn's book, and Noah could practically feel the moisture from David's salivation in his responses.

Noah was also relieved that his demon, the block that had once left him unable to write, had gone away. But how could it not, with the material Quinn was handing to him? Noah's only concern as fall turned to winter, and winter began to pass quickly—that being his primary writing window, since David wanted a more-or-less-complete manuscript no later than April—was that the dirt on Kitty was so juicy and substantial that Quinn risked becoming a minor player in his own memoir.

Not to worry, Noah told himself. *I'll fix that in the editing.* In the meantime, there were stories to document.

Kitty's battle with the bottle, for example. She hid the problem from most of Hollywood through the 1960s, but it was tough to hide all those stashed liquor bottles from the husband with whom she shared a home. That wholesome perky screen persona bore much more resemblance to *The Days of Wine and Roses* when Kitty wasn't in front of the cameras.

Then there were her parenting skills. Or, put more accurately, her *lack* of parenting skills. Young Q. J.'s mother didn't really want to be a mother, and showed it through her lack of attention. The story in which the post-divorce Kitty completely forgot to buy her four-year-old a single Christmas present would definitely be in the book.

She was cheap and abusive toward her household staff, although that was almost a cliché in a Hollywood tell-all, but she was also a merciless backstabber. Many actors had felt her wrath, although few knew where to assign the blame. Kitty would excise people from her films for the smallest, most innocuous offense, with as much surgical precision as she had disappeared Jimmy Beloit from *When the Stars Come Out.* Her genius came in never letting them know she had sacked them. She would comfort some poor, fired actress in her dressing room, joining her in running down the director or whomever, and never confess that Kitty had been behind the deed.

Not to mention the hapless actor Bert Cooper, whom she had married at a young age and then promptly divorced when his career flatlined. Three years later, when he drowned himself in the Pacific Ocean, Kitty—her own star in ascension—couldn't even be bothered to send flowers, and left out all mention of him when she penned her own autobiography.

Oh yeah, thought Noah. She was a gem. What had David Carlyle called her? A tigress? It was becoming increasingly clear that she was something much more dangerous than a tigress.

The Gay Hollywood angle Noah had originally hoped for was present, but it was more Gay Lite than Gay. In a sense, that was understandable. Quinn was gay, but he really hadn't done anything about that aspect of his sexuality until he met Jimmy, and since the two of them had been a couple almost since the day their eyes met on the set of *When the Stars Come Out,* he had managed to avoid interjecting too much tawdriness into his life story.

But still, there *were* stories. A few friendships had to be cloaked in anonymity, because the gay actors in question were still alive and more or less closeted. Noah could use the names of a few other actors, but many of them were unknown in 1970 and remained unknown in 2006. Quinn did confess to drunkenly making out with Cesar Romero after a dinner party; and, of course, there was the hot-and-heavy flirtation with Rock Hudson, about which Quinn was surprisingly coy, but if he had any true bombshells of the homosexual variety, he wasn't dropping them.

No, this would not be a revolutionary gay autobiography. No hustlers or diseases or shocking marquee names.

But as a story of one man and his short, tempestuous marriage to a major Hollywood star who could have single-handedly beat down Joan and Bette simultaneously, it was pure gold.

And, for Noah, there was a definite bonus beyond the gossipy intrigue: time with Bart.

When Noah began writing with Quinn, he had commuted from his father's apartment to stay at Quinn's house for a few days of interviews on most weeks, returning to Manhattan to write. After the DVD fiasco, though, Quinn all but ordered Noah to spend most of his time in Southampton. It made sense, after all, and it cut down on their growing telephone time, but it also made Bart a constant presence in Noah's life . . . not that either one of them had a problem with that.

Within the first hour of Noah's tenancy, Bart had cleaned out the dresser and closets of a guest room, which promptly filled with Noah's clothes . . . . although it was understood that the man who wore the clothes would stay in Bart's room. The room became not only his wardrobe but also his office, complete with a desk for his laptop, high-speed Internet, and a fax machine. On some days, when Quinn's hip was being particularly uncooperative, Noah even conducted his interviews in the room, as Quinn reclined on the bed.

And now that he had a daily opportunity to watch the interaction between Quinn and Jimmy, he found his mind increasingly wandering to his own relationship. What if he did end up spending decades with Bart? Would that be so bad?

In late November, knowing that he would not be back in the District of Columbia for a while, Noah—Bart in tow—made a quick trip south to clean out and sublet his apartment. That was the weekend he finally told Bart that he loved him, and Bart, of course, wasted no time in saying those words back to him.

They cuddled on Noah's couch in the almost-vacated apartment, naked under an afghan and lost in the afterglow of the words that moved their improbable relationship to another, much more serious level.

"I have to admit," said Bart, holding Noah's body tightly. "You caught me by surprise. I didn't see that coming at all."

"Me either," said Noah, shifting until he could see Bart's face. "I mean, I've been thinking the words, but I always thought you'd be the one to go first."

Bart laughed. "Because I'm the romantic one, right?"

"Exactly."

Bart slid his hand along Noah's flesh, feeling his tight, trim body. He was everything Bart had ever wanted. But even though Noah had professed his love, there was still an outstanding issue.

"Let me ask you something," he said, as his hand came to rest on Noah's hipbone. "This is great, but . . . as I recall, you have a problem with long-term monogamy."

"Maybe I've been wrong."

"Why, Noah Abraham! I don't think I've ever heard you utter that sentence before!"

Noah laughed. "Probably not. But I'm not in the same place I was a few months ago when we met. And I want to take a chance." He shifted a bit more until he could kiss Bart and did, adding, "I think we're great together, and if this is going to work, you're the one to make it work."

Bart kissed him back. "You must be a great writer, because you know just the right words to use with me."

As they worked through the winter, Noah continuously buffed the narrative, taking Quinn's often-rambling stories and putting them in proper order before jazzing them up with his own literary spin. The words on paper may have seldom been the exact words that came out of Quinn's mouth, but the old man, regularly reviewing the manuscript for continuity and errors, almost never objected. The tragic "popcorn" analogy was as close as he had come to putting his foot down.

It was late March, as Noah was trying to put a final polish on the manuscript, when Bart walked into the guest room-cum-home office and closed the door.

"How's it going?" Bart asked, as he sat on the bed.

Noah looked up from the manuscript. "It's coming along. Maybe another week or two."

"Good." He was silent for a while, and Noah's attention was about to return the pages in his hand when he added, "So what happens next?"

Noah set the papers on the desk. "What do you mean?"

"When you're done. What happens? Do you go back to Washington? New York?"

Noah didn't have an answer ready for him. He hadn't thought through what he would do when the book was finished.

"Not D.C.," he said. "The apartment is sublet until the fall. But maybe New York. I suppose I can always move in with my father and Tricia for a while." He paused. "Any thoughts?"

"Not really. It's just that . . . well, you've been out here for almost six months, and it's like we're taking a step back."

Noah sighed. "If you have any options, I'm listening."

That evening, over the dinner table, Quinn exchanged a glance with Bart and said, "You know, Noah, I've been thinking . . ."

Noah looked up from his plate of chicken and sausage over linguine, a Jimmy Beloit specialty. "About?"

"When the book is done, I don't think you should leave."

"Why is that?"

Quinn sat up stiffly. "Are you arguing with me?"

A knowing smile came to Noah's lips, and he looked across the table at Bart.

"I know a conspiracy when I see one," he said. "All right, Quinn, I'll stay. At least for a while."

"Good." Quinn cleared his throat. "Then after dinner you can help Bart with the dishes."

On April 7, 2006, David Carlyle answered the ringing telephone in his private office at Palmer/Midkiff/Carlyle Publishing. He instantly recognized Noah Abraham's voice.

"Do you have any news for me?" asked David. "We're getting very tight with the production schedule."

"I'm going to make you a very happy man today, David. The manuscript is finished."

Noah was right. David was *very* happy.

Chapter 9

I could understand Kitty's anger at me after my indiscretion.
For all her faults, she didn't deserve to walk in on that scene that
afternoon at Jimmy's apartment in Venice. That was one tough
moment for her.

But I could never figure out why she assigned so much of the
blame to Jimmy. The way she tried to destroy him and his career
seemed a little over the top to me. Even by Kitty Randolph's stan-
dards. Maybe it had to do with attacking the weak. Although I
don't think Kitty ever appreciated quite how strong Jimmy really
was . . .

When she was a little girl in Millville, New Jersey, growing up within sight of the factory where her father blew glass for a living, young Kathy Fisher took dance lessons. Her father considered them a waste of money, although he looked the other way. Her mother considered them a necessary introduction to the social graces. And Kathy, well . . . she was only seven years old. It would be years before she would have her own agenda.

The dance classes led to beauty pageants, and in 1952 Kathy Fisher was crowned Miss Cumberland County. It was there that a "talent manager," an occupation he assumed for himself on the spot as he watched the virginal teenage girls walk the stage at the county fair, first took her under his wing. Two months later, Kathy was no longer virginal and no longer single.

Soon, and through no fault of her new husband, Kathy found a role on the stage of a Philadelphia theater. At that point—earning her own income and now, thanks to the older girls in the chorus, wise enough to understand that her husband was little more than a garden-variety pedophile—she filed for divorce. And she never spoke of that marriage again. It ceased to exist. The creep went back to stalking southern New Jersey county fairs and Kathy Fisher moved on.

"Kathy Fisher?" asked the next smooth-talking man she would marry. "That's . . . *banal.*"

She didn't know what the word meant, but Kathy Fisher soon became Kitty Fisher, a name apparently less banal. The second husband also soon disappeared. But by then she had adopted his last name and, after scrubbing his existence from her life, she reemerged as Kitty Randolph.

She was a worldly twenty-one-year-old by the time the actor Bert Cooper came to Philadelphia to star in a play. And after Kitty had once again been wooed and wed she thought, *Finally, I have a husband I can actually list in a biography.*

Bert Cooper was a chronically depressed mess who could stay in bed for seventy-two hours at a time, but he *did* have a real acting resume dating back to adolescent roles in the 1930s. Kathy—no, *Kitty!*—thought she had married an icon. He took her from Philadelphia, set her up in Hollywood, and got her those all-important screen tests, which led to her first film roles.

Too bad about him, she thought, as she sat in the sunroom of her Bel-Air mansion almost fifty years later, sipping something bubbly and nonalcoholic. *Poor Bert.* But that hadn't been her fault. Theirs was an age-old Hollywood story, one career ascending as another was falling into the Pacific Ocean. The fact that Bert had *literally* fallen into the Pacific—on purpose—was not her fault. He had always been so sad . . .

Her fourth husband—*no, second,* she reminded herself, because the continuity of her Official Life Story was important—well, he was another story.

In an earlier period in her life, Quinn Scott would have disappeared from her biography as effectively as husbands number one and two had vanished. But when they married she was already a screen legend, and there was no hiding it. And so for more than three decades the ghost of that relationship had followed her.

It wasn't just that she had learned he was gay a few years into the marriage, although that was quite bad enough. It was that even after she made arrangements for Quinn to go quietly away, industry gossip kept growing. Her ex-husband, it seemed, was not merely gay, but gayer than gay. And when rumors finally reached her that Rock Hudson was preparing to go public and not only profess his homosexuality, but also his love for her ex-husband, well, that had to be stopped.

And she had stopped it. For thirty-six years.

And then, a few months earlier, word came from reliable sources on the East Coast that Quinn Scott was finally stirring after decades of dormancy. That would not do. Her lawyers were immediately dispatched to put out the fire, and she thought no more about it. Quinn knew better than to take her on in 1970, and he would certainly know better than to try it in 2006. Also, she had very good lawyers.

Kitty had moved on, and so should he. Discreet people—*proper* people—did just that. Why on earth would he dredge up old skeletons so many decades later?

And yet . . . there it was, in black and white, staring at her from an inside-page of *Variety*. Barely remembered actor Quinn Scott's autobiography would be released in September, and—lest any reader forget—*Variety* had to add that he had once been married to Kitty Randolph.

As she read the short item over and over again, she thought herself remarkably calm. Much calmer than she had the right to be. She had the right to be furious, but she wasn't.

The fury would come a few hours later, when the Valium wore off.

Books are not just written. Books are published, printers churning out page after page, more sophisticated than the days of Gutenberg but still following the same general principle.

In the case of Quinn Scott's autobiography, *When the Stars Come Out*, factories in three different states were all churning out the same pages and binding them the same way. And Johannes Gutenberg met Henry Ford as volume after volume rolled off the presses; the unexciting but necessary production side of publishing.

Before that came the writing and editing—David Carlyle's touch on Quinn Scott's book, as told to Noah Abraham, was notably light—and after that came the promotion.

Which is how Lindsay Flynn came into play.

Nine out of ten clients would agree: Lindsay Flynn was a pain in the ass. She was pushy, she was insistent, she was abrasive, she was annoying. On a professional basis, she had almost no redeeming personal qualities.

But all ten of those theoretical clients would still retain her. Because they weren't hiring a dinner companion, or even a hooker. They were hiring a publicist, and Lindsay Flynn—for all her flaws, or maybe because of them—was among the best.

David Carlyle was one of those clients. After the spectacularly dramatic meltdown of Palmer/Midkiff/Carlyle's overworked, underpaid, in-house publicist Angela Keenan—who finally cracked one afternoon when the local pharmacy ran out of nicotine gum, although the meltdown was bound to happen eventually—David reached out to Lindsay Flynn Communications, and he never looked back.

But while David had never looked back, he also didn't look forward to their occasionally necessary face-to-face meetings. Not only did he consider her pushy, insistent, abrasive, and annoying, he also tagged her with what he considered perhaps the worst of character traits: she was crass.

On the Wednesday morning she was due in his Sixth Avenue office for their first meeting in four months, David, steeling himself for the visit, was alarmed to note that he was sweating. As an oversized man, he was used to a touch of perspiration, but not in his office, which building management kept at a fairly consistent sixty-two degrees 365 days a year. Lindsay Flynn had just that effect on him. Disgusted with himself, not to mention the effect that one woman—a consultant, at that—could have on him, he wiped his brow with a monogrammed handkerchief and prepared for her visit.

And then she was there, suddenly braced in the doorframe to his office. "David!" she exclaimed through an affectedly stiff lower jaw. She was short and painfully thin, wearing a mismatched ensemble of varied stripes, her hair an unnatural yellow for any age, let alone her fifty-something years. And when she spoke through that clenched jaw, mimicking something she must have picked up that she thought made her look and sound sophisticated, the veins in her neck bulged unattractively. *Crass*, he thought again. *Just plain crass.*

But infusing the unwashed masses with class and poise was his avocation; his paycheck came from selling books. So he welcomed her into his office with air-kisses and feigned good cheer.

"Lindsay, dear! Please have a seat."

"Oh, I will," she promised, and David found himself strangely hypnotized by those throbbing neck veins, popping like strings plucked on a guitar. "But first I need to make a quick call. Do you mind?"

Well, yes, he *did* mind. But rather than argue the point he shrugged in resigned agreement, and she hit a speed dial button.

"Rosalyn? It's Lindsay Flynn." As she chattered along about something that, to David's ears, sounded somewhat less than urgent, he wondered again why he kept retaining *this woman* for PMC publicity purposes, and how she could possibly have any measure of success. Yes, unlike fashion industry publicists, she didn't need to be chic and refined to fit in; and unlike event publicists, she didn't need to be ready to appear before the camera at a moment's notice. But dammit, she was a *publicist*! Just because the only people she communicated with were other ink-stained publishing-industry types was no reason she couldn't be truly sophisticated, rather than affecting that faux sophistication that was more reminiscent of high-school theatrics than true refinement.

Lindsay flipped off her cell phone and sat. David looked at her across his desk, noting unpleasantly that she sat like a trucker, with her legs spread apart. He did not consider himself a misogynist, but he had to force a crude thought about the female anatomy out of his head before he continued.

"Thank you for coming."

"Not a problem. So what's up? Glenda Vassar again?"

"No," he said, referring to PMC's best-selling, although regrettably bipolar, romance novelist. "Glenda is in Maine, breathing in the fresh air and writing very, very, very slowly." Only in his last "very" did he let slip his impatience. As one of the Good Guys, David Carlyle wanted his writers to be emotionally healthy. But he also wanted them to produce, because production meant paychecks.

He continued. "Lindsay, we have a new book coming out in a few weeks—a very special book—and I think you'll find this assignment quite interesting."

She leaned forward, resting her elbows on her splayed knees. "Try me."

"*When the Stars Come Out*, by Quinn Scott."

Confusion crossed her face. She squinted. "The *Philly Cop* guy? Or his son?" She didn't wait for an answer. "The father! Of course! *When the Stars Come Out* was his last movie!"

There were, David realized, some benefits to hiring a woman of a certain age, even one with all her rough edges intact. Not having to explain somewhat recent history was one of them.

"Exactly," he said. "Quinn Scott is writing his memoirs." He smiled. "And . . ."

"And?"

"And he's coming out."

She gasped, and almost swallowed the gum he realized she was somewhat discreetly chewing. "He's a gay? Quinn Scott is a gay?"

"Gay as, uh, *me*."

"Gay as you? *That* gay?"

"Well . . ." He wasn't sure if he should be offended, but in any event he lost his opportunity to rebut when her cell phone rang. She held up a finger, signaling him to wait.

"Veronica, hi! I'm in a meeting. But wait until you hear—"

"Careful," David cautioned her, and, for once, she fell silent.

"Never mind. I'll have to call you back." She closed the phone, terminating the call, and said, "Are you sure about Quinn Scott?"

"Very sure."

"But he was married to Kitty Randolph!"

"Yes, he was. And that's why you're here. Quinn has written quite the tell-all, and I think there are countless PR possibilities."

"Right," she agreed. "Maybe I can get him on *Oprah.*"

"Uh . . ." David lifted a finger, stopping her. "I don't want to tell you how to do your job, but I need to warn you about something." He cleared his throat and continued. "You need to understand that Kitty Randolph is a killer."

"*I'm* a killer," she replied confidently.

"Well, there are killers, and there are *killers.* Kitty Randolph is a *killer.* I thought I already knew that she was tough, but after reading these memoirs . . . I had no idea. She's already threatened us with her lawyers."

"Whatever," said Lindsay. "I can handle her."

"I just want you to be discreet," David said. "The next thing you need to know is that no one remembers Quinn Scott anymore."

"*I* do!"

"Let me rephrase that: no one who is younger than fifty remembers Quinn Scott." Lindsay flinched. "Don't worry, I'm right there with you in the older demographic. The point is that you're going to have your work cut out for you reintroducing him to the world. You're going to have to essentially reinvent the Quinn Scott of the 1960s. The book only works if people think of 'the gay guy' as the macho, rough-hewn action star of the past. There will be quite an educational component to this."

"I should meet him."

David thought about that. An analogy involving water and oil was all that sprung to mind. "I'll think about that, but it's probably unnecessary. You'll want to meet with his ghostwriter, though: Noah Abraham."

"When? Where? Give me a number."

Five minutes later she was out of his office, armed with Noah's contact information. David said a silent prayer for the young writer, then wiped down the chair where Lindsay had been sitting.

If Lindsay Flynn had to choose the first word to describe her mood as she left David's office, it would have been "enthused."

The second word would have been "petrified."

She knew that old fuddy-duddy David Carlyle didn't care too much for her, and she really didn't care. Whatever doubts he had about her ability—so notable on his pudgy little face as he sat in judgment of her from behind the desk inherited from Daddy—were his own business. Lindsay knew that she was competent, and she had a healthy respect for her own abilities and creativity.

But, she wondered, why would the contemptuous editor entrust her with such a high-profile PR campaign? Was there a trap door here somewhere?

Yes, he had warned her about Kitty Randolph, but Lindsay dismissed that as the women-hating blather so typical of the gays. Maybe Kitty *was* a bitch; if so, she had met her match in *this* publicist, and that was that.

So it was a great assignment . . . unless David Carlyle was setting her up to fail. As she walked determinedly south on Sixth Avenue, she decided that she would not let herself fail. The Quinn Scott public relations blitz would be so thorough, so professional, that even that woman-hating homo David Carlyle would have to be impressed. Without another thought, she banished the word "petrified" from her brain and proceeded on, barreling through the crowds on the sidewalk.

After all, she had work to do. A lot of work. Which meant that she had no time to be nice to the people sharing her sidewalk.

Yes, she would show David Carlyle. By the time his book was released, Quinn Scott would be even more famous than he was forty years earlier. And everyone would know that Lindsay Flynn had done that for him.

Waiting impatiently for a light to change, she thought again about her flippant comment about booking him on *Oprah*. Well, why not? Her audience was the right demographic—mature enough and liberal enough to accept and embrace Quinn's homosexuality—and the ratings were still through the roof, after all these years. Better yet, one of Lindsay's dear friends—she couldn't quite remember his name, but she was sure they considered each other dear friends—worked there, and if she could find his card back at the office, she would give him a call.

Enthused. Yes, she was enthused. This was the big one, and she was going to ride it all the way to the end of her career.

Three days later, even as *When the Stars Come Out* was rolling off the presses, a cell phone rang on a sun-filled patio in Bel-Air, California. The phone's owner, a tan, rather featureless man in his late forties, wearing white shorts and a white polo shirt, looked at it as it chirped, briefly considering if the call made it worth putting down his joint. Looking closer, he saw a 212 area code in the caller ID display, which meant it was a call from New York, which meant it was probably worth taking. It could be his broker, after all, and brokers took precedence in the volatile stock market of recent weeks.

He snuffed the joint out and, exhaling, answered on the fourth ring, a split second before the caller would have been sent to voice mail.

"This is Dean."

It wasn't his broker. But he was glad he took the call anyway.

After signing off, he walked briskly into the house. He made a beeline directly for the sunroom, where he knew she would be sitting, reading some dreadful script that she had convinced herself would make mountains of money.

"Yes?" she said, looking up at him over the rims of the reading glasses perched halfway down her nose. He thought she looked much younger than her seventy years, but, then again, that was one of the reasons he liked to get high when she was headquartered at home.

"Interesting news," he said. "Guess who's trying to get booked on *Oprah?*"

"I don't have time for this, Dean," she said, returning her attention to the script.

"Quinn."

She looked up again, confused. "Q. J.? I don't understand . . ."

He shook his head. "Not Q. J. *Quinn.* Your ex-husband."

Kitty Randolph stood and made her five-foot-one frame stretch until she looked eight feet tall.

"How do you know this?"

He smiled. "Because *your* production company pays out lots of nice little annual stipends to a lot of people in the industry, precisely so we don't get blindsided by things like this. And in this case, our guy at *Oprah* got the call."

"Why?" she demanded, fire in her aqua eyes. "Why would Quinn want to go on *Oprah?*"

Dean shrugged. "You know the rumors, Kitty. That autobiography . . ."

"I thought we stopped that."

"The lawyers threatened. It didn't work." Over the seventeen years of their May-December marriage, he had learned how to convey absolutely nothing in his voice when she was riled. It was safer that way. "But this one, well . . ."

"It was supposed to go away!" She knocked the script off the table. "His biography was supposed to have gone away!"

"I guess he didn't get the message."

"We told them we'd sue, didn't we?" Dean nodded. "So why are they doing this? Do they think I was bluffing?"

"You were," he said, sticking his neck out by telling the truth.

She shot him a contemptuous glare. "Don't talk to me like that, Dean Henry."

"Sorry, Kitty."

She began pacing across the oriental rug. "You should call the lawyers back," she said. "And then . . . I want his balls."

Dean rolled his eyes, a gesture he only dared because her back was to him. Still, she seemed to sense it, and turned to face him.

"Did you say something?"

"No, dear." He paused, then added, "But the lawyers, well . . . you realize that they don't think they can win, don't you?"

"I don't care. I want them to sue."

"It's more publicity for Quinn."

"It's *defamation!*" she screamed. "He is trying to *defame* me!"

"We don't know that."

"Good Lord, Dean, use your goddamn head! He's going to write that he's gay! What else could he have to write about!"

"Uh . . . well, that's true."

"Exactly."

"No, I mean it's true that he's gay. So how is that defamatory to you?"

She tilted her head and spoke slowly, as if trying to explain a complex concept to a child. "It's defamatory because he's going to say that I married a gay man. Which makes me look stupid. And naïve. And . . . and it's defamatory because he's going to make the world think that the same dick that was inside Kitty Randolph was also inside men's asses! Goddamn it, Dean, what are you not understanding here?!" With that, she kicked the script, which slid inelegantly across the rug and onto the marble floor.

Dean closed his eyes, hoping to remove Kitty's peculiar mental image from his head.

"Kitty," he continued, eyes still closed. "If Quinn's memoirs are factual, the lawyers say there's nothing they can do. They tried to threaten his publisher, and that didn't work. Following through isn't going to do anything except give him more publicity, which is the last thing you want."

"You're all pathetic," she said, brushing past him as she made her way to the circular staircase just outside the sunroom's French doors. "You, the lawyers, all of you: *pathetic*!"

His voice betraying frustration, Dean called after her as she began to mount the stairs.

"What do you want us to do, Kitty?"

"Never mind," she said, disappearing from his sight around the curve of the staircase. "If the most expensive team of lawyers in California can't make this go away, I'll take this to a higher level."

"Meaning?"

He saw her head peer over the railing, seventeen feet above him. "*Meaning* that I'm going to take care of this myself."

When she was gone, Dean frowned. Then he walked back out to the patio, because it was suddenly the perfect time to get high.

Six days later, New Yorkers were celebrating a rare, temperate Tuesday in early August. With the atmosphere free of oppressive heat and humidity, David Carlyle decided to walk to work, and, as he did, he realized he was in one of his best moods ever.

Although he had worked at PMC for more years than he cared to admit, David had never seen a new release rolled out with such heightened security. The only description that the publisher's fall catalog had given was "an explosive memoir and instant bestseller" scheduled for a September 2006 release, and the company had even taken pains not to send out advance review copies. When Quinn Scott's biography hit the shelves, few in the industry would have more than a couple of day's notice.

Ideally, he would have liked to have had months to promote it. But Kitty Randolph's lawyers had at least succeeded in tightening the PMC veil of silence. *When the Stars Come Out* was strictly embargoed, and all players—even, to the best of his knowledge, the loathsome Lindsay Flynn—were doing an extraordinary job of keeping their mouths shut.

As David strolled casually down Sixth Avenue, late for an appointment and not really caring, he would certainly have been a bit more concerned had he known that, in addition to *Oprah*, Lindsay had already gotten a jump on her PR efforts by reaching out to virtually every television show that featured guests, including a UFO-oriented late-night cable access show. She was proud of her industriousness; he would have been less pleased.

But his good mood held all the way until he reached the revolving doors and entered the building housing Palmer/Midkiff/ Carlyle, at which point he remembered that his first appointment—with Noah Abraham, for which he was already late—would be pleasant enough, but it would be followed by what could only be described as pure hell. And then he wondered why he didn't just retire.

When the elevator doors opened, David strode purposefully down the aisle separating row upon row of cubicles, en route to his private office tucked at the far end of the suite of offices. At the end of the aisle, he saw Noah waiting for his 10:00 appointment. It was 10:15.

"I apologize for the delay," David said, motioning Noah in to his office. As they sat, the editor began fussing absentmindedly with stacks of paperwork on his desk, moving sheets from pile to pile, then back again, with no real purpose except to convey general busyness. "And I also apologize in advance that our meeting will have to be cut short. Trust me, I am not looking forward to that. But one of my authors is in town, and she's going to be in a very bad mood. As usual. I'm afraid my Tuesday morning will be spent getting kicked in the teeth."

"Your metaphors are so colorful."

David arched an eyebrow. "Metaphor? Oh, how I wish." He reshuffled the papers again and said, "Now, what's on your mind? How are you and Quinn feeling about the book?"

"Quinn's, well . . . He's been getting . . . funny."

David didn't like the sound of that. "Funny?"

"I talked to Lindsay Flynn on the phone—"

"Oh good. She talked to you."

"Yeah. Anyway, she said something about a book tour?"

David tried to remember if he had promised Quinn a book tour. He didn't think he had, and if Lindsay had taken the initiative, well . . . she shouldn't have done that.

"I have to admit," he confessed, "that I don't recall."

"She said something about twelve cities?"

Twelve cities? Oh, no, David would have remembered *that*.

"Uh, I think Lindsay is getting ahead of herself," David said. "I may be able to work a few things out, but PMC doesn't normally send authors on tour."

Noah bit his lip. "Oh."

"Is there a problem?"

"Well . . ." Noah took a deep breath. "First, let me say that he's been very pleased with all the support you've given him."

David glanced at his watch, and, sounding more abrupt than he meant to, said, "Get to the point."

"He sort of has his heart set on a book tour."

David sighed. "I'll see what I can do. Maybe New York-Philly-Boston."

"Um . . ." Noah knew this was going to be awkward, but he also knew if he didn't raise the issue now, it would probably come back to haunt him in the future. "Actually, he was sort of hoping to get more than twelve cities."

David laughed at the absurdity. It was one thing to take Lindsay's ridiculous promises seriously, and quite another to want to build on them.

"This is the same man who a year ago wanted nothing to do with a biography?" Noah nodded. "Good Lord. I swear, half the time I think writers have bigger egos than actors."

"And he's both."

"Indeed." David paused for a moment, thinking over the latest development. "So why the sea change in his attitude?"

"Now that he's dictated his life, refreshed his memory . . . well, he thinks he has a story to tell."

"He does," David agreed. "And it's a story available to everyone with twenty-five dollars, come September."

Noah didn't reply, so it was up to David to draw him out.

"So what is this story he wants to tell? Okay, somehow you got him to mention Kitty Randolph, and good for you, because *that* is the story here. But there will only be so much play in that. Some national publicity—book reviews and all that—should take care of that. What else is on his mind?"

"*His* story," said Noah. "Not so much Kitty's, but his."

David sighed. "In other words, we're back to square one. If he's all excited about being another retired actor to come out of the closet, that's admirable. But that story has been told. Richard Chamberlain . . . Tab Hunter . . ."

"That's not the story. He wants to tell a story of . . ." Noah paused, closed his eyes, swallowed hard, and forced the word out. "Love."

"Love? So we're back to that again!"

"Yes. Love."

David stared at Noah, searching for words. When they came, his voice was strangely lyrical, although accompanied by the dripping sarcasm he had really hoped to avoid on his very pleasant walk to the office.

"Yes, of course. Love is a beautiful thing, isn't it, Noah? Love, well . . . love makes life worth living. Love makes even the harshest aspects of life tolerable. It makes the world go 'round, they say, and it's also a many-splendored thing. And for Quinn Scott to know love is . . . well, it's as if Quinn Scott has personally, with his own two hands, reinvented the universe. I daresay that the world will never be the same, now that Quinn Scott has written the story of love!"

"I know, I know—"

"I think I'd better order extra printings of his book right away! This will outsell the Bible! And please tell Quinn that I will now personally make arrangements for his book tour. Not just twelve cities, either. Will fifty cities be enough? No, of course not. How about eight thousand?"

Noah held up a hand to stop him. "David, I'm on your side . . ."

"Do you think he'll write me another book, Noah? I could really use a how-to on world peace."

"David . . ."

"If we're going to give him a major tour to promote his book on wrinkly, naked, old-guy gay love, it's the least I can do."

Noah sat back, wishing the stream of sarcasm would finally end. Which, abruptly, it did.

Unfortunately for Noah, David only stopped to lean forward across his desk, his eyes blazing. One pudgy finger jabbed across the desk, punctuating each clipped syllable. He was now solidly in a black mood, having done a complete emotional U-turn in a few short minutes.

"Noah, I would like you to take a message back to Quinn Scott. Feel free to be blunt, or feel free to be diplomatic, but—whatever you do—make sure that this gets through to him. PMC wrapped up a lot of money in his biography, via his advance, *your* advance, advertising and publicity, and production, and we have received very little in return. When this book hits the shelves next month, I want him ready to get out there and talk."

"Gotcha."

"And not on my dime."

"Gotcha."

"And while he is free to talk about his love for Jimmy Beloit, what the world *really* wants to know about is Kitty Randolph. He would be well advised to keep that in mind."

"Gotcha."

"I should have written this project off, but I am taking a chance on his memoirs because, for some strange reason, I feel an obligation to his courage—not *unprecedented* courage, but courage—in coming out at his age. I hope that it will provide some comfort to other gay people, and help them find their own paths. But . . ." He stopped abruptly, then shrugged. "You know the rest."

"I know," Noah agreed. "Quinn has to get realistic about what he's accomplished."

David nodded sadly, and rubbed his temples. "Don't get me

wrong," he added. "We've got a good book here, and I'm pleased that PMC is publishing it. But Quinn Scott no longer controls the agenda. The readers do." He leaned forward. "More importantly, *I* do."

"I'll tell him," said Noah, nodding sadly himself. "If he doesn't see the reality . . . ?"

"If it comes to that, *When the Stars Come Out* won't be the first disappointing book to be remaindered and pulped a few months later." David lost himself in shuffling papers again for a few moments, then looked back at Noah. "So tell me . . . just what is so special about his love? Longevity?"

"Well, *yeah!* Thirty-six years. The Stonewall Era. And they're still together and going strong."

"Very sweet. And as someone who can't seem to make it past the two-week mark, let me add, that's commendable. But I'm afraid it's of limited appeal."

"I know. But that was his incentive to write the book. He wants people to remember the story of Quinn Scott and Jimmy Beloit."

"I can't sell the story of Quinn Scott and Jimmy Beloit."

"I know." Noah extended his hand. "I hope this doesn't reflect badly—"

"On you? Not at all." His eyes brightened. "And you did, finally, deliver me a publishable manuscript. Granted, it wasn't that Washington exposé I contracted for all those years ago, but I do think this will sell well. At least, it will sell well unless your actor decides to bore prospective readers with talk about his relationship."

David rose from his seat and began walking Noah to the door, never taking a break in his monologue.

"Quinn's book has enough dish to make it interesting. I would have liked more, but I'll take what I can get. He does narrate a courageous, compelling story, and I do thank you for drawing it all together. But the relationship angle is . . . well, I know that was his incentive to make this very public statement, and—again—I think it's wonderful. For both of them. But it's just not what's going to sell the book. These men are not Bogie and Bacall; they're not Tracy and Hepburn; they're not even Demi and Ashton. They're just two very nice old men living on Long Island who have shared a life together . . . which is nice, but not sexy."

"I understand."

At the door, the men shook hands for what was supposed to be one final time.

"If you want me to talk to him . . ."

"No," said Noah. "It will be better coming from me."

"If you need backup . . ." David stopped, looked over Noah's shoulder into the endless row of cubicles behind him, and muttered, "Oh God," as his normally limp handshake grew noticeably weaker.

Noah turned and saw nothing at first, until he noticed a short, well-dressed woman steaming toward David's office, her head only occasionally visible over the cubicle walls. Finally, she turned a corner and strode straight at them. In her wake, the PMC drones—the people who did everything from answering phones to mailing out review copies to copyediting—began to steal away to the other side of the office, as if seeking safety.

"Carlyle!" she snapped when she was just yards away from the doorway. "We have an appointment!"

David glanced at his watch. "Yes, we do. In three minutes. Right now I'm finishing my . . ."

She pushed past Noah into David's office.

". . . other meeting."

"I have a plane to catch, so we'll start now." Her southern drawl was all honey, even if her words were not.

"Margaret . . ."

The ugly grimace that had been her face softened, as did her voice. Now she was a lady . . . although that was largely a matter of degree, since there was still a very hard edge to her.

"Who's he?" she asked, pointing to Noah and trying to smile.

"Noah Abraham," said David, "I'd like you to meet Margaret Campbell. Margaret, Noah is cowriting the Quinn Scott autobiography that we'll be releasing in a few weeks."

"Who?"

"Quinn Scott," Noah volunteered. "He was a big actor in the '60s."

She shrugged. "Norman, I do apologize for interrupting your meeting, but I hope you won't mind, since it was almost over. And I do have that plane to catch."

"Uh . . . it's Noah."

"Of course it is. But David and I have some very important items to discuss regarding my next book, so if you could just run along . . ."

When she trailed off, David saw an opportunity to jump in and defuse things a bit by appealing to her ego. "Margaret probably needs no introduction, but you might know her as the Grande Dame of the American Mystery."

"According to *People*," she added, and Noah couldn't be sure if she considered that validation, or was deploying self-deprecating humor.

"Love your books," he said, and hoped there was no follow-up; because although he *had* heard of her, he had never read her books.

"Thank you. Now, if you wouldn't mind leaving us alone . . ."

David's eyes pleaded with Noah to stay. But there wasn't much Noah could do about it, because Margaret Campbell was clearly about to liberate a pound of flesh from his ass, and she would not let anyone stand in her way.

"I'll just be going," Noah said, nodding at David.

"Um, yes, I suppose." They looked at each other, momentarily ignoring the Grande Dame of the American Mystery, and said their good-byes. "Give Quinn my—"

"Mmmm," mumbled Margaret, loudly and impatiently, after which she faked an exaggerated cough.

David walked Noah out of his office, then leaned close and whispered, "You'd better get out of here. She's about to blow."

"She seems fine."

"Trust me. I've published twelve of her books. I know the beast quite well." He stopped; then, swallowing his words, gasped, "Oh God."

Noah glanced behind him, scanning the office for the new incoming missile. And when he saw it, he, too, gasped.

The PMC office drones, chased away by Hurricane Margaret, were now popping up from the cubicles, chattering in a hushed but excited buzz, and craning their necks.

"What's going on out there?" asked Margaret loudly, no longer pretending to be a genteel southern lady.

In the doorway, ignoring her, David and Noah both whispered, at the same time, "Kitty Randolph."

"Who?" Margaret asked, not quite hearing them. David shushed her.

Kitty Randolph— head to toe in Chanel, wrists adorned with Cartier—sashayed slowly down the well-worn industrial carpeting as if she were walking a red one. Though short—no taller than Margaret Campbell, David thought—she commanded respect and authority as she made her measured way down the aisle, smiling ever so slightly.

A particularly brave editorial assistant popped up from behind his cubicle wall, proffering pen and pad, and she stopped, brightened her smile, and signed under the PMC logo. She had done it, by her own estimate, twenty-two thousand times over a fifty-three-year career, and she was proud of her ability to make each autograph seeker feel like the first.

After signing her name, she walked determinedly but politely to the doorway where David and Noah stood, frozen in what each could not decide was awe, fear, or a little of both.

"Excuse me," she said, smiling even as she stared down David. "Would you happen to know where I could find David Carlyle?"

"That . . . that would be me."

"Mr. Carlyle," she beamed, taking David's hand and making every effort not to recoil when she felt the cold dampness. "I am so pleased to meet you. I'm Kitty Randolph."

"You, uh, you need no introduction."

"I hope you don't mind me bothering you. That very nice receptionist asked me to wait in the conference room, but I wanted to see the publishing world in action." In reality, that very nice receptionist was, at that moment, hiding in a bathroom stall, having been reduced to tears by the not-so-very-nice Kitty Randolph, who would not take no for an answer. The office manager would find her forty-five minutes later, still traumatized by the encounter. But, for this brief moment, upon meeting David Carlyle for the very first time, Kitty Randolph dripped more sweetness than she had ever dripped on the screen, and that was saying a lot.

"Yes, well . . . welcome to the publishing world in action."

"May I sit down?"

Noah came out of shock just long enough to realize that it was the perfect moment to escape before he was detected, but was swept along as Kitty backed the men into the office and, in an act she hoped was perceived as humble, in that it involved a tiny degree of manual labor, took the initiative to close the door. David didn't quite know how to tell her that he had never closed the door in the thirty years he had had his own office at PMC.

"Who is she?" asked Margaret Campbell loudly, shocking David and Noah, who had forgotten she was there.

"Margaret," said David, with a hollow, nervous laugh. "You certainly remember the great star, Kitty Randolph."

"Who?"

Kitty put another smile on her face, but this one was clearly strained. She was not amused. "Please call me Kitty," she said. "Just Kitty."

"So you're a star." Margaret looked her up and down. "Have I seen you do dinner theater or something?"

Kitty's strained smile flickered. *Who did this little obnoxious hick think she was?* She let the thought out and was then able to ignore it.

"I think you're confusing me with someone," said the actress.

David leapt between the women, partially blocking their view of each other, and nervously said, "Ms. Randolph—er, *Kitty*—this is Margaret Campbell, the best-selling author."

"Really? Very nice to meet you, dear. I had no idea you were still writing."

His back was to her, but David knew Margaret Campbell well enough to know what she was thinking, and he felt her eyes piercing him en route to Kitty's fragile smile.

"Uh, yes, she is," said David. "Her most recent book will be released in two months. If you'd like, I can get you an advance copy . . ."

"That won't be necessary. I only read serious literature." She took a few steps away from the door, the better to keep all three of them in sight. "Mr. Carlyle, let me tell you why I'm here, although I suspect you can figure it out."

"Please," said David, wanting the meeting—no, the *day*; no, the *week*—over.

"I understand that this company will be publishing my ex-husband's autobiography. And I don't want that to happen. It would be . . . so traumatic for me."

"Yes, well . . ." David took forever to finish his thought, but finally gathered up the nerve to blurt out, "It's being printed, the publicity has started; I'm afraid it's out of my hands right now."

"That's too bad," she said. "Because there are arrangements we could make, if you happen to think of some way to stop its release."

"Such as?"

"Well, it's no secret that I'm not pleased with the publisher of the first three volumes of my autobiography. Possibly, we could reach an agreement for Palmer/Midkiff/Carlyle to publish volume four."

"Really?"

Again, she flashed that sweet, sweet smile. "Well, not if you're going to publish Quinn's book, of course. But if that didn't happen, I'd certainly have my literary agent contact you."

"So what you're saying," said Margaret, and David let out a moan, "is that if David kills the book, you'll screw him over."

Kitty Randolph no longer made an effort to smile. It was enough of an effort for her to keep the ugliness off her face. "Mr. Carlyle," she said, "Do you think we could talk without these other people present?"

David shook his head. "Given the circumstances, I think witnesses are appropriate."

She sniffed. "Very well, then. You will have your witnesses. And here is what they are going to hear: if Palmer/Midkiff/Carlyle releases my ex-husband's book of lies, I will own this company within the year." She locked her gaze on Margaret Campbell. "And the first thing we're going to do is cancel *her* contract."

"Let me ask you something," said Margaret, rising to the verbal challenge. "Have you ever been fictionalized?"

"Excuse me?"

"Look out," David whispered as an aside to Noah. "This could turn into *Godzilla Vs. Mothra.*"

"I mean," Margaret continued, "has anyone ever used you as a fictional character? Because I need a model for a nasty old bag who fucked her way to the top of Hollywood, and I think you'd be perfect."

"Now, Margaret," said David, trying again to squeeze between the two women in the office, which was growing smaller by the minute. "We don't need any unnecessary provocation."

"Oh, let the gnome speak," said Kitty haughtily.

"Really, both of you!" David was growing visibly upset. "Can't we deal with each other like adults?"

David was poised to say more—exactly what, he did not know—when his phone rang. Without a second thought, he leapt at the temporary reprieve and grabbed the receiver. No doubt he was about to have a long conversation. Even if it was his dry cleaner calling.

"David Carlyle," he said, and his expression immediately darkened. "Yes, Lindsay, yes . . . Thank you, I know . . . No, I don't think that's advisable. And in the future . . ." David glanced at Kitty Randolph from the corner of his eye and stopped himself. "Never mind. We'll talk about it later."

After he hung up, he pasted on a cheery smile and slowly turned to again face the glowering Kitty Randolph.

"I do apologize for the interruption, Ms. Randolph."

She waved him away. "I don't want your apologies, Mr. Carlyle. You know what I want. Since you aren't receptive, you'll be hearing from my lawyers."

"The First Amendment . . ." he began, but she stopped him.

"I don't give a flying fuck about the First Amendment, Carlyle. I care about something more important: my good name." She yanked the door open then stopped, slowly turning back to them. "Tell me why this story has to go public after all these decades. Why do you feel you have to humiliate me now?"

David took a deep breath to regain his composure before answering. "Because Quinn Scott has an interesting story to tell."

"Quinn Scott has nothing to tell," she said. "He's a has-been, and if it weren't for me, he'd have been a never-was. I made him, and I broke him, and I'll break him again, along with the rest of you. I'm only surprised he had the balls to do this."

"You made him do it," blurted Noah, and he instantly regretted it.

"Excuse me?" She began to close the door again.

"Never mind."

"No," she demanded. "Tell me what you meant."

Noah braced himself against a credenza. "He didn't want to write the book. But then you had to be petty, and cut Jimmy Beloit out of the dance sequence in *When the Stars Come Out*, and, well . . . this is the result."

She eyed him suspiciously. "What's your name again?"

"Noah. Noah Abraham."

"And how do you know this?"

Now that Noah was on Kitty's radar screen, he gained some bravery he could afford to lose when she was focused on everyone except him. He let go of the credenza, took a step forward, and said, "Because I collaborated on the book with Quinn."

She cocked her head and smiled, strangely appreciative for his confession. "So you're the ghostwriter."

"I'm the ghostwriter."

"I see. So this is just one big act of revenge by the homosexuals, is it?"

Shocked, the men looked at each other, jaws open. Even Margaret Campbell, still surly in her chair, seemed stunned.

"You *do* band together," Kitty continued. "You're loyal to each other, I'll give you that. So Homosexual Quinn is upset that Homosexual Jimmy is cut from a movie, so he works with Homosexual Noah to write a book out of vengeance, and then Homosexual David publishes it. And all the homosexuals pat each other on the back in congratulation because they've ganged up on an old woman. Very classy." She turned to Margaret and added, "And their lesbian friends seem eager to help, too."

Margaret was surprisingly calm. She even smiled as she said, "Old lady, if I were a lesbian, you would turn me straight."

Kitty Randolph again opened the door and angrily spat out, "You'll be hearing from my lawyers." Then she turned to the room for one parting shot, delivered directly to Noah.

"By the way, Jimmy Beloit was a very bad dancer."

And with that, she was gone.

It took perhaps thirty seconds for anyone to speak, but finally David said, "Well, that's that."

"That's that," Noah agreed. "She's not happy."

"We knew that going in," said David. "I just didn't think she'd be paying us a personal visit to express her displeasure. It somehow seemed more . . . frightening."

"Frightening," Noah agreed.

"And 'homosexual' this and that? A bit anachronistic, wouldn't you say?"

Noah shrugged. "She's a product of her times, I suppose."

David turned his attention to Margaret, still sitting in the corner. "You were quite well behaved. For you. Thank you."

"She's nothing. I could have destroyed her, if I wanted to. Actors . . . they can't keep up."

"Still, thank you for your support."

"Think nothing of it. I did it for one reason and one reason only. Because your ass belongs to *me*, David Carlyle. Not her, *me*. And don't you forget it."

"I'm sure you won't let me."

"Exactly." She turned her attention to Noah and said, "Now that the drama is over, would you excuse us? David and I have something very important to discuss, and I'm sure David doesn't want you to see him cry."

Several minutes later, as he passed through the still-vacant receptionist's office, Noah could have sworn he heard David cry out from pain from somewhere deep inside the PMC network of offices.

Chapter 10

Kitty had always been good at protecting her image. She was publicly graceful with her fans, as well as her fellow professionals who were within listening distance. As her husband, I was one of the few people privileged to see the real Kitty Randolph,

Even after our divorce, she was all-Kitty, all the time. Imagine my guilt and shame when, one Christmas Day, her nanny called me in tears to tell me that Kitty was passed out on her bed, and she had forgotten to buy even a single present from Santa for four-year-old Quinn Jr. . . .

The people at *Oprah* were not returning Lindsay Flynn's calls, and that made her unhappy. So far, she had Quinn Scott booked on most of the important talk shows, although, given various noncompete clauses, some of the appearances were weeks apart. Still, she really had her heart set on *Oprah*, and continued to hound her contact on the show.

In turn, her contact, who now seldom took her calls, updated Dean Henry at least every other day, and took great pains to assure him that Quinn Scott would never appear on the popular talk show. Dean seldom relayed those messages to Kitty; they just sent her into more spirals of rage. Given that her lawyers had washed their hands of the case, her husband was now her only target, so he tried his best to keep to himself, spending hours on the terrace getting high.

But *Oprah* was one thing; it was quite another keeping Quinn Scott off every other talk show in the country, and Dean watched helplessly as advance publicity for the book began to steamroll. Damn satellite feeds! At its most difficult and inconvenient, all Quinn Scott had to do was pop into any television studio in New York and he'd be beamed to Oklahoma City or Tampa or Portland . . . and it often wasn't even *that* hard. Too many interviewers were willing to make the trek out to the Hamptons to sit down with their subject, and he was only too happy to talk to them.

Gone was the taciturn Quinn Scott of legend. This new Quinn Scott was welcoming, gregarious, and, worst of all, a great interview. All that and the book wasn't even out yet. Dean Henry knew that Quinn was waiting to divulge the juiciest details until the publication date, and, the way things were shaping up, it wasn't going to be pretty.

For now, the public relations juggernaut was only mildly embarrassing to his wife. So she had a gay ex-husband. Big deal. Half the women in Hollywood had a gay ex-husband, or even a gay *current* husband. Dean could tell. He could feel their eyes following him at the A-list parties, where he and Kitty, the ultimate Hollywood power couple, were a staple. He knew that they were watching him because they thought he was one of their own, which annoyed him. *Just because a man is fastidious and a good dresser*, he thought, *doesn't make him gay*. It was such an ugly stereotype.

No, Kitty could survive the "gay ex-husband" gossip. Maybe she'd even be seen as stronger for it: having been victimized by Quinn Scott's deceptions, people would rush to sympathize with her. But that was the easy part.

What worried Dean was what Quinn *didn't* say in those prerelease interviews. He hinted, but he didn't say.

And as Dean shaved in the master bathroom, the television blaring nearby in the bedroom, he heard it again.

"I don't want to get into all the details before the book is on the shelves," Quinn Scott's gravelly voice said, "but let's just say that you'll see a side of Kitty Randolph you've never seen before."

The razor nicked Dean's chin and, as blood oozed, he let loose a stream of profanity.

Across the nation, hundreds of trucks rolled away from dozens of loading docks. As they left the distribution centers, each carried a special cargo: carton after carton of *When the Stars Come Out*, an autobiography by Quinn Scott, with Noah Abraham.

As the ground activity was underway, there was also activity of the electronic sort. Two days before the official launch date, pre-orders made *When the Stars Come Out* the top seller on Amazon, and the gay book club InsightOut had already reordered twice to meet the demands of its members.

In his office, David Carlyle read the unfavorable review of Quinn's book in *Publishers Weekly*, then tossed the magazine aside. It didn't matter. It didn't matter what *PW* wrote, or the *Times*, or the *Post*, or any other reviewer. He knew that this book was review proof.

David Carlyle was a happy man . . . so happy, in fact, that for the first time in weeks he could put the Kitty Randolph confrontation out of his head. *She* had been banished.

Or so he—and everyone else—thought in those first euphoric days.

* * *

Four days after the biography's official release date, Margaret Campbell—Grande Dame of the American Mystery, according to *People*—stood in Elaine's, the famed Manhattan restaurant and celebrity magnet, before 125 guests culled from society, journalism, and publishing, and raised her champagne flute, wishing it were a tumbler of her beloved bourbon.

"I don't know why I have this honor," she began, in a southern accent exaggerated slightly for the night. She had her own character to play, after all. "Actually, I do know. It's because I'm the best-selling novelist Palmer/Midkiff/Carlyle has ever published, and ever *will* publish." The crowd chuckled, as she knew they would.

She continued. "I have the honor tonight of introducing a man who has just set the publishing world on fire. Four days ago, his autobiography hit the bookshelves, and now it's hard to find a copy. He has shaken up Hollywood, and a lot of reputations are never going to be the same." The crowd laughed, knowingly and collectively.

"Ladies and gentlemen, on behalf of PMC I'm proud to introduce . . . Quinn Scott!"

A flurry of flashbulbs erupted as Quinn made his way through the applauding crowd, shaking hands as he pushed his way to the front of the room where he was greeted with a kiss on the cheek. She faded to the background as he motioned for silence. Once they complied, minutes later, he cleared his throat and began speaking.

"So this is a book party," he said, and the industry professionals gave his throw-away line a laugh, since they liked nothing better than self-reference. "I really have nothing to say that isn't in the book, except to thank you all for coming. This has been a remarkable experience." He took a step to the side, as if prepared to cede his spot at the center of the party, then stopped. "I must be getting old; it almost slipped my mind that I owe a few people some thanks."

His eyes found Jimmy in the crowd. "My companion, Jimmy Beloit, has meant the world to me for all these years. I hope this book does him justice, because it can't really be put into words. Oh, and thank you, Margaret Campbell, and, of course, David Carlyle and all the folks at PMC. Thank you."

He scanned the room, finally finding Noah, who stood against a wall with Bart. "And there's Noah Abraham over there. With my assistant, Bart Gustafson. Cute couple, aren't they?" Bart blushed. "You know, when Noah first approached me about writing a book I told him . . . well, I can't really repeat what I told him." Another laugh. "But I'm glad he kept after me and worked with me, because he was right. I *did* have stories to tell."

By now, the 125 guests—as well as most of the restaurant staff and Elaine herself—had heard the stories, even if they hadn't actually read the book. The minute the book was released even the most respectable newspapers had a field day with Quinn's revelations. Not really his homosexuality, which was considered tame in the days of tell all, tell all the time. As David and Noah had accurately predicted, that revelation generated next to no interest.

The buzz came, as they knew it would, from the stories about the real Kitty Randolph. Just days after the book's release date, she was already beginning to supplant Joan Crawford in the public mind as the epitome of the self-involved, wicked bitch. And the media couldn't get enough of it. When word came that even *The New York Times* was planning a story—tentatively titled, "In the Age of Confession, Can a Star Ever Keep Her Secrets?"—it was clear that the limits of media obsession with Quinn's book knew no bounds.

Quinn finished his brief remarks and was mobbed by the party guests, the literati and glitterati elbowing each other to get close to the elderly retired actor who had lived such a quiet existence for decades.

The book party had been covered by *Entertainment Tonight, Hollywood's Hottest Stories,* and even the morning news shows, not to mention *People, Us, New York,* and, of course, *Haute Manhattan.* A reporter and photographer were there from *The Advocate,* prepping a story on Quinn and his book for a late September cover. Photographs were posted on the *New York Social Diary* Web site, and then copied and posted by dozens of gay and literary blogs.

And Kitty Randolph had watched, read, and browsed every word and image.

She had tried—*oh, how she had tried*—to stop the Quinn Scott publicity machine, but she faced a rude awakening in the realization that, in the modern days of high-speed Internet connections and hungry mainstream journalists, her power was limited. She could threaten, but she couldn't control—especially with the media, the bloggers, and the public savoring every juicy detail of her life.

Now when she turned on the television or radio, she could be fairly certain to hear someone eventually describe her as a lush, a negligent mother, a control freak. It was almost too much to bear. Even the hosts on late-night talk shows—shows on which she had appeared so many times, and always with a smile on her face—were getting laughs at her expense. *Well, screw you, Leno! Johnny would have never treated me that way!*

When she found Dean in the kitchen one morning a few days after the book launch party, Kitty confessed her frustration.

"It's ridiculous! I can't believe that not only did someone publish Quinn's lies, but every entertainment show in the country is giving him airtime." She spun to face her husband. "And *you* can't seem to do a damn thing about it."

"Neither can you," he said, under his breath.

"What? What was that?"

"Nothing."

"There has to be some way we can stop this. We're just not thinking hard enough. We have to be creative."

The kitchen was silent for a few minutes as Kitty tried to be creative and Dean tried to be invisible. But when it was clear that she wasn't going to go away, he spoke.

"A counteroffensive."

"Excuse me?"

"You've got to get yourself out in front of the public as much as he's getting out there. But you'll be giving your side of the story."

"People *know* my side of the story," she protested. "I've been a star for half a century."

"They have short memories," he observed. "Right now, all they know about you is what's in Quinn's book."

She stewed about that briefly, then asked, "So what am I going to say to make them change their minds?"

Dean had already been idly pondering that question for a few days, so he was ready with an answer.

"Laugh it off."

"There is nothing funny about this."

He shook his head. "Here are your talking points: Quinn is an old man who's obviously in mental decline; he doesn't really remember those things he's written. Someone is taking advantage of him. They're trying to make a quick buck through the false memories of a doddering old man and your good name."

She put a hand on her hip. "And who are we claiming is manipulating Quinn?"

"He had a coauthor, didn't he? That sounds like a candidate for the prime suspect to me."

Kitty Randolph was not the sort of person who liked to give interviews. Too many things could go wrong in an interview. Yes, you could try to connect with the person asking the questions, and maybe they'd make you look good and overlook the occasional flub, but, more commonly, they'd use every bad camera angle and verbal tic.

Still, she had long ago accepted the fact that she had to give an interview every now and then, especially now that she was seventy years old. It was a cruel fact that, as rich and powerful as she had made herself, she had to trot the old bones in front of a camera at times just to prove that while she had perhaps aged a bit in her appearance, she had lost none of her allure.

But those interviews were on her terms, and she could take them or leave them as she saw fit. She was, after all, Kitty Randolph, and if anyone wanted to behold the essence that was Kitty Randolph, they had only to rent one of the almost two-dozen movies she had made between 1957 and 2004, or even watch one of her semiannual appearances on Q. J.'s ridiculous television show, *The Brothers-In-Law*. Other than that, fans could wait and hope to catch her whenever she felt the whim to acquiesce to an interview request. Which was at some undefined point between almost never and next-to-almost never.

That was, of course, when the interviews were on her own terms. But as in war, when even the most committed pacifist might take up arms in response to a first strike in order to protect life and liberty, Kitty had been forced into a series of interviews because Quinn, that gay ex-husband of hers, had fired the first shot. She could either let him and his smutty autobiography overwhelm her, or she could fight back. And through forty-nine years in the entertainment industry, no one and nothing had *ever* overwhelmed Kitty Randolph.

Which is why she was sitting in the sunroom, cameramen and lights coiled all around her, ruining the beauty she had created to surround her, as a crew member clipped a tiny wireless microphone to the lapel of her ecru Dior dress.

She smiled at the crew from *Hollywood's Hottest Stories*, one of the many syndicated entertainment shows that had long pursued her but, until now, had not met with success. When they actually looked at her, rather than at whatever it was that they should be doing, they smiled back. She now felt as if she had allies in this particular battle of the War Against Quinn. They would make her look good; they would take her side. Even the gay-looking man carrying a clipboard, the one in the baggy pink shirt and loose khakis, would choose Kitty over Quinn, and that's all that mattered.

A sunny blonde walked efficiently into the sunroom and extended her hand.

"Ms. Randolph," she said, "I'm Mary Hoyt. I'll be conducting the interview with you and your husband."

Kitty smiled and took her hand gracefully. "It's a pleasure, Mary. And please call me Kitty. I'm looking forward to . . ." She stopped, Mary Hoyt's words finally hitting home. "Did you say me and *my husband?*"

"Yes," chirped Mary. "Mr. Henry."

Kitty's smile faltered for a moment, until she remembered that everyone was supposed to love her and, *damn it*, they would love her.

"Dear," she said, as sweetly as possible, "I'm afraid Mr. Henry doesn't give interviews. He's an agent, you see, not an actor. He's more a . . . 'behind the scenes' type."

The blonde turned away and called to the gay-looking man in the pink shirt.

"Alan, didn't you tell me that Dean Henry would be sitting in on the interview?"

"All confirmed," he said. "Ms. Randolph and Mr. Henry will be interviewed together."

Kitty gently touched Mary's wrist, pulling her closer. She was losing control, and she didn't like that . . . although she couldn't let the interview team know that, of course.

"Mary," she said, "Who said that Dean would consent to be interviewed?"

"I did," said her husband, as he strolled into the sunroom.

Kitty stood. "Darling, could I speak to you for a moment?"

Dean correctly guessed that it would not be a pleasant experience.

When they retreated to the kitchen, out of earshot of the crew, she spat out, "What the hell are you doing?"

"Relax," he said, trying his best to not only be casual, but also not show fear. "I'm doing this for you. Look, you've got an ex-husband problem, so how better to combat that than with your current, loving, heterosexual husband, sitting next to you for the interview? It's perfect."

"It's ridiculous," she said, affecting a pout. "And I don't want you to do it. You come off as . . ." She paused and looked for the right word. "You come off as too doting."

That's not what she wanted to say. What she wanted to say was that, compared to the masculine Quinn Scott, her fifth—but third official—husband came off as a big wimp who had only married the old lady for her money. And not only that, but she had seen him on videotape before, and on camera he came off as downright effeminate. She didn't need the world to think that she was in the habit of marrying every homosexual who came along. The entertainment industry had enough women carrying that reputation around.

But Dean, unable to read her mind and unwilling to try, simply smiled and said, "It will be fine, Kitty. And in any event, it's too late to back out. *Hollywood's Hottest Stories* is already promoting this interview. How will it look if I don't appear?"

Significantly more heterosexual, she thought, but actually said, "Dear, this is *my* side of the camera we're talking about. You know the agenting side, and I know the acting side. And I think we should stick to what we know."

Dean smiled at her and walked away.

"Where are you going?" she demanded, as she followed him out of the kitchen.

"To the interview, of course," he replied over his shoulder.

"Didn't you hear a damn word I said?!" Kitty stopped, suddenly appalled, as she realized that she had not only walked into the foyer, she had walked directly into Mary Hoyt at the crew from *HHS,* who were waiting for her outside the sunroom.

Instinct took over. She tittered and, speaking directly to Mary, whom she had quickly sized up as her most important prospective ally, said, "Please excuse my language. I don't know how this happened, but a mouse found its way into the kitchen and I was trying to get Dean to kill it." She took a few steps toward Dean and took his cheek in one hand, squeezing, she knew, a bit too hard. "Dean is such a darling he wouldn't even kill it. Isn't that right, darling?"

"Mmmph," he mumbled.

"I got upset, and I apologize for my language. I'm just . . . so frightened of mice!"

Her nails pushed just a bit deeper into Dean's cheek and, again, he mumbled an agreement. She finally let go of him.

"In any event, I'll just call an exterminator after the interview."

"I can kill it for you," said the gay-looking guy in the pink shirt.

Kitty flashed him that famous smile and didn't commit. It was easier that way.

Watching *HHS* a few days later, as Kitty Randolph and Dean Henry began their interview with Mary Hoyt, Quinn said, "I'm surprised she let him on camera."

"Why is his cheek so red?" asked Noah, but no one answered.

"So," Mary said on screen, "for the past few weeks America has been buzzing about the autobiography written by your former husband, Quinn Scott."

"Can I stop you for a second, Mary?" Kitty didn't wait for an answer. "I was probably old enough to know better when I married Quinn, but in those days, well . . . we just didn't know enough about gay people. Not like today, when they're all over the place." She laughed a laugh that said "just kidding." "And I felt bad—*deceived*, even—to learn that Quinn had taken advantage of me like that."

"Huh?" said Quinn, but Jimmy shushed him.

"My heart was broken, Mary, and it took me a long time to recover. However, you may not know this about me, because I come off as delicate and vulnerable, but I'm a survivor. When Quinn walked out I told myself, 'I will survive.' And I did."

The blonde interviewer nodded sympathetically, then changed course.

"So tell me," she said. "Your ex-husband's autobiography paints a picture of Kitty Randolph that is anything but delicate and vulnerable. He claims that you're manipulative, greedy, and, well, 'the "B" word.' Do you care to comment?"

"The 'B' word?" Kitty asked.

"Bitch," said Dean from his perch at her side.

"Oh . . . Uh, I guess all I can say is this. Quinn is the person who had sex with men in our bed while we were married. Quinn is the person who tricked me into marrying him, even though he was a homosexual. And, after all these years, Quinn is the person who wrote all those nasty words." Tears appeared in her eyes and her voice cracked. "I was faithful, I married him because I was in love, and, even thirty-six years after we divorced, I have been discreet and not attacked him." She looked straight into the camera, her eyes still glistening. "Now you tell me which one of us is manipulative, greedy, and the 'B' word."

"Any other thoughts?" asked Mary, as she handed Kitty a tissue. "Are you angry at him?"

"No," she said, dabbing at her eyes. "No, despite everything, I'm not angry at Quinn. Because I don't remember things the way he does. In fact, I'm quite certain that some of this never happened."

"Really?"

"Quinn hasn't been well," she said. "I haven't seen him, but mutual friends tell me that the last few years have been hard on him."

"What the fuck is she talking about?" asked Quinn, staring at the box.

"And I really, truly think that he's being manipulated into saying all these horrible things, all in the interest of making money for other people."

"Other people?" asked Mary. "Who?"

"Oh, I don't know, and really shouldn't speculate. Maybe his publisher . . . maybe his writing collaborator . . . who knows?"

Noah pointed to himself. "Me?"

Bart nudged him and whispered, "Manipulator."

"Interesting," said Mary, and she did, in fact, look interested. Which annoyed the hell out of Quinn.

"Let me add something," said Dean, tilting his body slightly toward the camera.

"That's her husband?" asked Jimmy. "Is *he* gay, too?"

"*My* gaydar just went off," Noah agreed.

On screen, Dean continued. "I really want your audience to

know what a great woman I'm married to, Mary. She's just as beautiful now as she was when I first laid eyes on her as a small boy, watching that screen as she stole the picture from Judy Garland in *The Mabel Normand Story*."

"That was the gayest sentence I've ever heard," said Jimmy.

"And can we laugh at the fact that he just indirectly mentioned how much older she is than him?" added Bart.

"Oh, yes," said Quinn. "I wish you would. Because if she's going to beat the crap out of anyone more than she's beat it out of me, that would be Dean Henry."

Kitty turned off the television set and turned to her husband.

"And *that*, dear, is precisely why I don't want you to do interviews."

"I thought it went well," said Dean.

"You thought it went well? Which part, Dean? The part where you told the camera that you had a schoolboy crush on me? Or the part where you came off like my *second* gay husband?"

Dean didn't respond. It was safer that way.

Kitty stood and began pacing the room. "So far, this counter-offensive isn't working. He goes on TV, I go on TV. He goes back on TV, I go back on TV. Back and forth, back and forth. Sometimes I think that all we're doing is giving him more publicity." She threw herself down in an armchair and the room fell into a tense silence.

After several minutes, Dean found the courage to speak.

"Maybe we should give up."

Her eyes flashed and nostrils flared. "Give up?!"

"He probably would have dropped from the radar weeks ago if we'd ignored him."

"Darling, have you forgotten that this isn't about Quinn Scott? This is about *my* reputation. And I am *not* going to ignore him."

Dean sighed and slumped a bit deeper into his chair.

A few days later, Quinn took a phone call. When he cradled the phone, he looked at Jimmy and, shaking his head, said, "Well, isn't that the damnedest thing."

"What's that?"

"That was the guy who produces Q. J.'s show. They were having a meeting this morning and thought . . . well, they asked me to be a guest star." He slowly stroked his chin. "Sixteen years without work, and now they want me."

"Do you think Q. J. . . . ?"

"Doubt it. Maybe, but I just don't think the boy has that much pull. Not to mention the fact that, remember, we've barely had any contact since he was a toddler. I can't imagine Q. J. rallying to my defense right now, after all these years."

"So what did you tell him?" Jimmy asked.

"Hell, yes, I'm going to do it. It'll be wonderful to be on a sound-stage again."

"I'm surprised Kitty didn't try to stop it."

"Me, too. Me, too. She must not know about it yet." He sighed and sank back on the couch. "But when she finds out . . ." The men looked at each other and smiled. Then they burst into sustained laughter.

"She'll go wild," said Quinn, when he finally caught his breath. "She'll be bouncing off the walls. Katherine and that little mouse of a husband of hers. I wish I could be there to see it."

"But you just know she's going to try to stop it," said Jimmy, a note of sobriety in his voice. "You remember what nightmares she made out of your last few roles."

"I remember." Quinn shook his head. "Poor Angela Lansbury. But . . . look, Jimmy. My name is hot right now and Q. J. is my son, so the producers are playing it smart and looking for ratings. That's all. If Katherine fucks with me, that means she fucks with *The Brothers-in-Law*. And *that* means she fucks with Q. J. Trust me on one thing: Katherine will never hurt him or his career. Never. Say what you will about her—and I have—but she was always a classy actress, and for her to make guest appearances on Q. J.'s show must be so humiliating for her that it proves she has great maternal love."

"If you say so."

"I know so." Quinn began the lengthy process of lifting himself from the chair as he added, "This little guest spot, with my son, will be my moment of triumph, and there isn't a damn thing Katherine dares do about it."

*   *   *

Mark R. Cassidy had never intended to become a television producer. In fact, his aspirations had once been far more modest. Reared on a steady diet of *The Match Game, Password, To Tell the Truth, Hollywood Squares,* and as many other celebrity-driven game shows as he could take in, Mark R. Cassidy was going to be a famous celebrity game-show contestant. Oh, there would be other facets to his career, of course, such as guest appearances with Merv Griffin and Mike Douglas, but mostly he was going to be known as that funny guy in the center square. And it couldn't get any better than that for Mark R. Cassidy.

But reality—in the form of rent, groceries, and, increasingly, bar tabs—reared its ugly head, and Mark had to face facts. Without preexisting celebrity of some sort, he really had no idea how he was going to get the plum position sitting next to Brett Somers. And, beyond that, he had no idea how to develop preexisting celebrity. So without a way to get from Point A to Point B, which would eventually lead to Point C—Point C being the land of Wink Martindale, Peter Marshall, and Gene Rayburn—he had no choice but to get a real job while he waited for the fates to align. It was a tough blow for a twenty-three-year-old, but no one said life would be easy.

Twenty-two years later the fates had still not aligned, and Mark R. Cassidy knew that destiny had passed him by. Now he was a fat forty-five-year-old, prematurely embittered by the collapse of his unrealistic dream. Now he made his living spending sixty-hour weeks overseeing second-tier actors through their paces on a string of forgettable situation comedies. *Hal & Shari . . . The Doug Stone Show . . . Leaded & Unleaded . . . T. J. & Becks . . .* and, most recently, *The Brothers-in-Law,* which he not incorrectly considered the nadir of a mediocre career.

Mark R. Cassidy now knew a few things he had not learned from Charlie Weaver and Charles Nelson Reilly, and that made him sad as well as bitter. He now knew he would never win an Emmy; he would never be known outside the lower rungs of his industry; he would never find workplace satisfaction; and he would never, *ever,* play a round of *Celebrity Jeopardy.*

And so, embittered, he did what bitter people have done and will always do through eternity: he took it out on his subordinates. If Mark R. Cassidy was going to be miserable, *everyone* was going to be miserable. And he had his own unique way to spread the misery.

The "MRC Memo" had become a reviled standard on his sets. The MRC Memo criticized everything from the temperature of the coffee to horsing around by the writers—and, oh, how he hated the writers—to untimely pregnancies, and while he had never actually recommended an abortion, he hoped his pregnant and impregnable starlets would be smart enough to read between the lines. His dictates were always reviled by cast and crew alike, and they were also almost always ignored, but they achieved their desired effect, because almost everyone on a Mark R. Cassidy set was as miserable as Mark R. Cassidy.

And that was even *before* the Monday morning staff meetings, which he had made so singularly unpleasant that, in anticipation of them, few people were able to have an even slightly pleasant Sunday. Mark R. Cassidy had even managed to spoil the Lord's Day, and that made him slightly happy, in his own miserable, bitter way.

His bosses—those seldom-seen, seldom-heard-from suits at Porch-Star International—were aware of the situation, and occasionally even paid a friendly call to gently suggest that he ease up whenever incipient crew mutiny was detected. But for all his flaws and general unpleasantness, Mark R. Cassidy was delivering them a product that was, for all its on-screen mediocrity and off-screen unpleasantness, inexplicably popular and, more importantly, profitable. So with an eye on the bottom line and an "if it ain't broke, don't fix it" attitude, PorchStar made a conscious decision not to fix it.

The only people involved in *The Brothers-in-Law* who usually escaped his wrath and contempt were the actors. That was because Mark R. Cassidy knew that he could drive a set designer or costumer out of the industry, but actors . . . well, sometimes they could rise above their mediocrity. The problem, as he saw it, was that in the entertainment industry one never could predict which ditzy actress in a walk-on role was going to be next year's breakout star. For that reason—and that reason alone—he generally treated his actors with slightly more sensitivity.

Although it tried him at times. Especially when that actor was Q. J. Scott.

Take the incident two weeks earlier, during the taping of a Very Special Episode. In the scene, Q. J.'s character had just learned of the death of his beloved third-grade teacher, the woman who had turned his young life around after catching him cheating on a test.

As the camera zoomed in, framing Q. J.'s face in an extreme close-up, MRC felt that something was wrong, but he couldn't quite put his finger on what that something was. Then, as Q. J.'s eyes welled, he figured it out.

"What the fuck is that?" he hissed at the cameraman.

"What? Oh . . . the brown thing?"

"Yeah, the brown thing."

"I dunno."

Together, they stared into the monitor, watching a small brown . . . *thing* slide slowly down Q. J.'s cheek.

"Cut!"

MRC stormed across the set as the director looked around, wondering who had stolen his thunder and yelled "cut." When he was inches from Q. J.'s face he took one finger and, very gently, he plucked the offending brown thing off the actor's damp cheek.

A contact lens. A brown contact lens. A *fucking brown contact lens*!

MRC looked into Q. J.'s left eye. It was the normal hazel color, favoring green. He looked into his right eye. It was chocolate brown.

He looked again. Left: hazel. Right: brown.

Fingertip: brown.

"When did you start wearing contact lenses?"

"The brown ones?" The actor smiled, then noticed the lens on MRC's fingertip. "Oh, did I cry that one out? Sorry . . . they're new. I'm not used to them yet."

"They're new?" He scowled. "How new?"

"Three days ago."

MRC did the math in his head. If Q. J. had changed his eye color three days earlier, that meant that it had changed only two episodes after the episode where *the fucking script was built around his fucking hazel eyes!*

Not to mention the fact that it just wouldn't do for an actor to change physical characteristics like that. It wasn't done. Hair style? Maybe. Slight weight gain or loss? Maybe. Eye color? No way. You might as well just go out and get pregnant. Or lop off a limb.

So MRC did what any good producer would do. He flicked the offending lens to the floor, then reached for Q. J.'s right eye.

Long story short and less painful to relate: it made for a long night of shooting.

But still, MRC thought he had done an admirable job keeping his cool. Any common crew member would have been summarily fired—summarily *executed*, if there were any justice in the world—but he had allowed Q. J. Scott's idiotic contact lens gaffe pass with only expressed unhappiness and minor retinal discomfort. Mark R. Cassidy did not have a tantrum, and he did not scream, and he thought he had been extremely diplomatic toward the actor. Of course, the director and the cameraman—both of whom should have caught the problem instead of him—were out of a job before the week was over, but that was show biz.

Yes, Q. J. deserved punishment. But MRC kept in mind three things: (1) despite his pedestrian acting skills, Q. J. was a two-time People's Choice Award winner; (2) he was an actor, and therefore—given the inexplicable whims of the public—he could be the next Brad Pitt before MRC had the chance to kick him off the sound-stage; and, most importantly, (3) his mother was Kitty Randolph, and it was probably unwise to threaten harm to the progeny of Kitty Randolph. Because even though they hadn't been put to much productive use in recent years, Mark R. Cassidy still valued his testicles.

"Here's the thing, Q. J.," he explained to the actor, when shooting on that Very Special Episode ended at 3:47 AM that night and the cast and crew were numb with exhaustion. "I want you to understand why you can't have brown eyes."

"But I was wearing the cream sweater," he said. "I thought it would be a good contrast."

MRC swallowed his sigh, and thought that color-coordinated morons were possibly even more dangerous than regular morons.

"You know why thirteen million Americans tune in to *The Brothers-in-Law* each week? Because we give them consistency. Week in and week out, they know what to expect. Jason says this, you say something else, and we wrap it all up in twenty-two minutes. Twenty-two minutes, a few laughs, a dab of poignancy every now and then . . . The audience is happy, I'm happy, the suits at PorchStar are happy, Proctor & Gamble is happy. End of story. So when you suddenly have brown eyes, well, it screws up that consistency. It throws off the formula. Understand?"

Q. J. nodded, but, looking into his now-hazel eyes, MRC knew that his words had flown right over the actor's head. And he made a mental note to check Q. J. Scott's eyes every shooting day in the future.

Actors—especially actors whose mothers were not only celluloid icons, but also moguls in their own right—were one thing. Writers were quite another, and MRC was not alone in that opinion within the industry. With rare exception, he considered them expendable and interchangeable, and on a show of the caliber of *The Brothers-in-Law*, hardly worthy of their screen credit. Teenagers could—and, he thought, sometimes did—write this insipid crap.

Which is why MRC got a secret thrill when the call came from Stanley Roth, the show's almost-never-seen executive producer, which in this case meant he was the financial lifeline to PorchStar International, not a *real* producer. The call came late on a Monday morning, shortly after a crew meeting in which he had torn several new orifices in a production assistant.

Stan Roth got straight to the point. "Directive from the top. Mark. Episode 92 needs a major rewrite."

MRC allowed a smile to cross his lips, and was surprised it didn't hurt. Episode 92 was scheduled to shoot in two weeks, and a major rewrite would infuriate the writing team. Better yet, depending on the extent of the rewrites, this "directive from the top" could have a ripple effect, requiring subsequent scripts to be rewritten.

Still, he had to ask: "Why?"

"We want to take advantage of the Quinn Scott story."

"Who?"

"Quinn Scott. Q. J.'s father?"

MRC thought about that. Something made him uneasy. "Isn't that the fag?"

Stan Roth cleared his throat. "If you're asking if Quinn Scott is the *gay gentleman* you've been hearing about lately, then the answer is yes."

"So you want me to do some stunt-casting here?"

"Think of it this way," said Roth. "Forty years ago or so, Quinn Scott was on the screen with John Wayne . . . Sal Mineo . . . Bette Davis, I think. This isn't stunt-casting; it's his comeback. So we put him in the show and publicize the hell out of it. 'Special Guest Appearance!' 'Quinn Scott's Comeback!' 'Philly Cop Back on the Small Screen!' "

"Whatever you want to call it, Stan."

"We can milk this for months, Mark. But make sure the writers make the episode self-supporting, just in case the Quinn Scott phenomenon looks like it's going to die and we have to rush it on the air out of sequence."

"So we're casting this guy for a Very Special Episode, all because he's got a book out." The idea clearly annoyed MRC, and in this case he didn't care if he showed that side of his personality to Stan Roth.

"And," the executive producer added, "he's the father of Q. J. Scott. Don't forget that. We already have our hook."

"That also makes him Kitty Randolph's ex-husband."

"That's for PorchStar to worry about."

MRC was about to respond when the line went dead. And there was only one thing to do after being so abruptly dismissed by Stan Roth of PorchStar International, so he got on the phone with head writer Denny Levinson and told him that Episode 92 needed a total overhaul to accommodate an appearance by Quinn Scott.

And making a twenty-seven-year-old head writer cry in frustration brought another smile to MRC's lips. Two smiles in one day; it was almost too much to bear. It was almost—dare he think it?—better than being the center square.

Now he just had to hope that the father wasn't as big an idiot as the son. And Mark R. Cassidy didn't hold out much hope for that.

Chapter 11

Television is tough. Don't let anyone tell you otherwise. After three and a half seasons in *Philly Cop*, that is one of the few things I know for certain.

Even though I was in my early thirties for most of that experience, it was probably all that running and jumping over rooftops that ruined my hip . . .

Chris Cason couldn't believe his good fortune.

Only a few years earlier, he had been living in Tacoma, working at a Barnes & Noble, and only daring to dream of the day when his name would be as well known as those thousands of authors mocking him from their perches on the bookshelves. Over the years he had met many of the people attached to those names—Janet Evanovich, Glenda Vassar, Diana Gabaldon, Andrew Westlake, Margaret Campbell, and many more—and yet, somehow, he had still not been able to break into their league.

Life in Tacoma had been just that unfair, he thought, because, as an avid and discerning reader, he knew that his novel-in-progress was a genre-busting diamond in the rough, and not all that rough, at that. *Ant*—a horror/erotica hybrid with a neo-Marxist point of view about a race of mutant Ant-Women and the scientist who is their creator, oppressor, and, yes, lover—was admittedly in need of some trimming, but Chris Cason was convinced that very few passages in its 624 pages would have to go, and even those could be recycled for the sequel.

The problem was, how does an aspiring writer convince a publisher to read it, when the aspiring writer lives in Tacoma? And the answer, of course, was to move to New York.

So he quit his job at Barnes & Noble, packed up his Chevy Cavalier, and was ready to drive east—Washington State to New York State, nonstop if necessary—until fate intervened. In this case, fate came in the form of a friend of a friend, from whom he learned of an opening as a production assistant in the entertainment industry. Reasoning that *Ant* would make as good a movie as a book—or, better yet, a *miniseries!*—and also reasoning that the Cavalier was much more likely to make it to LA than New York, Chris Cason headed straight south.

The Cavalier made it to northern California. Undaunted, Chris made it the rest of the way to Los Angeles, and was soon working for PorchStar International, an entertainment conglomerate that produced a wide variety of mediocre television shows, all of which could have benefited from Chris Cason's artistic input if he was inclined to stoop to that level.

Now, by day, he roped off streets for outdoor shoots and delivered scripts to actors and, yes, he also got yelled at. A lot. But by night, he had transformed *Ant* into a 300-page, five-hour screenplay, and that was what was important. Every small-time actor, director, writer, or crew member who had ever yelled at him—which constituted pretty much everyone he had ever worked for—would be sorry when *Ant* made Chris Cason the new Spielberg . . . no, *bigger*: the new *Orson Welles*.

For now, though, he would bide his time and be patient. Because, like the Ant-Women, vengeance would eventually be his.

In the meantime, there were people to meet and contacts to make. And little did the suits at PorchStar International know, but they had just ordered him out to LAX where he would, in the process, make his biggest contact yet.

He stood outside the arrivals gate, straining his neck and hoping he would recognize him. And, yes, there he was, still familiar from his younger days, and looking quite similar to the photo on his book jacket. It was, indeed, Quinn Scott, slowly walking toward him with his entourage.

Wait . . . entourage? For some reason, Chris had not expected an entourage. The goal was to talk to Quinn Scott one on one, mano a mano. He didn't want to compete with those . . . those . . . *other* people. But after thinking about it for a few seconds—ever the thinker, his brain *whirred* into action faster even than the brain of an Ant-Woman—he decided that maybe the entourage was a good thing. One might be his future agent, another his future publicist . . . Quinn Scott and his crew might be the goldmine that Chris Cason had waited for so patiently for too many years.

For his part, Quinn Scott—grumpy and limping slightly after five hours in an airplane—looked down the corridor at the edgy, Brillo-haired thirtysomething man waving at him and, turning to Jimmy, said:

"What the fuck is that?"

"That," Jimmy replied, not much happier than Quinn, "is probably your ride."

"Fuck."

"Mr. Scott?!" asked the man, and without waiting for an answer added, "I'm Chris Cason. On behalf of PorchStar International, welcome to Los Angeles."

Quinn grunted. When Chris proffered his hand, the actor passed him his carry-on bag.

"Uh . . . yes." Chris looked at the bag in his outstretched hand. "I'll, uh, carry this for you."

It was not quite the reception Quinn had expected. This moron was clearly nothing more than a studio gofer, and Quinn had anticipated an executive. Maybe even one of the actors, although he silently hoped the reunion with his son would be private and brief. Very, very brief.

Things had clearly changed in his decades away. Once he was the star, and got the star treatment. Now even his newfound celebrity didn't warrant an executive, and that realization annoyed him. He supposed he should have been grateful that the studio had even sent a car, but . . . he wasn't.

In one sense, it was good that Quinn had been largely retired for the previous three decades, because—as the airline crew and many of his fellow passengers could testify—he was a bad traveler. He was too impatient to sit in one place for hours at a time, and the hip made extended trips uncomfortable. Even when he was young and working, he regularly passed on roles if he'd have to travel a great distance. Flying cross country was still a great imposition to him, one he was only willing to undertake to prove to the world that, contrary to his ex-wife's assertions, he was still mentally sharp and every bit a skilled actor.

The next time, though, they were going to have to come to him. Even if they had to move the entire damn show to New York to do it.

Their SUV fought traffic along freeways long-forgotten to Quinn. He looked out the window, only vaguely curious about their direction or how long it would take them. Next to him, Jimmy sat and stared out the opposite window, thinking quite different thoughts.

Jimmy Beloit prided himself on never looking back, but—as familiar sights came into view, then disappeared behind them at a slow thirty miles per hour—he couldn't help but feel the slightest twinge of nostalgia, the memories of a career cut abruptly short fighting their way to the surface. He wondered what would have happened if he had never met Quinn, and therefore had never been cast out of this Entertainment Eden. Would his career trajectory have played out as he planned, from dancer to actor? He knew that was a question without an answer, but he couldn't keep it out of his mind.

"Can you believe we used to live here?" he asked.

Quinn looked out at the bumper-to-bumper traffic on the 405. "What were we thinking?"

The four passengers—Quinn, Jimmy, Noah, and Bart—had been content to trust their driver, but all of them were beginning to have the vague sense that the trip to the hotel was taking far too long. If they had known some of the daydreams occupying Chris Cason's brain—for instance, kidnapping them until Quinn agreed to help bring *Ant* to the screen—they would have been even more concerned.

But they weren't being kidnapped. They just weren't being taken straight to their hotel. Quinn was the first to notice that something was wrong.

"Why are we almost to Encino?" he asked. "You missed our exit. The Bel Age is in West Hollywood. Off of Santa Monica."

"Construction," said the driver, as if that were a reasonable explanation.

Quinn grumbled, but sat back in his seat. He really didn't know Los Angeles anymore, so even though he remained convinced they were lost, he opted not to be a backseat driver.

Eventually, Chris looped east finally and, a few miles later, exited the 101. After quick left and right turns, he pulled up to a gate.

"Where the hell are we?" asked Quinn, peering through the window at a row of warehouses sitting beyond the gate, protected by fencing and two lonely shacks, each populated by one lonely security guard just waiting for a reason to raise the gate or lower the gate or otherwise do something besides fidget.

Chris allowed himself a smug smile. He did, after all, know something the big actor guy did not. "Welcome to Lilliane Studios. Home of *The Brothers-in-Law*."

"Huh?" Quinn squinted, and realized that what he thought were warehouses were actually a string of soundstages lining the paved lot. The security guards each leaned forward, staring back at Quinn and the SUV.

Chris turned the key and the engine came back to life. He eased the vehicle forward a few feet to the nearest guard shack and, when the guard's head was even with his window, said, in his most authoritative voice, "Chris Cason."

"ID?"

"Of course." He flashed a laminated card, and was rewarded when the guard pushed a button. The gate slowly began to open.

"I don't want to see the studio," said Quinn, in a tone of voice that Jimmy had learned to avoid over the past thirty-six years. "I want to go to the hotel."

The driver ignored him and drove. When he reached the fifth building—more of a Quonset hut than a building, Noah thought— he again pulled to a stop.

"Okay!" Chris said brightly. "Let's get out!"

"No."

With a sigh and a nod of his head, Chris opened his door and climbed down from the vehicle. Inside, Quinn turned to Jimmy and said, "I just want to go to the hotel. Is that so fucking hard to understand?"

"Of course not," said Jimmy. "But maybe if we humor him . . ."

Quinn's response was to fold his arms across his chest. He was absolutely not going anywhere.

"Uh, I don't want to cause any problems," said Noah from the backseat, "but my legs are cramping. Can we get out for just a minute?"

Quinn exhaled sharply, unfolded his arms, and finally opened his door. As he descended carefully from the vehicle, Chris Cason appeared, offering him a steadying hand, which Quinn took reluctantly.

"Long time since you've been on a studio lot?" asked the younger man.

Now on the ground, Quinn abruptly dropped Chris's hand. "Should've been one day longer."

When the others had also reached ground level, Chris said, "The producers wanted to have you take a look at the soundstage before we start rehearsing."

Quinn wasn't happy. "Which is why I'm here."

"Which is why you're here." With that, the production assistant began walking toward the double doors leading into the building, and the others followed at a slower pace, taking their cue from Quinn.

Inside, Chris turned on a bank of lights, dimly illuminating the spacious interior. The main set, surrounded by three false walls, was positioned in the middle of the room, opposite a tier of bleachers which would accommodate a live audience when it was time to tape.

Quinn stood, hands on hips, drinking it in.

"Much different than it used to be?" asked Bart.

Quinn thought about it. Yes, it was different, but someone who had only been on a soundstage a handful of times in the past thirty-odd years expected change. Since the answer was self-evident, he chose not to speak, leaving Bart's question hanging, unanswered, in midair.

He looked at the set, carefully designed for maximum mobility and minimal visual clutter. The living room of *The Brothers-in-Law* looked pretty much like every living room in sitcom land: forgettable couch; forgettable armchairs; forgettable china cabinet displaying forgettable fake china. The front door was stage left; the fake stairs to the nonexistent second floor were stage center; the entrance to the kitchen—make that, the kitchen *set*—was stage right.

Quinn felt immediately comfortable with the familiarity surrounding him, even though he had never been a situation comedy actor and had only seen his son's show three or four times. His sets had been from the world of action, and a lot of it was filmed outdoors. But the soundstage of *The Brothers-in-Law* was familiar in a different sense, in the sense it would feel familiar to anyone who had ever spent more than a day watching network television. All those generic television living rooms looked alike.

The others watched Quinn, wondering what pangs of nostalgia he was feeling, and completely unaware he was not feeling nostalgia . . . at least not in the truest sense. He was thinking what any other television viewer would have felt at that same moment: as if he had walked into the living room of every situation comedy ever made.

Somewhere in the dark periphery of the room they heard faint footsteps approach, and then a man's silhouette appeared, backlit in the doorway. Slowly they turned, one by one, and tried to see who the new arrival was, but they saw only his shape.

"Can we help you?" asked Chris Cason, the closest thing to an official presence in the room.

The man was silent for a moment. Until he said . . .

"Dad?"

Voices fell silent—even the echoes fell silent—as they looked at the silhouette that was Quinn Scott's son.

He took a few steps toward them and then there—in the flesh, dimly lit by the overhead lighting—stood two-time People's Choice Award-winner Q. J. Scott, looking nothing whatsoever like his father, but every bit like his on-screen image.

"Q. J.?" Quinn faltered briefly. Awkwardly, he continued. "It's been a long time."

The son took a half-dozen rapid steps until he reached his father and embraced him. At that exact moment, light suddenly flooded the room, and there was a scattering of applause at the emotional moment from the men and women who had, to that point, been hidden in the shadows. Chris Cason smiled, knowing that he had done his task—delivering the package—very well indeed.

As the others made themselves known, emerging from the shadows to applaud the father and son reunion, Quinn began to pull back, but as he struggled to disengage, Q. J. gripped his father all the harder.

And then came the flashes.

"What the fuck?" snarled Quinn, as he finally pulled clear of his son. He scanned the room, confused.

Q. J. grinned. "It's a very special moment, Dad."

Quinn shook his head, not quite sure if he was supposed to be angry. "Photographers?"

"We sold the exclusive, Mr. Scott," said the portly man who was approaching with a manner oozing with whatever the opposite of friendliness would be. Despite the man's unpleasant manner, Quinn was afraid he, too, wanted a hug, so he took two steps back. "I am Mark R. Cassidy, associate producer of *The Brothers-in-Law*. Welcome to the set."

"Yeah, I'm thrilled," said Quinn, who was now certain that he didn't mean it. "So you sold the photos?"

MRC forced a smile, which came out as something like a modified frown. "We're working with a reputable industry photographer, Quinn—can I call you Quinn? Anyway, our *reputable* photographer will only work with *reputable* media outlets. It's all on the up-and-up."

Quinn didn't like anything about this man, which is why he found himself reluctantly saying: "I was having a private moment with my son."

Off to the side, Q. J. rolled his eyes and said, "Dad, geez! You're embarrassing me! We do this all the time when Mama visits the set!"

"What, with the photographers and everything?"

"Well . . . no, not always. But sometimes. And then I hug her."

Quinn rolled his eyes. "Save the hugs for your mother. She needs them more than I do."

The photographer sidled around the room, hunting for a good angle. The Scotts were not cooperating, doing their own dance of estrangement. And every time he did get a good angle, that bastard Mark R. Cassidy was in the shot. The photographer wondered if Cassidy remembered firing him from the set of *The Doug Stone Show*. Probably not; the fat fuck had fired thousands of people, and most of them were grateful just to be away from him. He found a particularly bad angle at which to capture MRC's image and popped off a dozen shots in rapid succession.

Q. J. spotted a tall, balding man standing near the set and waved him over. As he approached, Q. J. said, "Dad, this is Bernie Bernstein. He's our director."

"Nice to meet you, Mr. Scott," said Bernie, taking his hand. "Welcome to *The Brothers-in-Law*. I'm looking forward to working with you."

Quinn shrugged. "Thanks. I'm sure it's an . . . uh . . . experience working here."

Bernie's smile dropped, and something unspoken passed between them as he agreed. "Yes, it's always an experience."

Turning back to his son, Quinn asked, "So is there anyone else I have to meet?"

"Well, there's . . ."

"Good. Now I want to go back to the hotel."

* * *

"So then the Ant-Women finally realize that he's been their oppressor all along, and they . . . oh, look, there's the hotel."

Finally, Quinn—and the rest of them—thought, as the Bel Age came into view. Chris pulled the SUV into the entrance and came to a stop in front of the hotel entrance.

"Can I help you with your bags?" he asked.

"No," said Quinn tersely, and without a thank-you. "The bellhop will get them."

"In that case . . ." Chris handed the actor an envelope. "Here's the script."

Quinn looked at the packet, afraid to take it from his hands. "Is this for *The Brothers-in-Law?* Or your ant-man movie?"

Chris fought the urge to correct him. He had been talking about Ant-*Women!* Hadn't the actor been listening?

"It's for *The Brothers-in-Law!* But I'll definitely get you a copy of *Ant* before shooting wraps!"

And, again, Quinn did not say thank you.

Safely in their suite, three floors above the smaller room shared by Bart and Noah, Quinn and Jimmy showered, ordered room service, and, as they relaxed in their Bel Age robes, Quinn began to leaf through the script.

"So how long has it been since you've seen Quinn Jr.?" Jimmy asked, when he saw Quinn's attention wander from the printed page. "Ten years?"

"More than that. Not since . . ." He struggled with the memory. "1990? Maybe even before that."

"How did it feel? You seemed a bit awkward."

Quinn looked back at the script. "My hip hurt. And I'm trying to read."

"No, you're not. Tell me how it felt?"

He closed his eyes. "It felt . . . strange. Listen, I know he's my son, and I shouldn't feel this way, but when he was hugging me, it was like I was being hugged by a wholly owned subsidiary of Katherine. The two of them cut me out of his life—not just her, but him, too—and he doesn't feel like family anymore." His eyes opened and he looked to Jimmy. "Does that make me a bad man?"

"No," said Jimmy. "Just a bad father."

"Thanks. Now I feel much better." His attention went immediately back to the script.

* * *

"And how was your father, dear?"

Quinn Scott Jr. held his cell phone tightly and worried about how to answer the question. He had been hoping she wouldn't ask, but now knew he should have prepared an answer.

"Uh . . ."

"Q. J.? Darling, are you still there?"

"Yes, I'm here. He looked . . . uh . . . old."

"Old?"

"Old*er*."

On her end of the phone line, Kitty sighed. "Well, of course he's gotten *older*. You haven't seen him in almost twenty years. What did you expect?"

"And he looks . . . uh . . . well, he limps."

"Darling, let me put this another way. Did he look tired?"

Tired! *There* was a word he could have used!

"Yes! Yes, he looked tired."

"Did he look sad?"

Well, no, he didn't really look sad. But he did look . . . "He was pissed off."

"Language, darling."

In the privacy of his own home, Q. J. blushed. "I mean, he was angry."

"He probably wasn't getting his own way. Your father can be a baby sometimes. Remember that if he tries to boss you around on the set."

"Yes, Mama."

"Okay, dear, I have to go now. Please let me know how he treats you, and let me know if he causes your show any difficulties. Love you! Bye!"

Q. J. Scott looked at the cell phone in his hand, and wondered if his mother would ever give *him* the opportunity to say good-bye at the end of a call.

Pocketing the phone, he walked the length of his living room to the wet bar, where he made himself a martini and contemplated calling Amber, the Jet Blue flight attendant he had met the previous week who, according to her text message, was back in town. But to hook up with her, he'd have to make a round-trip to Burbank, and he wasn't in the mood. After all, this had been a significant day in his life—reunited at last with his estranged father—and he thought he'd prefer solitude over sex. Which *also* made it a significant day in his life.

Martini glass precariously in hand, he ambled over to the wall-length window and looked out at the lights of hundreds, maybe thousands, of houses, glimmering in the hills. One of them even belonged to his mother, Life was good, he thought, sipping his drink and staring into the twinkling nighttime panorama. Life was good . . .

Q. J. heard his phone chirp and took it from his pocket. Amber had texted him—*r u coming over 2 get me?*—and it suddenly occurred to him that the twinkling nighttime panorama was too precious not to share with someone.

Plus it made a great backdrop for sex.

The next morning, Quinn, accompanied by Bart, drove onto the studio lot. They parked, and as they walked to the soundstage Quinn noted the presence of a van emblazoned with the logo for *Hollywood's Hottest Stories.*

"What are they doing here?" he asked, almost to himself.

When they entered the soundstage, he could see for himself what the *HHS* crew was doing there. They were apparently going to tape the taping of a television show.

"Mr. Scott," said Bernie, the director, when he saw his guest star enter the cavernous room, which caused other members of the cast and crew to turn in Quinn's direction.

"Reporting to duty," said Quinn, as he limped to the set. He looked around and, not seeing him, asked, "Where is Q. J.?"

"He'll be here in a little while. Q. J. and Jason generally arrive a bit later." Bernie glanced at his clipboard. "I'm going to have everyone do a run-through of the script in a few minutes, so if you wouldn't mind staying near the set . . ."

"No, not at all." Quinn pointed to the corner of the room, where lights and a camera bearing the *HHS* logo were set up. He recognized correspondent Mary Hoyt, the woman who had recently interviewed Kitty, standing just out of the light, clutching a microphone. "So what's that all about?"

Bernie smiled. "They're going to be capturing your comeback for posterity. So remember to knock 'em dead."

Later, Bart watched from the bleachers as the actors sat on the living-room set and read through the script, their voices echoing through the spacious room. Bernie and the writers watched, conceptualizing the staging and consulting on the lines of dialogue that fell flat . . . which, in the case of *The Brothers-in-Law* script, constituted a great deal of dialogue. Occasionally Bernie would have a discussion into his headset, obviously with an unseen superior, probably that foul Mark R. Cassidy. And *Hollywood's Hottest Stories* was capturing it all.

During the first read-through the actors meshed well, although Bart could sense tension between Ron Palillo—whom he remembered from reruns of *Welcome Back, Kotter*—and an actor named Joe Gramm, a gray-haired man with a deep, mellifluous voice who was playing his cousin. Their squabbling was only compounded when Gramm kept calling Palillo "Horshack," the name of his *Kotter* character.

"Call me Ron," the actor would correct him, to which Gramm would invariably reply, "Whatever you say, Horshack," leading to another tense go-around. Bart could only guess at their professional history, but it didn't look good that day on the set.

More importantly, Bart was pleased to see that Quinn was holding his own on the soundstage. He was a bit rusty, and bungled a few of his lines, but for someone who had only acted a few times over the previous three decades, he was keeping up, more or less, with the professionals.

After they finished the reading, Bernie called for a break. Bart was about to join Quinn when he saw Q. J. enter the studio; instead, he settled back onto the bleachers, allowing father and son to have their private moment. He need not have bothered; the reunion was quickly over.

Q. J. strolled up to his father and, once again, embraced the older man. As Quinn tried to wriggle away Q. J. said, "Isn't it great to be working together?"

"It would be a hell of a lot better if you'd stop hugging me."

Q. J. smiled and released his father. "You're so funny. Listen, I'm going to run to my dressing room and get ready. I'll see you back on the set." With that, he was gone. Quinn was not disappointed.

But Quinn would think that a bear hug from his son was close to heaven when the other star of *The Brothers-in-Law* graced the set a half hour later.

It was well known by those in the entertainment business, as well as by those who had kept their *People* and *Us* reading current, that Jason St. Clair was not supposed to be the star of *The Brothers-in-Law*. The former teenage underwear model was expected to become, eventually, a middle-aged underwear model, while John Stamos was to have played Ted Huntley on the network for eight to ten years, and then in reruns in perpetuity. But Stamos and the producers could never make a contractual love connection, and Jason St. Clair's twenty foot billboard image was in the right place at the right time—the right time being when a particularly lecherous casting director was stuck in traffic at its base—and so, after a few quick rewrites to subtract twenty years from Ted Huntley's age, a star was born.

Or rather, a *superstar* was born, because Jason St. Clair soon took the nation by storm. Good genes helped, of course; he was, quite simply, beautiful, with clear green eyes, enviable bone structure, and lustrous dark hair. The rest of the package—especially the torso, which managed to lose its shirt in every other episode, especially during sweeps—came from the gym, but what would one expect from a former teenaged underwear model? If there was a flaw, and it was minor, it was his excessively dry skin, but that disappeared under constant applications of very expensive moisturizer, so it could be ignored.

Beyond the physical wealth, though, Jason St. Clair won the airwaves over with his cheery, laid-back personality. On the screen and in interviews, he came across as genuinely sincere and unspoiled, appreciative of the fact that, four years earlier, his talents extended no further than taking off his pants, looking at a camera and flashing a smile or pout.

And as Jason St. Clair walked onto the set, trailing a small en-

tourage of handlers, that was exactly the personality Quinn was expecting.

But that's not what he got.

"What the fuck are all these people doing here?" Jason raged,
seeing too many unfamiliar faces among the cast and crew. "Bernie?!"

Bernie seemed to shrink. "Good morning, Jason. We're about to
start clearing the set."

The young actor tossed his hair. "The set is supposed to be clear
before I come down, Bernie. This is a fucking waste of my time."
He turned to Quinn and demanded, "Who are you? Bernie?! Who
is this?!"

"Quinn Scott," Bernie and Quinn answered at the same time.

"And that means *what* to me?"

"That means," said Quinn, remarkably polite, "that I'm playing
Uncle Jake in this episode."

Jason snapped his fingers. "Wait a minute. I know who you are.
Q. J.'s father, right? The guy who was married to Kitty Randolph?
The gay guy?"

"Yes, I was married to Kitty Randolph," confirmed Quinn. "And,
yes, I'm Q. J.'s father. The gay item isn't really relevant."

"Well . . ." Struggling, the young actor offered his hand to the elderly homosexual. "Welcome aboard. Sorry I yelled."

"No need to apologize. I've been on sets before."

"In that case, you'll understand when I tell you that this is a professional set, right? I don't believe in outtakes, and I don't believe
in goofing around. We get the shot in a few takes and move on.
And that's why I'm a little leery, Mr. Scott."

"Please, call me Quinn."

"Right." Jason shot a quick look around the set. "Let's talk for a
second, okay, Quinn?" Quinn agreed, and Jason shouted, "Five minutes!"

"Five minutes," agreed Bernie, although he was annoyed because
calling breaks was *his* job.

Jason motioned for Quinn to follow him to a slightly more private corner of the set. As they walked, the young superstar said,
"Can I level with you?"

"Please do."

"This whole thing doesn't make me very comfortable."

"*What* whole thing?"

"This is stunt-casting," Jason explained. "You know what that is?" Quinn nodded. "Listen, I'm just being honest with you. I don't have the studio hire *my* father for sweeps week, you know what I mean?"

Quinn stopped. "You do realize that I'm not just Q. J.'s father, don't you?"

"I know, I know . . ." Jason tried to do "conciliatory." "You also wrote that book."

"This is about more than the book . . ."

Jason was barely listening. "And the gay thing, well . . . more power to you, old man. I really appreciate my gay fans, and I think it's great that you're like eighty years old and their new icon. But still . . ."

Quinn was offended. "You have no idea who I am, do you?"

Jason shrugged. Hadn't he just told him that he knew who he was?

"I am an actor. I worked with John Wayne . . . Robert Mitchum . . . Rock Hudson. I'm not just here because I'm the gay guy who happens to be Q. J. Scott's father!"

Jason St. Clair thought about that for a few seconds, then offered Quinn a tight smile and said, "Yes, you are."

"That little bastard," muttered Quinn, once he was in the privacy of his dressing room. Someone had been kind enough to set up a small bar in a corner of the room, but he ignored it. "Who the fuck does he think he is?"

Moments after Jason St. Clair had extended his claws and started scratching, Quinn had thrown his script to the floor and stomped off the set, leaving general confusion in his wake. While slugging that smug prick would have been satisfying, he knew that it would have also doomed this comeback, modest as it was. In which case the dressing room was the safest place for him to let off steam.

Bart tried to be a calming influence. "He's just a kid. Ignore him."

Quinn looked at him. "*You're* a kid, and *you* don't talk to me like that." He stewed some more. "I'll bet he doesn't talk that way to Horshack."

"Unless you don't want people calling you 'Philly Cop' all week, I'd suggest you start calling him 'Ron.'"

"Eh."

Finally convinced by Bart that it was the professional thing to do, Quinn returned to the set. His discarded script had been retrieved by one of the crew, and actor and dialogue were quickly reunited.

It was the last good thing that would happen to Quinn that afternoon. Or for the rest of the week, for that matter.

When Bart arrived back at his hotel room, his face was grim.

"What's the matter?" asked Noah, taking his eyes off the television, where that night's edition of *Hollywood's Hottest Stories* was just beginning. Bart picked up the remote control and turned off the TV.

"I don't even know where to start. He lost his script a few times, and kept screwing up his lines, and . . ." He paused. "The thing is, he started off good. The first time the cast read the script he was fine. But then he had a run-in with Jason St. Clair, and everything went downhill. It went downhill *fast.*"

"Couldn't Q. J. do anything?"

"His son is an idiot. He probably has to wear a timer to remind him to breathe." Bart rubbed his face. "I don't know . . . maybe this was a bad idea. Maybe Quinn has lost it." Looking at Noah he added, "By the way, it gets worse. This isn't just a case of Quinn screwing up and pissing off a few actors. *Hollywood's Hottest Stories* is on the set this week, and they're capturing every moment."

"I was just watching that," said Noah, reaching for the remote. "Turn it back on."

"Not tonight. But starting tomorrow . . . ugh, it's going to be horrible. If Quinn can't get his act together, he's going to look *so* bad."

Upstairs, the same conversation was being played out in Quinn and Jimmy's suite.

"I can't understand it," said Quinn. "It was like I was being sabotaged."

Jimmy placed a hand gently on his shoulder. "It's been a while, Quinn. I'm sure no one expects you to bounce right back. Don't be so hard on yourself."

But the next day was no better. If anything, Quinn showed further deterioration. His poor performance was the one thing even Ron Palillo and Joe Gramm came to agree upon.

"Alzheimer's," said Palillo.

"Has to be," agreed Gramm.

They were not the only ones. And that night, when *HHS* began airing the first of its four-part series "going behind the scenes of one of television's hottest shows," the entire American viewing public was given a sneak peek at the befuddled wreck formerly known as Quinn Scott.

"It's not me," he insisted, after the first segment was over. "They gave me the wrong damn script."

Jimmy nodded supportively and held his partner.

Chapter 12

Sometimes, I think life would be better if it was scripted. Those awkward moments, inappropriate comments, embarrassing situations . . . they would be gone, unless they were essential to the plot. Choosing the wrong path: gone. Loving the wrong person: gone.

But I guess that's what makes it life. The movies are nice—no, the movies are wonderful—but they aren't a substitution for life. The only thing they have in common is that you can have popcorn in both of them . . .

Noah woke up in the middle of the night to the sound of Bart's fingers lightly tapping on his laptop keyboard.

"Isn't it a bit early for porn?" he asked.

Bart didn't immediately answer, so Noah slid himself down the bed to where Bart sat at the hotel room's faux-oak desk, his face illuminated by the blue light spilling from the monitor.

"Whatcha doing?"

"Research," Bart finally said. "I had a hunch, and I wanted to see where it took me."

Noah stifled a yawn. "And where is it taking you?"

"Nowhere. Yet."

"So come back to sleep."

"Not yet. I'm wide awake. But you should get back to bed. One of us needs to be well rested."

"In a second . . ." Noah sat on the edge of the bed and watched Bart's tapping on the keyboard, straining to read the screen as he typed. Finally, he realized what he was doing.

"Bart . . . stop and come back to bed."

"Not yet."

"You're a good man and a loyal employee, but you have to face facts. We were wrong. Quinn isn't the actor he used to be."

"I think he is," Bart said curtly, never taking his eyes off the screen. "Have you lost your faith, Noah?"

"No. I have faith in the *man*. But the actor, well . . . remember, he hasn't been in front of a camera since 1990. He's rusty. He's lost his skills."

"I don't think so. I think someone has been screwing around with him."

Noah sighed, sinking back into the comforter. "Who? Q. J.?"

Bart shook his head but still didn't look away from the monitor. "No. I don't think so. I don't think the actors have been involved in this."

"Maybe Kitty sent in Ron Palillo as her secret agent."

Bart didn't reply.

"Look," Noah continued, "it's not like people are making this up. We've seen it ourselves every night on *Hollywood's Hottest* . . ."

"We've seen what they want us to see."

"So what do you think?"

"I don't know what to think. But I'm sure that there's something going on."

Noah watched him as he earnestly conducted search after search, no doubt coming across the same fruitless information over and over and over again. His eyelids began to grow heavy, and although he wanted to be by Bart's side throughout the long, frustrating night, he felt himself begin to drift off. His last conscious thought was a fervent wish that he had the same faith in Quinn that Bart had.

But he didn't.

Some time later, as Noah lay half-covered by the bedsheet in the gray area between sleep and consciousness, he sensed Bart hovering over him. He cautiously opened one eye and, in fact, there he was. Seeing Noah's eyes flicker open, Bart leaned forward and kissed him, then whispered, "I love you."

"I love you, too," Noah answered, by rote. "Are you coming to bed?"

"No. And guess why I'm not coming to bed."

Noah was silent. It was too damn early to be playing games.

Bart got right to the point. "I think I found it, Noah!"

"Found what?"

"Proof! Proof that Kitty is behind this!"

Noah was skeptical. "You have proof? What did you find?"

"Lilliane Studios."

"Where they shoot *The Brothers-in-Law*?"

"That's it," said Bart. "And do you think it's a coincidence that Kitty Randolph's first role in 1957 was a small part in a movie called *Charmed, I'm Sure*, and her character was named . . ."

"Lilliane?"

"Lilliane Porch, to be exact."

Noah finally, breathlessly, joined in Bart's sensation of discovery, popping up in bed as he said, "Porch, as in PorchStar International . . ."

Bart nodded. "Her fingerprints are all over everything. Worse, it's all right out in the open. She might as well have called it Kitty International, or Randolph International. It's all too obvious."

"But it wasn't," Noah reminded him. "And who would know? As Lilliane Porch, she was on screen for . . . three minutes? . . . and she had two speaking lines. It's a role that doesn't even make most of her biographies."

"It doesn't," Bart confirmed, as he again took his seat in front of the laptop. "I've been trying to track something down for hours, and I've read almost everything about her on the Internet, so trust me on this."

"I do." Noah crawled down the length of the bed until he was positioned behind Bart, then cradled him from behind, staring over his muscular shoulder at the screen. "I do."

Bart sighed. "Okay, now that we have the knowledge . . . what do we do with it?"

"Tell Quinn?"

"Well, duh. But what else? How do we rescue his career? How do we get him out of this mess?"

"The trades?" Noah suggested.

Bart scoffed at that. "Kitty Randolph owns fifty percent of this town, and probably as many industry reporters. So forget about blowing her out of the water in *Variety*."

Noah had to acknowledge his logic. "So . . . uh . . . what are the other options?"

Bart began to power down the laptop, then turned to his boyfriend and said, "I don't think there *are* any options. That's the frustrating thing. We're out of them. We can't go to the trades, we can't go to the crew . . . shit, Quinn can't even go to his son." He slumped forward, staring at the now-black monitor. "And even if we were to get someone's attention, who's going to give a fuck? So Kitty owns PorchStar and Lilliane . . . so what? I know it, and you know it, but who's going to call it any more than a coincidence?" He sighed. "Kitty has Quinn's nuts in a ringer. She won! And the only thing Quinn can do is write another book about it to plead his case. Of course, if he were to write it, no one would read it, let alone publish it, because they think he's a senile old man." In frustration, Bart slammed his fist on the desk. "We are fucked."

* * *

Although he got no more than an hour's sleep that night, Bart dutifully drove Quinn to Lilliane Studio the next morning. As they traveled from freeway to freeway, the older man noticed that Bart was uncharacteristically quiet.

"Bad morning?"

Bart nodded. "I didn't get a lot of sleep."

And now that he had an explanation, Quinn returned his attention to *The Los Angeles Times* for the duration of the ride.

At the studio, Bart followed Quinn to his dressing room, closing the door tightly behind him.

"You can just hang out," Quinn said, turning his attention to the script that was waiting for him. "I won't be needing you."

"I can do line readings with you," Bart said sullenly.

Quinn shook his head. "I'm not sure that's going to do me much fucking good anymore. They keep changing these damn scripts on me . . ." He picked up the daily script and, almost instantaneously, announced, "And goddamn if they didn't do it to me again!"

"Huh?"

"Look!" Quinn shoved the script under Bart's nose. "Now Uncle Jake has a fucking Norwegian accent. What the *fuck* does a Norwegian accent sound like? Swedish or something?"

Bart shrugged. "I guess so."

"Fuck!" Quinn threw the script back on the table. "What are they trying to do to me? And I'll bet you anything I'll go out there and give them a fucking Norwegian accent and that fat fuck Cassidy will be screaming that it's supposed to be French or something, and I memorized the wrong script!"

"About the scripts," said Bart, but Quinn talked right over him.

"Something is going on here. I made movies for more than a decade! I was Philly Fucking Cop! I *know* how to read a fucking script!"

"Well, about that . . ."

Quinn was about to let Bart speak when they heard a knock at the door.

"Get that, will you?"

When Bart opened the door, Ron Palillo and Joe Gramm stood outside.

"Everything all right?" asked Palillo.

"We heard some noise," Gramm added.

"Everything's fine," said Bart.

"Just fine," snapped Quinn.

Palillo took a step forward into the dressing room. "You know, Quinn, if you'd like help with line readings . . ."

"Listen," said Quinn, making no attempt to hide his temper, "I was Philly Cop before you ever dreamed of being Kotter! I know how to act, dammit!"

"Uh . . . I wasn't Kotter. I was *in* Kotter, but I wasn't—"

"Bart, close the door."

Bart shrugged apologetically to the actors and closed the door.

"Wet-behind-the-ears actors," muttered Quinn. "They think they can run laps around the old man." He turned and hollered at the closed door: "Well, I've still fucking got it!"

"Okay, Quinn, I really have to talk to you."

The actor eyed his assistant up and down. Cautiously, he asked, "About?"

"This is a setup. The whole thing." And, with that, Bart detailed what could only be an elaborate scheme to discredit Quinn.

When he finished, Quinn was silent for a moment. Then he broke into a broad smile.

"Lilliane Porch," he said, chuckling. "I should have figured that one out myself. But you did good work, Bart. Real good work."

"You know this isn't over yet."

"Of course it is," said Quinn. "We've got her. You nailed her. The bullshit ends right now."

Bart pointed to the script. "So what are you going to do about Jake's accent? Try to fake Norwegian?"

"What do you mean?"

"What I mean," Bart said, "is that just because we're on to them doesn't mean they're not still running the show. Literally, in this case. You don't know who's working with her, Quinn. It could be any of them. It could be *all* of them."

"Even Kotter?"

"Yes, even Kot—I mean, Horshack. I mean, *Ron Palillo*. It doesn't matter who it is, though, because unless they decide to stop fucking with you all on their own, they've got you."

And Bart would not have believed it if he hadn't seen it for himself, but tough guy Quinn Scott actually looked like he was going to cry.

"It's a disaster, David. A total goddamn disaster!"

Lindsay Flynn was on the line with David Carlyle, having just updated him on the implosion of the Quinn Scott publicity machine. It was bad enough when Larry King's people cancelled an appearance, but now she was even losing radio interviews in gay-friendly markets like San Francisco, Denver, and—most gallingly—right here in New York City. She hadn't intended to take out her frustration on the book's editor—the frustration rightfully deserved to be directed at the senile old man who was making a fool of himself at that moment on a Burbank soundstage; probably trying to fake a Norwegian accent or something—but Palmer/Midkiff/Carlyle was paying for her services, so that's where she directed her buckshot.

For his part, David was every bit as frustrated and unhappy as Lindsay. He wasn't concerned when Quinn's difficulties on the set of *The Brothers-in-Law* began appearing in the gossip columns, because it was ink, and therefore it wasn't all bad. But as the week dragged on and the stories escalated at a rate David had theretofore thought impossible for a guest appearance on such an insignificant television show, he was growing alarmed. His concern had little to do with Quinn Scott's nightly humiliation at the hands of Jay Leno and Jon Stewart, and everything to do with the word coming back from his sales team: *When the Stars Come Out* had flatlined. Only one month after the book's official release, it had lost its luster, and now—in a reversal the likes of which he had never before seen—returns were outpacing shipments. If things continued as they were trending, the book was on course to set a record as the all-time *worst*-seller.

He had, of course, heard from Noah about the Great Lilliane Porch Conspiracy, or whatever they were calling it out there on the West Coast. While it was good to know that Quinn Scott was not mentally incompetent, David also agreed that the situation was out of their hands. He could only hope that Kitty Randolph would relent in her vendetta before PMC was forced to pulp the entire first printing of *When the Stars Come Out*.

But he didn't hold out much hope. Hoping was for people much more optimistic than David Carlyle.

He hung up the telephone, leaving a very frustrated, angry Lindsay Flynn talking to dead air. She didn't catch on until the off-the-hook tone began blaring in her ear.

"Hold it," said MRC's voice through a loudspeaker. "I'm coming down."

The cast and crew were still as statues—all except Jason St. Clair, that is, who folded his arms cockily, because he knew his breakout stardom put him beyond MRC's wrath—as metallic footsteps reverberated, the cue that the big boss was descending from his office to the set. Moments later, Mark R. Cassidy was on the soundstage with all those contemptible people.

He eyed each person on the set, and, as he did, they took a step back. Except Jason St. Clair. When his eyes finally reached Quinn Scott, he held his gaze.

"Norwegian?"

"That's what the script . . ."

"Why in hell's name would Uncle Jake have a Norwegian accent? He's from Indiana, or some place like that."

"Midland City," said a crew member.

MRC spun to face the offender and said, quite crisply, "Shut the fuck up." Then, returning to Quinn, he said, "And can I see this script? The one where it says you're supposed to swim a fjord or something?"

Quinn was holding the script, so he handed it over. MRC leafed through it and said, "So where do you see anything Norwegian?"

He took the script back and, as he turned the pages, knew immediately it wasn't the one he had carried onto the set. And therefore there would be no references to a Norwegian accent.

"It's not the same script."

"So let me get this straight. Someone gave *you* a special script? *You* got the Norwegian version, and everyone else got the American version? Is that what you're trying to tell me?"

Quinn didn't bother to answer. And in any event, he was too focused on the few moments the script had been out of his hands. He had briefly set it down on a table at one point, and that kid Jason

St. Clair had asked to see it to refresh his memory for a few minutes, but other than that . . .

Jason St. Clair. Of course. Why wouldn't the breakout star of Katherine's show starring Katherine's son shot at Katherine's studio be in on the plot? Quinn turned and glowered at the handsome young man, who was perched indifferently on the couch that served as the centerpiece of the set. He had been nothing but trouble from the beginning, and now Quinn knew why. He looked over to where Jason stood near Q. J.

Jason noticed Quinn's glare. "Looking at something?"

"Not much."

Off to the side, MRC suddenly felt excluded. *He* was supposed to be the badass around here, but now it looked as if the old hack and the hot young star were going to be mixing it up, and he couldn't have that. It would be tantamount to losing control. So he stepped between them—at no risk of personal danger, since Quinn and Jason were still separated by twenty feet—and said, "Okay, I want you both to shut up. I don't know what's going on here, but I want it to end right now."

"Here is how this ends," said Quinn, tossing the script to the floor. "This ends when everyone stops fucking with me."

"Nobody's . . ."

"I get incorrect scripts . . . I get the wrong information on blocking . . . Every hour there's a new fuckup, and you know what? It's not me." He looked around the set. "Yes, I know what you're thinking. I was starting to think it, too. But now I know that my ex-wife owns this show and this studio, and it's all beginning to make sense. I don't know which one of you is doing it—although I have my suspicions—but I'm putting you on notice that it stops right now."

And with that, he stormed off the set, leaving all of them—even Mark R. Cassidy—dumbfounded in his wake.

Not to mention more convinced than ever that Quinn Scott had lost his mind.

As Q. J. watched his father leave the set, he thought, *Mama owns this studio? Wasn't that something he should know?* And then he called his stepfather, to demand an explanation.

*   *   *

Quinn sat on the bench, staring at his image in the dressing room mirror and not liking what he saw. He could deny his reality for four decades, through banishment from Hollywood and a host of physical ailments, but, face to face, he couldn't deny that he had become the man who now stared back at him.

He was getting old. He was entering the sunset of his life that he had always believed was so far away.

The old man in the mirror still looked, more or less, like the young man on celluloid . . . the man he always thought of, when he thought of himself. But the dark brown hair was now thinner, and gray; the square jaw was now framed by jowls; the broad shoulders sagged; those eyes—those gray eyes that had first captured Kitty's imagination, then Jimmy's—were weary and surrounded by a relief map of wrinkles.

He continued to stare at his reflection, as if seeing for the first time the old man that Quinn Scott had become. It was still a handsome face, he thought; it just wasn't the face he expected to see, even though he had watched its slow decline over decades. That was in increments; this was sudden. And that, to Quinn, made all the difference in the world.

And Kitty had won. Yes, he knew he hadn't lost his mental acuity, but that was a small, personal victory. That's all. To know that he had not become a senile old man, but was the victim of Kitty's manipulations, was only a personal victory because the rest of the world—his audience, his fans, his *readers*—would never know that. To them, Quinn had tried to return from obscurity for one final, humiliating moment, embarrassing himself and guaranteeing his quick and merciful disappearance once again from public life. Forever.

And the image they would always remember—the kids and the handful of survivors who still remembered *Philly Cop* and *When the Stars Come Out*—would never be the Quinn Scott of the '60s, nor would it be the handsome actor striding proudly out of retirement as he simultaneously strode out of the closet. No, they would remember the doddering actor who they believed couldn't remember his lines, wrote a book full of false memories, and, possibly worst of all, had physically decomposed into the gray, jowly old man in the mirror.

"Dammit," he muttered, and he would have continued to mutter and stare if he hadn't been interrupted by a knock at the door. "Go away!"

The knock—three raps, the same as before—came again.

Quinn took another look at himself in the mirror, then tried to shake off the image. He knew he wasn't seeing anyone different; it was the same face he saw every day. But there was a new weariness to it, and he couldn't get that out of his head.

Again, three knocks.

"Hold on!" Annoyed, he rose slowly from the bench and walked the few steps across the tiny room to the door, ready to rip into Bart or Horshack or whoever else was bothering him at this moment, which he wanted only for himself. But it wasn't Bart or Horshack who stood in front of the door when he finally opened it.

"Sorry to bother you," said the man Quinn recognized as Dean Henry, nervously shifting his weight from foot to foot outside the door. He glanced around to see if anyone was watching who should not be watching. "Can I come in?"

"I don't know that we have anything to talk about."

"I think we do. May I?"

"Suit yourself." Quinn stepped back from the doorway and Dean skittered in, making a point to close the door gently but quickly in his wake. Without so much as a glance he slid past Quinn and made a beeline for the actor's makeshift bar.

"Can I pour you one?" Dean asked, his back to Quinn and acting as if the dressing room and bar were his own.

"No." Quinn reconsidered. "Yes . . . yes, I think maybe I will."

Dean poured himself a vodka and tonic, noting unhappily that the bar was garnish-free; then, without taking an order, poured Quinn a stiff scotch and water. When he was done mixing he took both glasses and pivoted, offering the scotch to Quinn, and said, "Sit down."

Quinn hesitated, so Dean became a bit more forceful. "You know I own this dressing room, so please sit down."

Stunned by Dean's brashness, Quinn obeyed and sat back on the bench, this time facing away from his elderly reflection.

"So you know," said Dean, his eyes darting everywhere but to Quinn as he slurped his clear, fruit-free liquid.

"Know what?"

Dean smiled, but looked at his shoes instead of Quinn, pretending to inspect them for an invisible scuff. "You know about PorchStar."

The stony-faced Quinn merely said again, "Know what?"

This time, Dean looked up, and, although his glance was fleeting, he *did* make eye contact.

"I know you know, Quinn. There aren't a lot of secrets around here. I also know you don't like me, but—trust me—I'm not stupid." He paused. "You're fighting back. That fascinates me."

Quinn didn't give him the satisfaction of an answer. He just looked at him . . . not with anger, and not with curiosity. He looked at him with nothing but indifference.

Dean tried to match his stoicism, and managed to hang in there for thirty seconds or so, but finally he cracked.

"Okay, you don't have to talk," he said, tapping his index finger against his glass of vodka. "*I* know you know and that's what's important here." Dean made another attempt to make eye contact; this one lasted only for a few seconds before it fell away. "Anyway, I just wanted to say . . . I'm sorry."

Quinn cocked his head.

"I don't know what to tell you, Quinn. Things had to happen."

Again, there was silence, broken only by the faint ticking of a clock.

Dean played with his swizzle stick. He had expected anger, maybe even violence. Although he had hoped there would be no violence, because even though Quinn had a good twenty to twenty-five years on him, he knew that there was a good likelihood that the older man could pound him to a bloody pulp. Still, a good beating would have been preferable to the sphinx that sat a short two yards from him, inscrutable and unanswering.

Until the sphinx finally spoke.

"What I don't understand," said Quinn slowly, "is why."

"Why?"

"Why. Why did you go to such lengths to . . . well, to humiliate me? Why not just ignore me?"

With his free hand, Dean smoothed his pant leg.

"Honestly," he said, "that was my advice. But . . . she had other ideas."

"I see that now. She wanted me gone."

Dean nodded.

Quinn held his stony expression and sat, unspeaking.

"You know how she is," Dean finally said, stirring his drink, but not actually drinking. "She wants what she wants, and she gets it. In this case, she wanted to drive you into silence."

"But she didn't get it," Quinn said finally.

"She didn't?"

"Maybe she got the humiliation . . . yeah, she got the humiliation. But she didn't get the silence. Never the silence."

Dean gently crossed his legs at the ankle. "Here's the deal, Quinn. She won. Understand? She got the humiliation, and maybe she can't physically shut you up, but she's essentially silenced you. After the *Brothers-in-Law* debacle, who's going to listen to you?"

"Lots of people," said Quinn, hoping his bluff was not too transparent.

"No one," snapped Dean. "It's not an accident that *HHS* is on the set this week. Thanks to Kitty, everyone thinks you're a doddering old fool who's being manipulated by other people for . . . whatever reason. And I'm sure she's already thought of that reason, too. Money . . . fame . . . one of those things that holds a peculiar fascination for people, but ultimately comes off as a big negative. She's always ten steps ahead of you, Quinn. She always has been."

"So you say."

"No, this is something I know. Because she's always ten steps ahead of *me*, too." And finally, in the way a nervous man can only do with someone who is in the same boat, Dean Henry made eye contact. "But back to the main question: who is going to listen to Quinn Scott now? Larry King? I heard that booking fell through. Barbara Walters? No chance. Are you going to get booked on Leno or Letterman? Hell no. They're openly mocking you on *The Daily Show*, for chrissakes! Four nights in a row! Last night they said that you weren't even gay, that you just forgot you're heterosexual." Dean again smoothed his pants against his leg and shook his head sadly. "The sad thing—the knife-twist that Kitty really did well—is that when the talk shows stop talking to you, they'll be thinking that they're doing you an act of kindness. Because the doddering old man can't make a fool of himself if no one will interview him."

Quinn nodded, digesting the completeness of Kitty's plot. She had indeed cut him off, even more effectively than she had banished him thirty-six years earlier. He looked at Dean, who was still, remarkably, maintaining eye contact, and asked, "Why are you telling me this, Dean? Why now?"

"My conscience."

"An agent with a conscience?"

Dean had to smile at that. "You want the truth? Here's the truth: I never would have told you if I didn't know you had already figured it out, okay?"

"Go on," Quinn prompted him.

"Listen, we all know that she's a horrible person. We all know that what people see on the screen is an illusion. A Kitty Randolph biography would make *Mommie Dearest* look like *The Sound of Music.* Your book proved that . . . well, in those few weeks in which anyone was taking you and your book seriously, that is. But we have to live in the world as it is, and—in this world—Kitty Randolph is the queen."

"It doesn't sound as if you like her very much," said Quinn, with more understanding in his voice than should have been there.

"I have to live in the world as it is, too."

"I used to know that feeling."

Dean broke eye contact and stared into his drink.

There was silence in the room for a moment, until Quinn rose from the bench and cleared his throat.

"Queens fall, Dean. Regimes are toppled. Leaders are forced into exile. And Kitty Randolph is only as powerful as you let her be. If you stand up to her, your world won't come to an end. I did, and mine didn't."

"Yours didn't? It looks that way to me."

"I have love, Dean. Katherine can take a lot away from me, but I own that. And what do you own? A few things, yes, but not love,"

Dean waved the sentiment away. "Love is overrated."

"Spoken like a man who's never had it and doesn't expect it."

It was Dean's turn to clear his throat. He noticed that his leg was shaking slightly. "She would scream if she knew I was here talking to you right now. That's not standing up to her?"

"You skulked in here," said Quinn. "You made sure that no one was looking and slipped right through the door. That's standing up to her? I don't think so."

The agent hunched forward, resting his forearms against his

legs, consciously risking wrinkles in his suit pants to emphasize his feigned comfort and at least partial sincerity.

"I'm just another guy she's got by the balls, Quinn. You get kicked enough, you get a little gun shy. That's all. Yes, I suppose I'm afraid of her just a bit, but not as much as you seem to think."

Quinn leaned forward, mimicking Dean's posture until their faces were too close for Dean's comfort.

"If that's true, let me ask you a question."

"Shoot." There was a slight hesitation in Dean's voice.

"Why don't you just come out?"

Stunned into silence, Dean froze in position until he finally found his voice. "Ex . . . ex . . . Excuse me?"

"Just come out."

"C-c-c-come . . . come out from where?"

"Come out of the closet."

"B-b-b-but I'm not in. In a closet, that is."

Quinn shook his head. "You mean, she knows?"

"Kn-kn-knows what?"

"That you're gay."

Dean sat up sharply in his chair, almost—but not quite—spilling his drink, and squealed, "*What?!*"

"So . . . wait," said Quinn. "I'm confused. Does Kitty know you're gay? Or not?"

"I'm not gay!!" Dean shrieked.

Now it was Quinn's turn to be confused. "You're not?"

"No! What would make you think . . . ? I am *not* a homosexual, Mr. Scott. I am 100-percent heterosexual! In fact, I'm . . . I'm . . . I'm *shocked* that you think I'm gay. What would ever . . . ? Okay, yes, I'm a bit fastidious. But that doesn't make a man gay."

"Well, you set off my gaydar . . ."

Dean was sputtering. "Gaydar? What the hell is gaydar?"

"It's that feeling gay men have that tells them someone else is gay."

Dean fumed, fumbling for words. "That's the problem of the gays. Not me. I don't do anything . . . *gay*. I am totally non-gay. Uh . . . un-gay. *Whatever!*" He stopped for a moment, then squinted at Quinn. "Were you just trying to pick me up?"

"Of course not," said Quinn, appalled. "Don't insult me."

"Insult *you?*!!" Dean surprised even himself with his fury, let alone the words spilling out of his mouth. "Why would *you* be insulted? Am I somehow undesirable? Unworthy of you?" He stopped himself and smoothed his lapels, then, calmed by the grooming ritual, continued. "Because I'm not, Quinn. If I weren't so heterosexual, I'd be a great catch for any gay man."

Quinn waved him away. "I'm sure you would be. In your own way. But it's not that," he said, although, in part, it was. "Not every gay man wants sex from every other gay man. That was the insult. I'm sure some people would find you attractive."

"But not you."

"Not me," confirmed Quinn, before adding, "No offense."

"None taken." Dean stewed for a moment, then asked, "Just out of curiosity, *why* not me? Do you think I'm unattractive?"

"Shut up, Dean," said Quinn with finality. "We aren't going down that road."

"I should hope not."

"We aren't."

"Good."

"*Shut the fuck up for two seconds!*" Dean shut up. "If I offended you, I apologize. But we're getting sidetracked. What we should be talking about is how you can reclaim your very heterosexual life from Katherine."

"You seem to be more certain than I am about that."

"Let me tell you what I see," said Quinn, talking a gulp from his glass of scotch before continuing. "I see a man who wants to be free, but is afraid of the consequences. A man who is a lot like I was, back when I was married to her. Am I right?"

"I told you," said Dean. "I am not gay."

"And I believe you," said Quinn, not quite convincingly. "But there are many more reasons to want freedom besides coming to terms with your sexuality. Take being your own man, for one. Being your own *heterosexual* man."

"I'm quite content."

"You say that. But I think the reason you came here this afternoon had nothing to do with your conscience. You came here because you don't want Katherine to win. Not this time, at least."

Dean thought about that. In truth, he wasn't quite sure why, exactly, he had come to Quinn's dressing room, except that, thanks to Q. J., he knew that Quinn had figured out the PorchStar connection and some damage control would be necessary, and the only way he could control the damage was by giving Quinn a warning. He just didn't expect that warning to be turned back on him.

Or did he? Unsure of his own motivations—unsure about anything, except his 100-percent unquestionably heterosexual status—Dean chose not to challenge Quinn's hypothesis. Instead, he nodded vaguely and said, "For better or worse, Kitty is my wife. I live in her world, and we know what that's like." He stood and straightened himself. "Consider this nothing more than a heads up, Quinn. And an apology. It isn't right—I *know* it isn't right—but this is the way things are. It's over."

As Dean began walking to the door, Quinn stood up from the bench and stopped him with, "Let me tell you something, Dean."

Dean glanced at his watch. "Quickly."

"I've waited thirty-five years for my comeback, and you can wait for five more minutes." When Dean timidly nodded his acquiescence, Quinn continued. "I have missed this business—missed acting—for almost half my life. This *Brothers-in-Law* show isn't much, but it *is* my last hurrah. In thirty years, I'll probably be dust. No one will remember me, or my movies, or . . . or even this show. They won't remember you, they may not even remember Katherine."

Dean scoffed. "She'll make sure they remember her."

"No doubt." Quinn ran his hand absently along an old—and, of course, incorrect—script, perched on the edge of the bureau. "But this isn't about Katherine. And it's not about you, either. For the first time since 1970, this is about Quinn Scott. And it's *only* about Quinn Scott."

Dean was silent.

"And you," added Quinn, jabbing Dean gently in the chest with one finger, "are going to make this moment happen for me."

"I don't think so," said Dean, shaking his head. "It's over, and the sooner you accept that, the sooner you can move on."

Quinn sat back down. His weary eyes were watery. Dean still kept his distance, although he now towered above the older man.

"I don't know what to say, Dean," said Quinn, resignation in his voice. "I could fight you—" Dean recoiled "No, not physically fight you. I could fight this debacle on the set. But until you're willing to give me the same freedom from Katherine that I've tried to give you . . . I don't know what to say."

Dean nodded. "I know. Me neither."

And with that, he quietly and quickly left the dressing room, not bothering to first check to see who might be watching.

Dean thought about their conversation through the entire ride home, letting it distract him so much that he missed his freeway exit and had to backtrack. There were things he now wished he had said, and, as he replayed the dressing room drama, he deftly inserted his new lines into the conversation, to the point where he started to become confused about what really had been said, and what was in his head.

"Your time is up, old man." Dean either said or wished he had said, "Pack up and hit the road."

"You're afraid of her, aren't you?" Quinn either asked or didn't.

"I'm not afraid of her, and I'm certainly not afraid of you." Okay, that was one line Dean was certain he had made up in his head, because he was afraid of both Kitty and Quinn, although for different reasons. Still, it felt good to give the old man his imaginary walking papers and point him in the direction of obscurity. He wouldn't be dust in thirty years. More like ten.

He slowed as he pulled into the driveway and poked a button on the dashboard. As the security gate swung open with a metallic groan, he began to feel indignant that that faded TV cop Quinn Scott had the audacity to question not only his motives, but his masculinity.

Gay? How could he even suggest such a thing? After twenty years in the business Dean knew many gay men and lesbians, of course, but there was nothing gay about him, and he could not understand why people kept making that mistake. And if it was bad enough when some random straight guy was confused about Dean's sexual orientation, it was doubly bad when a self-avowed homosexual like Quinn Scott said it, what with their mythical "gaydar" and everything.

The gate was almost fully open, and Dean decided that he should take up a sport as a hobby, to butch up his image. Because if people considered him a bit too fey, a bit too . . . gaydar-able, a little "butching up" would be a good thing. And what was more butch than sports? He knew some people who were in a volleyball league . . .

And then there were Quinn's allusions to his unhappiness. True, Dean was not as happy as a man with tens of millions of dollars in the bank was supposed to be, but he was still happy. His marriage to Kitty Randolph had brought him nothing but contacts, professional success, lots of money, three nice big homes, a stepchild, an ulcer, migraines, and . . . lots and lots of happiness. And, yes, it *was* happiness, dammit. Just a different kind of happiness.

And as for Quinn, he was obviously transferring his feelings onto Dean, which made Dean more and more furious as he drove the Jaguar up the driveway and past Raul, the gardener with the brown skin and wide shoulders, who today was shirtless and sweating in the hot—

Dean came to an abrupt stop.

An abrupt, crinkling, shattering stop.

Into the rear of Raul's truck.

"Fuck!" he muttered, as the shirtless, sweaty gardener ran across the lawn toward the wreck.

Chapter 13

Sometimes, it's hard for me to look back and remember that I was once married to Kitty Randolph. It was a lifetime ago—a lifetime in which I finally allowed myself to have a life—but the faint echoes of our relationship still reverberate in my ears.

I feel sorry for the men and women who have found themselves in her path over the past thirty-five years, but mostly I feel sorry for Kitty. She has always been a real star, but she has never let herself be a real human being . . .

"They're all laughing at me," Quinn told Jimmy as they sipped wine at CarnivALLA, the city's hottest new restaurant.

"Who?"

"All of them." Jimmy scanned the celebrity-packed dining room, not seeing a soul so much as glancing in their direction.

"Honey," said Jimmy. "You've got to take it easy. They don't even know who you are."

"After being in the gossip columns for the past few weeks? They know who I am. I'm the senile old gay man."

Jimmy sighed. "Maybe they know the name, but they don't know the face. So if they're laughing at you, at least they think they're doing it behind your back."

Quinn put down his fork and glared at Jimmy. "I know what's going on. I know what they're saying on Leno and the other shows. She's ruining me!"

"Keep your voice down. Nobody's saying anything about you, Quinn, so just relax."

He shook his head. "I know all about it. Dean Henry told me things that you–supposedly my partner—won't tell me."

Jimmy sat back, trying to control his temper. He was used to Quinn's tantrums, but it had been a long time since one was directed at *him*. And the fact that he, along with Bart and Noah, had entered into a conspiracy of silence to keep Quinn in the dark over the jabs on the late-night talk shows mitigated the self-righteousness Jimmy felt at that moment. Instead, he tried a different approach.

"So when did you start believing everything that Dean Henry tells you?"

"When he started telling me the truth."

"And how do you know he's being truthful."

"Because he didn't try to sugarcoat what's been happening on the set," said Quinn, once again starting to pick at his steak frites. "He admitted that it was all a setup, and that Katherine was trying to destroy me. After confessing that, why would he lie?"

Jimmy shrugged, acknowledging Quinn's point.

"In fact, the only strange thing," continued Quinn, "was when he said he wasn't gay."

"Really?" Jimmy was genuinely surprised, but not so surprised that he didn't think to ask, "Uh . . . and how did that topic happen to come up?"

"I encouraged him to come out."

Jimmy put his head in his hands. "I see."

"Yeah, I know," said Quinn. "I went somewhere I shouldn't have gone. But he just seems so . . . gay. Doesn't he?"

"Well, yes. But it's still not your business. That's between Kitty and Dean, and we should hope they have much misery together."

"Anyway," Quinn said, remembering that he was supposed to be mad at his lover and toughening up his voice. "Dean told me all about the talk shows and the gossip columns." He popped a bite of medium-rare steak into his mouth, chewed briefly, then asked, "Why did I have to hear it from him? Why didn't I hear it from you?"

It suddenly occurred to Jimmy that, despite his quickly diminishing appetite, a bite of salmon would buy him some time. It did, but only forty seconds . . . and then it was time to fess up.

"You're right, Quinn," he said, realizing that the only way he was going to get out of this with minimal damage was to fall on his sword right away. "I should have told you. But I didn't want to distract you."

"Same with Bart and Noah, I assume."

"Yes."

Quinn sighed heavily and returned to his food. The men passed most of the meal in silence—Quinn spurning Jimmy's occasional attempts at conversation—until, over coffee, Jimmy finally said, "I hope this silent treatment isn't going to last for too long. Will you please accept my apology?"

"I suppose."

"I know I should have told you, but it was just so trivial and mean. I couldn't see how anything good was going to come out of telling you about it."

"Maybe not," said Quinn, dabbing at the corner of his mouth with a napkin. "But at least I would have known. Now I'm just paranoid."

Jimmy reached across the table and took his hand. "Don't be. First of all, no one here recognizes you. Secondly, well . . . you're film-ing tomorrow. A nice dinner, a good night of sleep, and you'll knock it out of the park. And then the rest of it will be forgotten."

"We'll see," said Quinn. "First, let's see if the script they hand me tomorrow is the same one I've rehearsed, for the very first time this week. Then let's see if they've changed the blocking overnight with-out telling me, or moved that damn sofa."

"At least we know your mind is sound," said Jimmy. "We know that everything bad that has happened is because of your ex-wife, not you."

"We know it. But the rest of the world doesn't know it . . . and they will probably never know it."

"Then it will be our little secret."

Fifteen minutes later, after paying the check, as he put his credit card back in his wallet, Quinn asked, "Did you really think it was me? Did you think I had lost it?"

"Well, we know that Kitty . . ."

"No," said Quinn. "Before we found out about that. Did you think I was just another old guy who was too far past his prime? Even for a second?"

"No," Jimmy lied. "I love you, and know what you can do."

"Okay," said Quinn, as the wallet slid into his breast pocket. "I'm glad you had so much faith in me. Because I sure didn't."

They walked out to the sidewalk, where Quinn gave the valet the claim check for his car.

"And another thing," he said, sourly. "This hip. When we get back to New York, I want to see the doctor. It's just not right."

"Yes, dear."

"Don't patronize me. It hurts."

"Mmm-hmm. It hurts? Or are we setting up an excuse?"

Quinn pivoted slightly, so he could face his partner. "I hope you don't doubt me."

"Of course I don't doubt you. But it's a fairly new hip, and—"

"I said it hurts, so it hurts."

Jimmy knew well enough to keep his mouth shut until the car was brought around. When it arrived, Quinn set off for the driver's seat.

"Are you sure you want to drive?" Jimmy asked. "I mean, with your bad hip and everything . . ."

Quinn glared at him over the roof of the car; and, again, Jimmy fell silent. In fact, they both rode in silence all the way back to the hotel, where it was only in that traditionally silent sanctum—the elevator—that Jimmy finally dared to speak.

"We're quite a pair, aren't we?"

"What's that supposed to mean?"

"Two old men who went to LA hoping to capture a bit of the old glory. You with your bad hip, and me not getting any younger, and here we are trying to break back into something we haven't done since we were young men. Thinking we can reclaim the old glory."

"We're young enough," said Quinn. "As long as we're not dead, we're young enough."

They fell silent again when someone else got on the elevator, and stayed that way until they were safely back in their hotel room.

"What time is it?" Quinn asked, when the door was closed.

"A little after ten thirty."

"Put on Leno."

Jimmy shook his head. "Oh, no you don't. I'm not going to let you torture yourself."

"Then I'll do it myself." Quinn picked up the remote control from the bureau, aimed it at the television, and began pushing buttons. Finally, Jay Leno appeared on the screen, and Quinn dropped the remote on top of the bed.

Dick Cheney joke . . . George Bush joke . . . Ted Kennedy joke . . . another Bush joke . . . Martha Stewart joke . . . and then . . .

"So I think you've heard that Quinn Scott is trying to make a comeback." Laughter; a week's worth of jokes at Quinn's expense had already warmed up the audience. "Well, word here in Burbank—" More laughter; Burbank was always good for a laugh. "Yes, word from here in Burbank is that he's doing a great job. The only problem is that he thinks he's appearing in—"

The screen went black.

Quinn was confused for a moment, until he saw Jimmy standing behind him, remote still pointed at the set.

"What the fuck are you doing?"

"It's my way of telling you to let it go," Jimmy said, tossing the remote to the floor. "What did you want to hear him say? *Bedtime for Bonzo? The Boys in the Band? Will and Grace? Brokeback Mountain?*

Honestly, Quinn, why do you want to witness this . . . this . . . humiliation?"

Quinn didn't reply. Instead, he limped toward his lover until he was close enough to land a blow. Jimmy cringed . . . but Quinn merely bent down and retrieved the remote. Then he turned and zapped the television back to life.

The Tonight Show audience was laughing about something, but it no longer had to do with him. He watched it for a few moments, taking none of the words in, then pushed the off button once and dropped the remote control back to the floor.

Quinn still stared at the dark screen, his back to Jimmy, and remained in that position when he finally spoke.

"I wish you wouldn't try to protect me from myself."

Jimmy's voice was husky; Quinn knew he was trying to fight tears. "I love you, and I don't want to see you hurt."

At that, Quinn turned to him. "Thank you."

Jimmy finally let the tears flow, and, as he dabbed at his damp cheeks, said, "Let's go to bed."

Grabbing a tissue from a box on the nightstand, Quinn gently touched Jimmy's face. These scenes—what he cantankerously would describe as "the waterworks," when the moments had passed and the pain was eased—didn't happen often, but every time they did it broke his heart. He knew that Jimmy would die for him, which is why Jimmy had worked so hard to keep the cruel jokes of late-night television from him, even after Quinn knew and the jokes were being told to his face. He wondered if Jimmy knew he would die for *him,* too; and that, in fact, every time he saw him hurt, he died just a little bit.

Over the years, and increasingly in recent years as they aged, Quinn had wondered what would happen when one of them was gone. While they had talked about it over the years, the talks had been built around the practical concerns: life insurance, bank accounts . . . the things a surviving spouse would need to know. They had never discussed the inevitable in emotional terms, never discussed how the one of them who was still alive was expected to recover. As he embraced Jimmy, Quinn silently resolved to address the issue—no matter how difficult it was—before it was too late. They weren't young men anymore, but they also weren't obscenely old. Still, the aches and pains were warning signs that their bodies weren't immortal. And the late-night comedians were warning signs that, at some point, their minds were fragile, too.

But that would wait for another day. At that precise moment, Quinn Scott was only interested in comforting Jimmy Beloit, the man who had tried so hard to comfort *him.*

Jimmy had regained his composure. As the men sat on the bed, he said, "Sorry about the waterworks."

Quinn smiled. Jimmy had made a quick recovery. That was one of the good things about growing old together: they knew each other well enough not to dwell on things—tempers and setbacks and general malaise—they had confronted hundreds of times in the past.

Quinn rolled Jimmy slowly on his back and kissed him, letting his tongue slide inside his partner's lips. Those lips . . . still as soft as they had been all those years ago, the first time the young actor had been kissed by the younger dancer. His hand slid inside Jimmy's shirt, brushing his silky, almost hairless chest, every bit as taut and muscled as it had been when he was a professional dancer. In fact, Quinn sometimes had to wonder what, exactly, had aged on Jimmy's body as it progressed from its twenties into its sixties. Not his ass; it was as perfect and rounded as it had been in his youth . . . not his waist; still only thirty inches, at most, even after a holiday binge. His legs and arms still bent with a suppleness belying his age. Only Jimmy's hair, gone silvery gray; and his flesh, grown tawny and wrinkled from years in his beloved sun, showed his age . . . but otherwise, this Jimmy Beloit was instantly recognizable as the Jimmy Beloit of 1969 . . . the cute young dancer caught in the romance of The Glance.

As he slowly undressed, Quinn's self-appraisal was harsher. His waistline—always rebelling against him, even in his younger days of physical activity and stardom—was notably thicker, and the rest of the body had softened with it. His chest was still expansive, but now it was also spongy, If he was still an intimidating presence—and he knew that, rumors of his senescence aside, he was—it was because he knew that clothes could hide almost every flaw. Jimmy could walk into a room naked and be admired; Quinn could be . . . well, perhaps not admired, but he could draw attention. But only if dressed.

His hand continued to stroke Jimmy's chest, and he felt his partner's hands reach around him, slide under his shirt, and begin
kneading his back. That, too, reminded Quinn of their first time
together . . . the way the experienced dancer had put him at ease,
walking him through his first homosexual encounter with gentle-
ness and understanding. He had spent hours with Quinn, asking
for no more than he was able to give, knowing that time would ultimately prove to be the best teacher. What Quinn would have hungrily and awkwardly devoured, Jimmy taught him to savor. That
Quinn was an apt pupil was fortunate, but—even if that had not
been the case—he knew that Jimmy would have waited.

Being together was their destiny in September 1969, and it was
still their destiny, thirty-seven years later. Of the many things Quinn
Scott knew, that was the fact of which he was most confident.

On the bed, Quinn pulled away from Jimmy.

"What?" Jimmy asked.

"I'm taking my fucking pants off, you fool." Jimmy smiled at
that; he was in the mood.

Quinn and Bart arrived at the dressing room at 8:00 AM, both
having had a rather pleasant night of sleep, which was especially
surprising since both men had been up half the night making pas-
sionate love with their respective partners.

On the ride to the soundstage, Quinn had cleared the air with
Bart about the minor deception involved in keeping him in the dark
about the repercussions of Kitty's reign of terror. Bart, not knowing
exactly how much Jimmy had told Quinn, wisely kept quiet, beyond
his profuse apologies. Quinn—tired and still possessing a certain
after-sex glow—accepted them and assured him that the matter was
in the past. As long as it never happened again.

Ever.

Quinn's script arrived. He flipped through it and was pleasantly
surprised that, for once, it was the same script that had arrived
shortly after Dean had left his dressing room the day before, and
which—not with enthusiasm—he had nevertheless rehearsed. Not
that that meant anything, of course, if everyone else was reading an
entirely different script. Maybe they *all* had Scandinavian accents

now. Still, it was progress. He would just make sure that Jason St. Clair and the others stayed away from it on the set.

Later in the morning, while Bart was away, leaving Quinn to rehearse in peace, there were three light raps on the dressing room door. Quinn already knew Dean Henry's knock, and, sure enough, Kitty Randolph's third husband stood before him when he opened the door.

"Christ," said Quinn, looking Dean up and down. "What happened to *you*?"

"Fender-bender," said Dean, asking, "Can I come in?" as he entered, without waiting for an answer, his neck braced and forehead bandaged. Quinn closed the door behind him.

"I see you got the correct script today," Dean said, spotting the pink pages on the table.

"Or so I hope."

"No, that's the right one." Dean smiled. His teeth were a white not found in nature. "It's over, Quinn."

"What's over?"

"The games." He sat in an easy chair, pulled a joint from his jacket pocket, and asked, "Mind if I smoke?"

"What is that?"

"What Mitchum got busted for." Without waiting for an answer, Dean lit up a joint and took a deeper-than-advisable drag.

"Let me guess," said Quinn, waving away the proffered marijuana. "You're on some heavy painkillers, aren't you."

Dean giggled. "'Fraid not. Just this." He held up the joint with one hand and waved the smoke away from his face with the other. "Not even last night, after the accident. And believe me, I *asked* for painkillers."

"So what happened?"

"Some guy hit me. Anyway, I need to make a bit of a confession. When I left here yesterday, I was ready to destroy you."

"Uh . . . okay."

Dean, awkward in his neck brace, tried to rest his head against the back of the chair, but the position wasn't working for him. "Oh, yeah. I mean, you were the tough guy, and I was the wimp, but I was going to show you who was the boss. Think I'm a milquetoast because I don't stand up to Kitty? I'd show you. Think I'm gay? I'd show you. Uh . . . no offense. I mean, it's great that you're gay, but that's not for me."

"You're just attracted to much older, domineering, wealthy women."

Dean thought about that for a moment, and decided to drop it. The joint was going right to his head, but still he sensed a trap.

"Anyway," he said, trying to keep his thoughts clear, "I was totally going to bring you down today. You think the past week has been rough? I was going to make your name a bigger joke than . . . than . . . someone with a name that's a big joke. Um . . . Tori Spelling! Yes, I was going to make you a bigger joke than her! And then . . ."

"What?" asked Quinn, not as curious as he would have been had he not been distracted trying to think of who Tori Spelling might be. Wasn't she the U.S. Secretary of Education?

"Then I had the accident. And while I was sitting there for hours in the emergency room, waiting for someone to notice I was there, I got my head together." Dean painfully turned his neck to get a better look at Quinn and, making full, unbroken eye contact, said, "And I realized you were right."

"You're gay?"

"*No*!! Not about that! About Kitty!" His voice dropped to a near-whisper as he added, "She's a bitch. She's an evil, manipulative, conniving, abusive bitch."

"I know," said Quinn, nodding in agreement and thinking of a few other words that could be tacked onto Dean's list of negatives.

"She's . . . well, she's just plain mean." Dean took another drag, and again his offer to Quinn was declined. "Mean, mean, mean . . . And you know what else?"

"What?"

"She had a boob job when she was sixty-five. How fucked up is that?"

"Uh . . ."

"Right. Pretty fucked up." Dean began to giggle again, and slapped his hand against the arm of the chair. "Just decided to get her titties lifted for whatever reason. Totally fucked up." He paused and tried collecting thoughts. "Uh . . . so anyway, Quinn, get out there this afternoon and hit one out of the park."

Quinn looked at his dog-eared script. "I'll try."

"You'll try? Guy, this is *The Brothers-in-Law*, not Shakespeare.

You'll be fine." He dropped the joint into a half-empty water glass and began to struggle to his feet, as Quinn offered him a hand. "Thanks. And listen . . . no harm done, right?"

"I hope not."

"I'll make it all good for you. Leave it to me." Dean stumbled a few steps toward the door. "Remember: I'm on your side now. And nothing is going to stop us."

"Can I ask you a question?" asked Quinn, as Dean started to turn the doorknob.

"Shoot."

"What exactly happened last night to bring this on?"

Dean thought back to the accident . . . the ride to the hospital . . . the long hours in the emergency room . . . the way the young Mexican, Raul, now wearing a shirt, had stayed by his side through the entire ordeal. And at those memories, he smiled, turned to Quinn, and said, "The bitch never even called the hospital to see if I was all right."

That day on the soundstage, Quinn hit all his marks and knew all his lines. It was, he thought, like he had never left the business. While there were screwups—the sort of screwups that sent Mark R. Cassidy into a rage, Bernie into exasperation, and Jason St. Clair back to his dressing room, where he threatened to not return to work for the rest of the day—they came from Q. J., that unfortunate spawn of his loins. Quinn wondered if his son would have stood half a chance if he had raised him, rather than that shrew of an ex-wife and her feckless husband.

Oh, he wouldn't have become an actor—if Katherine didn't put an end to that career option, talent would have—but there were still a lot of choices for someone of Q. J.'s personal demeanor. He could have been a bank loan officer. Or a car salesman. Or a telemarketer. Somehow, he would have found a way to survive.

Then again, for better or worse Q. J. had earned two People's Choice Awards, so he was doing something right. And if he was doing it through likeability, rather than talent, more power to him. If he were smart, he was putting his money in the bank like his father had done . . . like his stepfather, Dean, for that matter. Stockpile it now, and escape from Katherine later. It was a sound financial policy for anyone within the larger-than-life web of Katherine Randolph.

They were filming the final scene of the episode, and for once everyone—Q. J. included—was at their professional best. Quinn stood to the side of the set, behind a fake wall, waiting for his cue.

"I'll miss Uncle Jake," he heard his son say on camera.

"Hey," said Jason, and Quinn knew from rehearsals that the actor was wrapping his arm over Q. J.'s shoulder. "He's not dead. He's just going back to Midland City."

"Which is a fate worse than death," said Q. J., earning a laugh from an audience that was strangely undemanding, given the hours they had spent sitting in chilly bleachers watching take after take of the same scene.

"You're gonna have a long time with him," said Jason. "A long time."

A production assistant—Quinn noted with only a trace of annoyance that it was that insufferable one named Chris who kept talking about those damn ants or whatever—cued him, and he reached for the doorknob. It turned, and he walked through the door into the bright lights of the set.

"Uncle Jake!" said Q. J., leaping up from the couch.

Quinn frowned and grumbled, "Stop screaming! Are you trying to kill me?" The undemanding audience laughed, as he knew they would, since they had laughed each of the four times he had made the same entrance and said the same line.

"How are you feeling?" Q. J. asked solicitously.

"I'm not dead yet."

"Told you," said Jason. Another laugh.

It was Quinn's turn again. "I'm packing my bags and getting out of your hair. You don't need an old man around."

"But—" Q. J. began, but his father—no, his *Uncle Jake*—cut him off.

"Young man, I came here because I thought you needed your uncle's guidance and companionship. But I learned something. You don't need me." As rehearsed, Quinn put one hand on the shoulder of each of the younger actors. "You've got each other, and that's all the companionship you'll ever need."

"*Awwwwwwwww,*" said the audience.

Back to the cantankerous old man: "Now get my bags and let me get the hell out of here."

Q. J. and Jason scrambled, and the audience began applauding, and suddenly Bernie was yelling "Cut!"

And that was that.

For a half minute, the set was general confusion, with cast and crew moving randomly onto or off of the set, until Jason St. Clair jogged to the edge of the soundstage and, addressing the audience, said, "Ladies and gentlemen, the cast!" As he announced each name, the cast member took his or her spot next to him.

"Mary Ann Rolison!"

"Debi Bain!"

"Ed Henzel!"

"Paul Berlioni!"

"Joseph Lee Gramm!"

"Ron Palillo!"

"Quinn Scott!"

"Q. J. Scott!"

Hitting his mark, Q. J. motioned to Jason and—returning the favor, as he had done at the wrap of every episode since Jason became the true breakout star of *The Brothers-in-Law*—screamed, "And Jason St. Clair!!"

At which point, the cast joined hands, raising their arms triumphantly as an already enthusiastic crowd went wild, jumping to their feet and applauding what appeared to be the entire cast, but was really only Jason St. Clair. Jason knew it . . . they *all* knew it . . . everyone, that was, except Q. J., who took bow after bow.

Jason finally broke the human chain, dropping Q. J.'s hand on one side and Ron Palillo's on the other. As the cast congratulated themselves all around him, he strode up to Quinn and offered his hand.

"I owe you an apology," he said.

"For what?" Quinn asked.

"The way I behaved on the set. Specifically, the way I acted toward *you.*"

Quinn waved him away. "Don't worry about it." He was actually wondering if the young actor would mention the sabotage, but correctly assumed that he wouldn't.

"No," said Jason, unwilling to walk away without delivering his full, and carefully rehearsed, apology. "I was a punk, and you were the consummate professional, and I should have treated you with respect."

"Well . . ."

"And I shouldn't have touched the gay thing. I mean, I actually admire you for your courage."

Quinn allowed himself a slight smile. "It's very big of you to say that, Jason. But don't worry about it . . . I've got tough skin."

Jason snapped his fingers at someone out of Quinn's field of vision, and seconds later the gofer appeared with two books.

"How about an exchange?" the younger man said. "I'll give you a signed copy of my new book, and you sign my copy of *your* book. Fair?"

Now Quinn allowed himself a broader smile, and took the volumes. "Fair."

He opened the copy of *When the Stars Come Out,* took a pen from his pants pocket, and jotted: "*To Jason, Who Someday Will Be One of the Greats! Quinn Scott.*"

It was only then that he noticed the other book, and thought to ask, "Uh . . . you wrote a book?"

"No," he said, with a laugh. "I didn't write anything. But I posed for 138 photographs—shirtless, swimsuits, underwear, et cetera—and the books are flying off the shelves." He winked at Quinn. "I probably should be more careful with the beefcake image, but I figure if it's making me a lot of money, why not?"

"Why not?" Quinn agreed.

"Just one thing," Jason added, as he autographed Quinn's copy of *Jason St. Clair: A Life in Pictures.* "Promise me you won't, uh . . . *you know,* when you're looking at these pictures. It would kind of creep me out if I knew that someone I respected was spilling seed over my Speedo shots, y'know?"

"Oh, Christ," muttered Quinn, but his demeanor lightened when the younger man looked up and he saw he was smiling. "Don't worry about this old pervert, kid. I've got a wrinkled old man standing over there who is still the only male flesh I lust for."

Seeing them look in his direction, Jimmy waved. The actors waved back.

*   *   *

Much, much later—after almost everyone had gone home and only a few technicians still worked on the stage—Quinn finally allowed himself to say good-bye to the set. He walked slowly into the darkness, arm in arm with Jimmy, limping slightly from the damn hip that would never give him peace. Tonight, though, his hip was an afterthought; he had found his peace on the set of *The Brothers-in-Law*, and no one—least of all Katherine—could take that away from him.

Ten yards behind Quinn and Jimmy, Noah and Bart also ambled slowly into the night air.

"It was a good night, right?" asked Noah.

"The best." Bart's eyes turned to the skies. "But, alas . . . no stars have come out."

Noah couldn't suppress his smile as he watched the older couple walk ahead of them, supporting each other not only physically, but in ways he could only dream of.

"I wouldn't say that," he said. "I think the stars came out tonight quite brilliantly."

Bad news, they knew, spread fast; good news, not so fast. And as fast as Quinn Scott's reputation had been shattered through the manipulations of Kitty Randolph and Dean Henry, it should have taken much longer for Quinn to regain his reputation. But that was decidedly not the case.

Everyone had his or her own theory. Quinn thought his speedy rebound came from a public that embraced his performance as Uncle Jake. Noah believed that the same public wanted to cheer for the elderly man who had come out of the closet and into the limelight, and when he showed he still had his acting chops, they were quick to disregard the vicious rumors. Bart saw it as a simple case of good winning out over evil. Jimmy saw it as his lover's reward. And Lindsay Flynn thought—no, *knew*—that his rebound had everything to do with her publicity efforts, and left herself a note to bill Palmer/Midkiff/Carlyle for an appropriate bonus.

But some things aren't quantifiable, and they all—with the exception of Lindsay Flynn—knew that, so they were careful not to ascribe too much to a specific cause. If the answer was magic, then it was magic that rehabilitated Quinn's laughingstock image within a week and a half.

They knew they had turned a corner when Lindsay fielded a call wondering if Quinn might be once again available for an appearance on *Larry King Live.* The show's booker was apologetic about the earlier cancellation, blaming an unnamed and now allegedly fired underling for not promptly rescheduling. It was a transparent lie—even the booker knew it was flimsy—but no one wanted to dredge up the past, so the apology was accepted and the interview rescheduled.

Within a week, David Carlyle received more good news. The book sales that had gone soft were now rebounding, due to both that long-absent good ink and the revival of Quinn's publicity tour. Although the numbers weren't quite back to where they stood before *The Brothers-in-Law* debacle, they were stronger than David would have ever believed when Noah pitched him the idea one year earlier.

And three weeks after departing Burbank—once again in good graces with the industry that had shunned Quinn for more than three decades—the phone rang in the Southampton house. Jimmy answered, and heard Noah's voice on the other end of the line.

"Aren't you supposed to be closing down your Washington apartment?" asked Jimmy.

"I am. The plan is to be out of here by the end of the month. But PMC just tracked me down with a message to pass along to Quinn."

"He's fighting with his physical therapist right now."

"Just tell him to give this guy a call when he gets a chance." Noah reeled off a name and phone number. "Get this. He's interested in optioning Quinn's story."

"Optioning? As in a movie?"

"Exactly."

Which led to an item a few weeks later in *Variety* revealing that Quinn Scott had reached a development deal with a major motion picture studio, and that *When the Stars Come Out* could begin production by mid-winter. Among the names bandied about in association with the project was Quinn Scott Jr., who was said to be interested in playing his father.

And, of course, none of it—not the talk shows nor the book sales nor that her son wanted to portray her ex-husband in a major motion picture—made Kitty very happy.

But she was about to get a whole lot unhappier.

Chapter 14

You know what they say: what goes around comes around, and usually at the most inappropriate moments . . .

When the call came from Stan Roth, officially the executive producer of *The Brothers-in-Law* but, in reality, Kitty Randolph's hand-picked agent overseeing all her interests at PorchStar International, Kitty and Dean were just finishing a light breakfast spent in near-silence over the butcher-block table in the center of their kitchen. Even though more than a month had passed, he was still in the doghouse for letting Quinn escape the show's taping unscathed, and had been consequently blamed for everything good that had happened to Quinn since then.

As Kitty took the call in the sunroom, Dean reflected on their withering relationship. Every time he started to dig himself out, something new would arise—the *Larry King* interview, the movie deal, the book's debut on the nonfiction bestseller lists—and he'd be right back in that doghouse. He was beginning to wonder if things would ever get back to what passed for normal in the Randolph-Henry household.

Kitty had been unreasonable—that was the only word to describe her behavior. The public was mildly titillated by Quinn's depiction of her, but—so far—her reputation hadn't unduly suffered. A few late-night talk show jokes, but that was about it. Most people, especially the people who populated the entertainment industry, wrote off Quinn's memoir as little more than an ex-husband's revenge on an ex-wife. This was Hollywood; it was expected.

As for the movie, Kitty should have known that she couldn't stop it. As powerful as she was in that town, the almighty dollar was much more powerful. When Quinn began appearing on all the major talk shows and his book hit the *Times* bestseller list, her chance of quashing any resulting movie vanished. There were a lot of people who would do almost anything for Kitty Randolph— mostly because they feared her—but none of them would zero out their bank account for her. Of course, she had managed to separate Q. J. from the movie—that had been easy, and even her idiot son was sharp enough to realize the long-range consequences of crossing her—but, still, the movie would be made. And she was just going to have to accept that.

When she walked back into the kitchen he could see the concern on her face.

"Is something wrong at PorchStar?" he asked, trying to sound like a concerned husband.

"I don't know. Stan told me that Jason has scheduled a press conference."

"Jason St. Clair? About what?"

"I just hope," she said, "that he's not jumping on the Quinn Scott bandwagon."

"What do you think . . . ? Oh." Not many people knew much of anything about their efforts to discredit Quinn on that television soundstage, but Jason was an exception. "You don't think he's going to . . . *name names,* do you?"

"He's an actor," she said, in a voice that could cut glass. "Which means that he's capable of doing something incredibly stupid at any given moment. I don't like it when my employees hold press conferences. If Jason has something to say, he should say it through PorchStar. Don't you agree?"

"Agreed." His voice was weary. He didn't agree; he had simply given up.

"Then do something about it."

Dean looked at her, confusion etched on his face. "Do what?"

"I don't know," she said, standing. "*Something.* Do *something.* For once in your fucking life, do *something!* Get Jason on the phone and talk some sense into him. If he wants more money, give him more money. If he wants me to fire Q. J., tell him we'll fire Q. J."

"You'd fire your own son?"

Kitty rolled her eyes. "Of course not, you moron. I'm not giving him more money, either. But tell him whatever he wants to hear *now,* and we'll deal with whatever his problem is *later.*" When Dean didn't immediately respond, she shouted, "Are you deaf? Do what I tell you to do."

And that is the moment when Dean Henry, who had dutifully obeyed his wife without question for almost seventeen years, felt the past few months of discontent bubble over. He summoned every ounce of courage in his body, stiffened his neck in its brace, and said, definitively, and in a voice that could not be dismissed:

"No."

Kitty spun and walked away from him, toward the foyer, adding,

"And please call me on my cell after you've talked to Jason. I want to make sure that this is done properly. Oh, and I'll be having lunch with Cloris Leachman today at CarnivALLA, so I won't be back in the office until late afternoon."

"Did you hear me?" Dean demanded, beads of sweat forming on his brow.

She stopped and turned to face him. "Hear what, dear?"

"Did you hear me when I said 'no?' "

"I'm afraid I missed that. And what did you say no to?"

Dean felt his resolve begin to falter. "Uh . . . Jason."

"Oh yes, the 'no.' No, you don't know what his press conference is about. Yes, yes, I heard that. But now you'll find out and—"

"No."

Kitty's face was awash in confusion. Dean was afraid he was going to have to explain again, until confusion gave way to anger.

"Excuse me?"

"*No. No,* I am not going to get Jason to call off his press conference. *No,* I am not going to offer him more money, or Q. J.'s head, or anything he wants. *No,* I am not going to do whatever you tell me to do. Never again."

She took three steps toward him, edging from the foyer into the kitchen. He took two steps back, stopping when he felt the refrigerator door dig into the small of his back.

"Dean," she said, her voice deceptively reasonable. "Dean, I don't know what this is all about but . . . Is this because of the accident? Did you get a head injury? Maybe one that is still undiagnosed?"

He shook his head, and the room was quiet for a moment until Kitty said:

"In that case, are you *asking* for a head injury?"

"What do you mean?" he asked, but—after he dodged the vase that was suddenly hurtling toward his head—he knew exactly what she meant. The vase smashed into shards somewhere behind him; following it came every other loose item at hand: the mail, keys, a small picture frame . . . With the exception of the keys, which glanced off his shoulder, he managed to avoid the onslaught.

When she was finished, Kitty stormed up to him and slapped him.

"Never—*never*—say no to me again, Dean Henry. Or I will destroy you. Now pick up that phone, get Jason's agent and his publicist on the line, and demand that he call off this nonsense."

Dean felt raw fear. He was afraid of disobeying Kitty, and he was afraid of obeying her, and he was afraid of making any move whatsoever which, by default, condemned him to disobedience, which frightened him into even greater immobility. He had never before crossed the line with her, and now he had not only crossed it, he had hit the point of no return before he even realized what had happened. And it felt . . .

It felt strangely liberating. Dean Henry felt like a free man for the first time in years. Seventeen years, to be precise.

While Dean was warily enjoying his epiphany, Kitty repeated herself, and added an additional threat.

"Call him. Do it or get out of my house."

He blinked. "*Your* house?"

"*My* house."

"*Our* house."

"*My* house!" Her scream rattled the windows. "Call Jason St. Clair or get out of *my house*!"

Get out of her house. Finally, Dean thought, they wanted the same thing. And in a moment of peaceful determination, unfettered from his usual emotions of fear, guilt, and shame, he calmly said:

"Do you know how much money I have in the bank, Kitty?"

"I beg your—"

"Thirty-two million dollars. And change." Dean paused for effect, relishing the slightest tic that took hold under his wife's right eye. "You know what that is, Kitty? That's my fuck-you money. That's the money I know I can fall back on, which is why I can stand here and say: fuck you."

"What?"

"Fuck you!"

"*Fuck you!!*"

"No, fuck you!!"

"Fuck you! Fuck you, fuck you, fuck you!" And then, capping her four-"fuck you" performance, Kitty picked up the fruit bowl and slammed it into the side of Dean's face. The last thing he remembered seeing was a single red apple rolling across the tile until it disappeared through the door to the foyer.

It was the second time that Raul the Gardener had to take him
to the emergency room that month.

Four dozen reporters. Twenty or so cameras. Not bad, thought
Kelly Rhule, Jason St. Clair's publicist and number one fan, who
was certain that Jason would have fallen in love with her had she
not had the great misfortune of being born thirty-three years before him. Despite her pleading and prying, she had no idea what
Jason was about to announce, but he had good instincts and she
was confident that it would be great for his career, as well as remu-
nerative for her.

Yes, for a former underwear model, Jason had great instincts . . .
which, come to think of it, was one of the reasons he was no longer
an underwear model.

Ordinarily, Kelly Rhule would never have allowed a client to call
a press conference without knowing the subject. But the way in
which he had kissed her cheek two days earlier and told her not to
worry about a thing, that Jason had everything under control,
well . . . she melted. She giggled just reliving that moment in her
head. He was such a sweet boy, and he had *such* good instincts. He
was going to go a long way, and Kelly would be at his side through
every step. If she couldn't be his lover, she would be his surrogate
mother, and what good boy doesn't love his mother? If that wasn't
the same as physical love—the soft sensation of naked flesh pressed
together in a sweaty, animalistic frenzy, hair wild and eyes ablaze
with passion . . .

She took a deep breath and thought, *If that isn't the same, it's the
next best thing.* Then she took another deep breath.

And, as she had known, they were all here: the trades and the
weeklies and the networks and the syndicated shows. As they shuf-
fled in and jockeyed for position, she waved to them, and they
waved back. In fact, she was waving to a late-arriving crew from
Entertainment Tonight when her cell phone rang. She excused herself and answered.

"How's my girl?" said His voice, and her heart fluttered.

"Everyone is here," she said. "*Everyone.* Where are you?"

"Just pulling into the parking lot," His voice said. "Let me pop into the green room and fix myself up, and I'll be right out. Can you hold them off for . . . mmm . . .seven minutes?"

"Of course," she said, and she did.

Jason St. Clair pulled his Prius into a parking spot, sprinted unnoticed through the lot to a back door, and slipped into what passed as the green room, which—to start—was actually gray. And which was also clearly a former locker room, into which someone had squeezed a couch. But there was running water and a mirror, and that's all that mattered to Jason St. Clair. With a brush and gel, he worked some quick magic on his windblown hair, then brushed his teeth and moisturized just enough for his skin to regain its elasticity, followed by a few quick dabs of makeup to hide the shininess from the moisturizer.

And then he was ready. He looked at his watch. Seven minutes and twenty-seven seconds—not bad—then dialed Kelly's cell phone.

"I'm ready," he said, when she answered.

She excused herself from a discussion with someone from *Variety* and walked out of the room through a side entrance, prompting immediate conversational buzz, followed by near-silence, from the assembled reporters.

"I heard he wants more money," said the Associated Press entertainment reporter. "One million per episode."

"Yeah?" replied the stringer for *People*. "I heard he has cancer."

"Really?"

The stringer's voice fell to a hush. "Inoperable."

Backstage, Kelly Rhule found her charge and said, "So, any hints for me?"

Jason smiled his maybe-million-dollar-per-episode smile; certainly no less than $700,000 per, or they'd walk. "You—and the rest of the world—will know everything in just a few minutes. Can you wait that long?"

"I guess I'm going to have to."

Jason leaned down to the fifty-something woman, his most loyal handler among a small corporation of loyal handlers, and planted a gentle kiss on her cheek. She blushed; he knew she would.

"I'll introduce you," she said, walking out front through the curtains, leaving Jason behind for one last opportunity to rethink things.

Kelly looked out over the room from her perch on the stage, four feet above the crowd, and tried to do a quick headcount. Seventy-five? Eighty? It was a good number, and—if she were right, and Jason was about to read the riot act to PorchStar Productions—it was the right audience. She tapped the microphone and, hearing that it was on, said:

"Thank you all for coming. I am Kelly Rhule, Jason St. Clair's publicist—"

In the middle of the crowd, someone yelled, "Kelly!!"

"Yes, well, thank you. But since no one else is here to see me"—appreciative laughter—"I want to get right on to it and introduce my client, and a great actor, Jason St. Clair."

Jason bounded onto the stage. The press tried hard to be objective—they were there at his behest, after all—but most of the people in the room still applauded his entrance. Jason thanked Kelly, led her to the stairs and down the six steps to ground level, then took over the podium.

"Here's how it's gonna work," he said, smiling and oh so friendly, but determined. "I have a statement. I'm gonna read that statement, and then I'll take a few questions. But not too many, because I have a feeling we're gonna be talking for a while, and there's no sense ruining a beautiful day in L.A., right?"

"Told you," whispered the stringer for *People*. "Cancer."

Jason towered above them, a Greek God with a microphone; a perfect human being, from his hair to his skin to his muscled-but-not-too-muscled physique to his "aw shucks" manner. As the sea of admirers looked on, Jason took a piece of paper from his back pocket, unfolded it, and began reading without sounding like he was reading.

"First of all, I would like to say that the years I've spent as a member of the cast of *The Brothers-in-Law* have been great. They really have. I've met a lot of great people: the production team, Q. J. Scott . . . oh, and, of course, the great actress, Kitty Randolph. I guess you could say I've learned a lot from the Randolph-Scott family."

Jason waited for the laugh he expected. Only two old-timers got it, so he continued.

"Recently I met a third member of that family, Q. J.'s father, Quinn Scott. I guess I don't have to tell you who he is . . ."

This time he got his laugh. Jason smiled.

"I feel some shame, because I didn't treat Mr. Scott with the respect he deserved on the set. As you know, I am a perfectionist . . . and, as you also know, Mr. Scott had some problems on the set which, it turns out, were unrelated to his skills as an actor."

A smattering of applause. Jason smiled.

"As the week went on, though, I gained a great appreciation for Quinn Scott. He is a brave man. Now, I have to admit that I was a bit put off to learn that my costar was going to be America's newest gay icon . . ."

Laughter. And Jason did not smile.

". . . but—could I have quiet please? Thank you. But as I got to know him, I got over my own, um, prejudices. And then I took the time to read his book, and, well . . . I had heard that the book would make older gay people brave, and help older gay people embrace their sexuality, but I have to disagree. I think a lot of people—young and old, gay and straight, male and female—can learn lessons from Quinn Scott's journey. I know that I did. I am glad I read *When the Stars Come Out*, and I think everyone should read it."

The Los Angeles Times reporter leaned over to Kelly Rhule and whispered, "Where's he going with this?" She could only shake her head in confusion.

"And I know this," said Jason, noticing that his knuckles were white from their grip on the podium, "because I am gay."

The room was silent, except for the thump Kelly Rhule's body made as it slumped to the floor.

The silence continued.

"What?" the *People* stringer finally asked.

"I'm gay."

"Happy gay or homosexually gay?" asked the reporter from *Variety*.

"Homosexually gay."

"You mean you don't have cancer?" asked the stringer.

Jason St. Clair looked at him. "What?"

The stringer withdrew. "It was just a rumor."

Jason shook his head. "Listen, folks, I know you're probably surprised, and—to tell you the truth—I'm sort of surprised that I'm sharing this with you. But Quinn Scott's courage has led me to this place, and I don't want to play the rumor game anymore. I, Jason St. Clair, star of *The Brothers-in-Law,* am a gay American actor. And I'm proud of that, and will always be thankful to Quinn Scott for giving me the courage to come out of the closet and state this publicly. Now if there are any questions . . ."

Epilogue

So now we're to Act Three. I don't know all the specifics of how the third act will play out, but I can tell you that this story has been far more comedy than tragedy.

It always is, when the stars come out.

That's a wrap. Cut and print.

"Coming up after our break, Barbara Walters talks to film legend Kitty Randolph. Her life, her loves, and her losses. Stay tuned."

A Jaguar commercial came up on the screen and Quinn Scott turned from his perch on the ottoman, pulled close to the television to accommodate his eyesight. Yet another damn thing that was failing him.

"Do you think I'm a love or a loss?" he asked.

"Both," said Jimmy, sitting behind him on the couch. "But I couldn't begin to tell you which in which order."

"Don't start, guys," said Bart, on the couch between Jimmy and Noah. "You're going to talk straight through the interview."

They sat in silence, watching the luxury car zip along a generic mountain highway. Finally the screen shifted abruptly into a McDonald's commercial. Fast, expensive cars could hold Quinn's attention; but not fast, inexpensive food.

"I've been waiting two months for this fucking interview," he said gruffly.

"Language," Jimmy cautioned.

"Fuck language. If that bitch starts with me . . . Noah, we're calling your father, right? And we're suing her into oblivion?"

"That's right, Quinn," said Noah, indulging him. "Oblivion."

"Oblivion. She'll be washing dishes in Hoboken when I get through with her."

"Actually," said Bart, "Hoboken is quite upscale these days."

"I meant Hoboken, Indiana," said Quinn, with a determination that almost made one believe that's exactly what he had meant. If anyone had been inclined to challenge him—which no one was, of course—he short-circuited that thought when the McDonald's commercial ended and he "*shushed*" his companions into silence.

On the screen, lights gradually illuminated Barbara Walters, transitioning her from silhouette to full-color interviewer. And then she spoke. Enthusiastically.

"Kitty *Randolph!* For over fifty years, she's been a Hollywood icon. The naïve ingénue ..." A very young Kitty, circa 1957, appeared on the screen, bickering playfully with Mickey Rooney in some long-forgotten movie.

"The sophisticated woman looking for career and love, with a song in her heart ..." Kitty, circa 1970, and, yes, it was a clip from *When The Stars Come Out.* Her costar and then-husband could be seen off to the side of the screen, visible for only a split-second before Barbara Walters moved on.

"The television pioneer ..." Circa 1974. A fortyish Kitty, wrapped in a sensible sweater as she and her TV family filled the screen. No critic would have ever claimed that *The Kitty Randolph Show* made her a television "pioneer," but no critics were conducting this interview.

"The survivor." Circa 2004. Kitty in a classic clip from *Marriage Penalty,* about to unleash her foul mouth on George Clooney.

The introduction continued: "Over the years, Kitty Randolph has had her share of triumphs—three Academy Awards, an Emmy, and tens of millions of fans—but she's also known heartache."

Quinn muttered, "*She* knows heartache," and Jimmy quieted him.

"And now she's here with us tonight. Kitty Randolph. Thank you for joining us."

The camera shifted to Kitty, sitting very ladylike in a studio chair and wearing a white Valentino dress that managed to make her look virginal and worldly at the same time.

"Thank you, Barbara." If the viewers had never met Kitty, they would have been prepared to believe anything she said. "Thank you for having me here tonight."

"You've had a tough year."

Kitty nodded in mournful silence. A tear—one very discreet, very believable tear, if you had never met her—appeared in the corner of one eye.

"It has been ... difficult. But you go on. You have to go on." She dabbed at the insincere tear.

"Your husband left you, and your ex-husband and frequent costar in the 1960s, Quinn Scott—"

"Yes, Quinn ..." said Kitty, a wistful smile on her face.

"He wrote an autobiography and revealed he was gay. Did that hurt?"

Kitty dabbed again. "It did hurt me, Barbara, but mostly I hurt because, well . . ." Dab. "Because I never realized how difficult his life had been."

"*What?!*" snapped Quinn, and Jimmy hushed him.

"He was hard on you in his autobiography."

Kitty bobbed her head, her expression somber. "Yes. Maybe deservedly so. You see, when we divorced all those years ago, I didn't really understand. Now, of course I knew gay people—they are some of my best friends in show business—but I couldn't understand how Quinn could say he loved me, but also be gay." Dab. "Those were different times. We all had a lot to learn."

"So you just didn't understand . . ."

"I didn't," Kitty agreed. "But I learned, and I came to understand, and I'm a better person for that. And now Quinn and I are closer than ev—"

"*What?!*"

"Shhh," said Jimmy. "She's just saying what she has to say."

"Since when did you become so forgiving?"

"Shhh."

"In fact," Kitty continued, "When Jason announced he was gay—"

"Jason St. Clair," said Barbara Walters, filling in the blanks. "The star of *The Brothers-in-Law*. Which your company produces."

"Yes, Jason St. Clair. When Jason came out, Quinn was right there to help him. And I am so proud of both of them for what they've gone through. Individually, and together. I'm grateful that I could . . . well, I'm grateful that I could serve as a bridge between two generations of great gay actors."

"She's making it sound as if she brought us together," Quinn snarled, and once again Jimmy shushed him.

"And Barbara," said Kitty, now positively glowing, "this is a bit awkward for me, because I'm a private person and I just *hate* to toot my own horn. But thanks to the inspiration I've received from people like Quinn Scott and Jason St. Clair, and the things I've been able to do to help gain greater visibility and acceptance for the gay and lesbian community in the motion picture and television industries, I'm being given a lifetime achievement award next week from the Gay and Lesbian Alliance Against Defamation."

"GLAAD," noted Barbara Walters. "The group that promotes positive depictions of gays and lesbians in the media."

"*Do you believe this*?!" growled Quinn, and this time none of them could pick their jaws up off the floor to silence him.

Kitty Randolph turned to the camera and, with the warmest smile, added, "The award isn't for me, though, Barbara. It's for all those hardworking gay men and lesbians in the arts; Quinn Scott, and Jason St. Clair, and my good friend, the lesbian novelist Margaret Campbell. It's for all of them."

Somewhere in Chapel Hill, North Carolina, Margaret Campbell sat alone in her very comfortable living room, eating sorbet from the container and watching Kitty Randolph label her a lesbian on national television.

"Bitch," she drawled, taking another scoop from the container. "This is not over."

At the same time, in Manhattan, David Carlyle powered off his cell phone and began the process of disconnecting all seven landlines in his Fifth Avenue co-op.

"Your marriage fell apart this year," said Barbara Walters, and Kitty nodded. "That was the marriage to Dean Henry, the Hollywood agent. Tell me what that was like."

Kitty paused a long time before answering. Then, after seeming to compose herself, she seemed to bravely press on. "It was traumatic. I was devastated. I was deeply in love with Dean, but I'm afraid the age difference was just too much for us to get past."

"I'm sorry."

"Thank you, Barbara." With a smile, she again stared into the camera. "But . . . well, I hope this isn't sharing too much, but it's probably for the best that Dean and I went our separate ways. There were some financial irregularities . . ."

"Really!"

"Oh, no! Oh, I don't want to make it sound as if Dean *stole* from me! No, that would be up to the Grand Jury. I just meant that I think Dean would be happier in a less intense financial atmosphere. My financial holdings are complex, and I think he was in over his head, which is probably why my auditors can't seem to find thirty million dollars." She laughed. "Silly Dean . . . he probably accidentally shredded the paperwork. We'll figure it all out."

In his newly rented West Hollywood apartment, Dean Henry bolted upright in bed.

"You bitch!" he shouted. "You bitch! Oh, you wouldn't dare try to . . . ! Oh, fuck, she *would*!"

"Hmmphh," said the slumbering brown body next to him.

"You have to admit it was pretty funny," said Noah much later that night, sliding his naked body a bit closer to Bart's under the sheets.

"I just can't understand how she gets away with it. It's . . . it's appalling. And no one ever calls her out."

"Sure they do. How many husbands have left her? Is it three now, including Dean? And don't forget Quinn's book. That's at least a few times she's been called out in a very public way."

"But she keeps going," said Bart. "And four times over fifty years . . . well, that means she wins a lot more than she loses."

Noah shrugged. "She's a survivor. Survivors survive. Every time a husband leaves or something bad happens, like the book, she gets right on damage control. She spins first, and she spins best, and she keeps spinning until she has everything back in control. So it's not that she doesn't get called out; she just keeps control. Did you see what she said about Dean and the missing money? That was amazing. She basically sat there on national television and accused her ex of stealing thirty million dollars. Even if he didn't take it, she's guaranteed his life will be a living hell for the next decade."

"You sound like you admire her."

"Admire?" Noah thought about that. "I have come to have a healthy respect for her, but I wouldn't say I admire her."

"So you don't want to be like her?"

Noah laughed. "I know you don't quite get my type-A personality, baby, but I consider myself one of the good guys, and I use my energy for good, not evil." Noah leaned closer and gave Bart a soft kiss on the lips. "I promise to never be like her, or admire her, or . . . well, if possible, I'd like to not think a whole lot about her anymore."

Bart returned the kiss and said, "Deal."

"You awake?"

There was no answer, so he asked again. "Noah, are you awake?"

Silence, followed by a mournful, "I am now."

Bart didn't answer, but Noah heard him move through the darkened bedroom. Then he felt something land next to him in the bed.

"What are you doing?" asked Noah.

"Your clothes. Get dressed."

"Why?"

"Because it's cold outside," whispered Bart. "And keep your voice down."

Noah pulled the comforter off his body and struggled in the darkness to pull himself into a sitting position. "Why are we going outside?"

In the moonlight he saw Bart's smile. "Maybe a walk on the beach. Maybe a trip into town. Maybe a special surprise."

Noah glanced at the clock on the nightstand. "It's 2:47. That's AM, by the way. And it's cold out."

In response, a pair of his jeans fell into his lap.

"Christ," said Noah, accepting his fate and climbing out of bed. "I should have just gotten a pet. Even dogs don't have to be walked in the middle of the night."

When he was dressed, Bart took Noah by the hand and led him through the quiet house. The stairs creaked slightly as they descended, then walked through the kitchen to the back door.

"I know what you're going to make me do," said Noah, as they walked onto the dewy lawn.

"I knew you'd figure it out. Now be quiet." With that, he wrapped one brawny arm around Noah's shoulders and walked him to the gazebo.

They climbed the two steps and Bart reached down to push the 'play' button on the boom box. The lush opening strains of "When the Stars Come Out" began to play, and Bart took Noah in his arms.

"You know I don't dance," said Noah.

"I know you *say* you don't dance. But no one is here except for us . . . and the stars . . . so you'll dance."

And under the stars on a cold Long Island night, they did.

And as their bodies moved slowly together, swaying to the rhythm, Bart moved his mouth next to Noah's ear and softly sang:

> *When the evening falls, my dear,*
> *And when my dream time calls, my dear,*
> *You'll be with me,*
> *Of that, no doubt,*
> *I'll see your face when the stars come out.*
> *We have the moon, we have romance,*
> *We have to take this one last chance,*
> *So take my hand,*
> *And take me out,*
> *To somewhere where we'll see the stars come out.*
> *We'll fly, so high,*
> *But our feet will never leave the ground,*
> *I'll swoon, 'neath the moon,*
> *And when our dance is done,*
> *Under the morning sun,*
> *You'll hold me close, and turn the sun around . . .*

In an upstairs window, Quinn and Jimmy—awakened by the sound of bodies moving through the house—stood watching the couple dance in the gazebo.

"I guess this means that they've caught us," said Quinn.

"No doubt," Jimmy agreed. "But imitation is the sincerest form of flattery, isn't it?"

"It is. Look at them. They look . . . cute."

" 'Cute'? Why, Quinn Scott! I don't think I've ever heard you use that word before."

"Don't get used to it."

They stared out at the gazebo for a few more minutes, lost in a world that they had created, but which was no longer theirs alone.

"You know," said Quinn, when the dance was drawing to a close. "I think we did a good job raising those kids."

Jimmy leaned into his lover and kissed him.

Quinn looked back out the window. "Noah can't dance."

Jimmy laughed. "Yeah, he's a bit stiff."

"You'll work with him, right?"

Jimmy nodded, and the two men stared out the window, watching the dancers and the dance and the stars.

Later that year . . .

Dan Rowell was nervous as he waited at the Clarendon station for the Metro from Northern Virginia into downtown Washington, D.C. But he knew what he had to do on that blustery day in late November, and he was prepared to see it through.

The train came and he hesitated, only boarding seconds before the doors closed. Turning around and going home would have been too easy, and he had to fight doing things the easy way from this point on. His long, personal journey had brought him to this moment, and he couldn't—he *wouldn't*—let himself back out.

Today Dan Rowell was going to tell his employer, the conservative senior United States senator from the state of Ohio, that he was gay. And if that meant the termination of his employment, which is what it almost certainly meant, he would persevere and he would survive.

After all, the famous actor Jason St. Clair had come out of the closet, and he was still working. In fact, Dan had read a number of interviews in which Jason St. Clair said that he was happier than he had ever been in his life. And that other actor—the old guy who had written that book; the one who had been married to Kitty Randolph—he had done it, too. If Jason St. Clair and the old guy could do it, so could Dan Rowell.

As his ride continued into the center of the federal government, the memory of the old actor's book made Dan Rowell think of another book, one he hadn't thought about in quite some time. What had ever happened to that project? Dan couldn't even remember the writer's name anymore; only that he was fairly arrogant, and clearly couldn't understand why a gay man in Dan's position would stay in the closet. The way he seemed so puzzled when Dan had told him that he chose to be asexual, rather than risk his job . . .

Maybe that guy wasn't altogether wrong, he thought, as the train approached the Foggy Bottom station. But, for Dan, there was a right time and a wrong time. And a few years earlier had been the wrong time. Hell, he didn't even want to use his real initials during that interview. What initials had he asked the writer to use? G. C.? Yes, that was it. He had used the senator's initials, which, he supposed, was subversive in its own way.

In any event, he was fairly certain that the book had never been written. Too bad, too, because the new Dan Rowell—the man who was about to come out to his United States senator—would have been amused to read his words again from today's perspective.

The doors finally opened at the Capitol South station and he took a deep breath.

QUINN SCOTT

Filmography

b. October 18, 1934, in Pittsburgh, PA
m. Kitty Randolph (1966; divorced, 1970)

Movies

1958:   The Fresh Kill
1958:   Port Richmond
1959:   Mariner's Harbor
1960:   The Outerbridge Crossing
1961:   Attack on Tottenville
1961:   The Glory of St. George
1963:   Father Cappadanno
1964:   It's a Mad, Mad, Mad, Mad World (cameo)
1964:   The New Brighton Story
1968:   Darling, I'm Darling
1969:   Sweet Svetlana
1970:   When the Stars Come Out

Television

1966–1969 Philly Cop
1978:   The Love Boat (guest appearance)
1980:   Kolchak: The Night Stalker (guest appearance)
1990:   Murder, She Wrote (guest appearance)
2006:   The Brothers-In-Law (guest appearance)

KATHERINE ("KITTY") RANDOLPH

Filmography

b. June 14, 1936, in Millville, NJ
m. Bert Cooper (1957; divorced, 1958)
m. Quinn Scott (1966; divorced 1970)
m. Dean Henry (1989)

Movies

1957:	Charmed, I'm Sure
1957:	Passport to Bermuda
1958:	She's Our Doll!
1958:	Betty and the Pirate
1959:	Penelope Van Buren & Her Secrets
1959:	Hello, Cowboy; Hello, Cowgirl
1959:	The East River Story
1960:	Fort Lee Love Song
1961:	That Gal & That Guy
1962:	The Mabel Normand Story
1964:	Sister Helen
1966:	Phone Book!
1968:	Darling, I'm Darling
1969:	Sweet Svetlana
1970:	When the Stars Come Out
1980:	Disco Trade School!
1992:	National Lampoon's Milwaukee Vacation
1996:	Gramma
1999:	The Family Dunnigan
2000:	The Family Dunnigan II: Beyond Rehab

2002:   Intervention
2004:   Marriage Penalty

Television

1972–1974:   The Kitty Randolph Show
1979:   The Carol Burnett Show (guest appearance)
1980:   Fantasy Island (guest appearance)
1996:   Stephen King's The Clown in the Scary
             Lighthouse in Maine (miniseries)
2002–2006:   The Brothers-in-Law (recurring guest
             appearance)

Featuring

Ron Palillo
Joseph Lee Gramm
Edward Henzel

And, as the Stooges,

Greg Crane
Craig McKenzie
Steven Seegers
Andrew Westlake

With

Camille as "Camille"

*   *   *

Edited by

John Scognamiglio

Written by

Rob Byrnes
based on his original story

Represented by

Katherine Fausset

*   *   *

Executive Producers

Lynette Kelly
Mark Siemens
Shaun Terry
& Michael Rao

Associate Producers

Wayne Chang
Greg Crane
Patrick Doyle
Byrne Harrison
Douglas A. Mendini
Jeffrey Ricker

Title Sequences by

James Daubs

Casting by

Paul Donelan

Costume Design by

Wayne Chang

Original Score by

Michael Holland & Karen Mack

Los Angeles Location Scouting by

Scott Schmidt
& Byrne Harrison

* * *

Stunts

Rabih Alameddine
Margaret Campbell
Becky Cochrane
Matthew Crawford
Diana Gabaldon
Kim Hogg
Bob Iovino
Illyse Kaplan
Timothy J. Lambert
Bob Liberio
Denise Murphy McGraw
Paul Parrott
Pam Paulding
OFR
Chris Shoolis
Brian Scribner
Candace Taylor
Robert Widmaier
Mark Zeller

*   *   *

Catering by

Posh
The Townhouse
O.W.
Freddie's Beach Bar
JR's
& Michael Rao

Mr. Byrnes's Hair by

Tim Vermillion

***

Dedicated to

the Best Boy & Key Grip,
Brady Allen

*   *   *

A
Kensington Publishing Corporation
Production

(c) MMVI by Rob Byrnes

*   *   *

No animals were harmed during the writing of this novel.